THE
COLLECTION

Also by Shannon Stoker

The Registry

THE
COLLECTION

A REGISTRY NOVEL

SHANNON STOKER

wm

WILLIAM MORROW

An Imprint of HarperCollins*Publishers*

HarperCollins books may be purchased for educational, business, or sales promotional use. For information please e-mail the Special Markets Department at SPsales@harpercollins.com.

FIRST EDITION

Designed by Diahann Sturge

Library of Congress Cataloging-in-Publication Data

Stoker, Shannon.
   The collection : a Registry novel / Shannon Stoker. — First edition.
      pages   cm
   ISBN 978-0-06-227174-7 (pbk.)
I. Title.
PS3619.T6453C65 2014
813'.6—dc23
2013035984

14 15 16 17 18   OV/RRD   10 9 8 7 6 5 4 3 2 1

For Andy

Acknowledgments

Thank you to my agent, Paula Munier, especially for listening to me when I go a little crazy. To my editor, Amanda Bergeron, I am in awe of your skills. To the entire HarperCollins team for your insane abilities and assistance. To my family, especially my parents, who don't mind a midnight phone call every now and then. To my friends, thank you for being there. To Katie and Dalmy, who always let me know when it was break time. To the Alms family, Laura and Mary Lynn, for being an awesome help. To GBPL for fostering my love for books. Finally, thank you to Andy and Nucky, whose help means the world to me.

THE
COLLECTION

Chapter 1

THE REGISTRY: A CULTURAL TRADITION OR A HUMAN RIGHTS ISSUE?
—Global Reporter

The waves were thrashing in all directions. Mia tried not to look down as she flung herself from the helicopter. The noise from the propellers and the sirens signaling the imminent crash flushed all thoughts from her mind. Right before Mia hit the deep blue water one idea worked its way back in: she didn't know how to swim.

In that second she reached her arms out and kicked her legs, as if she could fly away. This only made her landing more painful as she slapped against the surface and then slid under. The salt water filled her nose and burned her eyes. All of the scrapes on her body filled with fire from the water's invasion. She was sinking. Fast. She clawed toward the surface and tried to kick her way up, but nothing was working.

Mia ignored the pain and turned her head toward the rays beaming down through the crystal clear waters. She let out a gurgled scream. For a moment her concentration was broken. She heard the metal machine crash into the water, the propellers coming to an eerie stop.

Mia looked over at the chopper. It had flown her to freedom and would now rest in a watery grave. She refocused her efforts on reaching air. She wanted so badly to take a breath. Mia tried to fight the urge, but her instincts overtook her will. She felt the water enter her lungs, and everything went black.

Pain brought Mia back to consciousness. She gasped hard at the air, but water spewed out of her mouth. Someone rolled her onto her side and started smacking her back, forcing the salty liquid out of her body. Mia alternated between coughing and forcing breath into her lungs. The face in front of her was hazy.

"I thought I lost you too," Carter said. "Why didn't you say you couldn't swim? I would have held your hand for the jump."

Mia felt relief; one of her companions was safe.

"I wasn't thinking . . . ," Mia said.

She scanned the beach. She propped herself up on her elbow and tried to stand. Her legs were like jelly and she fell down. Carter caught her and lowered her back to the sand.

"Take it easy, princess," Carter said. "You almost died."

"Where's Andrew?" Mia asked.

She wondered if he knew how to swim; she'd never bothered to ask. As if on cue Mia saw him step out of the water and onto the beach, waves nipping at his heels. Andrew's clothes were sopping wet; his sweatpants and T-shirt hung off his lean, muscled frame. Mia remembered he'd been ready for bed when they'd had to escape. She closed her eyes and a sense of calm filled her heart.

"We did it," Mia said. "We're free."

But the silence next to her was a reminder of the hefty price.

Carter pulled his hands off Mia's arms and slumped down. *Rod,* Mia thought to herself. *He didn't make it.* She stared at Carter, who was focusing on the sand. There were too many emotions flying around for her to know what to say. Carter's father was a great man. He had sacrificed himself not only for his son but for Mia as well. Before Mia could cry, Andrew fell down on the sand next to them. He was breathing heavily and almost laughing. Mia knew he shared her relief.

"Is everyone okay?" Andrew asked.

"No," Carter said.

"Physically?" Andrew corrected himself.

"Mia almost drowned," Carter said.

"You can't swim?" Andrew asked. The relief in his voice was replaced with a sharp tone. "Why didn't you say something? Mia, you could have died—"

Mia interrupted Andrew. "I'm fine."

She knew he was right. Mia didn't have a defense and didn't want to argue. Not right now at least. If Andrew was angry, it seemed he didn't have the energy to lecture. He took a breath and stood up, taking in their spot.

It was a small stretch of sand surrounded by a cliff about ten feet high. Rocks lined the area closest to the overhang.

"The tide's out," Andrew said. "We're lucky or else the waves would have smashed our bodies against those rocks."

"Tide?" Mia asked.

"The water levels change," Andrew said. "It's not important, but we need to get out of here now."

"Can't we sit? I need a rest," Carter said.

Andrew shook his head. "Someone saw that crash, and I'm not ready for a welcome party."

Carter let out a groan, but he stood. Andrew scanned the coast and pointed to a spot with a tall boulder. Mia started to stand, but her legs were lead. She knew she'd fall again. Carter paused by her and bent down. He scooped her up in his arms and carried her toward the cliff. Mia was grateful.

"Carter, I'm going to help you over first, then I'll pass Mia up to you, and then you two pull me over," Andrew said.

Carter sat Mia down on a smaller rock, then joined Andrew at his chosen point. Andrew stood on the large rock, making him tall enough to see over the bluff, but Carter was just a little too short. Andrew balanced himself and gave Carter a boost. He scrambled up the cliff with ease.

"I can't carry you up here," Andrew said to Mia. His cheekbones looked prominent and his deep brown eyes pierced her. "Do you think you can try walking?"

Andrew was never one to coddle. Mia's legs were shaky, but she forced herself up. If they were delayed she didn't want it to be on account of her. As she made her way over the rocks, her foot slipped under her, but she caught herself. Andrew never took his eyes off her and waved her along. She was close enough to grab his hand. Right when she reached for it a familiar noise filled the air. A motor. Andrew's eyes widened. He signaled for Mia to work her way against the cliff.

She moved as fast as she could. Once she was closer to the wall she saw two large rocks against each other with a space between them. Mia slid down; the boulders were tight and went past her waist, hiding her legs. She pressed her back against the wall of the overhang, barely fitting in the tight spot. She looked up and all she could see was the top of the bluff jutting out over her head.

The motor came closer.

"Andrew," Mia said, "what's happening?"

"Stay quiet," Andrew said. "Don't make a sound, no matter what."

"Come down here," Mia said.

Andrew never turned to look at her. Instead he brought a finger to his lips. Panic filled Mia. Why wasn't Andrew ducking down? Whoever was approaching could see his head peering out. The motor drew closer and then it was followed by a stranger sound: silence. Mia heard a bird in the distance and the waves rolling in. She knew Carter wasn't alone up there.

"Help me," Andrew said.

Mia looked over at him. He wasn't talking to her. She saw Carter's hand come down and Andrew locked arms with him before gliding over the cliff. Mia was alone now. She pressed her hands against the rocks and tried to force herself up. The space was too tight for her to bend her knees. She was trapped. Her struggles stopped when a new sound came. A car door opened and slammed shut.

"Well, well," a man's voice said. "What are you two doing out here?"

His accent was thick. He rolled his *r*'s. Before Carter or Andrew could answer he yelled in another language. Mia had never heard anything but English in her life. The strange sounds heightened her fear. The sound of another door opening came next.

"Just the two of you out for a joyride?" the same voice asked.

"Yes," Andrew said. "We're alone."

The man gave instructions in the other language. Mia flattened her body against the cliff as best she could. The hairs on the back of her neck rose, and she craned her head upward. She had the feeling someone was right on top of her.

"*Sí.*" The new voice was deep. Mia heard a foot turn and saw some dirt fall down right in front of her. "Two sets of footprints in the sand."

"This is no place for American boys," the leader said. "Let's get you out of here."

"No," Andrew said.

"It wasn't a question," the man said. "You're lucky I found you. Most would deport you right back over the border. Not me."

"We'll be fine on our own," Andrew said.

The voices started to trail off. Everyone was quiet. Mia wished she could see what was happening.

"Get in the car," the voice said.

Mia wanted to scream. Her companions were being taken. They were going to leave her here. She needed to help them, or at least join them in their capture. Instead, she did nothing but plaster herself against the cliff. She heard a shuffle and the engine coming to life. It zoomed away. Mia stayed frozen until the sound was too distant to hear.

She tried to calm down, her breath ragged as her mind raced desperately back to what felt like an eternity ago. When she'd been a happy, naïve little girl who could only think about a husband. She'd woken up, risked—and lost—the lives of people who cared for her, and at last escaped the Registry.

But for what? To die alone on a rocky beach. She couldn't react like the fierce fighter she'd been a few hours earlier. Now fear overtook her and she stayed still against the rocks.

It felt like seconds had passed when Mia snapped out of her trance. Her face was met with the spray of mist. Her legs were locked in place and new pains filled her body. The sun had moved across the sky and the water was coming in. She felt some splash against her ankles. A new, smaller wave rolled toward her and this time the water hit her shins. Mia was getting a crash course in what the tide was. Survival. Mia had to survive. It was the only way she would find Carter and Andrew. The only way she could make things right.

She pressed her palms against the rocks and tried to jump up. Her knees slammed into the boulders. It wasn't going to work. She twisted her body around and tried to force herself up again. The space was too tight; without her knees she couldn't get out. She started to claw at the wall of the cliff. Her hands found some edges and she pulled herself up. Everything hurt, but the water was up to her knees now and as soon as the wall got wet, climbing wouldn't be an option.

Mia worked her arms through the pain and climbed high enough that she could try to use her legs again. Her knees hadn't yet cleared the tight spot, but she thought she could sit. Mia readied herself for more agony and pushed herself back. Her rear met the hard rock and her tailbone throbbed. She didn't waste time thinking about it though. She wiggled herself back and soon her knees could bend again.

Moving the joints brought misery. Mia didn't stand; instead she slid herself out and onto another massive boulder. A wave came in, spraying the rocks and Mia. She looked down and saw the blood coming from her scraped kneecaps. Her hands were covered in cuts from grasping at the wall. Everything hurt, but she wasn't safe yet. Andrew's words filled her mind. Once the waves were tall enough they would pick her body up and slam it against the rocks.

She kept on moving. Mia made her way to the rock Andrew and Carter had climbed over from and stood up. When she held her arm in the air her fingers could just reach the solid ground. She went up on her toes to see if she could get a better grip. Now her hand was flat. She moved her wrist around, trying to see if she could grab hold of anything, but was met with dirt.

Another wave came in, hitting her feet. Soon the water would be high enough that standing on the rock wouldn't be an option. Mia was going to die here. *No,* she told herself. She wouldn't give up. She would never give up. Mia moved both her hands to the top of the ridge.

Mia needed to jump high enough that she could grab hold of the ground and pull herself over. One chance was all she had. If she missed it would mean slipping and slamming onto the rocks. A new wave came in, higher still, and Mia knew she was running out of time. This was it.

She bent her knees and kept her hands right above her. Mia forced her legs straight and jumped in the air. Slamming her arms down on the ground, she began grabbing at the loose dirt. Her elbows were bent right at the cliff's edge. It was seconds, but Mia knew she was failing. Her body was sliding backward. She kicked, hoping to find some footing, but none came. She continued to slide and braced herself for the hard landing.

Mia's hands were about to make one last attempt to grip the ledge when she felt something grip her wrists. *Andrew,* Mia thought. He'd made his way back to save her. The falling stopped.

Mia took short breaths. She wouldn't crash onto the rocks. Andrew was pulling her over. Mia opened her palms and grabbed on to his arms. She shut her eyes tight, scared she'd be tempted to look behind her and see the rocks below. She used her legs to propel herself against the wall and soon her head and shoulders were above the cliff. Her stomach and knees followed. She stayed on the ground, unable to believe she was alive.

The relief she had felt earlier returned, but not for long. She was so happy Andrew had come back for her. She felt safe from the rocks below . . . but now, without the pure terror of dying clouding her mind, the idea that it could have been Andrew was insane. Mia looked up, frightened to see who had offered her the assistance. The fear changed to shock. It was a woman. She was dressed in a skin-tight black dress and breathing heavily.

Mia couldn't know if it was from the injuries, the loss of her friends, or the shock of seeing a woman as her savior, but everything went black for the second time that day, and Mia collapsed in the dirt.

Chapter 2

*Statistics show that America is the safest country in the world.
The number of attacks against women is 93 percent lower than
the world average.*

—American Gazette

The jeep bounced up and down against the gravel road. They drove along the coast and Andrew kept his eyes glued on the ocean. His wrist hurt where it was handcuffed to the roll bar at the top of the vehicle. It made it difficult for him to sit down. Carter didn't have the option of trying to sit. His cuffed hands forced him to squat inches above the bench.

The open top created a wind tunnel, making conversation impossible. Andrew was left alone with his thoughts. He'd abandoned Mia. She was alone, trapped between two rocks. When his captors pointed their guns at him, he hadn't had time to react. Saving her would be impossible. He hoped she'd made it out okay and told himself he had done the right thing by leaving her.

They started slowing down. Andrew looked ahead; there was a town coming up. Instead of taking the road straight, the jeep veered left, closer to the coast. They drove outside the tiny village and the road started descending. Soon they were driving along a sandy beach and the speed picked back up. Sand was flying into Andrew's face.

He tried to keep his head down and avoid the assault of the tiny flecks, but it wasn't doing much good.

He felt something slide over his head. He fought, but part of him welcomed the shield. He opened his eyes again; now he was surrounded by darkness. Andrew tried his best to count and pay attention to the turns. If he knew the amount of time it was taking to travel then he could get back to the beach and back to Mia.

Mia. Her face kept creeping into his mind. Her eyes had been wide and brimming with tears, her chin shaking, and he had left her. Andrew told himself not to focus on that now. *Twenty-two, twenty-three, twenty-four.* Could she get out of there? It seemed like such a good hiding spot. *Twenty-one, twenty-two, twenty-three.* How could he have let this happen? *Twenty, twenty-one, twenty-two.*

It was useless; Andrew couldn't keep count. He couldn't focus on anything. His lack of control was more aggravating than the situation he found himself in. They started to slow down again. Andrew hoped that meant the bag would come off, but no effort was made to release the hood. The deceleration continued and soon they came to a stop. The motor was turned off and Andrew's ears rang. The front doors opened and someone unlocked his cuffs.

Andrew formed a fist and tried to punch whoever was assisting him but failed to make contact due to his blindness. His body lurched forward and Andrew was hanging over the car door.

"Whoa," the man said. "This guy's ready for action."

Before Andrew could attack again his hands were pinned behind his back and recuffed. At the same moment the car door was opened and he fell to the ground. His assailants snickered. They left him there and went to Carter. If Andrew's companion tried to put up a fight he made no noise in the process. Andrew tried to find the balance to stand up again, but before he could someone grabbed on to his elbow and hoisted him up.

He was being walked. Andrew was so unsure of his surroundings. He tried to listen for clues, but his hearing was still off from the wind. In the distance he swore he heard someone counting off. The walking stopped and Andrew was released.

"Welcome home," his captor said.

The black hood was yanked off. Andrew blinked uncontrollably while his eyes readjusted to the light. They were on a ledge, looking over a huge training facility. Andrew's eyes focused on the man counting off. There was a group of twenty or thirty men doing push-ups in sync with his numbers. Farther down there was an obstacle course and another group of men running as a unit around a large track.

Andrew's heart jumped. This was what he imagined basic training to look like. This was what he'd spent his whole life looking forward to: being part of a team and belonging. Training and working for a cause. That dream had vanished, but part of it was etched too deep to erase.

"Are we in America?" Carter asked.

"Better," their captor said. "You two are the newest recruits in the Mexico Militia."

Chapter 3

What about the problems plaguing our own country? Unemployment? The crime rate? Let's fix our homes first before wasting money overseas.

—*Comment from the* Global Reporter *message board*

A teakettle whistled. The sound was an alarm clock to Mia and her eyes fluttered open. She was on a small cot, with a blanket up to her chin. She forced herself up on her elbows and the blanket fell down. Her tattered pink sundress was gone; she was in a white tank top and shorts. Her hands were bandaged.

"You're awake." A voice filled the room.

Mia snapped her head up and saw the woman in black. She had curly red hair, and what Mia had taken for a tight dress was actually shorts and a tank top. She was tall and lean, her skin covered with freckles. Mia guessed the woman was in her thirties.

"Where am I?" Mia asked.

The woman offered a cup of tea. When Mia didn't grab it she set it down on a small table next to the bed. The woman walked across the room and pulled over a chair.

"I hope you don't mind I cleaned you up," she said. Her voice was unusual. She didn't have the same accent as the man who took Andrew and Carter.

"I need to find my friends," Mia said.

Mia pulled the blanket off her and saw that her knees were covered with bandages.

"What's your plan?"

"What do you mean?" Mia said. "You can't keep me here."

"Nobody is keeping you anywhere," she said. "But if you need to find your friends, what is your plan?"

"I don't know," Mia said. "Follow the tracks from the car that took them?"

"Is that a question?" she asked. "Because the answer would be, what time did the car leave? What direction did it head?"

"I don't know," Mia said.

"Well, sit and have some tea," she said. "What's your name?"

Mia was uncomfortable. She didn't know how to respond. She didn't understand so much of what had happened.

"Where's your husband?" Mia asked.

The woman let out a small laugh. "Are you a mind reader?" she asked.

"No," Mia said. "I've never seen an unmarried woman live like this."

"In a one-bedroom shack?"

"Alone," Mia said.

"You are an American refugee," she said. "That's what I thought. In most parts of the world—not all, but most—women can live with or without whoever they want."

"Are you from Mexico?" Mia asked.

"Ireland," she said. "Where women aren't equal to men—they're slightly better."

Mia let out a nervous laugh and the woman joined her. Mia had so many questions, not just about what had happened to Carter and Andrew. She heard her stomach growl. The hostess stood up and went to the far side of the shack. There was a tiny kitchen. A small hot plate for a stove and a cooler for a fridge. Mia looked around the small space. There were candles and a desk. No electricity. The redhead returned with a napkin filled with cookies.

"Best I can offer you right now," she said.

"How did I get here?" Mia asked before taking a bite.

"I heard the helicopter, saw it crash, and was scavenging the area. You threw some nice things out of that aircraft. Imagine my surprise when I saw a hand waving at me from the cliff. I was walking over when you must have forced yourself up. You were falling, so I ran to help. The thanks I get? You passing out on me."

"Thank you," Mia said.

"No," she said. "Thank you. I got several new pieces of ammunition."

The guns. Mia shivered. Grant's guns. Mia's former betrothed was the king of weapons. She looked over at the redhead, wondering what this woman could need them for.

"I'm Riley," she said. "I know what you're thinking, it's a boy's name, but my parents wanted a son."

"They wanted a son?" Mia asked.

"Carry on the family name," Riley said. "In most—not all, but most—parts of the world, parents are happy with a son or a daughter."

This made Mia smile. She was in that part of the world now.

"I'm Mia," she said.

"Well, Mia the American girl, it is nice to meet you."

"Likewise," Mia said.

There was so much more Mia wanted to know about this woman. Questions started filling Mia's head too fast for her to process them. Right as she was on the verge of exploding with curiosity her priorities came back to mind.

"I really need to find my friends," Mia said. "Someone took them."

"Who?" Riley asked.

"A man," Mia said. "I didn't see his face. I stayed hidden. I didn't do anything to help them."

"Were your friends girls?"

Mia shook her head.

Riley let out a sigh of relief.

"Then your friends are fine, part of the Collection now," Riley said.

"What do you mean?" Mia asked.

"You can't help them tonight."

"I have to," Mia said. "They need me."

"Need you to what?" Riley said. "To get yourself kidnapped? This is a very dangerous place."

"I can't stay here," Mia said. "I froze. I could have thrown a rock or done something, but I didn't. Now they're missing."

"They're not missing," Riley said. "I know where they are."

"Take me to them," Mia said. "Please."

Riley let out a breath. "No."

"Why not?" Mia felt the tears forming. "Please."

"You know why I am still alive? Living free in this place?" Riley asked. "Because nobody knows I'm here. There are lots of things you don't understand."

Mia ignored Riley and stood up. She walked toward the door. The aches came back full force. Riley rose.

"If you leave here, when you come back I'll be gone," Riley said. "If you stay and learn some patience, I'll help you find your friends. I promise you they're safe."

Mia's back was to Riley. She stopped and tried to process the situation. Mia was in a strange place and didn't have a clue how to proceed. This woman wasn't offering her the help she wanted, but it was help nonetheless. Mia spun around. Riley's face relaxed into a smile.

"Why are you helping me?" Mia asked.

"Because you haven't given me a reason not to," Riley said.

Tears rolled down Mia's cheeks. She didn't know if they were from grief or gratitude.

"Come back over here and have a seat," Riley said. "You tell me your story and I'll tell you mine. Then in the morning we'll make some progress on getting your friends back."

It was wrong for Mia to feel happiness over talking with Riley, a free woman, when Andrew and Carter were being held captive somewhere. But she couldn't battle the eagerness she felt for this conversation. She told herself it was all right. Riley knew where her friends were and had promised their safety. With little hesitation Mia went back to the bed.

"It all started this past year," Mia said. "My sister burst through our front door soaking wet . . ."

Chapter 4

AN AMERICAN TRAGEDY: GRANT MARSDEN WIDOWER BEFORE THIRTY
—American Gazette

The tie felt like it was choking the life out of Grant. He sat in the waiting room, an armed guard watching over him. It was obvious this young man was meant to intimidate Grant, but he had little effect. The suit was more bothersome.

It had been twenty-four hours since Amelia Morrissey and her two lost boys bested him. The memory made Grant's insides burn. It wasn't his fault though. The RAG agents who had raided the Rowe house, where she had been hiding, were responsible. Grant had seen to it that they received their punishment: death by his hand.

Grant was sure this hearing was only a formality. After the emergency, escape crews were on the scene in seconds. Grant's injuries were minor. A few bruised ribs and some scrapes. He had gone to the hospital mainly to get showered and to ready a private plane for his return. He was shocked when an armed guard met him there.

Instead of his luxurious jet, Grant was forced to travel up to the capital in a military helicopter, one of his designs that he was trying to improve. Even though Grant's residence was less than an hour outside the city, his request to change into his own clothing was denied.

This cheap suit had been brought to him instead. It barely fit and the fabric irritated his skin.

The door to the courtroom opened up. A man dressed in the same attire as Grant held the door. Grant rose and was waved inside the tribunal. The room was dark. There was one long bench; he went to stand behind it. Leonard, the head RAG agent, who had done little to help Grant in capturing Amelia, was already standing there. He wore a smug look on his face. Grant wanted to slap it off.

Grant took his place next to Leonard and looked at the judges. He recognized four of them immediately. They were the heads of the army, air force, navy, and marines. Grant had dealt with them personally on many occasions. He was on a first-name basis with all the older men. His eyes stopped when he saw the fifth judge.

Without hesitation Grant lowered his head and dropped to one knee. It was the grand commander himself. Now Grant's nerves kicked in. This was more serious than he had thought. Never in his life had Grant imagined being in the same room as the grand commander, let alone on the wrong side of the bench from him.

"Please rise," the grand commander said.

Grant stood up but didn't raise his head. This man deserved every bit of respect he could muster, and Grant was going to honor that.

"Grant Marsden," the grand commander said. "Your wife fled the country. According to this Recovery of Abducted Girls agent you had multiple opportunities to stop her and chose to ignore your options."

Fire rose through Grant. How dare Leonard try to pin this on him? Grant thought about moving the blame back to where it was most deserved but didn't think the grand commander wanted a game of he-said.

"Please respond to these allegations."

"Amelia Morrissey did not flee," Grant said. "She was abducted by a deranged truck driver and tragically lost her life in the rescue attempt."

Grant thought about the trucker who had died by Andrew's hand. He made the perfect scapegoat, giving Grant the chance to blame Mia's disappearance on someone. The room was quiet. Grant raised his head and looked at the judges. He was certain they knew he was lying, but this story would be easier for them to spin than one involving Mia's escape over the border. Grant felt a rush of boldness and decided to speak further, making sure the group was aware of his true plans.

"With your permission I would like to recover her body."

There was some discussion among the judges at this point. Their chairs were on a platform several feet high. The only light in the room illuminated their faces, giving them a commanding presence.

"It is true," the grand commander said. "Amelia did lose her life in a rescue attempt. It is wise of you to realize this."

The man looked down at Grant with raised eyebrows, indicating he knew this was a charade as well. The grand commander gave a wave of his hand. Leonard let out a small groan before slumping over the bench. His body continued to fall and then hit the ground. Grant's eyes went back toward the door. The man in the suit was putting his gun away.

"That, Mr. Marsden, is one of my favorite toys," the grand commander said. "The silent bullet. Before there was the silencer, but it still had that small whizzing noise. Now there's no sound at all, making it impossible for the victim to have even one second's notice of his fate. How did you create that?"

Grant felt his lips curve into a smile. The grand commander knew of his inventions.

"I'll have to take some with me to help bring my wife's body back," Grant said.

"No," the grand commander said. "Her body was destroyed in the rescue attempt."

Confusion started to work its way into Grant's brain. He didn't appreciate the lack of understanding; it wasn't something he was familiar with.

"There is no need to speak in codes any longer," the grand commander said. "You were partly at fault in this situation and you will receive a fitting punishment.

"Taking into consideration the advancements you have made for your brothers and country, along with the failure of the RAG bureau, a decision has been made. You are forbidden to leave the country. All travel is suspended."

Grant braced himself for the rest. But no other sound was made. If this was all he was facing, Grant was getting off light. He didn't appreciate that though. Knowing that Mia was out there living after betraying him was infuriating. She needed to be punished as well.

"Sir," Grant said, "I think it is in the country's best interest that Amelia be killed. What if she makes a public appearance elsewhere?"

"You think one little girl is going to make any difference?" the grand commander said. "Most likely she died trying to land that contraption you built. It would be a waste of our resources. Get her out of your mind. She beat you; move on."

Nobody beats Grant Marsden. He scowled at the comment.

"There was some media attention drawn to her abduction. You will play the role of the grieving widower. Talk about how you loved her and what a sad end she met. Young girls will swoon over you and they will take heed of Amelia's story. You're a public hero now. Congratulations."

This did not sit well with Grant. Grieve? Over a woman? Never.

"Once a sufficient amount of time has passed you will announce your engagement to one of my daughters," the grand commander said.

Grant's mouth hung open. All the men seated in this room were married to the spawn of the grand commander. It was an honor and meant the groom was slated for big things.

"That is all for today," the grand commander said. He rose and the rest of the panel followed him toward a door at the back of the room. He ushered them out, leaving Grant speechless.

"Someone will be in contact with you shortly," the grand commander said. "Your first appearance is scheduled for tomorrow. Close your mouth."

Grant snapped his jaw shut. The door slammed closed and a side door opened. He walked back out into the waiting room, giddy with what the future had in store for him. His happiness was facing a small obstacle though. *She beat you.* The words stung. The game wasn't over yet, and Grant knew just what he needed to ensure victory.

Chapter 5

At any given time multiple countries face civil war. The great nation of America has never been divided.

—American Gazette

The walk continued. Andrew was happy to have his vision back, but it didn't give him much relief. He and Carter were led into a large building made of clay bricks, which apparently kept the inside cool. A door was pushed open, and Andrew and Carter were thrown against a wall. Their handcuffs were undone.

"Strip," a voice said.

Neither Andrew nor Carter moved.

"Fine, have it your way."

Then a blast of icy water came at them. It was powerful and almost knocked Andrew over. He turned around, trying to make his back take most of the force. The temperature started to change and it didn't feel so bad anymore. Then the spray was shut off. Two of the men who had escorted them had buckets now. They flung the contents onto Andrew and Carter. Andrew tried to wipe his eyes; it was soap.

Without the handcuffs Andrew looked for the door. Before he could take a step the blast of the hose came back home, washing away the soapy residue. Andrew had to gasp for breath as the water fired toward his face.

"We're giving you some trust here," the man with the hose yelled. "If you break it the cuffs go back on."

The water was shut off again. A towel was thrown at Andrew. He took off his soaking-wet shirt and sweatpants and patted himself dry. Once he was dry enough a new outfit was tossed toward him. He pulled on the white scrubs. He hadn't seen anyone in these since his days in the orphanage.

Andrew had been getting close to thirteen, about to get tossed out into the real world. All the boys in his group were taken to a clinic where men dressed in these outfits gave them their last round of vaccines. The shots were supposed to keep them free of transmittable illness until it was enlistment time. They'd worked too. Andrew wondered now if the doses were no longer effective and he was susceptible to illness again, having missed his enlistment date and the boosters.

"Face the wall," the man said.

Andrew did as instructed. Carter did the same. When Andrew and Mia had first met Carter he'd been bold and outspoken, but he wasn't in this place. Someone grabbed Andrew's wrist and pulled it behind his back. It wasn't time to make a move yet. The image of those men training outside was too fresh. Even if Andrew did make it out of this room he'd never get past them.

The cuffs clicked back on. Andrew kept his face blank. It was a skill he'd mastered over the years. He glanced toward Carter, whose face was emotionless. Andrew was grateful Carter wasn't speaking out or mentioning Mia, but this behavior was too unsettling.

They were spun back around. Andrew wouldn't break. He didn't want to speak or let these men know what he was thinking. *Show no fear.* Carter didn't look fearless; he looked like a shell. A new man had entered the room. He was pushing a small table with four syringes laid out on it.

"What is that?" Carter asked.

Don't speak, Andrew said in his head. He didn't know if he was reminding himself or trying to magically communicate with Carter.

"Boosters," the man said. He was American. "You missed your enlistment date and we can't have the two of you getting sick now. Are either of you injured?"

Andrew kept his eyes glued to the wall. His leg bothered him from the accident. When Grant ran them off the road, Andrew had been flipped from the bed of the truck. His pain was not enough that it needed medical attention, and even if it had needed it, he wasn't about to let this man help him.

"I'll take that as a no," the man said.

Andrew felt the cotton swab on his arm. He didn't flinch when the needles entered his skin. The doctor did Carter, who was less composed, next. He rolled his arm away.

"Don't touch me," Carter said.

The empty shell of Carter was getting filled with rage. Andrew wanted to calm him down; this wasn't the time for fighting back. The doctor didn't seem bothered. He reached out and yanked Carter's arm toward him. Andrew expected a blowback, but this time Carter didn't protest. The emptiness returned to his face.

The doctor wheeled his table out. Two men walked over and grabbed Andrew's arms. The remaining two did the same to Carter. They were escorted out of the room and back into the hallway. Andrew was leading the way.

Andrew didn't stop walking or try to fight the men guiding him. He kept his stone face as he heard Carter struggle.

"Stop," Carter said. "You can't do this to us."

Carter's protests faded away. They were getting split up now. Andrew never looked back. He felt bad for Carter; he had a father who had trained him to act proud and strong. Carter never learned the lesson about getting in line and shutting up. Andrew knew they could make it out of here, but they needed a plan first. Screaming and fighting at this stage would only make it worse.

The escorts stopped moving and unlocked a heavy wooden door. It led into a small room. The floor was made of dirt. There was a table and two chairs. The men walked Andrew to the table and unlocked his cuffs. Andrew didn't turn around when they closed the door. He heard the lock snap into place.

Andrew rubbed his wrists where the handcuffs had been. He did a quick inventory of the room. The chairs and table were metal and none budged when he tried to move them. Andrew didn't understand how they were stuck to the ground. That was it.

There were no windows in the clay room. A single light hung from the ceiling; it was too high up to reach, even when Andrew stood on the table.

Andrew tried to keep calm and focused. He thought over the path here. They were driving fast, over sixty miles per hour, but the ride couldn't have been longer than ten minutes. Mia wasn't that far away. She was resourceful. Andrew was certain she'd made her way off the rocky beach before the tide came in. He wouldn't allow himself to think otherwise. Then she would have stayed close to that spot, knowing he'd come back for her. It would take a day or two, tops, for him to get out of this place. The best way to accomplish that was to not draw attention. Remain quiet, take in the surroundings, and form an escape plan.

He was trying hard to reassure himself, but guilt kept peeking through. He had led Mia out of America and into danger, then abandoned her on a beach. Andrew felt his heart rate increase and tried to calm himself down. She was fine. She would be fine. He told this to himself over and over, hoping he could convince himself it was true.

Andrew's thoughts were getting to be too much. He had no clue how long he'd been in the room. He was guessing at least three hours. He was growing restless. They didn't pay any attention to him. They were letting him sit here alone in a cell. Were they trying to break him? This was slow torture.

"Hello?" Andrew called out.

He felt stupid for trying to reach out. As time wore on only one thing remained true: Andrew was certain he had made the right choice leaving Mia on the beach—at least he kept telling himself that.

Chapter 6

I don't support the Registry, but if the American armed services hadn't stepped in, the state of West Austrachek might not exist.

—*Comment from the* Global Reporter *message board*

There was only one window in the tiny shack, but the sun shone brightly through. Mia sat up on the cot and her eyes danced across the space. Riley was gone. Mia didn't remember falling asleep. Panic replaced any peace the night's sleep had brought. She remembered Riley's threat. If Mia left, when she got back Riley would be gone. Instead she had tricked Mia into staying and then abandoned her in the morning.

Andrew and Carter. The thought of them brought a sick feeling to Mia's stomach. Riley had said they were safe and that she knew their location. That was a lie too, and Mia had fallen for it. She stood up; ignoring the aching in her bones, she went toward the door. Before she reached the knob, it swung open.

"Oh, you're up," Riley said. "I was about to wake you."

"You left me," Mia said.

"Relax." Riley put her hands on Mia's shoulders. "There's not exactly indoor plumbing here. You have to do your business outside."

"Ick," Mia said.

"What? You're that prissy?"

"My friends." Mia was eager to change the subject. "You said in the morning you'd help me find them."

"You don't need to find them," Riley said. "You need a way to get them back."

Riley walked past Mia and went to the makeshift desk in the corner. She reached under the rickety table and pulled out a black bag.

"Tell me where they are," Mia said.

"Don't get so worked up," Riley said. "You're alive and they're alive. Hold on to that thought."

"Are you playing some sort of game with me?" Mia asked. "I told you my story last night. You promised you'd help me."

"You fell asleep before I could tell you mine," Riley said. "You're a very bright girl, but you have a lot to learn."

"You can teach me whatever you want, as soon as I get Andrew and Carter back."

"You're reckless," Riley said. "I tell you where they are, you'll run over there and get yourself killed or worse. I can't have that blood on my hands."

"So you lied? You won't help me?"

"Lesson number one: learn to listen," Riley said. "I'll help you. But you want quick answers with even faster solutions. Life doesn't work that way."

Riley left the bag on the table. She stood up and walked toward the door.

"Come outside," she said. "I'll give you the grand tour."

Mia rolled her eyes and tried to rein in her frustration. Carter and Andrew needed her and she was no good to them cooped up in some shanty. She needed Riley to find them. Playing along was her best option. She walked outside.

Mia didn't know what she was expecting, but it wasn't this. The shack looked like it was falling apart on the outside. A gust of wind could have blown it over. Mia thought they'd be in the desert or close to the sea, but neither seemed true. It was hot and humid outside. The hut was surrounded by trees blocking the sun. Mia looked up and saw a mirror outside the window, guiding the sunlight in. The grass was long and thick, filled with the humming of insects. Mia wished she had some shoes.

Riley walked through a patch of trees and Mia saw some water. It was a small pond.

"This is where we clean ourselves and get our water supply," Riley said. "Don't do your business near it, please."

"You drink the water you bathe in?" Mia asked.

"I purify it first," Riley said. "I have a small kit."

"How long have you lived here?"

"Thirty-six days," Riley said.

"Why do you live here?"

"Now you want my story?"

"I always wanted it," Mia said.

"Well, clean up a little," Riley said. "Meet me back inside and I'll get our breakfast ready. Then you can sit and listen."

Riley smacked her hands together and left Mia by the pond. She let out a sigh and headed to the pond, ready to splash some water on her face and take in whatever story Riley was about to tell.

When Mia went back into the shack, Riley was at the table with a laptop flipped open. The screen was black and all Riley's typing was in green.

"How are you doing that?" Mia asked.

"Using a computer?"

"There's no electricity here," Mia said.

"Why would I need electricity?"

"Won't it die?"

"Ah, the American technology ban," Riley said. "Things in the rest of the world have changed a bit. Strangely, most of our inventions come from you guys."

"Huh?" Mia asked.

"Americans crave inventions," Riley said. "But they don't let their own people use them, just the military. Then they sell them off to the rest of the world."

"Why and how?"

Riley let out a groan. "One question at a time," she said.

Mia crossed her arms and Riley acquiesced.

"I don't know why," Riley said. "I've heard rumors it's to keep the people under stricter control. As far as how—again, this is a rumor— certain boys show talents at a young age and those are honed. They spend their whole lives inventing things."

"It doesn't bother them that they can't use what they invent?"

"I assume they can," Riley said. "But again, this is all a presumption. America keeps its doors sealed tight. A lot of the world doesn't know much about them."

Mia was still interested in how the computer was running. She pointed to the machine. "You didn't answer my first question."

"Updated. There's a battery in here."

"How do you charge it though?"

"It will die, but it's guaranteed for two years," Riley said.

"What?" Mia was confused. "How?"

"I'm not a computer expert," Riley said. "But with the first laptop, the battery lasted an hour; then someone said, 'I'll make it last longer,' so the new battery lasted eight hours; then another person came on and said, 'Longer battery life, please,' and the twelve-hour battery came. This went on for many years and now we have the two-year battery. It's like your cellular phones."

"Phones have batteries?" Mia said.

She had never given a second thought to the fact that the phones didn't shut off. Mia had never had access to one without her father's supervision and never questioned what made the things work. She was feeling a bit out of sorts about all the things she didn't know. Riley knew more than Andrew, Carter, or Rod though. Mia wanted to take it all in. Riley finished whatever she was doing and shut the lid to her computer. Then she turned her chair around and faced Mia.

"Did you build this place?" Mia asked.

"No," Riley said. "I found it and fixed it up."

"What would you have done if it wasn't here?"

"I have netting in my bag," Riley said. "I would have slept outside."

"For thirty-six days?"

"I've done it for longer."

"When?"

"How about you stop asking questions and listen for a little bit," Riley said.

Mia frowned and her cheeks grew warm.

"My name is Riley Hart and I'm from Ireland. I am an agent for the Irish people. Do you know what that is?"

The only agents Mia knew of were RAGs. She assumed Riley wasn't looking for runaway girls. Mia shook her head. She didn't even know where Ireland was.

"If the Irish government has a problem they come to me and I tell them the best way to fix it," Riley said. "I don't fix it myself. Instead I send other people in to fix the problem. I just tell them how to proceed."

Riley worked for the government. Now it made sense that she didn't have a husband. She must have been government property. Mia started to wonder if she'd escaped as well.

"I can read you," Riley said. "Your head is already off in the clouds. You're not focusing on what I'm saying. You're forming your own conclusions already. Don't."

Mia nodded and refocused on Riley.

"The people who carry out my plans, they're the intelligence agents. They work for me," Riley said. "I was foolish enough to fall in love with one of them. His name is Nathan Hart. He is my husband. He went missing during a mission five months and nine days ago. The mission failed due to less-than-perfect planning on my part. So I entered the field to track him."

Mia was forcing her lips shut.

"Do you see the difference between my story and yours?" Riley asked.

That was the whole story? Mia had so many questions.

"You went on and on for nearly two hours, giving unnecessary detail. I told my whole story in under a minute. Be concise whenever possible."

Mia nodded her head.

"Oh dear, you are about to burst. Ask your questions."

"You were a man's boss?"

Riley let out a laugh. "I am many men's boss."

"You're married to someone you love? And you're trying to save him?"

"I picked him out myself," Riley said.

Mia went a little cross-eyed.

"I forget, I can't joke about that stuff with you," Riley said. "There's no reverse Registry. We chose each other."

"Good," Mia said. She was looking for equality, not domination by women. "What happened to your husband?" she asked.

"That is not something you need to know," Riley said. "I got a tip he might be here and I'm scoping it out."

"What is . . . here?" Mia asked.

"That's not part of my story, dear," Riley said. "Keep focused on this conversation and remember your other questions for later. It's the best way to get information. Don't flip back and forth between topics."

The next question Mia asked was important. She wanted more information but needed an eloquent way to phrase it. If Mia asked where Ireland was, Riley would answer, but that wouldn't help Mia's current situation. There was so much she wanted to know, but her first priority remained Andrew and Carter.

"How do I fit in your story?"

"Now, that is a good question," Riley said. "I saw your small hand, thought you were a girl or a child. At first I thought it might be a trap, but my basic human decency required me to help you. Once you passed out on the sand I couldn't leave you there. You were pretty banged up and I figured you were the one who fell from the sky. Since I was taking your supplies I thought I owed you. Then once you talked about your friends' abduction I thought our goals might be the same."

"Your husband's in the same spot as Carter and Andrew?"

"I'm not sure," Riley said. "But if he's in this country that's where I'll find him."

"Why didn't the men who kidnapped the boys take the guns and helicopter stuff?"

"Because those two men are a much bigger prize than what was lying in the grass."

"Why don't you rescue him?"

"Nathan," Riley said. "You can say his name. And I'm not certain he's here. I've been trying to find that out for thirty-six days, but nothing has told me otherwise."

"I'm not waiting that long to get my friends back," Mia said.

"I wouldn't expect you to," Riley said.

She stood up, went to her desk, and brought back a small box. She flipped the lid open and it turned into a board covered with different-colored squares. Inside were many different pieces. Riley set them up along the squares.

"I'm going to teach you a game," Riley said.

"I don't want to play games," Mia said. "I want my friends back."

"Before you act you need confirmation that's where they're at," Riley said. "You won't get it right away. Even then, what will you do?"

"Whatever you tell me," Mia said. "You're the strategist."

"And when I'm gone and the next problem comes along—there are always more problems when you're on the run—what will you do then? Run into another strange Irish lady and let her do your dirty work?"

"You're just trying to stall until you find out about your husband," Mia said.

"Maybe that's part of it," Riley said. "But you're a smart girl, you've been through worse than most, and you can think on your feet. Listen to your gut; does it say I'm trying to help you?"

Riley continued setting up the board. She didn't acknowledge Mia's unresponsiveness. Mia wanted to learn from Riley. A piece of her felt guilty because she was after more knowledge than the necessities involving rescuing Carter and Andrew.

"You promise me they're not dying?"

"Quite the opposite," Riley said. "They're safer than you or me right now. This piece is called the pawn . . ."

Riley went on explaining the game and Mia hung on her every word. No thoughts or worries filled her mind. She was focused on learning the rules.

Chapter 7

GRANT MARSDEN TO MAKE FIRST PUBLIC APPEARANCE SINCE HIS LOSS; RUMORED TO BE DELIVERING IMPORTANT MESSAGE ON SAFETY FOR ALL FEMALES

—American Gazette

"Welcome back. For those of you just joining in, tonight's guest is Mr. Grant Marsden. Mr. Marsden, you recently lost your young wife. How are you feeling?"

Frustrated, Grant thought. He would feel happy when she finally died.

"I feel a lot of pain," Grant said. "Some anger too."

"Absolutely," Greg Finnegan replied.

The Greg Finnegan Show. Grant couldn't believe this was his first television appearance. People swore by Greg, citing him as the most honest man in America. He gave the people their news Monday through Friday at seven P.M. Grant thought the man was a phony. Nobody is honest all the time. Sitting in the studio in another suit and tie, Grant was trying his hardest to play the grieving widower. Greg Finnegan wasn't doing much to help that portrayal by asking personal questions Grant wanted only to give impersonal responses to.

Grant smoothed out his tie; it was made of fine silk. The suit was from his collection and at least the fabric was to his standards. His hair was parted down the middle and gelled back. Grant made sure to flash his smile whenever possible. He was the new poster boy for America.

"Do you think you'll ever find love again?" Greg asked.

This was killing Grant. Love was a myth and not something Grant ever bothered trying to obtain. But that wasn't a response he could provide. He had to phrase his answer in a way that would allow him to keep the respect of the male population and the admiration of the females. It was like a logic puzzle.

"All relationships are unique," Grant said. "I look forward to the day I am ready to start anew."

Grant knew this interview was some form of a test. He was surprised none of the questions had been provided beforehand with the answers drafted by the capital. Now Grant had to figure out what the test was for.

"Well, if there are any young ladies out there watching I'm sure they're hoping your next choice is them," Greg said.

Grant gave a small smile and a laugh.

"Is there anything else you would like the public to know?" Greg asked.

"Yes." Grant turned his head so he could talk directly into the camera. "I want to speak to the young ladies out there who are watching. This was a tragedy. It is a dangerous world out there for girls. Remember to listen to your fathers and, when the time comes, your husbands. That's the only way to protect yourself."

"Wonderful advice from a humble man," Greg said. "Thanks to all our viewers for tuning in. See you tomorrow."

"Cut," the director yelled.

Greg Finnegan pulled off his microphone. Grant did the same.

"This will air in a few hours," Greg said. "Your story is very compelling. Poor . . . Mina, was it?"

"The focus isn't on her death, it's on me and my recovery," Grant said, ignoring Greg's question.

"Which, I might add, is remarkable," Greg said. "Has it even been forty-eight hours?"

"Her funeral is tomorrow," Grant said. "I am doing remarkably well."

He didn't appreciate Greg's undertone.

"I'll be in attendance," Greg said. His steely eyes belied his famous smile. "Don't worry. Everything will be edited and cut together. You'll show just the right balance of charm and mourning."

Grant loosened his tie, stood up, and walked off the stage. He hoped this media parade wouldn't last too long. There were other, more pressing matters that required his attention.

Chapter 8

Four years of mandatory service isn't enough. Why, each man should serve ten before accessing the Registry.

—Opinion from the American Gazette

A key slid into the lock. The turning metal broke Andrew from his trance. He jumped up from the ground and tried to brush the dirt off his white scrubs. There was nothing for Andrew to defend himself with, but the solitude was pushing his brain into overdrive and he welcomed any knowledge about his current situation.

Three men walked into the room, all dressed in camouflage fatigues. It was the uniform Andrew had spent most of his life coveting. The oldest of the three walked to the far side of the table and sat down. He was in his forties, with tanned skin and a cap covering his head. The two others were much younger. They carried rifles and stood on either side of the seated man.

"Please, Andrew, have a seat," he said.

Looking for options and seeing only one, Andrew sat down.

"My name is General Bolivar," the man said with a thick Spanish accent. "I'm here to welcome you and give you the orientation."

The man expected Andrew to speak, but he didn't want to break the silence.

"Your friend Carter has a much different attitude than you," General Bolivar said. "He was less responsive, had too many questions, howled at the door for release, and tried his hardest to attack my men. Why is it you two are so different?"

Andrew still didn't say anything.

"Maybe it is because he was raised in a loving home and you were tossed out by your country, forced to live on the streets."

This wasn't good. Andrew tried to keep his features still, but he worried about what else Carter might have told them.

"We're going to give you a new country to fight for," the general said. "A new cause to take up. I think you'll fit right in down here."

"I don't need a new cause," Andrew said.

"He speaks," the general said. "In that case I'll shoot you dead on the spot. If you try to escape I'll shoot you. If you give less than one hundred percent I'll shoot you. If you cause any problems I'll shoot you. Do you understand?"

Andrew nodded. One escape attempt was all he had. Andrew knew he needed to plan wisely.

"By leaving your country prior to service in their armed forces you are guilty of treason. I say treason against a disgraceful nation is not a crime," the general said. "You will join our cause. You will fight for us. You will belong and work as a team with your fellow soldiers."

For some reason this man's words stung to the core. Treason. He was guilty of that. He had no intention of joining this brigade, but if he was going to fake it long enough to escape he needed some motivation.

"What am I fighting for here? If this service is against my will, isn't Mexico a disgraceful nation?"

The two men lifted their rifles and pointed them at Andrew. He had struck a nerve.

"Everyone has that idea at first," General Bolivar said. "After your previous home invaded our country under the cover of stopping a war, they required the disbandment of the Mexican armed services. The militia is the only line of defense your new home has, and you will be a proud member."

"A militia isn't an army," Andrew said. "I saw maybe one hundred men training out there."

"You saw three hundred men training here. And there are another four hundred training off base, along with five hundred more on missions," General Bolivar said. "We are a new group and our numbers are growing."

"What will I be?" Andrew asked.

"A militiaman," General Bolivar said. "Your new name is Private Andrew Simpson. Your training starts today, Private Simpson."

"I can shoot a gun," Andrew said.

"And fly a helicopter," he said. "But that doesn't mean you're going to get either of those here. Once you can be trusted we'll move you up to weapons training and see what you have. Now you start at the bottom. We break you down so we can build you up. Gentlemen, please escort Andrew to his new room."

The two guards walked around the table and kept their guns pointed at Andrew the whole time. He rose from his chair and started into the hallway. *Break you down.* Andrew didn't like the sound of that. Now was the time for him to act strong. He couldn't show any weakness. The quicker he moved through this, the closer he would get to regaining his freedom and finding Mia.

Chapter 9

The world's efforts should be put into repairing the barren wastelands created during the Great War, not helping thriving nations.

—*Comment from the* International Reporter

The day was spent playing too many matches for Mia to keep count. Riley was a skilled player and didn't take it easy on Mia. Some of their games only lasted two moves. Mia never got close to winning.

"Checkmate," Riley said.

"Urg." Mia started pulling on her hair. "I don't want to play anymore."

"Why?" Riley asked, and she set up the board again.

"Because you keep winning," Mia said. "It's not fun for me."

"Well it's not fun for me either. You're not very good and there's no challenge here."

Riley moved her pawn forward.

"Then why are we playing?" Mia said, making a move.

"It's the only way you'll get better," Riley said. "The key to winning is guessing what my next move is. Staying one step ahead at all times."

It was Mia's turn again. She moved her knight out.

"I knew you would do that," Riley said. "Every fifth game you get bored with moving pawns and you move the knight. I also think it's your favorite piece because of its design. Guess my move," Riley said.

Mia stared at the board. Riley would move her pawn another space forward. Mia nodded her head. Riley made the move Mia predicted she would. The shock on Mia's face must have been enough for Riley to know she'd guessed correctly.

"See?" Riley said. "You've learned more than you know. Think like that for all the moves. Plot a strategy in advance and go with it."

Mia moved her knight back into place. Riley gave her a raised eyebrow. Mia thought she might have thrown her off.

"Want to make this interesting?" Riley said. "If you win this match I'll show you where I believe your friends are."

"I don't think it's fair to bet on something like that," Mia said.

"Use your head," Riley replied. "If you can beat me, it shows me you learned something and are capable of formulating a plan and not running in and destroying everything I've worked for. Does that phrasing work better for you?"

Mia focused on the game. She wanted to see Andrew and Carter. She tried her hardest to tune out any distractions. She guessed Riley's moves and was right some of the time. Pieces were being captured right and left. Then Mia saw it. Her chance to win. Riley needed to make one more move, then Mia could take the game.

"Checkmate," Riley said.

Mia stood up and let out a small scream. Riley smiled. Mia paced back and forth.

"Don't get so busy planning the win that you forget your defenses," Riley said. "But much better that time."

"Again," Mia said.

Riley set up the board for another battle.

Six games later Mia still hadn't won. Between matches she was feeling less frustrated though. Almost winning was more rewarding than losing by a lot every time. This match was intense. They were down to the final moves, on the verge of determining a winner. Mia had Riley set up to lose. She was down to just her king. Mia moved her queen into place.

"Check," Mia said.

Riley moved her king. Mia followed with her queen.

"Check," Mia said.

Again the same moves followed.

"That's not fair," Mia said. "This will go on forever. Making these same moves."

Riley put her hands on her lap, leaving her king in place. "And that, my dear, is called a stalemate."

"What's that mean?" Mia asked.

"There is no winner," Riley said. "Or if you like it better, we're both winners."

"Does that mean . . ."

"I'll show you where they're at," Riley said.

Mia let out a sigh of relief. Riley stood up and walked over to her desk. She pulled out a large backpack and threw Mia a pair of black pants and a black tank top.

"My feet are larger than yours," Riley said. "I'm going to stuff my spare shoes with socks. We have a long walk so make sure you're comfortable. Remember, nothing is going to happen tonight. I'm just going to give you a tour. Break this rule and I won't invite you back here with me."

Mia nodded. She wished there was some way to let Andrew and Carter know she was all right. That she was alive. Mia turned her back and changed into the black outfit. She looked at the small window and saw the light was starting to disappear.

"It's that late?" Mia asked.

"Better to observe at night," Riley said.

"How will we see anything?"

"I have some toys," Riley said.

She grabbed a tiny backpack and put two water bottles inside before flinging it over her shoulders. Mia made sure the black sock-filled tennis shoes were tight. They were ready to head out. Riley handed Mia some dried meat.

"We'll eat on the way," Riley said. "Let's go."

"How far is the walk?" Mia asked.

"About ten kilometers," Riley said. "Two to three hours."

"You don't run there?" Mia asked.

"No," Riley said. "I don't run unless I have to. It wastes energy and requires more water."

Riley opened the door and the two were on their way. The sun was dropping fast but the sky seemed lighter than she expected.

"It's darker at night where I'm from," Mia said.

"We're farther south here so the sun sets later," Riley said. "Some rules: Nobody can see us. We don't have to worry too much right now because they only leave the area by car and we'll hear the motor in time to hide."

The grass stopped and they started walking on a dirt road. They were along the coastline. Mia could hear the waves crashing. She guessed the tide was in again.

"Where would we hide?" Mia asked. "This is all open."

"In the dark it's easy. Just drop," Riley said. "Most people don't see what they're not looking for. I never head out in daytime."

"But you found me in daytime," Mia said.

"Special circumstances," Riley said. "A helicopter crashed. Right about where we are now."

"I was that close to you?"

Mia tried to look out into the ocean for remnants of the crash, but there was no sign of it.

"That's how I was able to get you home," Riley said. "Flung you over my shoulder."

"Can you tell me about where we're going?" Mia asked. "Where we're headed?"

"Puesta del Sol," Riley said.

"What's that?" Mia asked.

"Sunset," Riley said. "In Spanish."

"The men who took Andrew and Carter, they spoke a different language."

"Spanish was the official language of Mexico," Riley said. "Now it's English, but most of the residents are bilingual."

"Why did it change?" Mia asked.

"You want a history lesson?" Riley said. "Mexico was run by drug cartels. It was a very dangerous place. The government had no power or control and civilians were being murdered. They needed help, so they turned to their neighbor. America sent their army and crushed the cartels. Then they helped set up the new Mexican government, which supported English as a national language."

"The people weren't mad?" Mia asked.

"Not at first," Riley said. "They were happy the drug lords were gone. Time has passed though, and some rebels miss the old ways."

"So the American services?" Mia asked. "They help people?"

"Oh yes," Riley said. "The thugs of the world."

"What do you mean?"

"Countries are always fighting other countries," Riley said. "And sometimes they fight with themselves. Whichever side convinces America to help is the victor."

"This is a bad thing?"

"Not always," Riley said. "But the outcome is that America gets to do what it pleases. Even treat women like property and leave young boys to starve."

Mia reflected on this for a moment. America was eager to help other nations so that none of them would step in and help the American people.

"You said Mexico was dangerous? It's not now?" Mia asked.

"Most of Mexico isn't dangerous," Riley said. "This particular spot is. Puesta del Sol is off most maps. In a way you're lucky you landed here. Any other part of the country would have deported your gentleman companions back right away. But Puesta del Sol has another purpose for them."

"Which is?" Mia asked.

"Soldiers," Riley said. "They want your boys' bodies to enlist in their makeshift army. The two are part of the Collection."

Mia let out a snort.

"Andrew and Carter would never do that," Mia said. "They ran away from service."

"Well, these men won't give them the choice," Riley said. "And they specialize in brainwashing too."

"So I'm going to have to break into an army base and smuggle two new recruits out?" Mia asked.

"That would be the end goal," Riley said.

"How?" Mia asked.

"That's what I want you to tell me," Riley said.

"And you think Nathan's there?"

"The last time Nathan was seen he had a gun to the back of his head and was being walked onto a plane. That was more than five months ago. I've followed every lead and there's a chance he is here," Riley said.

"Then maybe we can make the plan together," Mia said.

"First let's canvass the area," Riley said. "Then we'll talk about plans."

Mia turned inward for a moment. She pictured Andrew and Carter being forced to enlist in a second service. Riley had mentioned brainwashing, but Mia didn't think she had too much to worry about. There was no way her two friends would fall under the spell of another military regime when they had both walked away from one already.

Chapter 10

Andrew had spent his whole life reading about the service. He'd seen several photographs of base life and hung on every word when postservice men described their time. He'd readied himself for an open room lined with bunk beds and trunks, large enough for several hundred men. This room did not compare.

It was the same idea, but on a much smaller level and with a dirt floor. There were ten bunks, none of which looked occupied. His guards remained by the door, not speaking or moving. Andrew heard footsteps and his eyes focused on the entrance. The key turned and the heavy wooden door opened. In came Carter, escorted by two of his own guards.

The young man's face was blank. His eye was red, on the way to turning black, and it looked like he'd gained a fresh bruise on his chin. Carter was defeated and dropped his head when he saw Andrew.

Andrew felt his rage flare. Not toward Carter, who had given these men information, but toward his captors, who had outnumbered and attacked an unarmed man. Carter was released by his guards and shoved into the center of the room. Andrew tried to make eye contact and give Carter a reassuring nod, but his counterpart refused to look at him.

A booming voice filled the room. "Welcome to your new home. I am Sergeant Randall MacLean. You will call me 'sir.' Do you understand?"

Andrew looked at the man. He was about a decade older than the two of them. He was small, not taller than five foot five, but his face and voice commanded attention and respect. Andrew was frozen.

"I asked you a question. Do you understand?"

Play the game, Andrew reminded himself. It was the only way he'd get a chance to escape. He had to convince these men he was on their side. Then he could find Mia.

"Yes, sir," Andrew said.

This caused Carter to look up.

"No," Carter said.

"What was that?" Randall screamed.

He stepped forward to Carter.

"What is my name?" Randall was practically on top of Carter.

"Sir," Andrew said. "Your name is Sir."

"I want to hear him say it."

"No," Carter said.

Randall backed up with a cruel smile on his face.

"You failed lesson one," Randall said. "You two are a team now and you share in punishment. I'll return in the morning. I expect you to know my name by then."

Randall left the room with the four guards behind him. They closed the heavy wooden door and the metal lock clipped over.

"Did they hurt you?" Andrew asked.

"No," Carter said. "I banged my head on a table." He rolled his eyes and looked away from Andrew.

"Don't draw attention to yourself," Andrew said. "Let's get through this."

"What am I doing?" Carter replied. "I'm not a soldier or a militia-man. Neither are you."

Andrew dropped his voice as low as possible and whispered into Carter's ear.

"If we don't play along they'll keep us here," Andrew said. "Act the part."

"My father taught me many things," Carter said in a whisper. "One of them is to have some integrity."

"Rod also taught you about taking care of other people," Andrew said. "We can't help anyone from in here."

"You don't say his name," Carter said. "He's dead. We left him and he's dead."

"What did you tell them about us?" Andrew asked. "Did you mention our—"

"No," Carter said. "Our names and where we're from. I didn't mean to tell them your name; it slipped. They asked if we served any time and I didn't mean to give away so much information. They poked fun at me for having a dad, but were excited you were raised on the streets. I didn't even tell them my dad was dead."

"Don't let him die for nothing," Andrew said. "We need to get out of here. Putting up a fight right now is wasting time."

"Maybe if I fight now they'll end this," Carter said.

"You don't want to die," Andrew said.

Carter let out a sigh and shook his head.

"We don't even know what their cause is," Andrew said. "All I know is that I need to get out of here. As fast as possible. We won't have a shot at that if we're locked in a cell."

Carter didn't have the chance to reply. Out of nowhere loud music filled the room. Both boys covered their ears. It was obnoxious, a ca-cophony of different instruments, drums and guitars making random noises. Andrew wasn't even sure it was actual music.

Carter tried to be heard above the sounds. Andrew saw his lips move but couldn't hear a thing coming out of his mouth. Andrew started moving around the room, but it was the same volume everywhere. It had only been a minute and Andrew thought his ears would bleed. He needed the noise gone now; he couldn't focus on anything. If these men wanted Andrew and Carter to stop talking there were easier ways to gain their silence.

Andrew gave up trying to talk. He waited for the noise to stop. It seemed like as soon as he got used to it the volume would increase or the instruments would change. It became impossible for Andrew to focus or think of anything but his desire for the noise to cease.

Chapter 11

EUROPEAN TAXES AND UNEMPLOYMENT AT AN ALL-TIME HIGH

—Global Reporter

The sky didn't seem too dark until the lights from the town became visible. The entire terrain had changed too. The lush greens and grasses disappeared and were replaced by a desert floor. The contrast sent a shiver down Mia's spine. If there was someone else walking around it would be hard to spot them in the darkness; of course, seeing Riley and Mia would be just as difficult.

"Is that where they are?" Mia asked, pointing to the lit area.

"No," Riley said. "That's Puesta del Sol proper. Never go in there."

"Why?"

"Trust me," Riley said.

Their path changed directions. Instead of walking along the coast, Riley started moving inland. They were going to pass the town on the opposite side. Mia wondered what made Riley so nervous. They were walking too far away from the small buildings for Mia to get a good look, but the area didn't seem threatening. The whole thing was about two blocks long. Behind the town was a patch of several small homes. Mia wouldn't have noticed them if some didn't have their lights turned on. Not more than three hundred people could have lived there, and that seemed like it would be pushing it. In the distance Mia thought she heard music. The town was celebrating.

"We're not very far from your friends," Riley said. "Do you see that house?"

Riley pointed past the town. The road wound upward along a hill. In the dark Mia wouldn't have noticed it, but there were lamps lighting the way. They were beautiful guiding lights. Mia's eyes scanned where they stopped; she could see the outline of a home.

"Not really," Mia said. "It's too dark."

"Here."

Riley handed Mia a pair of glasses. Mia wasn't sure how sunglasses would help her see in the dark but she slid them on. Everything was clear as day.

"How—"

"Your homeland," Riley said. "My team came in contact with an American. He didn't survive so they searched his person and found these. It was two years ago. Our government spent long hours trying to copy the technology, unsuccessfully. I doubt you know about these?"

"Do you think this is something created by one of those boys you mentioned earlier?" Mia asked.

"You'll have to ask a member of the American government," Riley said. "But as I mentioned earlier, it's just a rumor."

"Well, what happens to the other boys? The ones who are kept?"

"Supposedly, they're the ones who make the new technology; they're given the best education and kept highly medicated."

"What do you mean?" Mia didn't understand.

"It goes back to American secrecy," Riley said. "It's only one assumption."

Mia knew Riley wasn't comfortable discussing things she wasn't certain of.

"Your team kills people?" Mia asked. She changed the subject faster than she wanted to, but she didn't want to forget her other question.

"Only if they have to," Riley said. "They didn't kill the American. Didn't even know his name, if that's what you're wondering."

"Have you?" Mia asked.

With the glasses on Mia saw Riley's face fill with worry.

"Look at the house," Riley said. "Can you see it better now?"

Mia could. It was a sprawling white ranch with an orange roof. They were too far away for any detail. Mia wished the glasses had a zoom.

"A little," Mia said.

"That's Joseph Ruiz's home," Riley said. "He's the man in charge. This whole thing is his operation. The militia that has your men, they think they're preparing to fight for Mexico and protect their country, but they're only his personal army."

"The men don't know?" Mia asked.

"This militia thing is new," Riley said. "Two years old max. The man in charge of that operation is named General Ricardo Bolivar. I think he knows; before he was given the title of general the only military experience he had was running Ruiz's thugs."

"How did he start the militia then?"

"Disenchanted American youth," Riley said. "Your countrymen who are scared of service sneak over the border on a regular basis. Instead of being turned over for deportation, sometimes they fall into the wrong hands; it depends on who grabs them. General Bolivar got the idea to start buying them up. He recruited some local youth too. In two short years he's assembled more than one thousand well-trained soldiers."

"But what for?" Mia asked.

"The cartel wars might be long gone, but that doesn't mean that drug use left Mexico," Riley said. "I think Joseph Ruiz wants the militia to protect his drug running."

"So Joseph Ruiz is a drug dealer?" Mia asked.

The unserved boys who had shown up for work on Mia's father's farm brought her little knowledge of the outside world. One time when her father didn't know Mia was within earshot, she'd heard him talking to a manager about how one of the new hires was caught selling drugs to the other boys.

"A drug dealer," Mia's father had yelled, upset. "Can you believe it? Here? You need to get better at screening these boys."

Mia wasn't sure who the offending helper was, but several of the workers were gone after that day. At the time Mia assumed they were kicked off the property, but after learning from Andrew about the average young man's life, Mia wondered if the drug dealer met with a crueler fate. Later that night she had asked her mother what a drug dealer was; the response was that it was someone bad Mia would never have to deal with. She held on to the question though and asked her sister Corinna when she was home from finishing school for a long weekend.

"You know how if your stomach is upset Mom will give you a pill and it makes the pain stop?" Corinna asked. "Well, that's a drug. There are other kinds out there too, though. Some the government doesn't like, so if you're caught with them bad things will happen. Drug dealers are the people who sell these things."

"How do you know that?" Mia asked; she thought her sister was lying. It seemed too preposterous to twelve-year-old Mia.

"In the fall Mom and Dad will send you to a finishing school," Corinna said. "They don't teach you much but there will be other girls who know stuff there. You'll trade information with each other."

Mia smiled. She couldn't wait for finishing school. It was the best way to secure a match. Mia valued anything that would help her land a husband. She had never made it to finishing school, though. By the time the fall rolled around her parents agreed she was pretty enough that it wouldn't be necessary. At the time Mia's ego had soared from this announcement. Now Mia wondered how different her life would be if she'd had some form of education.

"I wouldn't call him a drug dealer," Riley said. "He's a mobster. Gangster. He has his hands in all sorts of illegal activity. The drug running is just a guess. Truthfully I don't know what he wants an army for, but it's probably nothing good."

The two continued moving, and Mia handed Riley back the glasses. The darkness offered Mia a new protection she welcomed. The two continued walking inland and north. Soon Puesta del Sol's lights were in the distance again. Riley stopped walking and took a drink from her water bottle.

"We're almost there," Riley said. "Reminders: Don't do anything to draw attention to us. We're just looking for information."

Mia nodded. She would give anything to get a glimpse of Andrew and Carter, though.

"Keep low and quiet," Riley said. She hunched down and started taking large steps forward.

Mia could only see flat landscape. She didn't know what Riley was trying to take cover from, but Mia followed her lead. Soon Riley dropped to a crawl. Mia joined her. A few more feet and Riley stopped. She lay down on her stomach and Mia fell next to her. Riley pulled herself forward, and Mia did the same.

The ground dropped away. Mia and Riley were at the top of a huge canyon. In the dark Mia would have missed the ground's absence and fallen off the cliff. Mia looked across the canyon and saw the opposite side had ridges just as steep. Riley handed Mia back the glasses and she put them on. This was a training facility. Mia saw a track circling the ground and an obstacle course of sorts. Her eyes scanned the field. She spotted several armed guards patrolling the area. Two of the four looked American. Their demeanor was that of any soldier. Nobody else was visible and that meant no Carter or Andrew.

"Where is everyone?" Mia asked.

"Below us, carved into the cliffs, is a housing unit," Riley said. "It's a giant relic created by past cultures. There are hundreds of rooms. That's where they have their offices and sleep, among other things. That's where your boys are."

"And maybe your husband?"

Riley nodded.

"Have you been inside?" Mia asked.

"Once," Riley said. "This is still an amateur army. They don't have any electronic security. Only those four guards."

"Five," a new voice said.

Mia heard a gun cock. She froze in fear.

"Keep your hands up and turn around," the man said. "Not too amateur to notice your break-in and change our rotation."

Mia rolled onto her back. This was it. Yet another time she was certain her journey would come to an end.

"A girl?" The guard laughed. He was American, not much older than Mia. He looked at her with a fire in his eyes.

"General Bolivar is going to love you," he said. Mia saw his eyes moving up and down her body. She looked away in disgust. "You too," he said to Riley. "Turn around. Keep your hands up."

Riley spun around onto her back.

"Another beauty," he said. "You're a little old, but I'm sure there's some use for you. Stupid girls."

He let out another laugh. Riley didn't hesitate. While Mia sat in fear she reacted with speed. She flopped back onto her arms and forced her feet in the air, flinging herself upward. Mia had never seen a body move that way. The guard was surprised too. Riley landed on her feet and kicked the barrel of his rifle down to the ground. She grabbed him by the shoulders and pulled him forward. The rifle served as a fulcrum and once he flipped over the weapon he was flung into the canyon.

"Come on," Riley said.

She reached down and pulled Mia up by the hand. Riley didn't give Mia the chance to ask any questions. Instead she started running through the desert. Mia's legs felt heavy again. The same way they felt after the helicopter crash. She was sure she was going to fall.

"Don't leave me," Mia called to Riley, who was several feet in front of her.

Riley turned around. "If you want to live, you'll run," she said.

Live, Mia thought. She forced her leaden legs to move under her and followed Riley as best she could. The gap between them widened, and Riley never slowed. They cleared the town and were back up by the coast again. Mia pulled on her inner strength and ran faster; otherwise she risked losing Riley in the dark desert. After what felt like forever Mia saw Riley slowing down to a walk. Mia continued moving fast until she was next to the redhead, who handed Mia some water.

"What was that?" Mia asked. "Were you going to leave me?"

"You need to learn to react," Riley said. "You froze there, then dragged your feet. I'm not going down with you."

"I can react," Mia said. "I saved Andrew from—"

"You need to respond for yourself," Riley interrupted. "If you can save others, you can save yourself. You froze on the beach that day, and you froze tonight."

"You said I needed to strategize," Mia said. "Which is it, form a plan or react?"

"Both!" Riley said.

Mia felt the tears sting her dry eyes. "I don't know what happened," she said. "I saw the way he was looking at me and I got so scared."

"He was American," Riley said. "They never suspect a girl is capable of anything but having babies. Our cover is blown."

"Nothing's changed," Mia said. "They knew someone was breaking in. The guard told us that. Now all they know is it's two girls."

"They'll start looking for us," Riley said.

"What if you killed him?" Mia asked.

Riley bit her lip and looked away. There was no way to get confirmation and Riley appeared to favor the idea of the young soldier surviving a dive into a canyon.

"Well, we need to start strategizing before they find us," Mia said. "I'll never leave my friends."

"You're not ready," Riley said.

"Get me ready then," Mia said.

The urge to cry vanished. Mia stared hard at Riley. The sky was lightening by the second. The Irish woman looked at the ground and started shaking her head. Mia's heart stopped, but when Riley lifted her head she wore a soft smile.

"Is that a yes?" Mia asked.

"We'll start tomorrow," Riley said.

She took another sip of water and then started walking. Mia felt a wave of adrenaline pass through her body. Tomorrow was the day they'd start plotting the retrieval of her friends. Mia thought about her freezing act tonight. Why hadn't she reacted? This hadn't been a problem for her in the past. Then the previous situations worked their way through her mind: trying to save Whitney in the back of the truck, pulling Andrew up from the railroad tracks, using her self-defense skills on Grant to protect Andrew. All of these situations did have a common denominator: Mia was more driven by the need to save someone else than herself. Mia's initial escape from her father's farm was self-interested, but since that time she'd evolved more and more into performing selfless acts.

Mia knew she wanted Andrew and Carter back more than anything, but she realized that in order to rescue them, she needed to learn how to save herself again.

Chapter 12

Being an American is a gift. Not appreciating that gift is a waste.

—American Gazette

The sounds stopped—at least Andrew thought they did. His head was so fuzzy he couldn't be sure. If they hadn't stopped, then his brain had shut his hearing off; either way he was grateful. Andrew looked at Carter for confirmation. Carter wore a look of confusion as well.

"Did it stop?" Andrew asked.

His voice sounded foreign to him. The simple sentence echoed through his brain. Carter had a similar reaction and nodded his head. Someone opened the door to their room. Both Carter and Andrew stood up straight as the sergeant walked inside, followed by two escorts.

"Well, are you going to wish me good morning?" he asked.

"Good morning, sir," Andrew said.

It was morning? Andrew had gone forty-eight hours without sleep or food. He didn't care at the moment, he was just grateful that the music had stopped. He looked over at Carter. If the other man didn't greet the sergeant with a "sir," Andrew would punch him. That was the thought Andrew had spent the last several hours trying to focus on.

"Good morning, sir," Carter said.

Andrew let out a sigh of relief.

"Very good," the sergeant said. "Get changed."

Carter and Andrew had spent a little bit of time trying to explore the room. Each of them had a chest filled with clothing. Andrew had thought about changing last night but didn't want to proceed without instructions.

"No breakfast today because you weren't in your uniforms this morning," the sergeant said. "If you want to eat you will follow the rules."

"Yes, sir," Andrew and Carter said.

While this was an annoyance, Andrew was happy to forgo food as long as the music didn't turn back on. He assumed next would be some form of strength training. He hoped they would go outside. Andrew knew there was a reason he wanted to head out there but couldn't put his finger on it. He let out a yawn. He was tired and didn't think physical activity would do him much good today.

The boys were escorted down the hall. Andrew tried his best to keep up. Carter's eyes had heavy bags under them. Andrew was sure he looked the same, but he needed to show these men how strong he was. That was the way to get respect. Andrew wanted their respect so he could survive, so he could . . . escape. Andrew's eyes lit up. Mia, escape. That was why he needed to get outside. The music had clouded his mind so much he'd nearly forgotten.

The group stopped and another door was unlocked. It was a spotless, shining bathroom. The walls and floor were covered in white tile. There were three toilet stalls and a mirror with a sink.

"You two will clean this dirty room," the sergeant said. "Once it is done we will start your training."

Andrew saw the cleaning supplies on the sink, but he didn't know what the sergeant was talking about. This room was flawless. Andrew didn't think it had ever been used. The mirror didn't have a single spot; everything was perfect. Carter's mouth hung open and his forehead wrinkled.

"Get started," the sergeant said.

"Where?" Carter asked.

"Call for me when it's done," he said.

With that he walked out of the room and slammed the door. A lock was flipped over. Andrew didn't understand why a bathroom would lock from the outside. Then it hit him.

"Am I imagining this?" Carter asked.

"Don't talk," Andrew said. "Don't do anything other than clean."

"Clean what?" Carter asked.

"Shh!"

The lock was already turning back. Andrew winced when the door opened up again.

"Since you two want to stand around and talk instead of work, I guess I'll need to motivate you," the sergeant said. "You'll work through lunch too."

The door was closed and Andrew preemptively covered his ears. The same music from the night before blared into the bathroom, and just like in their room Andrew couldn't find any speakers or figure out where the noise was coming from. This was a training exercise, Andrew knew. They were trying to break him, and he was scared because it was working.

Chapter 13

Americans must go through the same citizenship standards as any immigrant. They shouldn't be classified as refugees. Countries should worry about their own people.

　　　　　　　　—*Comment from the* Global Reporter *message board*

Andrew was kissing Mia. She was wrapping her legs around his while the wind breezed over the bed of the truck. Their embrace was broken when Grant's helicopter slammed into the bed.

"Don't worry," Andrew said. "I'll save you."

"No, it's my turn," Mia replied.

Then a knife whizzed past her head. Her eyes flew open. The knife was right in front of her eyes, sticking straight out of the wooden floor of Riley's cabin. This was it; the men who held Andrew hostage had discovered their location. Mia didn't think before shooting up and pulling the knife out of the wood. She readied it for her attacker, surprised to see Riley sitting in a chair with a grin on her face.

"That was pretty good," Riley said.

Mia's heart raced. "A knife? You threw a knife at me?"

Riley was seated at her desk. She clicked a button on her computer and music started playing.

"And you reacted," Riley said. "You didn't freeze up."

"You could have killed me," Mia said. "What were you thinking? Do you want me dead?"

"I was thinking I have great aim, and you want to save your friends," Riley said. "That and it's almost noon."

"I've only slept for seven hours," Mia said with a groan.

"Not everyone is so lucky," Riley said.

"I think I'm going to throw up," Mia said.

She started breathing heavily and leaned toward the side.

"That's the adrenaline," Riley said. "It kicked in with your wake-up call and got sucked out when the danger vanished. Don't get too comfortable. The danger is always around. Keep your body moving."

Riley stood up and gave Mia a shove. Mia stood up straight, but the heavy feeling in her legs returned.

"Keep it going," Riley said. "The more you stay still the worse you'll feel."

She started bouncing back and forth on the floor. Mia tried to echo her movements. She started to feel better.

"There you go," Riley said. "The color in your cheeks is coming back. Don't give in to the dread. Work through it. Now, when someone attacks you, remember this: If you give in to the fear you'll freeze. If you work through it you'll get some energy."

As Mia bounced up and down she realized she was moving to the beat of the music. It was happy and catchy, unlike any noise she'd ever heard before. It spread through her like an infection.

"What is this?" Mia asked.

"Pop music," Riley said. "An Irish band. If you can't think of a fight move, try and think of this song. It'll keep your body moving until an idea presents itself. Keep it quiet, like it is now, in the back of your mind until a move comes to you."

With the last comment Riley raised her fist and threw it at Mia. Mia lifted her arm at the elbow and blocked the punch, just like Carter taught her. Riley grinned at Mia's defense.

"I told you in my long, rambling story," Mia said. "Carter taught me some self-defense."

"Had to see the skills in action myself," Riley said. "Nice work."

Riley pulled her fist back and stopped moving. Mia couldn't believe how good she felt. She wasn't scared at all, even though minutes ago a knife was staring her in the eyes. Riley moved over to the computer and stopped the music.

"You've never heard pop music?" Riley asked.

"None like that," Mia said. "Mainly slow songs, some with twangs or classical music. I'm a terrible singer."

"They don't want you girls to wiggle your bodies around too much up there, huh?"

Mia shrugged. She wasn't so sure of the motivations in her world. Some of the questions that had raced through her head during their initial meeting returned.

"Do you know why?"

"They want you to seem pure?" Riley asked.

"No," Mia said. "I mean how the Registry came to be. Why America is the way it is."

"Oh," Riley said. "I know what everyone knows, not much more. America is a very private country."

Mia looked at Riley with eager eyes.

"Don't you want to start on your friends' case?" Riley asked. "What do you have as a plan to rescue them so far?"

"Not this time," Mia said. "You change the subject whenever you don't want to give an answer to something. I love those boys and I would do anything for them, but I need answers."

"It's part of your past," Riley said.

"But I can't move on unless I have some clues."

Riley let the air rush between her lips and they flapped against each other.

"For the last two hundred years or so, I don't know, maybe since the beginning of time even, women have been fighting for equality," Riley said. "All over the world, for the most part, they were seen as the weaker sex. Then about a century ago, maybe more, it started happening everywhere. Women were equals to men, including in America. Then there was a war."

"The Great War," Mia said.

"The Great War, World War III, the Great Conflict," Riley said. "Lots of different names for it."

"What was it about?" Mia asked.

"Does it matter?" Riley said. "America was important; they were late to join the fight and sided with the good guys. If America hadn't joined I can't imagine what kind of suffering would be in Ireland today. They were our saviors."

"So we were the good guys?"

"Once the war was done the world was in ruins," Riley said. "It wasn't fought on this continent. It was overseas, near my home, and in other places around the globe. We were too busy cleaning up, and then a few years later the Registry existed. America closed its borders but kept a huge armed force. They made it clear to the rest of the world they'd offer help in times of grave danger, and they still do."

"That doesn't explain anything," Mia said. "What caused the Registry to come into existence? How could everything change just like that?"

Riley looked away.

"Tell me," Mia said.

"They don't teach American history in Irish schools."

"You're an intelligence officer," Mia said. "You know. Tell me."

"Disease struck your homeland," Riley said. "When the soldiers returned home there wasn't much of a home to come back to. People were sick and dying."

"Didn't they get their shots?" Mia asked.

"Some," Riley said. "Not like we have today."

"No other country came and helped us?"

"They were all torn apart by the war," Riley said.

"So America steps in to help your country and you turn your backs?" Mia asked. "You didn't mind when all women became slaves?"

"I hadn't been born," Riley said.

"Why not step in and help now?" Mia asked. "You have a position of power; you can do something."

"International politics are a tricky thing," Riley said.

"There's nothing tricky about it," Mia said. "People are suffering and you choose not to help. Your country focuses on its own problems instead."

"I'm helping you, aren't I?" Riley asked.

"Because it furthers your own agenda," Mia said.

"That's cruel and untrue," Riley said. "Before the war there were one hundred ninety-six sovereign countries. Do you know how many exist today?"

Mia shook her head, but she wasn't ready to back down.

"Today there are ninety-three countries; tomorrow there might be ninety-two or ninety-four, because countries keep merging and revolting. Before the war Ireland was a small island; now it's a group of small islands and some large ones too. The whole world was rearranged!"

Riley's voice was deepening. Mia felt a pang of guilt. Over half the world was lost in a war.

"Me and you are starting our plan, and I don't even know if my husband is there. I may be putting his life in danger to get your boys out."

"Just because we were spotted last night and your timeline was pushed up," Mia said.

"Whatever the reason, I am helping you," Riley said. "Have you ever come across someone who gave you assistance without benefiting themselves at all?"

Yes, Mia thought. *Andrew.*

Right now she needed this woman's help to save him. Fighting over century-old problems wasn't going to help that, so Mia bit on her pride and shook her head.

"Then back to work," Riley said.

She clicked some buttons on her computer and a man's face popped up. He was older and distinguished. His dark hair was down to his shoulders and slicked back; his eyes were warm and welcoming. Mia thought he was the type of man American girls dreamed of marrying.

"This is Joseph Ruiz," Riley said. "He is smart, wealthy, well connected, and evil."

She flipped to the next picture. It was a beautiful woman, several years older than Mia but not quite Riley's age. Her thick, shiny black hair ran down her back.

"Dalmy Ruiz," Riley said.

Mia had never heard such a name. Riley pronounced it "Doll-Me" but that didn't match the spelling on the screen. She looked exotic. Mia thought it was fitting that Joseph had wed such a beautiful woman.

"The pride and joy of Joseph's life," Riley said. "His daughter and heir to his empire."

"She's too old to live with her father," Mia said.

Riley gave her a look.

"We're not in America anymore," Riley said. "Mexico supports its women. She is being groomed to take over Joseph's business."

"What's an heir?" Mia asked.

Riley rolled her eyes.

"If your father died, what would happen to your mother? His money? His land?"

"I never thought about that," Mia said. Her cheeks grew red and she looked down.

"Your mother would go into retirement; his land and money would revert to the government, which would sell it and make even more money," Riley said.

Mia looked up at her with wide eyes. If Riley knew this, she knew other facts about America. Mia couldn't ask another question though. Her focus needed to remain with the boys.

"In other parts of the world it would go to the spouse, the children, or any other person the father chose," Riley said. "That person is called an heir."

Riley clicked to another picture. It was an older man. He had the same dark features as the other two. He was heavier-set with cold, hard eyes.

"General Bolivar," Riley said. "You heard about him yesterday."

She clicked another button and the three pictures appeared next to each other.

"These are our three key players," Riley said. "If you want Andrew and Carter back you'll have to work through them."

"Strengths and weaknesses?" Mia asked.

"Hmm," Riley said. "Nice question. Straight to the point. I like it." She took a breath.

"General Bolivar's weakness is Joseph Ruiz. Joseph Ruiz, Dalmy Ruiz. Dalmy Ruiz, none known."

A father who cared about his daughter above all else, above money. This was a new concept for Mia, but it made the first step simple.

"Her," Mia said. "She's the key to getting the rest of them."

"And how will you accomplish that?" Riley asked.

"Study her," Mia said. "Learn what she does first."

Riley smiled and turned back to the computer.

"You're right. I would make you do the legwork but since we were spotted last night I don't think that's necessary."

She clicked a few buttons and Dalmy's face took up the whole screen.

"What do you know about her?" Mia asked.

"Not much," Riley said. "She's protected, dangerous, lives in her father's house. I think she's in charge of the girls in the town."

"So why not become one of the girls in the town then?" Mia asked. "Get close to her, take her hostage, and exchange her freedom for the men's."

"No," Riley said. "Too dangerous."

"What's so dangerous about being a girl in a town?" Mia asked.

"We shouldn't plan on an empty stomach," Riley said. "Go get yourself ready for the day and I'll get us some breakfast. Then afterward you can show me more of your self-defense skills. Try to think about other options too. Never turn your brain off."

Riley closed her laptop and Mia stood up. It was becoming easy for Mia to read Riley. Her sudden change of subject made Mia all the more curious about the town, but as she would in a game of chess, Mia decided to wait to make her move.

Chapter 14

FROM VICTIM TO HERO: GRANT MARSDEN REPRESENTS THE AMERI-CAN IDEAL

—American Gazette

"And now the deceased's husband will speak," the funeral director said.

Grant went to take center stage. Everyone was sitting outside on his back lawn. "Lawn" was an understatement. It was the acres on which his mansion and many secondary houses sat. He walked up to the podium and looked at the jar of ashes on display. He wondered what was inside, knowing it wasn't Amelia. After nodding at the contents he looked out over the audience.

It was his business acquaintances mainly, the heads of all the military departments and their wives. Some lower-level individuals he dealt with frequently. Members of his team and Rex, his most trusted assistant, assembled with other staff for his home. Greg Finnegan had brought his partner, and some of his media counterparts were present too. Strangers, but their cameras lined the back row and all were going to feature this speech at some point on their programs. Grant was disappointed that the grand commander hadn't attended. None of Amelia's family was invited, of course, because her family was Grant now. Ha.

Grant wasn't nervous about giving the speech he'd prepared; he hoped he could muster up some grief. He tried to think of different situations that would allow him to display some real emotions. Grant thought about what his mother and father must have been like, but Grant had had a good life and felt better off without them. He envisioned Rex passing on; that annoyed Grant more than brought tears. Then he decided if grief wouldn't come he would show the world his anger. That was easy to conjure up with the image of Mia flying off in his helicopter fresh in his mind.

"My wife is dead. I worked so hard and chose with caution, never thinking this was a possibility. I'm angry that my hard work went for naught and I'm angry that I lost so much. I racked my brain thinking of what I could have done to deserve this. I fought for my country, I work for my country, and I live for my country. Focusing on these strengths, I realized this is no punishment. This is an unfortunate occurrence that I will survive and grow from. People will learn from this. Protect your wives and daughters. I know when the time comes for me to wear the titles of 'husband' and 'father,' I will."

The speech was memorized and Grant took turns making eye contact with his audience. At the end he spoke into the cameras. He picked up the vase of ashes and took off the lid.

"This should symbolize not the passing of life, but a new start for myself."

With that Grant turned around and scattered the ashes behind him. The people in the crowd clapped. When he turned to face them they were standing. Some of the women were wiping away tears. It was perfect. He smiled with them and nodded his head. The grand commander was right; these people didn't want a victim, they wanted a hero, and Grant was playing his part.

After Grant had shaken hands with everyone present, they packed up their things and left. Grant's employees scattered back to their posts within his great estate. The last one left was Rex. Rex lived on Grant's property in one of the smaller homes. Today he joined Grant in the walk up to his mansion. Some people thought it was too large, but not Grant. It was a symbol of his wealth and he was happy to show it off. One of the television reporters had asked to schedule a tour, thinking the people would love to see the great house.

"I'm sorry, boss," Rex said. "Good speech. That must have been hard."

"It was," Grant said. "I should never have split up the team. My gut told me she was in the Gila Bend area. If I'd had you with me none of this would have happened."

"We can still make it right," Rex said.

"No," Grant said. "I'm forbidden from leaving the country. There are more pressing matters at play."

"Than your pride?" Rex asked. "I've been doing some research."

Grant hunched his shoulders down and put a defeated look on his face. He glanced around the property to make sure nobody was in view. Then he brought his arm up and nailed his employee in the gut. This caught Rex off guard, and the large man fell to his knees with his arms around his stomach.

"I didn't lose," Grant said.

He left Rex on the grass.

"Don't forget your place," Grant said. "I'm still the one in charge."

With those final words Grant walked into his giant house alone. He closed the door behind him and an echo sounded through the halls. He made his way toward the stairs, which were gold plated and lined with red carpeting. The whole house was red and gold, the colors of his country.

"Sir," Brandon, Grant's chief of staff, said, "it was a perfect ceremony. My condolences again. Can I bring you something to eat?"

"No," Grant said. He didn't bother to turn around and continued up the steps.

One of the main reasons he wanted a wife was so she could handle the staff. Housework was a woman's concern. Most men weren't willing to let their wives have a job, and Grant didn't think he wanted the type of woman who would be in his employment. Grant's wife should have been the one dealing with Brandon.

Grant turned down the hallway and into his bedroom. This room was the third largest in the house. He went straight for his closet, pulling off his suit in the process, feeling instant relief. Grant checked the cell phone he'd left there, upset that there was no call. Next he dressed in his normal attire—today it was blue plaid shorts and a baby-blue polo. He slid on his moccasins and left the pile of dirty clothes in the closet, knowing Brandon would pick them up later. He was the only servant permitted in Grant's room.

He was starting out of the closet when his pocket vibrated. He pulled out his phone and didn't recognize the number.

"Hello," Grant said.

"Please hold for the capital," a woman's voice said. The call switched to music.

Grant hated that women could work for the government but not for private citizens. Even though Grant was a government contractor he didn't have the right to that supply of workers. If he had then maybe a wife wouldn't have been necessary at all; he could employ the unmarried to run his household for him.

"Grant," the grand commander said.

"Sir," Grant said. "This is unexpected."

"You've done well," he said. "And that was expected. I'd like for you to come to the capital tomorrow. After lunch."

There was a click. The line went dead. Grant smiled; the grand commander was all business. Grant appreciated that. The personal phone call raised his spirits. His plan had been to head down to the workshop and start tinkering with inventions. He didn't see that happening anymore. The invitation to the capital would make it too hard to concentrate. Grant was thrilled. He tried to remember the last time he was this happy.

As a child in one of the government orphanages Grant was well liked by most of the boys and his teachers, but that didn't mean the feelings were reciprocated. He was much different back then, lacking the self-esteem he now possessed, plagued with shyness and a miserable stutter. He'd been released the same day as four others, including Erik, a pompous ass who teased Grant for his speech patterns.

While Grant had developed into a very different man, some of his characteristics had always been present, including his thirst for revenge. The five thirteen-year-olds had gathered on the street and debated where to look for work. Grant had spent years waiting for this moment—not to be free from the orphanage but to take his vengeance.

He walked up to Erik and acted as if he was going to whisper something into his ear. Instead Grant slid the butcher knife he had stolen from the kitchen out of his long-sleeved shirt and straight into Erik's gut. Erik didn't know what had happened, and the other young men weren't paying any attention.

"It's a hard world out here," Grant whispered. His stutter was gone.

Grant yanked his knife out and backed away. He enjoyed the look of terror on Erik's face. Erik brought his hands forward, covering his wound. Grant started walking away, not wanting to run or draw attention. He tossed the knife in a garbage can and rounded a corner. That was the first man he'd ever killed, and he had felt such vindication.

Yes, that was perhaps the last time he'd felt such pure glee. Grant wondered what his thirteen-year-old self would think of him now. Wealthy, adored, and receiving personal phone calls from the grand commander. Grant's smile faded.

Erik crossed you once and you took care of him; now you let little girls beat you.

Grant heard his own voice in his head. *No, the game isn't over. She hasn't won; I haven't shown my hand yet.* He knew his plan wasn't moving fast enough and doubted himself for a moment. Then the moment passed and Grant let himself relax a bit. Patience was a necessity to victory, and Grant knew she would come home in due time.

Chapter 15

America is a worldwide bully. If the Registry isn't stopped, how long until it spreads into other countries?
—Comment from the Global Reporter *message board*

"What if we break into Dalmy's house at night, take her hostage, and then trade her?" Mia asked.

"I told you," Riley said. "The house isn't an option. It's impenetrable."

"But you broke into an army base."

"I broke into an oversized, poorly guarded militia front," Riley said.

"Why don't we bust in there and break them out?"

"One person undetected was risky enough," Riley said. "Going in with two and moving out with four is a death wish."

"Five," Mia said. "We're looking for Nathan too."

"Five," Riley said. "That means locating the men, and I don't have a map or the aerial surveillance to get that information."

"You keep shooting everything down," Mia said. "The best option was still my first suggestion. We become Dalmy's girls, then hold her hostage. I can make a new friend."

"How will you explain our presence? An American and an Irishwoman wandering around in Mexico?"

"I'm here on my honeymoon and ran away from my husband,"

Mia said. "I stuck out my thumb and you picked me up. Then our car ran out of gas."

"Days after a helicopter crash?"

"Do you have a better idea?" Mia asked.

Riley was quiet.

"I think I should go alone," Mia said. "That way you can cover for me if anything goes wrong."

"Back to me saving you again," Riley said.

"Not me," Mia said. "Andrew and Carter. If something goes wrong, get them out."

"And what if the soldier who saw us is there?"

"You threw him over a cliff. I think the odds are in our favor that he's out of commission. Tell me what is wrong with this plan. A straight answer."

Riley paced back and forth. Her brow was furrowed.

"Don't lie," Mia said.

"Dalmy's girls . . . ," Riley said. "They're not her friends. They're her employees."

"I can cook," Mia said.

"They all have the same job."

Mia wasn't following. It still didn't sound too bad.

"I can only research so much on the Internet," Riley said. "I'm not sure what this town is all about, but the inhabitants are bad men. The women who live here work to please them."

"I thought the militiamen lived there," Mia said.

"No. They live on the base."

"So a town of bad men that has an army behind it and women please them? . . . Oh."

It took saying it out loud for Mia to understand what Riley was getting at.

"Please them . . . ," Mia said. "But that's illegal unless you're married."

"Only in America," Riley said. "It's the oldest profession in the world. So if something went wrong, that's the life you'd live."

"Never," Mia said. She wasn't ready to think about intimacy at all, let alone with a stranger.

"That's why your plan won't work."

"I'll get out of there before it comes to that," Mia said. "I have to save Andrew and Carter."

"We'll find another way," Riley said.

"There is none," Mia said. "We're running out of time. They know someone is watching them; how long until they look for us? Then we'll both end up Dalmy's girls."

"We could leave," Riley said. "You and I. Go back to Ireland, get some reinforcements, then break out your friends."

"And how long would that take? I'll never leave them. I know you won't leave Nathan either."

Riley was silent.

"I came up with a solid plan," Mia said. "It will work. Dalmy will take me in and when she's at her weakest I'll hold her hostage and trade her for the boys."

"They'll come after you," Riley said.

"I won't free Dalmy until I'm out of harm's way," Mia said. "If Joseph loves his daughter like you say he does, he won't chase me until she's safe."

"If it came down to it and you had to kill her, would you?" Riley asked.

"I've never killed anyone . . ."

The image of the RAG agent on the ground came to Mia's mind. She remembered slamming the rock into his face over and over. A shudder went through her body. How could she forget so soon?

"I would," Mia said. "If I had to I would kill her."

Riley raised an eyebrow at Mia's response. She nodded her head in agreement.

"Then it's settled," Mia said. Her voice was a bit shaky.

"No," Riley said. "We have the start of a plan. Now we fill in the rest, leaving no room for error."

"What's first?" Mia asked.

"Once the sun goes down a bit we head outside," Riley said. "You show me some of your fighting skills and we'll improve from there."

Mia expected to feel comfort at starting the rescue mission; instead she was met with a feeling of dread. She pictured Andrew and Carter dead in the bottom of a ditch. They were in army uniforms, guns in hand after losing a battle for a cause that wasn't even their own. Whatever risks Mia was taking were worth preventing that fate.

The cabin was growing dimmer. It was later in the day than Mia realized; she'd wasted most of the afternoon having her ideas shot down. After choosing their strategy Riley turned to her computer and Mia lay down on the bed. She stared at the ceiling, brainstorming about what might help her in her mission. She knew Riley didn't want to discuss it yet, and Mia didn't want to think out loud.

"Let's head outside," Riley said.

Mia was looking forward to demonstrating her self-defense skills. She'd used them before and Riley had only gotten a glimpse of what she was capable of. Riley turned around and faced Mia. She put up her fists and Mia did the same. Riley toggled back and forth on her feet.

"Hit me," Riley said.

Mia's mind flashed back to Carter's lessons. She doubted Riley's would end the same way. Mia knew Riley was right-handed and likely to move toward the right. Mia threw her first punch. She anticipated Riley's movements and tapped her in the stomach. Riley looked shocked.

"This is just sparring," Mia said. "I'm not going to hurt you."

Riley came forward and swung her leg at Mia. Mia bent down and put her arms out, ready to block the kick from Riley. Mia grabbed hold of Riley's leg and stood up with it, showing she would have knocked Riley to the ground. The redhead backed away. Mia could see she was running out of breath. A few more attempts were made, always with Mia being the victor.

"How are you so good at this?" Riley asked.

"I was trapped in a basement all day with nothing to occupy my time but practice," Mia said. "I've spent the last two days with you and you're easy to read."

"So you're anticipating my attacks?"

Mia nodded. Riley came at her with her right fist. Mia lifted her right hand, knowing this was a fake-out. She blocked Riley's left-hand punch.

"Enough," Riley said.

She dropped her fighting stance and moved away.

"Impressive," Riley said. "You don't attack though."

"The best way to stay alive is to keep on the defense," Mia said.

Mia was feeling proud of herself. She had just opened her mouth to speak when Riley dropped to the ground and spun her leg out. Mia fell onto the dirt with a thump. Before she could take a breath Riley was standing over her.

"I hate to break it to you, but a couple weeks in a basement is nothing," Riley said.

She reached her hand down and pulled Mia up. The pride vanished.

"You're still in good shape," Riley said. "If I was reading you I wouldn't have thought you could defend yourself at all, but you're no professional."

Mia gave Riley raised eyebrows as she dusted the dirt from her clothes.

"So you think I can handle one surprise attack?" Mia asked.

"That's one way to look at it," Riley said. "I think it's best if you avoid fighting at all. Then there's no need to worry."

"Not an option," Mia said.

"Someday it will be," Riley said. "Once you rescue your friends, what is your plan?"

"Guatemala," Mia said.

"You're close," Riley said. "It's the next country down. Several hours south of here."

Mia's eyes lit up. She had never dreamed it would be that easy.

"Why Guatemala?" Riley asked.

"I met someone on the Internet, a former American who is living there," Mia said.

"Do you think it's a trap?" Riley said. "American Internet is pretty closed off. You'd need special skills to hack into that . . ."

"What?" Mia asked. "Do you know a group of Americans who have those skills in Guatemala?"

Riley nodded her head.

"Where are they? What are they like?"

"You should know better than me," Riley said. "You're the one going to spend the rest of your days with them."

"It's not like that," Mia said. "Please, tell me what you know."

Mia was thrilled. She hadn't had the time to think much about S or their late-night chats. Mia would soak up everything Riley had to offer on her mystery correspondent's home.

"Some people out there want to help Americans," Riley said. "Women's rights, that sort of thing. There are small pockets in certain countries dedicated to that cause. I'm assuming that's what your contact in Guatemala is about."

"That's fantastic," Mia said.

"Is it?" Riley asked. "You escaped. Your friends are being forced to take up a cause now and you'd lead them into another. Why not live your life for a bit?"

"You're not living your life," Mia said. "All you do is move around the world searching for a ghost."

Mia regretted the words the second they left her mouth.

"I'm sorry. I didn't mean that," Mia said.

"It's fine," Riley said. "You're right. Maybe I don't want to see you head down the same path."

"Right now my path just leads to rescuing Andrew and Carter."

Riley nodded her head.

"Promise me your goals will remain uncorrupted," Riley said. "The world already has enough villains."

"Of course," Mia said. "You don't think the Americans in Guatemala are bad, do you?"

"I think they're extremists," Riley said. "Things aren't as black and white as they seem, Mia. Don't let your head get so locked in one direction that you can't see the destruction you leave behind you."

Mia was silent. Riley smacked at a bug on her arm.

"Come on," Riley said. "We have some more work if we're going to get moving on this."

Riley walked inside the shanty and Mia followed. She didn't understand what Riley meant about things not being black and white. To Mia they were. The way America treated all their youth—not just the females—was wrong. Mia shook her head. *One mission at a time,* she told herself. Right now it was rescuing her friends.

Chapter 16

The armed services receive multiple requests each year from other countries to train their units. That is how skilled American men are. Of course, their requests are always denied.

—American Gazette

Intense hunger now joined the other list of problems ailing Andrew. He moved the rag back and forth across the pristine sink, trying hard to block out the noises blaring over the speakers. He couldn't tell if they'd been in here for hours or days. It felt like months. Time was starting to lose meaning. The music stopped. Carter dropped his rag and stood next to Andrew. Carter's face was expressionless, and Andrew was sure his own was just as hard to read.

The door opened. Andrew's ears were ringing from the memories of the sounds played over and over. *Be strong,* he told himself. If he showed these men what he could handle it would stop soon.

The sergeant frowned. He paced back and forth in front of the men, eyeing them up and down. Andrew kept his eyes forward, posture perfect. Carter was doing the same.

"What is it you want?" the sergeant asked.

"Food, sleep, silence," Carter said.

Andrew whipped his head to the side, angry with Carter for

speaking, but the blond man kept his eyes glued to the sergeant and his face expressionless.

"And you?" the sergeant asked.

Andrew wanted the same things, but he was too afraid an outburst would result in more punishment. He couldn't handle any more. Andrew tried to guess what the man wanted to hear, but he was having trouble forming words.

"Silent," the sergeant said. He turned his attention to Carter. "Maybe we should have kept you separated. You come with me, and Private Simpson will stay here."

Andrew felt his fists tighten. Simpson was his new name now; he'd forgotten. He wanted to rage at Carter; this was his fault. Carter didn't put up a fight as the sergeant wrapped his arm over Carter's shoulder. The two left the room and Andrew was alone again. He debated screaming but thought any noise would burst his eardrums. He keeled over; his stomach was too empty. Andrew didn't understand why Carter was getting the praise and attention. This whole situation was his fault. Andrew was the good soldier, not Carter. Andrew had the discipline. He had to get outside, speed up his training so he could . . .

Again Andrew's thoughts betrayed him. Why did he want to get outside so bad? He stared openmouthed at the ground. He didn't think enlistment would be like this; he had thought it would be more formal. Was this enlistment? Andrew asked himself. It didn't matter. He had to show these men he was a good soldier; now that Carter was gone he could prove his worth. The noise returned at full volume. Andrew didn't bother covering his ears. He picked the rag back up and started wiping the counter.

Chapter 17

A global governing board should be created to monitor human rights around the world.

—Comment from the Global Reporter *message board*

The quiet was deafening. Mia stood on guard around the small patch of trees and relied on her ears to guide her, but they were giving her nothing to work with. She tried to ignore the pain in her thigh from the giant bruise growing under her shorts. Mia lifted her hand to touch the welt, and it was at that moment her attacker came barreling out of the trees.

Mia moved out of Riley's way and gained herself an extra second, but the redhead wasn't about to waste her lead. Mia tried her best to defend herself from the blows and still look for a moment to land one herself, but Riley was as quick as ever. Their sparring came to an end when Riley's fist broke through Mia's defenses and came just short of knocking Mia to the ground.

"That was better," Riley said. "I waited till you were distracted. It only takes a second."

"Me checking the bruise?" Mia asked.

Riley nodded.

"A lot of fighting is waiting around," Mia said. "I get bored and my mind wanders."

"This is a controlled exercise," Riley said. "The next step is to have you prepared for random attacks. We could be playing chess and I'll try to pounce on you."

"You'd risk your precious board?" Mia asked.

"It's all about the timing."

Mia swatted her arm and killed a mosquito. She didn't know why she bothered. After a week out here her body was covered in bruises and bug bites. Killing one wouldn't make that big of a difference.

"Do you think they'll attack me when I get to town?" Mia asked.

"They might," Riley said. "But not right away. If things go according to plan it will be you doing the attacking."

"Get close enough to Dalmy and find a way to hold her hostage. Trade her freedom for our men," Mia said.

She went over the plan in her head again and again.

"Don't let them know what you're capable of," Riley said. "Even though it's not much."

"I'm getting better," Mia said.

"I could take you with both arms behind my back," Riley said. "I don't have enough time to turn you into a fighting machine."

Mia frowned.

"Don't get down on yourself," Riley said. "You're doing fine for what we need."

"When will I be ready?" Mia asked.

She was getting antsy about Carter and Andrew. She couldn't begin to guess what they were going through.

"I don't know," Riley said. "Soon."

The days and nights were becoming a blur. All they did was play chess and work on Mia's defense abilities. She'd yet to beat Riley at either.

"I don't think I'll get much better," Mia said. "We should go now."

"And what will you do when you get our men back?" Riley asked.

"Leave," Mia said.

"How?" Riley asked. "On foot? Dragging Dalmy along with you?"

"I'll get a car too," Mia said.

"Can you drive?"

"I've driven before," Mia said.

She left out the part about not knowing what she was doing and the car running out of gas. Riley's eyes looked like daggers in the moonlight.

"By lying to me you're only hurting yourself," Riley said.

"I'm not lying," Mia said. "It might not have gone so well though. I can make Carter or Andrew drive."

"What if they're not capable?" Riley asked. "You need this planned out to perfection for it to work."

"I don't know," Mia said. "Can you teach me?"

"To drive?" Riley asked.

Mia nodded. "You must have some kind of computer program."

She welcomed a chance to switch up their current routine. Riley's daggers faded and a coy smile went across her face.

"I have something better," she said.

Riley turned around and started walking through their small wooded area away from the cabin. Mia did her best to keep up; she was more interested in avoiding stepping on a bug or getting smacked with a branch, so she didn't notice when Riley stopped walking and Mia almost ran right into her.

"Little notice next time . . ." Mia's complaints faded away when she looked up.

Sitting in the clearing was a vehicle, or at least the shell of one. Mia walked around the car. It had no roof and was high up off the ground. There were no doors and the paneling on the sides was missing.

"It's a jeep," Riley said. "A run-down one at that."

"How did you—"

"I found it abandoned about two kilometers north of here," Riley said. "I waited a week and nobody came back for it. It wouldn't start though, so I took my time pushing it back this way."

"Why is it so destroyed?" Mia asked.

"It broke down, so they took what they could from it and left it in the desert," Riley said.

"Does it start now?" Mia asked.

"Give it a try," Riley said.

Mia climbed up into the driver's seat. She remembered starting her father's car and felt around for the keys.

"Where are the keys?" Mia asked.

Riley gave her a frown.

"Cars haven't used keys in decades," Riley said.

"How does it start then?"

Riley walked over. Mia climbed across the center console and into the passenger seat. There was a single white button in the middle of the dashboard. Riley used her thumb to press it down and a light hum came over the vehicle.

"But won't people steal it this way?" Mia asked. "And the engine is so quiet."

"The buttons are normally fingerprint coded," Riley said. "I'm guessing not all military-style ones have this feature, because A, it's probably not traveling alone a whole lot, and B, multiple militia members need to drive it. Or option C: when the electrical panel in this thing fried it rebooted the fingerprint code."

Mia watched as Riley's hand moved down the dashboard. There was another panel with four buttons. She went over each of their purposes.

"Drive, reverse, harsh terrain, and inclement weather. You really only need the first two."

"What was that for?" Mia pointed at a space in the dash where something had been ripped out.

"Self-driving system," Riley said. "It looks like the militia wanted to keep that one."

"The car can drive itself?"

"Plug in a destination and it will take you there," Riley said.

Riley pushed the first button and the car moved forward. She was using her feet to accelerate the jeep. Once they were out of the branches the moonlight lit up the desert. Mia was overwhelmed by the beauty of the place. The car sped up and Mia's hair flapped around in the wind. Riley made a quick turn and spun the jeep back around. She sped up even more, but still the engine stayed at a dull hum. Soon they started slowing down. Riley turned the wheel left and Mia saw the patch of trees reappear. The vehicle slowed even more and Mia thought Riley was stopping too soon.

"Why don't you pull it all the way in?" Mia asked.

The dull hum was gone and Mia saw the buttons were no longer illuminated. They came to a full stop about ten feet away from Riley's parking space.

"This is a broken car," Riley said.

She jumped out and Mia did the same. Riley was already at the rear pushing and Mia joined her.

"Can you fix it?"

"I already did," Riley said. "Most cars are electric. In America you still use gasoline engines, which make more noise. I wish I had a backup tank now though. This vehicle's electrical board is fried. I can get her to drive about five kilometers at the most before she dies. I'm proud of myself for that accomplishment."

"You want me to learn to drive on a car that only goes five kilometers?" Mia asked.

"No," Riley said. "I want you to learn to drive on a computer program I have in the shack. Then maybe test this out a little bit once you have some skills."

"How will that help? Do you have a spare set of pedals in there too?" Mia asked.

"Don't be so wary of my technology," Riley said. "All you need is a pair of glasses and the simulator program. Trust me."

Mia was hoping for the chance to drive all over the desert. She reminded herself these lessons weren't about having fun; they were about saving her friends. She smiled at Riley as they pushed the car back through the trees. Even though it wasn't what Mia had anticipated, she looked forward to working with the computer program.

Chapter **18**

America is the most physically fit country in the world. Citizens spend more time outside and engage in more physical activities, resulting in healthier people.

—American Gazette

The lines on Andrew's hand were fascinating him. He liked to make his hand into a fist and watch the lines around his knuckles disappear and reappear. It was a distraction from the noise, but Andrew couldn't be sure the loud music was still playing. He wasn't sure of much anymore.

He knew he must have slept at some point, and eaten too, but neither of these basic human acts was in his memory. Andrew decided Carter was long dead by this point. At first Andrew was grateful he was still alive, but then he started to think dying would be the less cruel fate.

The noise quieted down. Andrew thought it might have been turned off, but the phantom sounds were still playing in his brain. He looked toward the bathroom door; it was still as pristine as the day he arrived here, whenever that was. The man dressed in a lab coat came in again. This was his eighth visit. Andrew thought that might mean he had been here for eight days, but it could have meant eight months.

The first five times the man came into the room, Andrew had tried to attack him. Every time, the three men who escorted the doctor beat Andrew back. He was easily outmatched. His stomach was still sore from their punches.

"Good morning," the doctor said. "Or is it afternoon?"

Andrew's lips were dry. He wanted to speak, to hear the sound of his own voice, but he wasn't sure he had one anymore. Two of the escorts came and grabbed Andrew off the floor. They hoisted him up and one pulled up the sleeve of his scrubs. Andrew looked as the doctor uncovered his tray. Each time before, there had been five needles. Five quick shots and Andrew was alone again. Today there was only one. He wondered if it was the final dose to end his suffering. The doctor loaded the syringe and walked toward Andrew. It was at this moment the fear of death crept over him. He wasn't ready to pass on.

With the little energy he had he raised both his fists and slammed his elbows into the guards' stomachs simultaneously. Both were caught off guard and dropped their grips on Andrew. He pushed past the doctor and made it to the door. The third man, the sergeant, stepped aside, and Andrew was almost in the hall. He heard yelling behind him and then a loud zapping noise. Andrew felt electricity explode through his body. He was stopped in his tracks and fell to the floor. His hand landed just beyond the threshold. Andrew moved his head up and watched his hand open and close into a fist and the lines in his palm disappear.

Chapter 19

Grant Marsden is living proof that mandatory service produces outstanding men with amazing contributions to our society. He is everyone's son.

—American Gazette

The drive to the capital took a little under an hour. As Grant drove up the hill leading into the city he took a moment to soak in the view. It was almost perfect. Short buildings made out of marble reflected the afternoon sun, making the whole area glow, but his eye was distracted by the monument. A single pillar that rose several hundred feet in the air, it was designed after a rook, a piece from an ancient game most had never heard of. Grant knew not only what the game was but how to play it, and he was quite good at chess.

The building was supposed to remind the country of its past and serve to honor those who protected America, but Grant saw it as an eyesore. He'd been to the top several times. While the view was beautiful, it wasn't worth how hideous the structure looked from the ground.

He drove past the Rook and straight up to the gate surrounding the Mission. The guard waved him through without checking any documentation. Grant smiled at his own notoriety. The Mission was the most important building in the world. It housed the offices for all the men who ran the country. Grant had once heard that before the Registry, the leader of the country slept in the same place he worked; he always thought that sounded inappropriate for a man of such stature. He reminded himself that that was when the country was weak. Now it was strong and would only grow more powerful.

Grant reached the front of the building. The exterior was a deep crimson. It was the only structure in the capital whose color stood out. As he cruised the parking lot he passed other vehicles and noted that they belonged to the most important people in the world. His fit right in. He slid into a spot and jumped out of the car.

It didn't take long for him to make it to the entrance. Again he was waved through by the guard at the door and allowed to bypass the security check. He wasn't sure where to go, so instead he took in the beauty of the structure. The interior had two large twin staircases that wound up to the second floor. Everything was trimmed in deep gold. Crimson and gold, blood and glory.

"I see you made it," the grand commander said from the top of the steps.

All of Grant's previous dealings in the Mission had been in the basement; now he was going up. He went to meet the older gentleman. As he rounded the stairs he noticed the man's outfit; he was wearing khakis and a pastel-orange polo. Grant felt a slight embarrassment, as he was wearing almost the same outfit, except instead of pants he had chosen shorts with penny loafers.

"Hello, sir," Grant said. He reached out and shook the man's hand. "To what do I owe the pleasure of this visit?"

"I was hoping it would be a casual one. I've been informed by your business partners that this is your usual attire, but I didn't think we'd be exact twins," the grand commander said. "I've never been one for suits myself, though at times they are a necessity."

"Well, I'm glad today isn't one of those times," Grant said.

"There is something about you. You're strong; it radiates when you enter the room. I'll have one of my wives bring me another shirt; then I was hoping I could give you a tour."

"*One* of your wives, sir?" Grant asked.

"A perk of the position. I keep that information quiet though. Eventually I'd like multiple marriages legalized for every man. It's just another way to bring in additional funds, but there is some fear it could destroy the middle class. Rich men would buy all the pretty wives and have all the pretty daughters, leaving only the lowest of the bunch for the rest of the men."

Grant felt this was another test. He took a moment before responding. "And if that happened the middle class might revolt. We need a joyful country for things to run smoothly."

"You are bright," the grand commander said. "None of my wives are from the Registry. When a man dies before his daughters come of age, we take them in. Some are sent straight to work if they won't generate a profit; others enter the Registry, where we take their whole fee—and some slip through the cracks."

Grant had always assumed the reason the grand commander had so many daughters was that he was fortunate, but now he realized it was because they had multiple mothers. The public wife, Nancy, did appear to be constantly with child. Of course it must be a fake stomach, designed to increase public awe of the commander.

"Genius, sir," Grant said.

"Stop with the 'sir' nonsense. Please, call me Ian," he said. "Shall we continue?"

Ian didn't wait for an answer. He started walking down the magnificent hall. It was lined with portraits, most of them showing the grand commander himself through the years. Each painting showed the man younger. Grant started to wonder how old Ian really was; based on the sheer number of pictures he should have been close to one hundred. Ian stopped and admired the first picture that was not his own.

"Our first grand commander, Aaron Miller, was a visionary," Ian said.

"Did you know him?" Grant asked. He knew the man's whole story. How General Miller rescued the country when it was at its weakest. He created the Registry and required mandatory enlistment. There could not be enough praise said about the man.

"No," Ian said. "I never had the pleasure."

They had walked past several more portraits of Grand Commander Miller when Ian stopped again.

"Our second grand commander," Ian said. "Gary Cleary. He built on his predecessor's ideals. It was his decision to put the technology ban into effect. Most people aren't privy to that information."

"I wasn't aware," Grant said.

"Commander Cleary led the country for sixty-three years," Ian said. "Him I had the pleasure of knowing quite well."

They continued their walk past many more portraits of Grand Commander Cleary.

"He picked me to take over," Ian said. "I was his protégé. Young, like you are now. We were still growing; some rebels tried to revolt. People remembered the old ways back then. It was harder to break them. He knew his time was up and I would continue on with his vision."

"I'm sure he'd be proud," Grant said.

"Thank you. I know you mean that, because you're not one of the yes-men who follow me around, and there are many of those. They are so eager to gain my approval that they lie and tell me everything I do is wonderful and only fill my ears with good news. Find people willing to let you in on the truth. It's the only way to survive."

Ian continued down the hall. There was an open door at the end, which led into a giant office. Grant noted it was almost as large as his bedroom. Ian made his way to the desk and used his phone to call for a shirt. Grant took a seat on a chair across from the desk. It wasn't long before a beautiful young woman came into the room. She rushed over to Ian with a blue polo. He stood up and she pulled off the orange one and dressed him in the blue.

"Thank you, Katherine, you picked just the one I wanted." To Grant he said, "I keep some extra clothes in a spare room here," Ian said.

His wife didn't make eye contact and bowed before turning to leave.

"Wait." He placed his hand on her shoulder. He spun her around to face Grant. She dropped her shoulders and the commander placed his hand on her chin; she couldn't have been thirty years old.

"Notice her small frame, thick brown hair, and brown eyes?" Ian asked. "Does she remind you of anyone?"

"Your wife. Nancy," Grant said.

"Very good," Ian said. "That will be all, Katherine. This way nobody questions the genetic outcome of our children. Even though Nancy hasn't borne me any in at least ten years, and the last three from her were boys."

Grant noted Katherine couldn't leave the room fast enough.

"Don't fool yourself though. I still count on Nancy for many things. She is the one who keeps all the other girls in line."

"And you're telling me this why?" Grant asked.

Ian took a seat at his desk. He leaned back in his chair and folded his hands together.

"I love this country. I love my job—don't get me wrong, it has many benefits, but it is a difficult one. Only a certain type of man can maintain the workload. I see that in you. Even though your wife may have escaped, it wasn't due to your lack of perception. It was because you enjoyed chasing her too much."

Grant swallowed at the last comment. He wanted to defend himself against the accusation and point out whose fault it really was, but he needed to keep his confidence in check.

"I followed her disappearance closely. I would have stepped in if she'd married another man, but I was so sure you would succeed and then we could turn it into a real hero story. But after she crossed the border I realized it was for the best. This way we can give you a proper wife who will play the public role."

"Role as?" Grant asked.

"I am not a young man. I have some health issues and need to train a replacement. I think if you were in this position there would be enough to keep your mind busy; you wouldn't allow a chase to continue. So far I have been correct. The people love you. They see you as a strong widower. A hero. All I need is for you to prove yourself a good leader."

"Sir—"

"Ian."

"I relish the opportunity to prove myself to you," Grant said.

"Then let's get started."

Grant curled his lips into a smile and shook the man's hand. He knew this moment should have been perfect. It was more than Grant had ever dreamed of accomplishing, but he couldn't enjoy it thoroughly. In the back of his mind all he could focus on was the comment involving Amelia's escape being his fault. It added to the fury he was feeling toward her.

"Ian," Grant said, "I would be honored to prove myself to you, but don't you think it's important that we ensure my wife is departed?"

Grant hated bringing a potential problem to the grand commander, but he hoped it would open Ian's eyes and allow him to hunt Amelia down. Instead the older man just laughed.

"I can tell it's important for you to close this, but forget about her. It is unlikely she'll reappear, and if it happens the only result will be an international public relations hiccup. All of her photos were removed from the Internet and nothing was handed out in print. No photo exists anymore. She'll look like an imposter if she steps forward."

Grant's stomach dropped. Saint Louis. It was there he'd ordered her photo plastered all over the city. Grant had never bothered to get approval. He'd had his private team distribute them.

"You seem uneasy," Ian said. "I know your pride is wounded, but don't let that stop you from moving forward."

Taking a breath, Grant forced his nerves down. He nodded to Ian, but now his head swam with the more pressing issue. If a single person had saved one of those photos and Amelia did reappear, it could cause an uprising. That was not how Grant planned to spend his tenure as grand commander.

Chapter 20

Citizens from other countries are not permitted in America. If you know of a person here illegally, notify your nearest government offices. They are a waste of our precious resources and want to undermine our greatness.

—American Gazette

A voice filled Andrew's head. The loud noise played in a quick spurt. A light flashed. Andrew popped his eyes open. He was sitting straight up at a table. A man in full military uniform sat across from him. Andrew looked around the room; it was made of red clay and a fluorescent light filled it.

"How are you feeling?" the man asked.

"Fine," Andrew said.

His throat was dry. The sound of his own voice echoed in his head. It was foreign to him. The man reached over and grabbed a pitcher of water. He poured a glass and set it in front of himself. Andrew wanted that water so badly. He couldn't take his eyes off it.

"What's your name?" the man asked.

Andrew didn't respond.

"Mine is General Bolivar," he said. He slid the glass of water closer to Andrew.

"Andrew," he said, still eyeing the water.

"Where are you from?"

"America," he said.

"Where are you now?"

Andrew opened his mouth, but no words came out. He wasn't sure how to answer. The loud music filled his head when he tried to remember. He winced.

"You're home," the man said. "Repeat that."

"I'm home," Andrew said. The noise went away.

"Did you travel here with anyone?"

"Yes," Andrew said.

"Who?"

"Carter," Andrew said.

"Who else?"

Andrew tried to think backward. The noise filled his mind. He tried to think through it, but the sounds were too much. The noise increased and the pain did too.

"I can't," Andrew said. "I don't want to remember."

"What can you tell me about Mia?"

Her face appeared before Andrew's eyes. He remembered traveling across the country with her, staying in Rod's basement; then the night they were leaving, he had been intertwined with her in the bed of a truck. Kissing her, smelling her hair, feeling his hand run up and down her back. Then a car accident. He tried to think of what happened next but the memory hurt too much. The noise came back.

"What happened to her?" Andrew asked.

"You don't remember?"

Andrew shook his head. The general smiled.

"She died," he said.

Andrew felt the world fall out from under his feet. He was floating, not sure how to respond. She couldn't have; he would remember that. His eyes went wide and he struggled for an answer.

"How?"

"A car accident," he said. "She never made it across with you two. Both she and Roderick Rowe died in the accident."

"You're lying," Andrew said.

The general looked disappointed.

"You and Carter crashed a helicopter into the ocean," he said. "There were no other footprints on that beach and nobody washed ashore. It was only the two of you flying over. If she were alive, would you have left her there?"

Andrew knew he would never abandon Mia, never.

"How did I get here?" Andrew asked.

"We found the two of you," the general said. "Walking aimlessly in the desert. Dehydrated and starving. We don't know how long you were out there."

Andrew squinted his eyes. He raised his chin and leaned back in his chair.

"Then how would you know about the footprints on the beach?" Andrew asked.

The general stood up and went to the door. He knocked twice and two armed guards walked in. Andrew rose from the table and backed up.

"Don't worry, we'll try again tomorrow," the general said. "Maybe day ten will be your lucky day."

The two men gripped Andrew's arms. He tried to push them off but they were too strong. As if he didn't have a choice, the memories came rushing back in. The memory of being trapped in the bathroom, the loud noises, the doctor stabbing him with needles, Carter being taken away.

"What are you doing to me?" Andrew asked.

He struggled harder when a doctor came in with another tray. His guards' grips intensified and he watched in horror as the doctor stabbed him with two quick injections.

"Don't fight it," the doctor said. "You've already set a record."

"The harder they are to break the better soldiers they will be," the general said.

Andrew felt his body go limp. His neck couldn't support his head any longer. Before he lost consciousness he promised himself not to forget, not to break. But he was already having a difficult time holding on.

Chapter 21

GRANT MARSDEN'S FORMER SUPERIOR IN THE SERVICE SAYS MARSDEN WAS BORN LEADER

—American Gazette

Another day and another visit to the capital. Grant was becoming accustomed to driving in but was starting to find his visits on the boring side. It was a lot of common sense that Ian insisted on explaining in great detail. Grant had started to think the man was out of touch with the average American male.

Grant parked his car and walked up the steps to the Mission. He was shocked to see Ian standing outside with a group of men. It looked like they were waiting on Grant.

"Good morning, sir," Grant said. "Am I late?"

"I thought today I would show you a special treat, something that will appeal to your interests," Ian said.

"Oh?"

One of the men opened up the door to an SUV parked in front of the entrance and Ian climbed in the back. Grant thought the elderly man looked like he could use some assistance but dared not offer any in case it gave offense. Grant waited till Ian was seated and slid in next to him.

There was a divider between the two and the driver. The car started up and they drove off through the capital.

"Tell me something," Ian said. "You are one of the very few private inventors. How did you fall into this trade?"

"A natural gift," Grant said.

"I suppose it's good we all keep some secrets," Ian said.

Grant gave the grand commander a smirk. His past was something Ian was not privy to.

"America is on the forefront of modern technology," Ian said. "Did you know that?"

"Of course," Grant said.

"Did you ever wonder how?" Ian asked. "You didn't create all the modern technological advances, did you?"

Grant laughed and shook his head. "I assume a branch of the military did," he said.

"Filled with poorly educated minds?"

"Some people are gifted, regardless of their education," Grant said.

"Wrong," Ian said.

Grant tried his best to give the man a smile without looking too condescending. He had the urge to reach over and wrap his hands around the grand commander's neck.

"One of the ways to keep a country successful is to have money," Ian said. "America is far and away the wealthiest country on the planet. We own almost all the major inventions outright, with the exception of yours and those of a few other private citizens over the years."

"I am aware of that fact," Grant said.

Ian raised his eyebrows and Grant regretted his choice of words.

"I mean, please, continue," Grant said.

"When sons are turned over to the government, some are sent into the general orphanages and others into more specialized fields," Ian said. "I'm showing you one of those fields today."

The car stopped. They were in front of an average-looking building. Ian waited for the driver to open the door and then exited the car. Grant followed him. It looked like any old office space.

"Every year about a hundred boys are selected for this life," Ian said. "People start to show certain talents as young as five years old. I'm sure you remember some of the general tests from your days as a boy?"

Grant nodded his head. He remembered thinking they were boring and unimportant, so he had just filled in bubbles at random. He was glad for his childhood laziness.

"The ones that score highest are brought here and trained. Their brains are honed and skills developed. These men are one of the backbones of our society."

The driver opened the door to the building and Grant followed Ian inside. There was an open gray room with an empty front desk. Ian walked toward the back elevator. The doors opened and the two walked in. Ian didn't hit a floor; instead he punched in a sequence with the keys. Grant tried to follow, but Ian blocked his hands. The elevator started moving down.

"One hundred per year," Ian said. "They don't all measure up and some are disposed of, but at any given time there are at least fifteen hundred men working here."

The doors opened up. Ian walked ahead and Grant followed. They stood on a balcony overlooking a massive warehouse. Men in nondescript gray clothing worked at a number of stations. Grant thought the room was large enough to span the entire capital. His laboratory didn't compare in the slightest. His eyes scanned the room and he saw some men working on a tank, others using chemistry sets—some men were even at work on a firing range in a sectioned-off area.

"Where are the rest of them?" Grant asked.

"They're all here," Ian said. "Walk with me."

Nobody paid them any attention. Everyone who walked by wore a look of hard determination.

"These are the most brilliant minds in the world," Ian said.

"Isn't that dangerous?" Grant asked. Ian had previously lectured him on the dangers of a highly educated population.

"They're controlled," Ian said. "Their education is completed at about fifteen to sixteen years of age, they work on the floor for about fifteen to sixteen years, and then their time is finished."

"Still," Grant said. "What if one escaped? Aren't you scared they'd cause an uprising?"

"They're served a steady diet of the best pharmaceuticals, created by their predecessors," Ian said.

"Human robots?" Grant asked.

He watched as one walked by. Grant debated poking him in the shoulder to see if he would stop moving.

"I suppose one could look at it that way," Ian said.

The wheels in Grant's mind started to turn.

"Why not create a formula that could turn someone into the perfect soldier?"

"Now, that would be dangerous," Ian said. "Create a killer, then try to release him into the population? That is an experiment designed to fail."

"As a country we would be unstoppable," Grant said.

"We already are," Ian said. "I strongly advise against altering the status quo. Things run smoothly. Keep it that way."

Grant nodded his head and made a mental note to keep any future plans he had for America to himself in front of Ian. The grand commander wasn't looking for a replacement. He was looking for a clone, and Grant was more than willing to fake that role till the position was his.

Chapter 22

GENHAN THREATENS TO INVADE NATROCK, FLEDGLING COUNTRIES ARGUE OVER RIGHTS TO THE BLACK SEA

—Global Reporter

"Are you certain you're ready for this?" Riley asked.

"I could do it blindfolded," Mia said. "I did already. Remember?"

"That was on a simulated course you memorized," Riley said. "This is a real vehicle."

"I wouldn't say that," Mia said.

Riley frowned at Mia's joke.

"Pretend this is a fully functional vehicle," Riley said. "Walk me through everything first."

Mia was seated in the driver's seat of the torn-apart jeep. Riley was next to her, trying her hardest to find a reason to deny Mia the use of the vehicle.

"I make sure the car is already running," Mia said. "Then I look at the auto-drive screen and pick 'disengage.' "

"And?"

"And then I wait till the screen gives me confirmation," Mia said. "Then I rip it out."

"Why?"

"Don't you trust me?" Mia said. "I know what I'm doing."

"You're young and rash," Riley said. "You'll only get one shot at this. Now, why rip it out?"

"Because that is the likely spot for the GPS chip," Mia said. "And then they won't be able to follow me."

"Very good."

"Then I put the car in drive—" Mia said.

"Wrong," Riley said.

"—after I check all the gauges to make sure there is enough backup fuel," Mia said. "You need to relax."

"What next?"

"I use the pedals and the wheel," Mia said. "Drive back here. Pick you up and drop off Dalmy. Then the five of us make our way down to Guatemala."

"How will you get to Guatemala?"

"You have the map," Mia said.

Riley glared at Mia.

"I drive ten kilometers west across the desert till we hit the main road," Mia said. "I drive straight down into Guatemala without stopping. Then once I enter the country I take my first left and drive up into the mountains. From there I make the fourth left, then the sixth right, then the next two lefts, all the while traveling along a steep cliff. I make sure to drive slow."

"Always be prepared," Riley said. "No plan will ever be foolproof. Someone may be with you to navigate, but you have to know the way yourself."

"Can I drive now?" Mia asked.

She had spent more than half of the past week on the simulator and was more than eager to test out her skills on an actual vehicle. Riley reached over and buckled her safety belt. Mia grinned and put the car into drive. Riley didn't share Mia's excitement as she whipped the car out of the trees.

Chapter 23

No true American male would ever consider marriage to a foreigner.

—American Gazette

"Mia's dead." Andrew said the words. They rolled off his tongue so easily but bit at his core.

"I am very sorry for your loss," the general said.

He handed Andrew a printout from an American website.

> *Grant Marsden continues to mourn the loss of his wife. She met her demise during a fatal car accident caused by her abductor. Marsden bravely tried to save her but was unable to stop the madman.*

Before Andrew could finish reading, the newspaper was pulled away.

"That's not what happened," Andrew said.

"Why don't you tell me what did happen then?"

"Grant Marsden is the madman," Andrew said. "Nobody abducted Mia; she ran away. I helped her; so did Carter and Rod."

"Was there a car accident?"

Andrew tried to remember. His head filled with intense pain.

"I don't know," he said.

"What's the last thing you remember?"

"Preparing with Rod," Andrew said. "He was teaching me to act like a soldier."

"Where was Mia during this?"

"Learning self-defense skills with Carter," Andrew said. "You said he's here? Can I see him? Maybe he remembers."

"We found the two of you walking aimlessly around the desert," the general said. "You were both very sick."

Andrew closed his eyes. He tried to remember the last few days but was met with intense pain in his head, like a noise was trying to burst through his eardrums. He winced and held his hands to his ears. The general stood up from the table and knocked once on the door.

A man dressed as a doctor walked in with a tray.

"This is Dr. Kashuba," the general said. "He's going to give you some medicine."

Andrew grabbed his arm. He was grateful these men had saved him from the desert but wasn't comfortable with a stranger injecting him with anything.

"He's been treating you for days," the general said.

"How long have I been here?" Andrew asked.

"A little over two weeks," the general said.

Andrew was stunned. He'd lost two weeks of his life and found out Mia was dead. He wanted to mourn her, but it didn't feel right. All he could feel was anger. The doctor gave Andrew a few quick injections.

"What are these for?" Andrew asked.

"You were late on your booster," the general said. "We don't want you to get sick again."

"Thank you," Andrew said to the doctor.

He gave Andrew a grin and walked out of the room.

"Do you have anywhere you can go?" the general asked.

"Are you going to deport me?" Andrew asked.

"I won't," the general said. "If you stay here I can offer you protection too, but if you leave this place I cannot guarantee your safety."

"What is this place?"

"The Mexico Militia," the general said.

"Militia?"

"Army," the general said.

Andrew couldn't process what was happening around him. He wanted to picture the last time he saw Mia's face, but every time he tried a sharp noise entered his mind. Andrew blinked his eyes a few times. The light in the room was making everything a little hazy.

"You've suffered from inflammation of the brain," the general said. "Your government put you in this position; they stole your friends and your memories, forced you to escape, and now they want to call you a traitor."

"It's America's fault Mia is dead?" Andrew asked. He blamed Grant.

"She felt the need to run from an unjust system," the general said. "If you decide to join our cause you can avenge her."

Andrew had run away from service. He didn't think he was ready to join another army. He thought of Saint Louis, lying in the same bed with Mia and turning her down. Now she was dead and Andrew had lost his chance to be with the one person who had ever really cared about him. His anger grew.

"You want to avenge her death," the general said.

Almost as if a switch had been flipped, Andrew thought about the general's words with sincerity. He did want vengeance for Mia. She deserved the tribute.

"You want to fight for Mexico," he said. "You hate America and are more than willing to take up arms with the militia."

"I am," Andrew said.

"Say it," the general said.

"America killed Mia," Andrew said. "I want to join your militia."

The general nodded his head and Andrew's feeling of anger turned into pride. He would fight for Mia's memory, he would repay the debt he owed the general for taking care of him, and he would become part of something bigger than himself. Andrew felt a wave of exuberance flow through him. He was home.

Chapter 24

Grant Marsden is constantly surrounded by friends, even though he would rather be at home with a wife.

—American Gazette

Grant spun the tiny black cell phone in his hands, willing it to ring. His plan should have come to fruition by this point. It had been almost three weeks since the fateful night. The night Amelia bested him. He was a patient man, but his patience was wearing thin. He had to put the phone down on his dresser or risk squeezing the thing to pieces.

Why was there no call? Had Grant overestimated the young man's love? Had they died in the helicopter? He'd been too busy with visits to the capital and press appearances to perform the necessary research. He remembered the last time he was so unprepared.

He had been in Miami, just out of the orphanage, all alone and not expecting to feel so . . . hungry. Sleeping on the streets didn't feel right to him, so he decided to learn a trade: picking locks. At first Grant would break into small empty apartments, a different one each night. Then he moved on to homes, waiting until the occupants were fast asleep and borrowing a couch. Except for some missing food, they wouldn't know he was ever there. As his skills grew, so did his tastes. He started sleeping in mansions, making a game out of eluding the staff members and the occupants. That of course required him to become familiar with security systems. He'd been living an easy life, until one fateful night he woke up on the wrong side of a shotgun.

Not wanting to relive his past, Grant decided to get proactive about his future. That involved settling the score with Amelia. He swallowed his pride and strode out of his room with one destination on his mind. Grant walked through his home and headed out back, toward the man who had made it clear he had some knowledge of the former Mrs. Marsden's whereabouts.

He's already shown me some of the facilities," Grant said. "I think he's a bit outdated."

"What do you mean?" Rex asked.

"Let's say I'd like to put the country's resources elsewhere," Grant said. "If I were grand commander people wouldn't have it so easy."

"You think people have it easy?" Rex asked.

"Unwed females are cared for, unserved men get to carry on as they please," Grant said. "And some unmarried men are a drain on our economy. Not to mention the females who work for the government. There are better ways to use our money."

"It's bordering on treason to talk like that," Rex said. "There's only one grand commander, and he holds that office until he chooses to move on."

"Well, let's say I have the inside track," Grant said.

Rex looked at the ground. His jaw was clenched. Grant thought he must be uninterested in political goals.

"So did you discover anything?" Grant asked.

He was sitting at the table in Rex's house. The military man had never bothered to set it up like a home; instead it resembled a tactical center. Grant apologized for his behavior at Amelia's funeral and he was not surprised to hear that Rex had ignored his instructions.

"Well, I went on an international server—don't worry, I masked the address like you told me; nothing can be traced here," Rex said.

"Speed it up," Grant replied.

"Based on the fuel left in the helicopter and the direction they were headed, our best bet is they crashed within one hundred miles of this spot," Rex said.

There was a map of Mexico with a blue dot on the southeast coast.

"This is undeveloped desert," Rex said. "Odds are in your favor that they died, either in the crash or from dehydration in the desert."

"So that's your news. She's dead?" Grant said.

"I looked for reports of a crash in the Mexican news and there weren't any," Rex said. "I couldn't believe that nobody saw the helicopter fly by or go down. So there's some reason it wasn't reported."

"Go on," Grant said.

"Have you heard of the thieves' paradise?" Rex asked.

"I'm not a criminal," Grant said.

"I called a contact who was stationed in Mexico during service," Rex said. "I told him someone stole something from me and fled to Mexico. Couldn't give him a name or any information outside of it being tracked to this area. He laughed and said that section of the country has a lot of folklore about it, including this city of thieves. It's a story; criminals want to retire, so they go live out their days drinking in the sun."

"If such a place existed—and I don't think it does—the authorities would shut it down," Grant said.

"Not if it was controlled by the authorities," Rex said. "I did some more digging. Most of that land is owned by a corporation, Puesta del Sol. The plan was to turn it into the next vacation spot for tourists, but it fell through. Now, the CEO of this organization is Joseph Ruiz."

Rex clicked a button and the screen changed to a picture of a distinguished-looking man.

"He doesn't own any other business except Puesta del Sol, and their only holding is this land," Rex said. "Even though all he owns is worthless real estate, he is a consistent donor."

"Donor of what?" Grant asked.

"Money, to everything," Rex said. "Politicians, hospitals, city parks, hundreds of charitable organizations."

"So you think he's doing something in this area that is generating a profit and buying off government interference?" Grant asked. "How does the city of thieves tie in?"

"My contact made a joke," Rex said. " 'Every thief thinks his sun will never set.' "

"Interesting," Grant said.

He crossed his legs and leaned back in the chair.

"If Amelia landed there what would happen to her?" Grant asked.

"Nothing good," Rex said.

Grant smiled at the thought. He had made up his mind to send Rex to Mexico before he came to visit with his second in command.

"It's a long shot," Grant said. "Be cautious and bring me some proof back."

"I already have my forged travel documents and a commercial plane ticket to the nearest big city. I leave in an hour."

"Have Brandon give you some cash," Grant said. "Leave no paper trail. This cannot get back to me."

Both men stood up and Grant shook Rex's hand. He headed toward the front door.

"About the incident," Grant said.

While Grant was an intelligence officer in the army, Rex had worked on the front lines. They were helping the people of Sudan end a civil war. It was the end of a battle and Grant was surveying the remains. Rex was his escort. A wounded enemy combatant was on the ground. Grant saw the flicker of silver against the sun as he raised his weapon. Without thinking twice Grant pulled his pistol out. Rex thought Grant was going to shoot him and tried to knock the gun down. Grant squeezed the trigger and ended the attacker's life. It only took Rex a moment to realize what Grant had done. That was when his true loyalty was born.

"Let's not mention it again," Rex said.

Grant did not appreciate being interrupted.

"I was going to say, I hope you remember your place from now on," Grant said.

Rex kept his face stone and didn't make eye contact. Grant cracked a smile.

"One last thing," Grant said. "If you find her and she's dead, bring back proof. If she's alive, don't alert her to your presence. Just trail her."

"Why?"

"Bringing a girl who the entire country thinks is deceased kicking and screaming over the border might draw some attention," Grant said.

"I can kill her there," Rex said.

"Not until you have my permission," Grant said.

Amelia deserved punishment from Grant's own hand, not a surrogate. Grant believed his initial strategy could still work. Rex was insurance. The large man nodded his head and they parted ways. Grant headed to his home and let out a yawn. Today was exhausting. Everything should have been perfect, but Amelia Morrissey continued to be a thorn in his side.

Chapter 25

Scientific advancements all but stopped outside of America. We need to start funding our scientists and engineers to become less dependent on America's inventions.

—Global Reporter

The moonlight shone down on Mia. She watched for rustling branches and kept her ears open for any movement. This time she was ready. She spun around right as Riley came barreling out of the trees. Mia lifted her arm to block Riley's swing. She lowered her arm to catch Riley off guard and tapped her in the stomach. The two continued sparring for several minutes, with Mia anticipating Riley's kicks and managing a few would-be blows. Riley still outmatched her, but Mia was holding her own.

"You're much improved," Riley said.

"Not perfect," Mia said.

"Nobody is," Riley said. "Not even me."

"How much longer till I'm ready?" Mia asked.

She swung her arm forward and Riley ducked her head out of the way. Mia moved to the side in time to avoid a tap from Riley in the gut.

"Enough for tonight," Riley said.

She dropped her defensive stance. Mia kept her shoulders back, still unsure if Riley was tricking her.

"I can drive now, I can fight, I have the plan memorized," Mia said. "I'm ready."

"Ready for what?"

"To rescue Andrew, Carter, and Nathan," Mia said.

"You're not," Riley said.

"It's been more than three weeks," Mia said. "I can't wait any longer."

Riley ignored Mia and walked back to the cabin. Mia wanted to scream. If she waited until she met Riley's standards, it would be years. She turned around and walked back to the shack, ready to plead her case to Riley again. She opened the door and saw Riley setting up the chess set, the same as every other night. Mia sat down opposite her and started putting up the pieces.

"I give my fake story to the first person I see," Mia said. "They call Dalmy. I go with her, wait until I have a chance, and take her hostage. Then trade her for the men."

Riley didn't look up as she made her opening move. Mia was quick to take her turn. Riley didn't say anything.

"I have forty-eight hours," Mia said. "Then I have to get out of there. If I don't find a weapon by then I run away. If I think they are onto me I run away."

"And what weapon will you look for?" Riley asked.

"A knife or a gun," Mia said. "Hold the knife to her throat, hold the gun to her temple. I keep myself in line behind her the whole time."

"What if we overestimated the love Joseph has for his daughter? What if he'd rather see her killed?"

"Then I'll die knowing I tried to save my friends," Mia said.

Riley frowned and narrowed her eyes. She continued with the match and Mia kept right on playing.

"That is a stupid thing to say," Riley said. "We don't move in until that isn't an option. We have one chance. I don't want to screw this up."

"Bad joke," Mia said. "I'm sorry, but one more week of practice won't make enough difference. Carter and Andrew have already been in there too long. I need to save them."

Riley was keeping pace with Mia's quick chess moves.

"The fact that you're able to make jokes about this situation tells me you're not ready. What if they're expecting you? What will you say if your boys ratted you out and the militia discovered you are alive?"

"Checkmate," Mia said.

"Very funny," Riley said.

"No," Mia said. "Checkmate."

Riley's eyes went wide and her mouth hung open a bit. She looked down at the board and examined the layout in detail. Mia didn't want to act smug, but after weeks this was her first real victory. The confidence she got from this win alone told her she was ready. Riley shook her head from side to side before looking up at Mia. She let out a loud sigh.

"Tomorrow," Riley said.

"Really?"

Riley nodded her head and scooped the pieces off the board. Mia's happiness from her chess win and the possibility of seeing Andrew alternated with feelings of worry. She closed her eyes and breathed heavily, knowing it wasn't time to show fear. Tomorrow the plan would come into play. Mia needed to hold on to that feeling.

Chapter 26

The modernized world should band together. If we combine our forces and take out America, peace will be restored to all women.

—*Comment from the* Global Reporter *message board*

Today was the day. Mia had spent the night going over the operation with Riley. It would be simple. Mia needed to act the part of the scared, naïve, lost girl Dalmy could take under her wing. Once they were alone Mia would display what a capable woman she really was and barter Dalmy for Andrew, Carter, and Nathan. Riley would watch from a distance; they'd meet up at the cabin and the five would head into Guatemala. Still, Mia was nervous. She started asking questions that had never occurred to her over the past several weeks but now seemed so pertinent.

"What if they recognize me?" she asked. "I mean, my picture was everywhere as the missing girl."

"You're not missing. You're dead. The government removed any evidence of you. Unless those men were following the case as it unfolded you'll be fine."

"How can they do that? How do you know that?" Mia asked.

She hadn't anticipated the feelings of anger she felt upon learning her identity had been demolished.

"I searched for information on you, once you gave me your name, that is," Riley said. "Your husband is front and center, but even he knows to focus the interviews on himself. He leaves any mention of you out."

"He's alive?" Mia asked. This whole time she had pictured him dead.

"Not even injured," Riley said. "Did you think you killed him?"

Mia shook her head. "Why are they leaving me out of the news?"

"In case you ever pop up again and claim you made it out alive. There will be no way for you to prove who you are, so you'll seem like a crazy person," Riley said. "Plus they want little American girls to swoon over your husband, and that can't happen if he's focusing on his dead wife. I have to say you bagged yourself a pretty big fish."

Mia wrinkled her nose.

"Even my grandma understands that saying," Riley said.

Mia had heard stories of grandmothers. She never thought anyone ever really had one though. The idea of generations of women guiding each other gave Mia another feeling of warmth.

"Your husband, he is attractive and wealthy, and smart too," Riley said.

"And cruel and murderous and evil," Mia replied.

"Time to get your costume on," Riley said.

She handed Mia the tattered pink sundress. There was some blood and ash, and it was stiff from the salt water. Mia pulled it over her head, alternating between remembering the brave girl who wore it when she fought Grant and the terrified, shaky one who froze on the beach as her friends were taken. She focused on the former, remembering flying over the border into freedom, emptying the helicopter of all Grant's weapons, and jumping into the unknown. Mia wondered what Riley had discovered among the wreckage of the chopper.

"You scavenged the beach, right? Did you find a plastic bag with some papers and money?" Mia asked.

Riley reached into a drawer and pulled out the see-through baggie. Mia's eyes widened and she grabbed for it. The getaway kit Rod had prepared. She dumped the contents on the bed and started sorting.

"Why didn't you tell me about this?" Mia asked. "This is important."

"According to that passport your name is Jeanette Rowe," Riley said. "Then you told me Amelia Morrissey and I wasn't sure which was accurate. By the time I realized I could trust you it had slipped my mind."

Mia grabbed the small blue books and flipped them open. There was a passport with a picture of her with the Jeanette name, one for Carter, and one for Rod. Andrew's was missing.

"They were part of an unfinished plan," Mia said.

There was a marriage certificate between Jeanette and Roderick, some strange-looking money, and a cell phone. Mia flipped the tiny device around, curious whom Rod had planned to phone.

"Were you planning on making some calls down here?" Riley asked.

"I don't even know how to work this," Mia said.

"I'll show you," Riley said.

She grabbed the phone from Mia's hand and flipped it open. On the keypad she started pressing numbers.

"Everyone has a specific phone number," Riley said. "To call me you have to enter a country code, but any American phone number is ten digits."

Once Riley was done pushing buttons she put the phone back in Mia's hands.

"Push 'send,' " Riley said.

Mia did and held the phone up to her ear.

"It's ringing," Mia said.

Riley nodded. After a few minutes a voice came on. It was Riley's. Mia didn't understand. There was a short noise.

"Hang up or leave a message," Riley said.

"How is this possible?" Mia asked.

"It's a recording," Riley said. "Then you speak and I'll get the option of listening to your voice later, and a transcript will be sent to me as well."

Riley leaned over and pulled the phone away from Mia's ear. She flipped the lid shut. Mia didn't want to ask the million questions she had about the device. There were more important happenings at the moment.

"Should I take this with me?" Mia asked. "Say my name is Jeanette Rowe?"

"If that's the same last name as one of those boys, I wouldn't," Riley said. "They'll realize you're with them."

"It's Carter's," Mia said. "Andrew's is CMW1408."

"That's a strange one," Riley said.

"If that guard woke up they'll suspect someone is coming anyway," Mia replied. It was starting to sink in that he couldn't have survived the fall, but Riley still didn't want to acknowledge this.

"Most American females aren't capable of sending a man over a cliff," Riley said. "And it was dark. He won't recognize you. We don't have to use this idea. The whole plan is canceled if you're not comfortable. I think you need more time anyway."

"I'm ready," Mia said.

"Then let's start walking before I change my mind," Riley said.

She opened the door of the small shack and walked outside. The two began heading north, toward the city. The afternoon sun made the walk much harder than Mia remembered.

"I'll take you as far as I can," Riley said. "But you'll enter the city on your own. Tell me the details again."

Mia repeated back everything they had worked on. Her secret identity, the inflection her voice required. There were no holes in the story.

"One change," Riley said. "Don't bother asking for Nathan. He's not here."

"I'm sorry," Mia said.

"New intel is sending me to Australia after this," Riley said. "Sometimes I think I am chasing a ghost."

"He's alive," Mia said. "If he wasn't you'd know."

"Sixth sense?" Riley asked. "Do you think your boys know you're alive and coming for them?"

"They have to," Mia said. "We'd never give up on each other. When did you find out?"

"Two weeks ago," Riley said.

"And you stayed," Mia said. "To help me."

"I'll see you through to the end," Riley said. "If you want to join me the offer is on the table. We could travel the world and I will teach you more."

"Carter and Andrew?" Mia asked.

"You're serious about the Guatemalan reserve, aren't you?" Riley asked.

Mia nodded her head. She appreciated Riley's offer, but she would never abandon Andrew. Never.

The walk continued in silence until the city appeared in the distance. Then Riley stopped.

"Remember, I'll wait for you at the shack," Riley said. "If anything goes wrong, get out of there and we'll find another way. Forty-eight hours is all you have. If it doesn't happen by then it won't. You'll need to run away."

"I know," Mia said.

Two days. That was all the time Mia needed. If she spent any more time undercover like this it would require too much. She winced at the idea.

"We can turn around," Riley said.

"Thank you," Mia said.

She leaned in and wrapped her arms around Riley. The Irish-woman stiffened up at Mia's touch. Then she returned the hug, her body relaxing.

"I'll meet you at the shack in forty-eight," Mia said.

"Good luck," Riley said.

Mia pulled away.

"You were wrong," Mia said.

"About?" Riley asked.

"My favorite piece is the queen," Mia said. "She's a woman and has the most power."

Riley smiled. Mia thought she saw Riley's eyes glisten but didn't say anything. Mia took a breath and turned toward the town. She closed her eyes as she walked, envisioning Andrew and Carter. They needed her. Even though she wanted assurance from Riley, Mia focused on the future and didn't look back.

Chapter 27

The fact that the Americans keep their borders closed is worrisome enough. They are hiding dangerous weapons. If they aren't stopped the whole world is at risk of another war.
—*Comment from the* Global Reporter *message board*

A bead of sweat rolled down Mia's cheek. Not a soul was on the street. It wasn't much of a street either. Only two blocks long. Mia followed the plan and turned into the first building on the left. The wooden doors swung open. It was a large room with a bar spanning its entire length. Unoccupied tables took up the center space and a balcony lined the upstairs.

"Hello?"

Mia's voice didn't echo against the wooden building.

"I'm lost," Mia said. "Can anyone help me?"

No response came. It was time to try the next building. Mia had just turned to walk out when a door behind the bar swung open. A man came out. His eyes widened when he saw her.

"*¿Qué es esto?*"

"*No hablas español.*"

Mia said the words Riley taught her. The man continued to speak in the foreign tongue. Mia repeated the phrase. He repeated himself;

she couldn't begin to comprehend what he was saying. She tried to speak again but he broke into English.

" 'You don't speak Spanish, you don't speak Spanish,' " he said. "No, I speak Spanish; it is you who cannot."

"I'm lost," Mia said. "Can you help me?"

"Pretty little American girls don't get lost," he said. "What are you doing here?"

"I'm lost," she said.

He reached behind the bar and pulled out a knife. The air rushed out of Mia's lungs. His hands went back down and he pulled out an apple, slamming it against the bar. He brought the knife down and sliced off a piece, handing it to Mia. She reached forward and took it from his hand, devouring the fruit.

"I'm so hungry," Mia said. "I've been walking for hours."

"From where?" he asked.

"I don't know," Mia said.

He gave her another piece.

"Where's your husband?" he asked.

"I'm not married," Mia said.

"Well, in that case I'll get ahold of deportation," he said. "Confirm your single status."

He started walking toward the back again.

"Wait," Mia said. "Your country doesn't deport unwed females. I know that."

"I bet you're married and dying to reunite with your husband," he said.

"No, please, not that," Mia said. "I'll kill myself first."

This raised an eyebrow. Mia relaxed; the plan was working.

"Have a seat," he said.

"Are you going to turn me in?" Mia asked.

"Not my call," he said. "I'm going to get someone who can help you. Eat the rest of the apple."

It was working. Mia was doing it. He kept his eyes on her as he walked into the back room. Mia left the apple untouched. It didn't take long for him to come back into the room.

"Someone is on their way to get you some help," he said.

"Thank you," Mia said.

The two sat in silence. He looked annoyed while she ate her apple. Once enough time passed it was time for phase two of the plan.

Mia thought back to the train station in Saint Louis. Grant was there with his thugs. Mia and Andrew almost outsmarted them, but Grant won. He held a gun to Mia's head. She was about to admit defeat when a force knocked her onto the tracks. Andrew pulled her to safety just in time for her to see a train wipe Whitney from sight. Mia's best friend died that day. She focused on that image until the tears started flowing.

"Hey now," the man said. "No tears here. I said we were going to try to help."

He set a box of tissues down.

"It's awful," Mia said. "I'm so tired and hungry and lost."

"I didn't mean to scare you," he said. "We don't get many strangers down here."

"But you pulled out that knife and you threatened to deport me," Mia said. "I can't go back there."

"Don't mind Henry."

The words were purred from the doorway. Mia turned to look as Dalmy Ruiz strolled into the bar. She was more stunning in person. Her thick black hair was shiny and it flowed down her back. Her white pants swayed at the bottom, making it look like she was floating, and her red tube top brought out the perfect tan in her skin. Mia looked like trash next to this woman.

"I heard you were in trouble," she said. "Maybe I can help you. Henry, get us some water and leave."

While Henry poured the glasses Dalmy shouted something in

Spanish. Two men walked inside dressed in military uniforms. They carried rifles and one walked straight toward Mia. She stood up and he started patting her dress.

"What . . . ," she said.

"A formality," Dalmy said. "Thank you, Ricky."

He walked back and guarded the door. Mia tried her best to look shocked by the frisking Riley had warned her about. She knew its purpose was to protect Dalmy. Mia glanced at the counter; Henry had taken the knife with him. The opportunity to grab a weapon was gone.

"I'm sorry about that," Dalmy said.

"Why did he touch me like that?" Mia asked, trying not to overdo the fear in her voice.

"A traditional greeting in this town," Dalmy said. "Now, tell me what happened to you and maybe I can help."

"Will you deport me?" Mia asked.

"No," Dalmy said. "I promise, but I can't help if I don't know what's wrong."

The way she rolled her *r*'s was beautiful. Mia tried not to get distracted. She used her shaky hands to take a sip of the water.

"Are you here with your husband?" Dalmy asked.

Mia nodded her head.

"On a honeymoon? Didn't go so well?"

Mia gulped and nodded some more. This was unexpected; Dalmy was telling the story for her. "How did you know?"

Dalmy let out a light laugh.

"Pretty young American girl in an exotic land," Dalmy said. "If you ran away you wouldn't be so far south."

"I don't have a clue where I am," Mia said.

"It's not important," Dalmy said. "What happened?"

"We got down here and he made me chop off my hair," Mia said. "I was so happy to get married, but after the ceremony he changed. He locked me in the bathroom of our hotel and I climbed out the window."

Mia started getting louder.

"I ran; I kept on running," Mia said. "Then I jumped in the back of a truck and lay down. I knew he was right behind me. But then the truck started moving. A few hours ago the truck parked and I got out and ran some more."

"It's okay," Dalmy said. "You're safe; he can't get you here."

"I saw another car," Mia said. "I dove inside and started pushing everything; it came to life and I drove off."

Mia paused and took a breath.

"I kept going straight," Mia said. "Then the road ended and it was desert. I didn't see the cliff until right when I was heading over. I opened the door and dove out. The car went right over. I almost died.

"I kept on walking. It was hours; the sun came up and I made it here. Am I still alive?"

"Yes," Dalmy said. "You poor thing. You're alive. That's quite an ordeal. What direction was the sun when you started walking, behind you or in front?"

"Behind," Mia said.

Dalmy turned around and nodded to the guards. One ducked out of the building. They were going to try to verify Mia's story. There would be no car, but at least they'd check in the opposite direction of Riley.

"I'm Dalmy," she said. "What's your name?"

"Jeanette," Mia said. "You have a beautiful name. In fact, you're beautiful."

"Not as pretty as you," Dalmy said. "Even with that awful haircut. Do you want a place to lie down? Maybe take a bath?"

"Please," Mia said. "I feel so dirty."

"Don't worry," Dalmy said. "I'll help you."

She wrapped her arms around Mia's shoulders and led her out of the building. The armed guard followed behind them.

Chapter 28

America helps the world. We should leave them in peace to live as they choose. We aren't the world police.

—*Comment from the* Global Reporter *message board*

A small dune buggy led them through town. When they reached the house on the top of the hill it wasn't the mansion Mia had expected. She thought her father's farmhouse was larger. They got out of the buggy, but Dalmy led Mia past the front door. They went to a side entrance Dalmy unlocked. It led right to a staircase. Riley hadn't predicted this part.

Mia climbed in front of Dalmy and at the top was a thin hallway. Four doors lined each side, and there was one at the end. Dalmy leaned over Mia and unlocked one of the doors. She opened it up to show a bathroom. Mia walked in first. Dalmy went to a cabinet and pulled out some towels.

"Get yourself cleaned up," she said. "I'll find you something more suitable to wear. Soap and shampoo are in the shower. Ricky will be in the hall; if you need anything, just yell."

"Thank you," Mia said.

"Feel better," Dalmy said.

Dalmy walked out through the bathroom door and Mia swore she heard the lock click shut. Mia walked over to the tub and turned on the shower. Next she searched the drawers, hoping to find a razor blade or any other type of weapon. Most of the drawers were empty. There was some makeup, a blow dryer, and cream hair remover. The closest thing to a weapon that she found was a toothbrush. Nothing was strong enough to hold Dalmy hostage with.

Mia let out a sigh of frustration. The steam from the shower filled the bathroom and Mia readied herself to bathe. If there was any silver lining it was the chance to get clean.

She took her time, making sure to assess every detail of her situation. Mia felt like she was living another person's life. The thought of impersonating a helpless girl in order to break two people out of a military base was absurd. Mia kept reminding herself she was more than capable and to keep calm. She shut off the water and dried herself off. When she stepped out of the shower there was a garment bag laid across the sink with a note.

I think you'll look perfect in this. If you're not too tired my father and I would love for you to join us for dinner. Be ready in an hour.

It was more of a command than a request. Mia was fine with that. She didn't want to waste more time pretending to sleep. If both of them were present it would be easier for Mia to make her move.

The short hair cut down Mia's blow-drying time. Once she was done with that she went through the drawers looking for makeup. She applied some light eyeliner and mascara. Mia put on some lip gloss and paused, staring at her reflection. Even with the short hair this act reminded her of her former self. The vain girl who looked in the mirror for hours. That girl was dead. Still, as she hung the garment bag on the shower rod and pulled the zipper down her breath almost caught in her throat. It was stunning. A short red dress that cinched at the waist with a flowing skirt. A layer of thin red chiffon would wrap around her neck, leaving her back exposed. A pair of red strappy heels were stuck in the corner. Mia slipped on the dress and loved the way the nice fabric felt against her skin. It was meant for a taller girl, but outside of that it was a perfect fit. Mia did a little spin and the skirt flared out. It was wonderful. Her concentration was broken by a knock on the door.

"Come in," Mia said.

The door creaked open and Dalmy stood in the doorway. She was wearing a baby-blue dress that matched Mia's in fineness.

"Red is a good color on you," she said. "Ricky, come here. Doesn't Jeanette look beautiful?"

His head appeared on the other side of Dalmy's shoulder. He nodded and moved back. It was a split second, but Mia managed to notice Ricky's hand graze Dalmy's waist. This sign of affection was met with no objection from Dalmy. Ricky was more than a body-guard. Mia filed that knowledge away.

"Are you ready?" Dalmy asked. "I hope you're not too tired."

"I'm fine," Mia said. "The last few days have left me so jittery I think I'll have a hard time sleeping anyway."

"I'm sure you'll sleep like a newborn tonight," Dalmy said.

She held out her hand and Mia grabbed ahold of it. The two walked down the steps. Dalmy dropped Mia's hand to unlock the door again. It only opened with a key from either side.

"I'm locked in?" Mia asked.

"Old house," Dalmy said. "We never had the locks updated. This part was where the servants lived."

The locks didn't look old. Mia stayed quiet as they rounded the outside. The ocean waves crashed along the coast next to them. Mia walked toward the edge and looked over. There was a road that no doubt led straight into the complex housing Andrew and Carter.

"It's dangerous over here," Dalmy said.

"The ocean," Mia said. "It's so pretty as the sun sets."

"I thought you'd have a problem," Dalmy said. "Since you drove your car over the cliff and all."

Mia nodded and followed Dalmy back toward the house. Inside she was screaming at her screwup. Dalmy was no amateur.

They entered the front door and Dalmy led Mia into the first room. It was decorated in beautiful colors. Mia didn't pay much attention to the décor though; she needed to stay alert in case any possible weapon presented itself.

"Have a seat," Dalmy said. "My father will join us in a few minutes."

"Thank you," Mia said. "For your kindness."

"I have some bad news," Dalmy said. "We may have to deport you after all."

"What? Why?" Mia said. She tried hard to show some tears.

"You're married," Dalmy said. "If you weren't spoken for it wouldn't be a problem, but if we're caught housing an American bride we could get in a lot of trouble."

"Please," Mia said. "There must be something you can do."

"There's one thing," Dalmy said. "But I doubt you'd be interested."

"Anything," Mia said. "I'll do anything."

Mia wasn't expecting the job offer so soon.

"If we were to hide you, it would cost us a lot of money and we'd be risking our lives," Dalmy said. "How could you pay us back?"

"I can cook and clean," Mia said.

"What about . . . entertain?" Dalmy asked.

"I'm not a good singer," Mia said.

"You have other skills," Dalmy said. "I'm sure the men in our town will appreciate them."

This was happening too fast. Dalmy suspected something. Mia closed her eyes to think for a moment.

"Maybe someone can give me some lessons," Mia said. "I can hone my voice."

"What about your body?" Dalmy asked.

"I don't understand," Mia said. "I can dance."

"Maybe the men would pay just to spend an hour in your company," Dalmy said. "Would that be all right with you?"

"Anything not to return to America," Mia said, quickly adding, "I can talk for hours."

"I think they'll pay quite a bit for a chance to *speak* with an American," Dalmy said. "You're the only one in the town."

An eager smile crossed Dalmy's face and her eyes glanced up and down Mia's figure.

"I can stay, then?" Mia asked.

Dalmy closed her lips but her smile remained. She wore a look of pure satisfaction.

"Yes," Dalmy said. "I think we can work something out."

A tall man walked into the room, breaking up the conversation. Dalmy stood to greet him and Mia did the same. He wore white knit pants and a blue shirt to match Dalmy.

"Jeanette, this is my father, Joseph Ruiz," Dalmy said.

"Please sit, ladies," he said.

Mia sat back down on the couch.

"Jeanette has agreed to join our team," Dalmy said.

"Welcome aboard," Joseph said. "No business talk tonight. This is a friendly visit. Dalmy told me your story. You have my deepest sympathies. I despise the way your country treats women."

"Thank you for taking me in," Mia said.

The two people she needed to free Carter and Andrew were right in front of her, and there wasn't a guard in sight. Mia wished badly that she had a weapon. Nobody was speaking. Mia didn't want them studying her movements.

"I didn't know the outside world was so different," Mia said. "There's no Registry here?"

"No," Joseph said. "If Dalmy ever finds someone who is her equal, it will be her choice to settle down. Of course, I still want some approval."

"Our countries are so close; why are they so different?" Mia asked.

"We have religion, morals that your country doesn't have," Dalmy said.

"What's religion?" Mia asked.

Dalmy coughed and Joseph smiled indulgently. Mia's question was legitimate; she'd never heard the term.

"It's not time for a theology lesson," Dalmy said. "But that's why unmarried women aren't deported. If you had come down here before your ceremony there'd be no risk."

"Let's go to the dining room," Joseph said.

Mia was eager to move on. Eating meant silverware, which meant a knife, or at least something sharp to eat with. Dalmy whispered something in Joseph's ear and he chuckled. Dalmy led the way down the hall with Mia sandwiched in the middle.

They made their way into the dining room and took seats around the table. Mia was shocked that there was no cutlery next to the plates.

"It smells good," Mia said. "What are we having?"

Someone entered the room carrying a tray. He was wearing a chef's uniform and stopped right behind Mia. He leaned over her and set three crispy rolls onto her plate.

"Flautas," Dalmy said.

"I just use my hands?" Mia asked.

Dalmy picked up one of hers and took a bite. She grinned before chewing the food. Mia picked up her food and did the same. Another strikeout for the night. The conversation continued with talk about the local weather and other cuisines. Mia tried her best to look interested, all the while scanning the room for some weapon. It was useless; her plan was failing.

They finished eating and the plates were cleared away. Joseph rose from his chair; Dalmy and Mia did the same.

"It was a pleasure meeting you," Joseph said.

"You as well," Mia said, bowing her head.

"I thought we'd head down to the town," Dalmy said. "I could get you acquainted with your new home, and maybe, if you feel up to it, you could start what we talked about before."

"Talking with men?" Mia asked.

"Privately," Dalmy said.

"I'm sure you'll be a natural," Joseph said.

Mia's heart jumped into her throat. This wasn't on the schedule. Riley assumed they'd give her at least one night before they sent her to work. Mia's tongue caught in her throat. She was freezing up, about to give herself away and ruin everything. Joseph and Dalmy waited for a reaction, but Mia gave none. The con was over and Mia was in trouble.

Chapter 29

A female brain is far less developed than its male counterpart. It is nature's way of reinforcing American ideals.

—American Gazette

Andrew's fist flew forward and the dummy fell back. He didn't feel any pain in his hand and he hit again. Sweat was dripping into his eyes, but he ignored the burn. Andrew didn't see the cushioned dummy. He saw an enemy, an enemy responsible for taking Mia away from him. He channeled his rage and threw his fist at the target again, this time remembering to follow through. He fell forward and a whistle blew.

"You're still fighting like a street urchin," the sergeant said.

Taking a couple breaths, Andrew felt a sting in his hand. He looked down to see a bit of blood on his knuckles.

"Watch Private Rowe," the sergeant said.

Andrew walked over to Carter and the sergeant blew his whistle. The blond man attacked the dummy's head with the inside of his forearm, then he lifted his leg and kicked the lower section. Carter did have a more formal style, but there was a certain passion missing. Andrew didn't think his blows would cause any real damage.

"Private Rowe is anticipating defenses," the sergeant said. "You are hitting aimlessly as if your opponent is already dead."

"I'm sorry, sir," Andrew said. He kept his chin up and spoke in a monotone voice, just like a real soldier.

"That's enough, Private Rowe," the sergeant said. "Private Simpson, your turn."

Andrew walked back over toward his dummy. He waited for the sergeant's whistle to blow. He stared at the dummy and watched as it transformed into an American, one decorated in the colors of his home. The whistle blew and Andrew began his attack, pretending the soldier was fighting back. An image of Mia flashed before his eyes and he kicked hard. He waited before attacking again and then visualized her face once more, this time attacking with his fist. He breathed heavily and waited again. He concentrated on her face and an image of her in his arms came to mind. He lifted his leg again and with a powerful kick knocked the dummy off its stand.

Pain flooded Andrew's head. The strange noises returned and he needed to crouch down. Mia in his arms? That never happened. The pain intensified.

"Private Rowe, get the doctor," the sergeant said.

Andrew didn't know whether to fight through the pain to see the memory or block it out. Before he had the chance to decide the doctor was kneeling next to him, pricking his arm with another injection. The pain subsided.

"You still have some lasting effects from your trauma," the doctor said.

"A loud noise," Andrew said. "It hurts."

"You'll be all right," the doctor said.

He stood up and pulled Andrew to his feet. Carter stood next to the sergeant with no sign of concern on his face.

"How are you doing, Private Rowe?" the doctor asked. "Any similar pain?"

"No, sir," Carter said.

"Well, you were only sick for three days," the doctor said. "Private

Simpson faced two weeks of the illness. Do you know what brought on the spell this time?"

Just like every time this happened, Andrew shook his head. The last thing he remembered was fighting the dummy. Everything else was on the cloudy side. He glanced over at his destroyed training doll and stopped the smile from appearing on his lips.

"Good work, Private," the sergeant said. "Good work, both of you. Hit the showers and get some sleep."

The doctor and sergeant left the training room. Andrew started to follow them, but Carter remained.

"Are you coming?" Andrew asked.

"No," Carter said. "I want to train longer tonight."

Andrew spun around and picked up his broken dummy.

"If you're staying, I'm staying," Andrew said. "We're a team."

"In memory of our families," Carter said.

"In memory of our families," Andrew repeated.

Carter nodded his head and went back to practicing. Andrew was glad they were staying late tonight. The harder he trained, the better he could honor Mia's memory.

Chapter 30

"Is something the matter?" Dalmy asked with a cold voice.

"Maybe I'm more tired than I thought," Mia said.

"It will be a short trip," Dalmy said. "I promise. Back here and in bed in under an hour. Unless you're not up for it, but in that case we may have to start the deportation process."

"I don't want to appear unappreciative, or unladylike," Mia said. *Think. Think. Think,* she told herself.

"Please," Dalmy said. "Be yourself."

"I wouldn't know what to say to a man," Mia said. "I've never been alone with one before."

"But your husband . . . ," Dalmy said. "Right? It will be just like that."

"Even we were never alone together," Mia said. "He celebrated with his friends too much on our wedding night and when we arrived here he locked me in the bathroom, angry at me because he chopped off my hair the night before."

"That's horrible," Joseph said. He sat back down and Dalmy did the same.

"So you've never known the private company a male companion can offer in any sense?" Dalmy asked.

Mia shook her head. She saw her hosts look at each other with large grins.

"An innocent girl," Dalmy said. "I think people might pay a large sum for her time."

"I agree," Joseph said.

Mia felt her skin crawl. Even if she hadn't known these people's true intentions she would have figured it out by now.

"We'll have to change the hair though," Joseph said. "Maybe some new clothes too. Ones that fit better."

"I'm free tomorrow," Dalmy said. "I can have the girls come by and help."

"I have the perfect idea," Joseph said. "A party. Here, tomorrow night, in Jeanette's honor, welcoming her to our small town. We can introduce her to the locals."

"Don't go to all that trouble for me," Mia said.

"Nonsense," Dalmy said. "It's for us too. We can show off our new girl, and who knows? Maybe someone will want to spend time with you here."

Mia nodded her head.

"It sounds nice," she said, her stomach turning at the idea.

"It's settled then," Dalmy said. "Tonight, rest up; we have a busy day tomorrow."

Dalmy called for Ricky and he came into the dining room. They spoke to each other in Spanish. Mia wished she knew what they were saying but decided it couldn't be any worse than the previous conversation.

"Ricky's going to walk you up to your room," Dalmy said. "He's going to keep an extra-close eye on you. It can be difficult sleeping in a strange place; we don't want you running off and hurting yourself. He'll be outside your door all night if you need anything."

Mia stood up and Ricky grabbed her arm.

"Is this necessary?" Mia asked.

"We have some strange customs here," Dalmy said. "Meeting you has been a gift and we'd hate for anything to happen to you."

Mia couldn't read Dalmy. She didn't know whether the woman was dropping the façade or was protecting her new investment. Probably both. Either way Mia's best bet was to continue playing the naïve girl. She gave a sheepish grin and Ricky led her out of the house.

Mia debated attacking him and pulling his gun, but she could tell his defenses were up and she wouldn't be successful. Mia wasn't good at initiating conflicts, only defending herself during them. In the morning, Mia would make her move. Dalmy would be nearby and if Mia got ahold of her Ricky would likely toss his gun. That was her best chance for now.

The back stairs were unlocked this time. Ricky led Mia up and to the end of the hall. He pushed open another unlocked door and let go of Mia's arm. He didn't wait for her to respond before pulling the door shut and locking it from the outside. Mia searched the room, happy when she found a small garbage can. Sickened by the night's experiences, Mia unloaded the contents of her stomach into the receptacle. A chill ran up her spine when she was done. Her confidence was faltering.

Chapter 31

The South Area is claiming Grant Marsden as their own, but the Northeast Area says it doesn't matter where he's from, but where he chose to settle.

—American Gazette

It felt like a good day to wear pink, Grant thought. He took off his silk pajamas and pulled on a pair of pink-and-blue-striped shorts. He chose a thin pink dress shirt and rolled the sleeves up, completing his getup with a pair of tan sandals. He heard the vibration of his cell phone and picked up the device.

"Did you find anything?" Grant asked.

He had expected to hear from Rex last night.

"Sorry for the delayed response," Rex said. "I found the town. The welcoming committee took my phone."

"Is my bride there?" Grant asked.

"I think so," Rex said. "I gave the cover story and I was invited to town by one of Joseph Ruiz's acquaintances. His daughter came to check me out, asking questions about Americans and if I was searching for my wife."

"So she's suspicious?"

"To prove myself I had to hand over quite a bit of cash," Rex said. "But there's something off about this place."

"Find the girl and get out of there," Grant said.

"They think I'm a high roller," Rex said.

"Do you need more money?" Grant asked.

"No," he said. "I buried some supplies in the desert before I made my entrance. I had to wait until it was late, then snuck out and dug them up. That's how I got this phone."

"Get confirmation on the girl and get out of there," Grant said.

This mission was poorly planned. Grant couldn't do much from a distance and wasn't familiar with Mexican culture.

"I thought you wanted me to trail her," Rex said. "What if she's here?"

"What makes you think that?" Grant asked.

"Well, after I flashed your money, Miss Ruiz invited me to an auction tonight," Rex said. "A virginal American is joining her team of working girls. Tonight's the unveiling."

"So you believe that Amelia is a prostitute now?" Grant asked.

"I doubt she has much say in it," Rex said. "From the look of this place the men here wouldn't have a problem with that either."

"What about her male companions?"

"Not here," Rex said. "I can hunt them down, but so far no sign of them."

This was unexpected. Grant's plan wouldn't work without Amelia's men. He debated his next move. Leaving Amelia to that lifestyle might be a fitting punishment for her betrayal.

"Maybe she will get what she deserves either way," Grant said.

"Boss?" Rex asked.

While Grant was working in the armed forces he'd visited a brothel or two, as all men had. He doubted his headstrong little wife would enjoy herself. But the pictures of her floating around Saint Louis were plaguing him. Leaving her alive was too big a risk.

"I want to kill her myself," Grant said. "But if there's no other option, win tonight, and when you're alone, shoot her in the head. No loose ends."

"Yes, sir," Rex said.

"Call me when it's finished," Grant said.

He hung up his phone. It was a fancy machine capable of accessing the Internet and never out of service range. The screen was created from synthetic diamonds and uncrackable. It could be submerged in water up to a mile deep without breaking and could locate any person with a cell phone in the world. The phone was indestructible. This type of technology wasn't available to the general public, but Grant's status afforded him many luxuries. He set it down on his dressing table and picked up its mate.

It was a standard-issue civilian phone. It flipped open and couldn't do anything but handle calls and text messages. This one was special though; its casing was dirty and starting to chip, but it was sturdy. This little piece of technology was supposed to bring Amelia back to him, so he could inflict the suffering on her she deserved. He debated destroying the machine, since his plan was falling apart. But Grant couldn't do that, not until he had confirmation of his wife's passing.

Grant's personal phone rang again, breaking his concentration. He looked at the number and picked up the call.

"Dr. Schaffer," Grant said. "Please give me an update."

Chapter 32

What if it was your daughter trapped in such a life? Wouldn't you beg for someone to step in and help?

        —*Comment from the* Global Reporter *message board*

The door to Mia's cell flew open. That was what she was calling her room. It was plain, with no windows or closets. The only furniture was a bed in the center of the room. Mia couldn't even find a loose nail to use as a weapon. She didn't remember falling asleep.

"Hello," a female said, greeting her. She was pretty, with long, dark hair. Two others followed her inside. "We're here to get you ready," she said. "For your big night."

"Where's Dalmy?" Mia asked.

She saw a guard with a gun close the door and turn the lock, keeping Mia inside this room with these women.

"She couldn't make it," one said.

The women carried several boxes with them. They set them down on Mia's bed and started taking out their contents. One was plugging a machine into an outlet, while another started holding up pieces of hair to Mia's head. The third grabbed Mia's hands and started cleaning her nails.

"What's going on?" Mia asked.

"I already told you," she said. "We're making you pretty. Stand up."

Mia did as she was told, still trying to process the situation. One of them took her measurements and wrote down the figures. Mia glanced down at the bed, which was now covered with makeup brushes and hair accessories. This was a standard makeover. A game Mia used to love playing with Whitney back at her father's house. This time it wasn't a game.

"So these men are going to pay to talk to me?" Mia asked.

The three girls giggled.

"Yes," one said. "Talk all night."

"Ow," Mia said.

She raised her hand to the nape of her neck; it stung from a burn.

"Sorry," she said. "Trying to get your new hair attached."

"By fusing it into my head?" Mia asked.

She had assumed someone was bringing her a wig.

"Extensions," the girl said. "Sit down again."

Mia did as she was told. These girls were moving fast. None of them could help her. She needed Dalmy; her life was the one Mia could trade for Carter and Andrew. Horrible memories of her appraisal invaded. The procedure that earned her a price tag for the Registry. This scenario echoed that, only this time it would be in person. In arms' reach of men who sought to buy her. There was no way Mia was going through that again.

"Stop," Mia said.

She pulled her hand away and stood up. The three girls looked shocked.

"I want to see Dalmy," Mia said.

"Are you getting nervous?" Dalmy said.

Mia spun around and there was her captor at the door, looking glamorous as ever.

"You three wait in the hall for a minute," Dalmy said, coming inside.

The girls got up and left. Ricky walked into the room. He shut the door. Ricky's rifle was gone; now he had a handgun hanging in a holster. It was easy for Mia to see. Her eyes went up and met Dalmy's; the woman wore a cruel smile.

"What's your husband look like?" Dalmy asked.

"Brown hair, blue eyes, average height," Mia said.

"What's his name?"

"Michael," Mia said.

"Last name?"

"Riley," Mia said. If she used Grant's real last name there was too much risk.

"Mr. Michael Riley, a brown-haired, blue-eyed American," Dalmy said.

"What's going on?" Mia was trying hard to fight her nerves.

"You show up one day before another American, with loads of money ready to toss around," Dalmy said.

Mia's eyes widened at that. Was Grant here?

"Are the two of you working together?"

"No," Mia said.

"Do you know what is expected of you tonight?" Dalmy asked.

"Yes," Mia said. "As I stated earlier, I'll do anything to avoid going back to my husband. What did the American look like?"

"Not like the man you just described," Dalmy said. "Jeanette, I want to believe you, really, but this might be too much of a coincidence."

"I'm just a girl who ran away from her husband," Mia said. "Nothing else."

If this new American man was somehow connected to Grant, Mia had more to worry about than just Dalmy's intentions. Dalmy's face seemed to relax a bit. She broke eye contact and started walking around the bed.

"Are you really a virgin?" Dalmy asked.

"Yes," Mia said.

"Your presence has caused quite the commotion, and the people are excited. You could pull in tens of thousands for us tonight."

"I went for a lot more than that in the Registry," Mia said.

"I'm sure you did," Dalmy said.

Mia couldn't read Dalmy. She wasn't sure if the woman was speaking sarcastically or not.

"I could have this man disposed of, if he is your husband. Would it bother you if I did?" Dalmy asked.

Mia was relieved. If Dalmy took care of whoever was here, that would clean up some problems. Whoever this American was, his presence was a blessing. It made it harder for them to connect Mia to Andrew and Carter. She thought twice before speaking up. Acting like someone who was indifferent to the death of another might spark Dalmy's curiosity even further.

"Ricky's gun," Dalmy said. "It didn't scare you. In fact, none of them do. Why is that?"

"I'm from a farm," Mia said. "I've been around guns my whole life."

"So you know what I want from you and you're on board?" Dalmy asked. "Is that your story?"

"I'll do what I have to not to get deported," Mia said.

Mia kept her eyes glued to Dalmy's. Both of them were trying to feel each other out.

"I have people watching that man," Dalmy said. "If he tries anything funny, I'll make the call and he's dead."

"I'm not with him," Mia said.

Dalmy gave a small laugh and started walking toward the door.

"Be a good girl and let these ladies make you beautiful. Life can be pleasant here. All things are more enjoyable when you're dressed for the part."

Dalmy opened the door and walked out. Ricky stayed; he was more than ready to pull out his gun if need be. The three girls came rushing back in and started working on Mia again. She didn't protest. Mia told herself nothing had changed. Tonight was the night she'd make her move. All she needed was a weapon.

Chapter 33

American women have a higher standard of living than most people. They are in good health, live in nice houses, and are treated like prizes. Citizens of Eastern Europe face starvation and the possibility of freezing to death every night. We should be more concerned with their health and safety.

—*Comment from the* Global Reporter *message board*

Besides a few bathroom breaks, Mia was never alone. Her makeover took hours. They waxed the hair from her body and spent over an hour painting her face. Her dirty, broken fingernails were covered with beautiful artificial nails and her short hair was transformed into long locks that hung down her back.

"How will I take these off?" Mia asked. She picked up a piece of her new hair.

"You don't," the girl said. "They'll grow out eventually; when it starts to look bad we'll put new ones in."

Mia tried to keep her eyes on the pair of scissors one of the women had brought. They were on the top of a box. Mia needed to swipe them. If she could hold them next to Dalmy's neck it might be enough to barter for Andrew and Carter's lives.

A new woman entered the room. She hung a garment bag and walked out. Mia tried to sneak her hand out and grab the scissors but at the last second the worker picked them up again and started cutting small pieces from Mia's hair.

"Why are you cutting my hair if you just put it on?"

"To make it look more natural," she said. "You're cleaning up very nicely."

One of the girls went over to the garment bag and pulled the zipper. Hanging was a long red dress. It was strapless, with a corset-style top that would pull Mia's waist tight. The skirt had a giant slit so her leg could pop out. One of the girls moved the dress and Mia saw a faint design in gold glitter shimmer across the fabric.

"They're going to fight over you in this tonight," a girl said.

"Why would I want them to fight over me?" Mia asked.

"Relax," a girl said. "You'll do great tonight, and you're so pretty."

"Why do you do this?" Mia asked.

The girl shrugged.

"I have a roof over my head; they treat me nice," she said. "It's not a bad way to live."

"So you're all here by choice?" Mia asked.

"Aren't you?"

"You live in a free country; you can do anything you want," Mia said. "I don't have that option."

"I want to work here," the girl said. Her tone became defensive. "Don't judge me."

"Sorry," Mia said. "I didn't mean to offend."

"You Americans never do," she said.

"So you've met other Americans? Dalmy made it sound like we're rare down here."

"You're the first female," she said. "There's a decent amount of males. They work below and come visit us on their nights off sometimes."

Carter and Andrew were now in those ranks. Mia doubted her men would ever participate in any goings-on around here.

"What work are they doing down there?" Mia asked.

"They help out around the town," she said. "With Joseph's business."

"Dalmy mentioned soldiers," Mia said. She hoped nobody reported that lie back to her warden.

"They act like they're soldiers, but the only war I've ever seen them fight is guarding deliveries."

"Some of them think they're so important," another girl chimed in. "Like working for Joseph is such a great honor. They call themselves militiamen and think they're going to lead Mexico in some rebellion. But I say, what rebellion? The people are happy down here."

The girls all had a laugh at that. "Brainwashing"; she remembered Riley using the term. Whatever they were doing to the men down there to make them so compliant, it was wrong. Mia watched the girl walk away from her, scissors in hand. She would love to get her hands on those. Mia watched as the girl tucked the scissors away with her other supplies.

One of the girls held up a mirror so Mia could see herself. She was shocked at the reflection looking back. Mia looked perfect. Her makeup was dramatic, the long hair was held away from her face by a gold headband, and curls flowed down her back. She hadn't looked like this since the night she met Grant. The memory of her vanity came crashing back and Mia looked away just in time to see the case carrying the scissors leave the room.

Like a gift, Mia's attention was drawn toward a clatter. She turned her head to see a pair of stiletto heels on the floor. They were gold with red-jeweled straps. One of the girls picked them up.

"I didn't notice these earlier," she said. "They're beautiful. You'll be stunning tonight."

Mia smiled. She had what she needed to rescue her friends.

Chapter 34

Selling clothing your wife created is tantamount to having her work out of the home. A real man would never allow such a thing.

—American Gazette

"Great job today," the sergeant said.

Andrew kept his face blank, elated inside. He was proud of himself. His whole life he had known he'd make the perfect soldier, and now he was showing off his skills. Today Andrew had channeled his anger correctly. He was turning from a street fighter into a man with real proficiency. It was different from the work Andrew expected in the American armed forces, but here he had more of a purpose.

"Tomorrow we'll move on to some basic weapon training," the sergeant said.

The elation only grew inside Andrew. He was more than ready to learn a new skill.

"Sir, may I speak, sir?" Carter asked.

Andrew didn't turn his head to look at him.

"Yes, Private," the sergeant said.

"I do not feel that I have mastered hand-to-hand combat, sir," Carter said. "I think it is important that I master one skill before moving on to the next, sir."

The sergeant's lips pressed into a smile. Andrew was jealous. He wanted the sergeant's approval. He wanted to be the best soldier.

"Private Simpson," the sergeant said. "How do you feel about this?"

"Sir," Andrew said. "Private Rowe is correct. We should be perfect."

The sergeant kept the smile but shook his head. He took a big breath before yelling, "Both of you, down on the ground. Push-ups, count out loud."

Andrew reacted and hit the floor. He started counting out loud in perfect unison with Carter.

"When I give you an order you accept that order," he said. "I am in charge. I set your training schedules. This isn't some workout facility. This is the Mexico Militia."

Anger returned to Andrew. He was a leader, not a follower. This was his fault; if he'd only spoken his true feelings instead of agreeing with Carter, the sergeant would have been praising him, not dishing out punishment.

"You call yourself soldiers," the sergeant said. "A real soldier listens to his superiors. He doesn't think he's better than them."

The two men continued doing their push-ups. Andrew felt like he could go for hours. He started raising his voice when he yelled the numbers out.

"Since you two aren't ready yet, tomorrow we will start at day one. You will tour the facility and learn the basic commands all over again. Does that sound like fun?"

"Sir, yes, sir," Andrew said.

"How about you, Private Rowe?"

"Sir, yes, sir," Carter said.

"I didn't stay stop," the sergeant said.

Andrew continued his push-ups with newfound determination. If they were going back to their first days of training he would make them count. He had to, for Mia. Serving to the utmost of his ability was the best way he could honor her memory.

Chapter 35

There is no single answer. Even if the Registry was shut down, that would leave generations of uneducated women to deal with, let alone their angry husbands.

—*Comment from the* Global Reporter *message board*

Mia paced back and forth across the floor. The red dress was a bit too long, but she knew if she put the heels on the length would be perfect. Instead she held the shoes in her hands. She listened to movement outside her room and sat on the bed, waiting for the door to open.

Dalmy walked in, with Ricky right behind her. Mia stood up and gave a twirl.

"Your mood has changed," Dalmy said.

"I feel beautiful again," Mia said.

"Everyone's downstairs waiting for your arrival," Dalmy said. "Get your shoes on and I'll escort you down."

"I'm not good at walking in heels," Mia said. "Especially down stairs."

"You'll get used to it," Dalmy said. "The American I mentioned earlier, he was invited."

"Why?" Mia said.

"If you don't know him, his presence won't be a problem," Dalmy said.

Mia nodded her head. She couldn't worry about the man downstairs being Grant. Andrew and Carter were her top priority. Dalmy gave Mia a smirk. The young woman was arrogant. Mia thought if it were Grant waiting downstairs, Dalmy might be his equal.

"Come on," she said. "You can put your shoes on outside."

Dalmy turned and walked out of the room. Ricky stayed put, likely to follow them down the steps. Mia started walking; right when she was in front of Ricky she let one of the shoes drop. Ricky's attention diverted to the fallen shoe and with the split second Mia had she swung her other hand around and drove the heel deep into Ricky's side as hard as she could.

He made a loud grunt and grabbed at his injury. Mia reached across his chest and pulled the gun out of its holster. Just as she'd seen Andrew do before, she unlocked the switch and pulled the top back, arming the gun. Her hand was shaky, but she had a weapon.

Dalmy's eyes were wide. She turned to run down the stairs, but Mia reached out and grabbed her by the hair, yanking her closer. Mia wrapped her arm around Dalmy and held the gun to her head.

"You killed him," Dalmy said.

Mia looked toward Ricky. His body was slumped on the floor. He let out another groan and forced himself up, his hand covering his side. Mia saw some blood on his shirt, but he was far from dead.

"You," Mia said. "Walk or I'll shoot her."

"Shoot her," Ricky said. "I don't care."

"Everyone knows that's a lie," she said. "Go."

Ricky locked eyes with Dalmy and Mia dug the gun harder into Dalmy's temple. The woman let out a small cry.

"Keep your hands up and walk," Mia said.

"You're a dead girl," Dalmy said through gritted teeth.

"Shut up," Mia said. "Walk."

The three traveled down the steps. They were met with a breeze from the night sky. Through the front windows Mia saw the men mingling. They were drinking glasses of champagne. Mia felt an anger burn inside her at the idea that these people could think of buying a girl's innocence as such a casual event. She couldn't let those thoughts take over though. This was about Carter and Andrew.

"You," Mia said. "Go inside and bring Joseph out alone. If anyone else comes with him I'll kill her."

Ricky nodded his head and walked into the house.

"The second my father gets out here your boyfriend is dead," Dalmy said. "You stupid girl."

"I wasn't lying," Mia said. "Whoever the American is, I'm not with him."

The front door opened and Joseph walked out of the house. His face was filled with worry. He saw Dalmy and started to run toward them. Mia moved the gun off her hostage and pointed it at Joseph. He slowed down.

"Are you all right?" Joseph asked.

"Daddy," Dalmy said. She was crying now.

"You have something I want," Mia said.

"You'll pay for this," Joseph said.

"Two American boys," Mia said. "Taken from the beach for your militia. I want them back."

"I don't know who you're talking about," Joseph said.

"I think you do," Mia said.

She lowered the gun and held it at Dalmy's knee. The hostage let out a cry.

"I don't, I swear," Joseph said. "We have lots of recruits, I don't get updated daily."

"They're not recruits," Mia said. "They're victims."

Mia looked down at Dalmy's knee, threatening to pull the trigger again.

"Names," Joseph said. "Give me their names."

"Andrew and Carter," Mia said. "Get them here now, with a car."

Joseph reached into his pocket. Mia lifted the gun back to Dalmy's temple.

"I'm grabbing my phone," Joseph said.

He pulled out a cell and hit a button. He spoke in Spanish. Mia needed this to work. She knew she wasn't capable of killing Dalmy. If these men called her bluff she didn't have what it took to follow through.

"They're on their way," Joseph said. "Let her go."

"I'll let her go when they get here," Mia said.

She felt a sharp pain in her gut. Dalmy had slammed her elbow into Mia, knocking herself free. Mia pulled the trigger on the gun— she didn't mean to, but it happened. Dalmy let out a loud cry and for a moment Mia thought everything was over. But Dalmy was still standing, frozen by the sound of the discharge. Mia reacted fast, reaching out and grabbing Dalmy's hair, then pulling her back.

"The next shot won't be a warning," Mia said.

Joseph looked like he was alternating between anger and fear. The men from inside started pouring out, having heard the gun go off. A few of them were drawing their own weapons.

"Don't," Joseph said. "Everything's fine, go back in the house."

Mia scanned the crowd, expecting to see Grant's face, but nobody looked familiar. Everyone froze.

"Get back in the house," Joseph repeated. He turned his attention back toward Mia. "You're making a mistake," he said. "Let her go and we'll forget this whole thing ever happened."

"That you kidnapped my friends or that you tried to sell me?" Mia asked.

"You were more than willing earlier today," Joseph said.

The sound of a car engine came in the distance. It was the same sound Mia had heard the day on the beach when Andrew and Carter were taken. The car came into view, but Mia was blinded by the headlights. The vehicle stopped next to Joseph. The engine shut off and the doors opened. There they were. Carter stayed seated in the backseat, but Andrew stepped out of the car. His face was blank.

"Andrew," Mia said.

There he was, standing with his shoulders back. His lean body was accentuated in a tight black shirt. He stared at Mia; his warm brown eyes were filled with confusion and his mouth hung open. She watched as his breathing increased and a perfect smile crossed his face. Andrew moved toward her. She wanted to meet him, but that would mean dropping the gun.

"You're alive," he said.

Even though Mia was holding Dalmy firmly against her, Andrew lifted his hand and touched Mia's shoulder. His hand felt so soft and sent tingles floating through Mia's body. She nodded at him and her smile matched his.

Their reunion was cut short when Dalmy tried to pull away again. Mia's attention refocused on Joseph.

"Andrew, get in the car," Mia said.

Andrew started backing up. Mia glanced to her left and saw him climb in the backseat. Carter remained still, staring at whoever had driven him to this place.

"Get out of the vehicle and back away," Mia said to the driver.

"Do what she says," Joseph said.

The other men moved behind Joseph. Mia started dragging Dalmy to the car.

"You have what you want," Joseph said. "Let my daughter go."

"I'm taking her with me," Mia said.

"That wasn't part of the deal," Joseph said.

"There was no deal," Mia said. "Don't follow me. Once I'm far enough out I'll leave her for you."

Mia slid through the driver's-side door and over to the passenger seat, pulling Dalmy in behind her so that the woman was seated behind the wheel.

"Turn the car on and drive," Mia said. "South."

The engine turned over.

"Don't worry, baby," Joseph said. "She'll pay for this."

"Drive," Mia said.

Dalmy's face was tear stained as she put her foot on the gas. Mia kept the gun firmly against her temple until the lights from the city couldn't be seen anymore. Then she backed off, still keeping the gun out. She turned to look at her friends. The wind was too loud for conversation, but one look at Andrew and tears started falling. It had worked; they were together again. Now all they needed was Riley and Mia's company would be complete.

Chapter 36

Smart, handsome, strong, single. Which lady will be lucky enough to become Grant Marsden's new bride?

—American Gazette

Grant was sitting up in his bed. He was watching a rerun of his second interview on *The Greg Finnegan Show*.

"I think the perfect girl is one who knows her place," Grant said. "It will make for a happier life for both partners."

"There you have it, ladies," Greg said. "The way into this man's heart."

The screen on Grant's phone lit up. He picked up the call within a second.

"Do we have a winner?" Grant asked.

"No," Rex said. It was hard to hear him; he was in a car and the wind was drowning out his voice.

"What happened?"

"She made a very public escape," Rex said. "Those boys are with her again. I'm trailing them now."

"Does she know?" Grant asked.

"I don't think so," Rex said. "I have my lights off, and I'm too far back. As soon as she stops she's dead."

Amelia was free once more. Grant felt his anger rise at that. She had beaten the town of Puesta del Sol, and she thought she'd beaten Grant. She was reunited with her friends too. Grant eyed the smaller cell phone sitting on his dressing table again.

"No," Grant said. "Don't kill her. If she's on the run again that means my original plan might still work. Keep close to her. I want to know her every move in case I need you to pull the trigger."

"You're the boss," Rex said.

"Tell me something," Grant said. "Is the blond boy still with her?"

"Both of them are," Rex said.

"Keep it that way," Grant said.

The call ended. Grant sat back in his bed. He was a concise man who knew what he wanted. Right now more than anything he wanted Amelia Morrissey to suffer and die. Grant knew he should just give Rex the go-ahead to take care of her; then Grant wouldn't need to worry about the pictures circulating around Saint Louis. Grant wasn't sure if it was pride, his need for revenge, or his desire to ensure Amelia was well and truly dead, but he wanted her back here.

During Grant's service days, killing a man who was lying on the ground close to death wasn't nearly as satisfying as taking his time with one who was healthy and whole, which is why he had excelled at interrogations. Grant was the best at sucking information out of people. He knew just how hard to push them without frying their memories. On one occasion a prisoner of war had been very forthcoming after spending the night with Grant. The man cried with relief when he gave Grant the information he needed.

"You did good," Grant said.

"Can I go home now?" the man asked.

"Yes," Grant said.

He stood up from the table and walked to the other side. The man's clothes were bloody from the small stab wounds Grant had spent the night inflicting. Some were starting to scab over already.

Grant pulled out another knife and slid it into the man's throat. He made a sick gargling noise as he drowned in his own blood.

Grant smiled. That was the type of death Amelia Morrissey deserved.

Giddy with the memory, Grant jumped out of bed and left his room. He wanted to check on his current insurgent.

Chapter 37

There should be no individual countries or governments. A ruling body that oversees the whole globe should be put in place.

—*Comment from the* Global Reporter *message board*

"Stop the car," Mia said.

They slowed down just outside Riley's shack. Mia expected her to come out. She turned back to Carter and Andrew.

"Are you two okay?" Mia asked.

"I'm . . . I . . . You're alive," Andrew said.

"I made it off the beach," Mia said.

Andrew crossed his eyes and he looked away. He lowered his head and covered his ears.

"What's wrong?" Mia asked. She turned around with her free hand and touched Andrew's wrist, hoping to give him some comfort.

Carter still sat with a blank face, looking indifferent to the whole situation.

"You were on a beach?" Andrew asked. "You died in the car accident."

Mia felt Andrew's hand push harder against his head, like he was trying to block something out.

"No, we flew over in the helicopter. Don't you remember? We

were scaling the beach when the militia drove up. You two sacrificed yourselves to hide me."

Andrew looked up. His eyes met Mia's and she could tell he was struggling to process what she was telling him. Before he could speak he squinted his eyes shut and lowered his head again. His face was filled with intense pain.

"What is going on?" Mia asked. She looked at Carter for some answers but he made no attempt at responding.

"Their brains are fried," Dalmy said. "Not that it matters. All three of you will be dead soon."

Mia momentarily forgot about her mission; they hadn't reached safety yet. Dalmy's tears were dried up now. She wore a wicked smile.

"Get out of the car," Mia said.

Dalmy opened the door.

"Stay here," Mia said to the two boys.

She pointed the gun at Dalmy and started walking toward the shack.

"Riley," Mia shouted. "It's finished."

They walked through the trees and the shack came into view.

"Sick," Dalmy said. "I'm not going in there."

"Shut up," Mia said.

"You think you'll be safe," Dalmy said. "You'll never be safe."

"Stop talking," Mia said.

"You have two boyfriends," Dalmy said. "You're too late, they don't care about you. They barely remember you."

Mia was starting to lose her patience.

"What did you do to them?" Mia asked.

"We break them down so we can build from scratch," Dalmy said.

"Riley," Mia shouted. There was no sound from the house.

They reached the front door and Mia pushed it open. It was abandoned. There wasn't any trace of a person having lived there. Even the cot was gone. All that remained was a plastic bag on the table. Mia lowered her weapon and grabbed the bag. There was a note taped to the side.

Mia,

There was no doubt in my mind you would be victorious. You're a born operative. It was time for me to move on. I added a map to your destination and a new number to your cell phone. If you're ever in trouble call me. I hope you find what you're searching for; remember, not everything is so black and white.

Something rolled back and forth on the table. Mia looked down to see the black queen. She reached down and picked it up, stunned her friend was gone.

"Did someone abandon you?" Dalmy said. "They were probably smart enough to know you're a walking dead girl stuck with two men incapable of forming their own thoughts."

Mia tuned out Dalmy's words. She lowered the gun, having no use for her hostage anymore, and walked out the front door of the house, clutching her new memento and the bag. She jumped in the driver's seat. Andrew and Carter stayed motionless in the back.

"Will one of you move up here?" Mia said.

Andrew climbed over and sat down. He kept his face straight ahead. Mia put her hand on his knee.

"I'm very much alive," she said.

"I can't remember," Andrew said. His forehead wrinkled, then his eyes closed and he raised his hands to his ears again.

"Don't try," Mia said. "Focus on the present. Look at me."

Andrew raised his head. She watched as the lines his pain was causing him vanished. He leaned over to her and wrapped his arms around her shoulders, pulling her into an awkward hug. She twisted her body and brought her arms up his back. His scent was still the same and she wanted to take in as much of him in as possible. He pulled away before Mia was ready.

"We need to get out of here," he said.

Mia pulled out the map and handed it to Andrew. There was a big red star drawn and a black dot with the words "you are here" printed next to it.

"Can you keep track of where we are?" Mia asked. It was a backup, in case Mia lost her way.

"Keep going west," Andrew said.

Mia drove off. There was no roof and the wind blew fast, causing her new hair to fly behind her. Mia had thought as soon as Carter and Andrew were safe everything would be all right again. She realized now that was a fool's dream. Mia thought about Dalmy's warning and found herself wondering if they would ever really be safe.

Chapter **38**

Humans occupy less than 1 percent of the Earth's landmass; larger cities should be rebuilt so people can operate on a global level.

—Comment from the Global Reporter *message board*

The drive was quiet. Once they reached the main road Mia knew it wouldn't be much longer until they entered Guatemala. The sky was at its darkest point and no other cars were on the road. Mia's concentration was broken by Andrew's voice.

"Pull over," he said.

"What?" Mia asked.

"Pull over, now." There was panic in his voice.

Before Mia could bring the car to a complete stop he was already opening the door and jumping out. The terrain was changing from desert to lush forests and they were very close to the ocean, as the road went right along the cliffs. Mia was scared Andrew was going to jump off, as he paced back and forth right next to the edge. He let out a loud scream. Mia jumped out of the car. She ran over to him.

"Andrew, what's happening?" she asked.

"You're alive," he said. "I can't remember. You have to tell me. Tell me everything."

Mia had never known Andrew to obsess over details. She didn't want to add to his pain but thought he needed to hear the truth.

"We made it to Mexico," Mia said. "We were on a beach scaling a wall. I was too tired so Carter carried me to a rock. Then these men showed up and they kidnapped the two of you."

"I left you on a beach?" Andrew asked.

"You didn't have any choice," Mia said. "It was for the best."

"Then what happened?"

"I don't know," Mia said.

"How long was I with them?" Andrew asked. "How much of my life did I lose?"

"Almost four weeks," Mia said.

His face changed into a ball of rage. Mia thought he was going to let out a scream.

"They had me the whole time," Andrew said.

"Why don't you tell me what you remember," Mia said. "We can work back."

"I was training with Rod, so I could pass as a postservice man," Andrew said. "Then I woke up at a table with General Bolivar. He said they found me wandering the desert. I missed my vaccine booster and was really sick. They nursed me to health.

"He showed me an article, about you dying in a car accident," Andrew said. "If I left someone would find me and deport me; if I joined them I could honor your memory."

The rage started to fade away. Andrew looked at Mia for reassurance. Mia didn't know what to say. She walked closer to him and placed her hands on his cheeks. He brought his hands up to her shoulders, as if she were giving him support. The sounds of the waves crashing and the bugs humming in the trees was taking over.

"You'll get your memories back," Mia said. "I'll help you."

She went up on her tiptoes and got as close to his face as possible. Andrew leaned his face down and pressed his forehead against hers.

Mia moved her face slightly to the left and readied herself to press her lips to his.

"Mia, you're really alive," Carter said.

Andrew turned his head and backed away. Mia hadn't heard Carter get out of the car. The three stood next to the cliff and Mia nodded her head.

"I thought you were dead too," Carter said.

Mia reached out both her arms and wrapped one around each man's waist, pulling them in. It took a moment, but they lifted their arms and put them around her too.

"Does that mean my dad's still here too?" Carter asked.

Mia pulled away and wiped a tear from her eye. She shook her head.

"He didn't make it," she said.

She saw Carter's jaw quiver. He looked away. She couldn't imagine the horror he was facing, finding out about his dad's death twice.

"Did he die in the car accident?" Carter asked.

"He jumped out of the helicopter," Mia said. "There was too much weight, so he sacrificed himself for us."

Carter couldn't hold in the sob. "How could I forget that?"

Mia knew he didn't expect an answer and she didn't have one to offer. Her not knowing what to say wasn't their biggest problem. Mia looked down the road; she didn't see any headlights, but the sky was starting to lighten and she saw the outline of a vehicle heading straight toward them.

"We need to move now," Mia said.

She jumped in the driver's seat as Andrew and Carter climbed into their spots. She turned the key and slammed her foot on the pedal. There was always the chance it was another driver, but Mia's gut told her it was Joseph or his militia.

The road started to curve and climb. She tried to pretend it was only a simulation, like the computer program Riley ran for her. Trees appeared on both sides, but Mia knew the cliff was just beyond the greenery. Mia was driving as fast as she could, but soon a bright light flashed in her eyes. The other vehicle was right behind them and its headlights were blinding her. Her body was flung forward as their car was hit from behind. She pressed her foot down again, trying to keep her eyes on the road. This was much different than a computer program.

Not wanting to give the other vehicle the option of sending her over the cliff, Mia moved to the left side of the road and hugged the jungle. Another bang from behind came, but Mia kept control of the car. Then the lights turned off. She heard the other car accelerate. She took her eyes off the winding road and looked to her right; they were starting to pull up next to her. She sped up, but they were too fast. The other vehicle came into view; it was the same type of car Mia was driving, a rugged outdoor machine, except this one was much larger.

If Mia tried to ram them off the road it wouldn't do any good. The other vehicle was right next to them now; Mia looked over to see four people in the car, three of whom had their weapons drawn and aimed at her. She slammed on the brakes just in time to see bullet holes form on the hood of the vehicle. The other car started to slow.

"It's the militia," Carter said.

"They did this to us," Andrew said.

Mia needed to calm herself down. She could do this; it was what she'd trained for. She slammed her foot on the gas, hoping to drive past them fast enough to avoid another spray of bullets. Mia kept her head down and her plan proved effective. They raced past the stopped car unscathed. With the sky lightening by the second, Mia was able to see a sign up ahead. They were entering Guatemala. She pressed her foot down as hard as she could, thinking if they crossed the border they'd be safe. The other vehicle was right behind her again. She raced over the border and the air left her lungs. Mia's sense of safety was false. Her body went forward again as she was jolted from behind. These people didn't care what country they were in.

The vehicle was pulling up to their side again. Mia didn't know if her brake trick would work this time. She was starting to duck her head to avoid their guns when Andrew stood up on his seat.

"What are you doing?" Mia yelled over the wind.

"I won't let you die again," Andrew yelled.

Mia lifted a hand off the steering wheel and tried to grab hold of him. The car started veering too far to the left and Mia was forced to grip the wheel and watch the road.

"Carter, stop him," Mia yelled. She knew her pleadings fell on deaf ears.

The enemy vehicle was coming up next to them again. Mia turned her head briefly to see their weapons drawn and pointed at her car. As soon as they were at matching speeds Andrew flung himself forward. Mia let out a scream as Andrew's legs dangled between the two cars. Mia and Carter both lurched over to grab Andrew's legs, but the enemy vehicle veered off the road into the trees. Andrew disappeared with them.

Mia slammed on the brakes. Carter jumped out of the backseat and sprinted toward the car tracks where Andrew had disappeared. The sun was rising behind them and the sky continued to lighten. Mia felt like the world was spinning as she chased after him. She couldn't lose Andrew, not now, not ever.

She and Carter ran through the trees; they were farther from the cliff than Mia had thought. She kept running until Carter held out his arm, stopping her. They reached the brink and there was the car, balanced perfectly on the edge, its front wheels moving up and down as if it might spill over any second.

"Andrew!" Mia screamed.

The man in the driver's seat was knocked out; there was a bloodstain on his forehead. The three armed men were gone, likely having flown out of the car and over the cliff without safety restraints. Then there was Andrew, his body in the back. He was half in and half out of the car with his head hanging out the window.

"Andrew, wake up," Mia pleaded.

Carter walked closer to the car and it made a creak. He backed away and moved toward the edge. Mia followed him. The waves splashed against the rocky cliff about fifty feet below. It wasn't a straight shot down though; the car would fall down a steep hill if it teetered over. Mia thought she saw a helmet float between the rocks before it was taken out to sea. The three men hadn't survived their fall. If the car fell forward Andrew was likely to share their fate.

"What do we do?" Mia asked.

"Go back to the car," Carter said. "Look for some rope."

Mia didn't want to leave Andrew, but she knew that was their best option. She dove through the trees, not bothering to stick to the path made by the road. Branches clawed at her arms and dress but she made it back. She searched her stolen vehicle, pulling open the glove compartment and looking in the backseats. The only thing in there was the gun Mia used to kidnap Dalmy, which wouldn't be much help now.

The familiar sound of an engine came up the hill. Mia froze, scared that a second wave of men was after them. Instead a huge truck came roaring past. It didn't stop for Mia. It turned straight down the path made by the other vehicle. Mia grabbed the gun and ran back to Carter, hoping she could protect him from whoever had just arrived. She made it through the trees just in time to see a metal chain being attached to the teetering vehicle holding Andrew.

Mia saw the chain was connected to the newly arrived truck. The driver got back in to start the engine. He had to rev the gas a few times, but soon the hanging car leveled itself out. Andrew was pulled back onto solid ground and Mia ran over to him. Carter was on the other side pulling Andrew out. He laid him down on the ground.

Mia knelt and put her ear to Andrew's chest. His heart was beating. She felt tears of relief roll down her face. The truck door opened and Mia diverted her attention, ready to thank their benefactor for his assistance. Her words fell silent on her lips as soon as he came into view. It was a face she would never forget. The man responsible for Whitney's death.

Chapter 39

The world should shift away from a view focused on individual countries and think on a global scale. Most of the African continent is still undeveloped from the Great War. Why not set up colonies for refugees and work toward a new world order?
—Comment from the Global Reporter *message board*

Out of instinct Mia pointed the gun she held at the large man's head. Mia's hand was steady now. He looked annoyed.

"Get back," Mia said.

"What are you doing?" Carter asked. "He just helped us."

"Carter, get Andrew to the car," Mia said.

She didn't take her eyes off the man. Carter groaned a bit as he picked up Andrew. He walked past her with the other boy slung over his shoulder.

"You're the other American?" Mia asked. "Why are you after me?"

The man walked over to the car that held the unconscious militiaman. He unhooked the chain and started to roll it up.

"I just saved your friend's life," he said.

"Answer my question," Mia said.

"Grant sent me down here to bring you back," he said.

"I should shoot you," Mia said.

"We both know you won't," he said.

He turned his back toward Mia and began kicking the front of the car. The militiaman was starting to wake up. The giant man leaned against the rear of the car and started pushing. It didn't take much for the vehicle to start moving.

"Stop," Mia said.

"See?" he said. "You won't even let me kill this man after what he just did. So put the gun down and we can talk."

"You're going to take me back to Grant?"

"No," he said. "I'm supposed to kill you, or watch you until you decide to return on your own."

"That'll never happen," Mia said.

"Grant seems to think it will," he said.

"Why are you telling me this?"

"Because you asked," he said.

"Why did you help me?"

"Following my orders," he said.

"So you're deserting your friend?"

"He's my employer, not my friend."

"You're responsible for my friend's death," Mia said.

"She threw herself on those tracks," he said.

"Because you were chasing me!"

"I guess I'm even then," he said.

"Not quite," Mia said.

"What happened?" the militiaman asked.

The large man resumed pushing the car. He kept his head down, but Mia had a clear view. She saw the militiaman scramble to pick something up from the front seat. Mia tried to yell "stop" again, but it was too late. The militiaman turned around, pointed his gun at Rex, and fired down. Mia raised her weapon and pulled the trigger, hoping to take out the militiaman.

She heard the large man let out a groan and fall forward, pushing the car off the cliff in the process. The militiaman screamed as his car rolled down the slope. Mia saw a bloodstain forming on her un-wanted assistant's right side. She dropped her weapon and ran over.

"You shot me," he said.

He sat up and held one of his hands over his wound. He raised his face and looked at Mia with wide eyes.

"It was an accident," Mia said. "Are you hurt?"

"Yes, I'm hurt," he said. "You shot me."

"I was trying to shoot him," Mia said.

"Great aim." The man let out a groan. Mia ran over to him and grabbed his free arm.

"Can you walk?" she asked.

Carter came running back through the trees.

"Are you okay? I heard the guns go off," he said.

Carter came over and took Mia's place. She went to Rex's other side and gave what assistance she could while Carter hoisted him up. Mia went around to his back and he lifted his hand off the wound.

"How bad is it?" he asked.

There wasn't a hole. It looked like Mia had grazed his side. Still, Mia saw some deep-red blood ooze out. She pressed his hand back down.

"I need to keep pressure on it," Carter said. He stepped back and took his shirt off, then balled it up and handed it to Mia. "Hold that against the wound."

Mia did as she was told. The man let out a groan. Carter ran over and picked up Mia's weapon, sliding it under his belt. He placed the man's arm over his shoulders and the two started walking.

"Where are you going?" Mia asked.

"We're taking him with us," Carter said.

"No," Mia said.

"He saved Andrew," Carter said. "We're not leaving him here to die."

"It's not a life-threatening wound," Mia said. "I mean, he can walk."

"And get an infection," the man said.

Mia kept pace and tried to hold Carter's black shirt against the wound. She wanted to object but knew Carter was right. Her hand stung from the kickback of firing the gun. Mia's nerves were fried. She didn't think she could take another problem. She should have known a border wouldn't stop Grant's pursuit.

Mia's heart skipped a beat when she reached the road. There was Andrew, awake and leaning against the car.

"What is he doing here?" Andrew asked. He seemed to remember the man from the train station as well.

"He saved your life and Mia shot him," Carter said.

Mia tried to look around the big man and see Andrew's reaction. One of his eyebrows was raised in confusion.

"By accident," she said.

"Open the side door," Carter said.

Andrew hesitated, but he seemed to know helping the man was the right thing. They made it to the vehicle and Carter assisted him as he got into the passenger seat. Mia's hand was pinned behind him, holding the shirt down over his wound.

"Mia's going to pull her hand out," Carter said. "You need to lean back hard on your right side. Keep the shirt and the seat pressed tight against the wound."

He readied himself and Mia slid her arm out. Mia got a look at his face. He was sweating badly and starting to lose some color but looked far from death's door. Carter buckled the man's seat belt and ran around to the driver's seat.

"We need to move fast," Carter said. "He's losing blood."

"Losing blood slowly," he said. "At least you missed all my organs."

Mia ignored him. Her plan was falling apart. She opened the back door and jumped inside, sliding over to make room for Andrew.

"Where are we headed?" Carter asked. "Maybe I can just type it in this thing?"

The auto-drive. Mia had forgotten to rip it out. She lurched forward and yanked the electronic equipment out of place, chucking it as far as she could. She saw the map on the floor and scooped it up.

"What was that for?" Carter asked.

"We're not far," Mia said, ignoring his questions. She studied the guide, even though she didn't need it.

Mia didn't know what her next step should be. Taking Rex to her sanctuary would be dangerous, but she didn't know where else to go and his condition was her fault. With little other option she decided to stick to the plan.

"Keep going up this road. Take your third left. Drive for about five kilometers."

Carter hit the gas and they started moving. Mia couldn't believe how badly she'd screwed everything up. It was her fault the militia was able to tail them, and to top it off they were now harboring an enemy. An enemy Mia had almost unnecessarily killed.

She turned to look at Andrew. He looked pale and there was some blood dripping down his forehead. Taking a cue from Carter, she leaned over and ripped some of the fabric from her red dress. She wiped his blood away and held the fabric over Andrew's wound.

"How are you feeling?" She leaned closer to him to ask over the wind.

"Fine," Andrew said.

"That was a stupid thing you did."

"I'd do anything to protect you," he said.

Mia wished she could take more comfort in that idea. If her time with Riley had taught her anything, it was the importance of strategizing. Mia didn't have a clue how to form a new plan now.

Chapter 40

Tune in to The Greg Finnegan Show *tonight, when your host takes you through a tour of the youth home where Grant Marsden was raised. Part of this week's feature "Grant Marsden: American Hero."*

—American Gazette

The Mission was growing more and more familiar to Grant. When his presence was requested again, Grant jumped at the opportunity. He needed a distraction. He didn't bother trying to ready his identification this time, and as expected he strolled right in with no problem.

"Grant, so glad you could make it with the short notice," Ian said. "I have a present for you."

The elderly gentleman tossed a small package to him. Grant flipped open the lid and saw a plain watch with a black wristband. Not his style, but he nodded his head in thanks.

"I notice you use your phone to check the time, but some people might find that alienating if you're in charge. You always need to connect with the people. You'll get farther if you face less opposition."

Grant pulled the watch out and slapped it on his wrist.

"So far everything about you has checked out splendidly," Ian said. "Soon I'd like to start taking you with me on public appearances. If the people associate your face with mine the transition will be smooth."

"I'd like that," Grant said, following as Ian started walking down a hall.

"Good, because we're going to start this afternoon," Ian said. "Some time ago an individual produced a video of one of our retirement facilities internationally. As predicted there was minimal response, but I think it best to have perfect foreign relations. We are going to head over to a facility and make a speech to the ladies who reside there. Then we're going to have a live press conference with reporters from the nations who expressed concern."

"I think it's noble we take care of the unwed women," Grant said. In truth, he assumed retirement facilities were another waste of government funds.

"It's strange you knew they existed. I don't believe we have major cause for concern. But this visit will settle any discomfort our allies feel. I'm sure you'll be impressed by what you see."

"There's nothing I enjoy more than gazing upon beautiful females," Grant said.

"I meant they are well taken care of. They have work to keep them busy and it's very sanitary. This video painted these places as some sort of death sentence."

"Where they're denied medical care?" Grant asked.

"Oh. I should have known you've seen it. Strolling on the international Internet?"

"I have the clearance," Grant said. "However you chose to operate it is for the good of the country. You have my full support."

"There is a system for everything. You'll learn that. The population can never grow too large. Many boys kill each other before they make it to service and not all of the servicemen come back alive. That makes for too many daughters with not enough husbands. There's a system allowing the females with some skills to enter more appropriate fields. But the rest still need a purpose in life. They produce goods, mainly for our troops."

"I think that would be more satisfying than other occupations," Grant said.

"It may seem harsh, but I imagine these women could face a worse fate."

When Grant was grand commander he would see to that. Grant was hanging on Ian's every word and hadn't realized they had already reached their destination. It was an ordinary door Grant wouldn't have given a second thought to. Ian pulled it open and behind was a thick wall with a keypad. The grand commander punched a code in and a door popped open to a set of stairs heading down. The walls were lined in thick steel with fluorescent lightbulbs attached. They made their way to a secret room.

"Is this a bomb shelter?" Grant asked.

"In a way," Ian said. "I think of it more as a fortress, and I am the only one with the code. Something I will pass on to you someday."

When they reached the bottom of the stairs Grant was shocked by what he saw. It was a server, not a special one either. It was large and a little dated.

"Is this the—"

"Master Registry," Ian said, finishing for him. "I bring someone down here and update it every three months. Most things are done wirelessly now, but this is not connected to anything. Completely unhackable."

"Why?"

"Why? I thought you were smarter than that," Ian said. "There are groups all over the world trying to break into our mainframe. Some have been successful, more than I like to admit. They're jealous of our way of life and think if they take the Registry away the girls will be free from some imaginary prison."

"Why only one though?" Grant asked. "It would make more sense to have at least ten mainframes all over the country."

"Ah, so you do see the importance. If there were ten there would be nine more I needed to protect from my enemies. There are some men who think they're better suited to act as grand commander. If someone like that gained access to a server they may try to use it to overthrow me. Since I am the only one who can ensure the Registry's existence I don't have to worry about that."

"What about the service records? Do you have a backup of those?" Grant asked.

Ian smiled and raised his eyebrows, unable to keep a smug look off his face.

"It's here too," Ian said. "A very fascinating piece of information. Your call number was AMT8583."

That number was burned into Grant's memory forever.

"Do you know that of all the boys in this country, only seventy-five percent make it into service? Twenty percent die, and five percent think they can dodge their duty."

"I'm surprised it's that high," Grant said.

"Which number?" Ian asked.

"Dodgers," Grant said.

"Almost all of those men are raised by mothers and fathers," Ian said. "The ones from those households who do enlist rarely survive."

"Did you keep any sons?"

"No," he said. "In fact the opposite. All my sons survive only for a few hours."

"I'm not sure I see the logic, sir," Grant said.

"Do you know who your parents are?"

"No," Grant said. "And I don't care to find out."

"I fear I would want to know their progress," Ian said. "See if they share any of my traits."

"I would think it would be inconsequential," Grant said. "Sons are worthless."

"Well, you're a stronger man than I for being so certain," Ian said. "This way all threat of temptation has been removed."

Grant nodded his head. He hadn't expected the grand commander to be so weak. Ian deserved no sympathy for putting down his sons. Grant didn't think that would be difficult, and in the process Ian was denying America additional soldiers.

"I wanted you to see this sooner rather than later. As long as this server is intact all will be well and any problem can be fixed."

With these final words they walked up the stairs and back into the hall, Ian firmly closing the door behind them.

"Sir, you mentioned organizations attacking the system through remote means. Why not send the army and take these groups out?"

"We don't fight our own wars anymore," Ian said. "All these people are stationed in neutral countries or areas close to radioactive zones. We know about them, though. An attack on them would mean an attack on their hosts. It is a delicate world out there, and any number of nations would jump at the chance to invade us; some countries even have females in their top leadership position. Our military serves two purposes. The first is to protect the homeland, and the second is to aid any country as I see fit. If there is a war about to break out, both sides always request our aid. Whoever we side with crushes their opponent. Any country we help must allow a military base on their soil, along with some other conditions. And we have a lot of bases around the world. If all these countries found a reason to band together and attack us, we would be outnumbered."

"But wouldn't our allies back our play then, against these rebels?"

"You are intelligent, but you have much to learn regarding diplomacy," Ian said. "You're handsome and you have charm, which comes in quite handy when dealing with foreign relations. The last thing we want is a war on American soil, and most of the world doesn't respect our way of life. If they were to attack us first though, our allies would have no choice but to give aid . . ."

"But if we throw the first punch everyone else will label us as aggressors and retaliate," Grant said, finishing his statement.

"Already catching on, I see," Ian said. "There is a lot of fighting in the world. Especially since we step in to help the smallest countries win their battles. As long as they need our help and we aren't hurting anyone they don't care what we do at home. Keep the service large and skilled."

Grant was already thinking about ways he would improve Ian's outdated ideas. He was curious about the retirement center. If it was as pristine as the propaganda showed he could think of an easy way to devote more funds to the men abroad and maybe even buy other countries' approval to take out these sects.

Chapter 41

The world is ever changing. There is no point in learning about other countries because they may disappear tomorrow.

—American Gazette

They traveled on through the mountains. Mia sat right next to Andrew, putting pressure on his head wound. He thought the stranger in the front seat was more deserving of medical attention but didn't want to pass up the opportunity to sit so close to her. She was alive; focusing on that was enough to get him through anything.

Mia leaned forward and signaled for Carter to take another left. They turned and Mia's hair hit Andrew in the face. She had long hair again. His final memory of her was with short hair. It should have taken months, if not years, for the length to grow out again. Andrew wanted to question her about how long he was really with the militia, because he was certain she wouldn't lie to him. Time wasn't making much sense to him.

The car started to slow down. Carter tried to rev the engine, but the speed didn't increase. This was a familiar situation.

"Pull over," Andrew said. "You're running out of gas."

"What?" Carter asked.

Andrew moved forward until his mouth was next to Carter's ear. "You're running out of gas," he said.

He looked at the dashboard. There was no fuel light; he assumed it was broken. Mia looked over at the gauges.

"There is no gas," Mia said.

"Well then, what's wrong?" Carter asked.

"I'm not sure," Mia said.

"How far away are we?" Andrew asked.

"Not far," Mia said. "According to the map maybe another five kilometers."

"I don't know what that means," Andrew said.

"Three miles, give or take," Mia said.

Andrew had never bothered to ask where she was this whole time. How she had managed to learn how to operate a vehicle or a new system of measurement. Nothing had seemed important at first, only the fact that she was here and breathing. The car slowed to a crawl.

"How are you doing?" Carter asked the man in the passenger seat.

"I've been better," he said. "But worse too."

Andrew looked at Mia; her nose was crinkled up. Andrew could tell she was struggling with her feelings toward the man.

"It was an accident," Andrew said.

"I was trying to stop the militia from hurting you," Mia said.

"Enough with the apologies," the man said. "Is there a doctor at this place we're headed?"

"Where are we going anyway?" Andrew asked.

The sun was all the way up in the sky now. Andrew felt his forehead sting as the sweat rolled into his wound. The car came to a complete stop.

"Can you walk?" Mia asked.

"I'm fine," Andrew said.

"Don't mind me," the man said. "I'm the one with the life-threatening injury."

"I'm sure you've been shot at before," Mia said.

Andrew almost wanted to laugh. It'd been so long since he'd felt that urge. Before the sound escaped his lips he realized Mia had ignored his question.

"Where are we going?" he asked again.

"There's a sanctuary for Americans here," Mia said. "We'll be with people like us."

She picked up his hand and replaced her own with it. Andrew felt the sting as he pushed the piece of fabric over his wound. Mia opened the car door and climbed out. She was covered in scrapes, but even with the tears in her long red dress she still looked beautiful.

"Why are you so dressed up?" Andrew asked.

He climbed out of the car. He couldn't believe he hadn't noticed her appearance when he first saw her.

"It's a long story," Mia said.

Andrew noticed she wasn't wearing any shoes. Her feet were covered in scratches. He started to take his off.

"Don't," Mia said. "They'll never fit me."

"Then I'll carry you," Andrew said.

"You look like you're going to pass out again," Mia said.

Andrew locked eyes with her. She was tired, but he recognized she'd never accept the shoes. He stood up again.

"Wait in the car," Mia said to the man. "We'll come back for you."

He started to open the door.

"I promise," Mia said. "If we were going to let you die we would have left you by the cliff."

He seemed to accept her answer and leaned back in his seat. Carter climbed out of the car and joined them.

Mia looked away from Andrew and started walking. She was clutching a plastic bag. Andrew and Carter followed her. The three walked in silence for a few minutes. Andrew tried his hardest to hide the difficulty he was having walking in a straight line.

"I can't believe you shot someone," Andrew said. He couldn't keep the smile off his face.

"It's not funny," Mia said. "I was trying to help."

"I can't believe you wanted to leave him for dead," Carter said.

"You weren't in Saint Louis," Mia said. "That man killed Whitney. And I wouldn't have left him. It just took a moment to come to the right decision."

The right decision; Andrew didn't think there was such a thing. Every choice carried significant repercussions that led to a series of uncontrollable events. This man's presence could be dangerous for them.

"How do you know about this place?" Carter asked.

"I made contact with someone here," Mia said.

"Man," Carter said. "We're busy taking up with the enemy and you're making all the plans."

"I found these people before we left America," Mia said. "I met them online. Through the same website your dad found us on."

Carter stopped walking.

"Before we left America? Do you mean before my house was invaded by government employees and my dad died in the car accident?"

"Your dad didn't die in the accident," Mia said.

"He's dead though," Carter said. His voice was getting louder. He took a step toward Mia. "This is all your fault," he said. "You thought you could contact strangers online and it wouldn't get traced back to us?"

"It wasn't like that," Mia said.

"Yes it was," Carter interrupted. He took another step toward Mia. "My father is dead because of you. I wish I never met you."

Andrew stepped in front of Mia. He didn't know what Carter was doing.

"We don't know that," Andrew said. "Stay calm."

"You're going to side with her?" Carter asked. "I know you're thinking the same way I am. You try to remember what happened and that noise comes crashing through. That's because of her."

"She saved us," Andrew said.

"And the militia found us wandering the desert," Carter replied sarcastically.

Andrew moved his eyebrows together. Carter turned and stormed off.

"Wait," Mia said. She started to walk out from behind Andrew.

"He'll be fine," Andrew said. "He's staying on the road. Let him walk alone."

Then Andrew started moving his feet. Carter's anger was misdirected. He was mourning his father, and Mia was an easy target. Still, Andrew didn't think it was wise for her to have contacted people over the Internet.

"I didn't mean any harm," Mia said.

"I know," Andrew said.

The two walked along the road in silence. Andrew thought about the previous day's events. He had been happy as a soldier. It made him sick to admit that, but life had been easier. He thought about the decisions that were in front of him, ones he'd have to make for himself. Up ahead Carter stopped walking. Andrew hoped it was to make amends. The three needed each other too much. As Andrew and Mia approached him Andrew saw Carter wasn't stopped; he was frozen.

"Carter, I'm sorry," Mia said. "But we don't even know how we were detected."

Andrew looked at Carter's eyes and followed them down to what he was staring at. Andrew took a step back as a man with a gun walked out of the trees. Mia gasped. Andrew spun around and more people with weapons drawn walked onto the road. He held his hands in the air. Lifting his hand off his wound caused a sting; Andrew felt the warm blood drip down his forehead. The three of them were surrounded.

Chapter 42

GRANT MARSDEN, TRENDSETTER: THE CASUAL CHIC LOOK IS SWEEP-
ING THE NATION

—American Gazette

The previous week's events were starting to take their toll on Grant's work. He finally had a free day with no press visits or meetings at the Mission. He sat in his basement working on several projects that needed attention. He was tinkering with an injectable knife, which allowed an assailant to not only stab their victim but also inject a poison at the same time. He wanted an automatic release where there wasn't even a button-push required.

Grant thought about the men in the training facility. These were people with formal education, working on classified projects. Grant could have easily ended up in their shoes, but he had picked up his trade in a more peculiar way.

*W*hat are you doing here?" the man asked.

"Looking for food," Grant said. He had only been out of the or-phanage for a few months. It was the first time he had been this close to a gun, but he wasn't afraid.

"I should shoot you," the man said.

"Then do it," Grant said. He took a step forward. Grant had six years to live through until he enlisted.

"Why aren't you afraid of me?"

"The way you're dressed," Grant said. "And the way you smell."

The man raised an eyebrow.

"You look bad and you smell bad," Grant said. "This is a beautiful house and it's not yours. You're trying to rob the place. If you kill me that means a loud noise, which will wake up the owner, who will kill you."

The man grew flustered at Grant's comments. Before he could speak a sharp whiz came through the air. The man lowered his gun and fell to his knees. Grant looked past him to see a man standing in silk pajamas and a robe. His dark hair was parted to the side with the previous day's styling gel in place. The house's true owner. Grant gave a smirk before the man shot him in the shoulder with a dart and Grant joined the dirty old man on the floor.

His concentration was broken when a knock sounded through the laboratory.

Grant rolled his eyes. His staff knew better than to disturb him down here. He had both phones in his pockets; if it was an emergency they knew to call. He ignored the sound but again it echoed through his private space. Grant got up from his table and stormed over toward the door. He looked at his security system and saw Brandon standing outside. Grant pushed the intercom button.

"Go away," Grant said.

"Sir, I am so sorry to bother you, but you have visitors."

"Tell them to go away," Grant said.

"It's . . . it's . . . the grand commander and his family," Brandon said.

Grant watched his employee's face glow. He did not share the house manager's emotions. Grant didn't appreciate surprises and wanted to continue with his work.

"Tell Ian he can . . ." Grant rethought his situation. "Tell him I'll be right up."

When Grant was running the country many things would change, and one of those would be that nobody would ever be allowed to interrupt his privacy. Until the position was his, though, Grant had to play along. He slid on his blue moccasins and grabbed the cardigan he'd brought down with him, pulling the white sweater over his yellow polo. He unlocked the door to his studio and climbed up the staircase.

The house had been built to Grant's specifications, and that included a secret tunnel system, making it easier to cross the giant structure. There were two entrances to his workshop; one was hidden behind a bookshelf in his office and only Brandon knew its location. Grant came out into the office behind his desk and started walking toward the foyer. There stood the First Family.

"Ian," Grant said. "What a pleasant surprise."

"I saw your schedule was clear and thought we'd pop in," he said. "This place is a compound."

"Just my humble home," Grant said.

"This is my wife Nancy," Ian said. "And I brought along my daughters Lyndsay, Tamara, Erin, and Nina."

The four girls giggled and bowed. Erin and Nina were the seventeen-year-old twins. Lyndsay and Tamara were just slightly older. All four were stunning.

"A pleasure to meet you," Grant said.

The five women bowed. Grant wondered which one was his future wife. Not that it mattered; any of the four would do.

"I wasn't expecting company," Grant said.

"We'd love a tour of your home," Ian said.

Grant nodded and called for Brandon. "Have some lunch ready in the courtyard for us in an hour," he said.

Brandon's grin couldn't be contained. He bowed and ran off toward the kitchen, knocking into a table on the way out.

"Let's start upstairs," Grant said.

The party moved up the stairs, the girls whispering to one another. Grant tried his best to keep a smile on his face, but the whole time his annoyance festered.

And finally we have the ballroom," Grant said.

It was larger than most banquet halls and could easily handle five hundred guests. The floor was made of gold marble. No event had ever been held here, but that wasn't the point of having a ballroom. The fact that Grant's home was large enough to house one was reason enough to have one.

"What's through there?" Nancy asked.

Ian turned and gave her a sharp look.

"I meant nothing," she said. "Only your house is perfect and from the outside I can tell it's still larger."

"You are observant," Grant said. "That's the east wing. I keep it closed off. I thought more employees would live on site, so it's mainly single rooms."

"Your servants don't live here?" Tamara asked.

"Some," Grant said. "I refuse to hire unserved boys. They should spend their preservice time in the real world, not sheltered in a giant house. Most of the workers have wives they like to go home to."

"What did you do for your preservice years?"

"I apprenticed for an engineer," Grant said. "He planned roads and sewage ducts, nothing ladies should concern themselves with."

"It sounds interesting," Nina said.

"It's not," Grant said. "Let's head outside to the courtyard. I have two swimming pools and some wonderful landscaping. I'm sure Brandon can round up some swimsuits."

This made the girls clap their hands with delight. He ushered them out of the ballroom and looked over his shoulder at the door to the east wing. He didn't want any more attention brought to it.

"Maybe while the ladies take in the outdoors you and I can continue with our conversations," Ian said.

"My pleasure," Grant said.

The grand commander started talking about foreign relations again. Grant was starting to see Ian less as a respected man and more as an outdated fool who made his teeth grind. This was the fourth time Grant had heard this speech in as many days. He couldn't think of a worse way to spend his time than listening to the old man babble on.

Chapter 43

The core principles of Affinity are trust, respect, and equality.
—Internal memorandum from Affinity

Nobody said a word as the three were marched down the road. There was no way to escape these people. Carter dropped his gun as soon as the men came out of the bushes and Mia didn't even have a shoe to hit them with. Mia was scared they were Joseph's men, another convoy sent to take revenge. She looked over at Carter; his eyes were hard and his chin pointed upward. She couldn't imagine the pain he was feeling.

Her attention switched to Andrew. He looked like he was in a different type of pain. His skin was pale, except for the dried blood. He was having trouble lifting his legs off the ground. Then it was too much for him. Mia gasped and tried to catch him, but he was too heavy for her.

"Andrew!" she screamed.

She starting patting his face. He wasn't waking up. The men aimed their guns at the two of them.

"He needs help," Mia said. "A doctor."

The men stared at her.

"Please," Mia said. "I'm not lying."

She tried to pat Andrew's face again, hoping he would come to. It was stupid to think he was unhurt after the car crash.

"We have another man with us too," Carter said. "Back at our car. He's been shot."

Mia cringed; she'd forgotten about Grant's henchman. Now if he died it would be doubly her fault. But Andrew still took priority.

"Please wake up," she said.

She turned her attention to the men.

"My name is Mia Morrissey," she said. "I'm an American. I made contact with someone called S. She told me to come to Guatemala. We're all Americans. Please, help us."

Someone pushed her aside. She was shaking.

"What happened to him?" the man asked.

"A car accident," Mia said. "He was unconscious for a few minutes, but he came to. Please help him."

The man held his fingers to Andrew's neck. He pulled open each of his eyes and slapped Andrew's face. There was no reaction.

"He has a pulse," the man said. "It's slow, but it's there. Get Dr. Drum."

One of the men took off running. The one examining Andrew started to speak.

"Turn their car back on," he said. "Reset the thumbprint key."

"Who are you talking to?" Mia asked.

The man knelt next to Andrew but looked at one of his counterparts.

"Run down to their vehicle, drive it up here," he said.

Another one of the soldiers took off running.

Time felt like it was standing still. A jeep came speeding down the road. It stopped and two people jumped out. They were dressed in beige linen clothing. One brought a small kit with her.

"Move back," the woman said.

One of the guards held his arms out and moved Mia away from Andrew.

"What's happening?" Mia asked.

She stood on her tiptoes and looked down to see the woman waving something under Andrew's nose. His eyes shot open and he started coughing.

"Move him into the back," she said.

Two guards hoisted a disoriented Andrew up and placed him in the back of the jeep. Mia watched his eyes start to shut again. His two helpers climbed in the vehicle and drove off.

"Wait," Mia yelled. "I can't leave him."

Her protests were unanswered as the car zoomed off. Mia was having a hard time breathing. She had lost him again. It was too much to handle. Her chest hurt as she exhaled. She stumbled back and one of the guards grabbed her wrist.

"You need to breathe," he said.

"Where are you taking him?" Mia asked.

She struggled against the guard's grip on her, but he only tightened his grasp. Their car came driving down the road. It didn't slow down but followed the car Andrew was in.

"Andrew," Mia yelled again.

"They're going to help him," the guard said.

He used his free hand to swing his rifle around his back.

"You're having a panic attack," he said. "Breathe like I do. Watch my mouth."

He started taking big breaths and Mia tried her best to mimic him. Once her breathing returned to normal he smiled.

"Who are you?" Mia asked. "What's going on?"

"My name is Zack," he said.

"Why are you kidnapping us?"

"We're not kidnapping anyone," Zack said. "Why are you driving through our space?"

"You jumped out at us with guns," Mia said. "Then you took my friend away."

"We saw your car," Zack said. "This is private property. One of your friends is dressed like a combatant, the other is shirtless with a gun, and you look like you're ready for a ball. We're just protecting ourselves. We took your friend to get medical attention. Did you think we were going to treat him on the side of the road?"

Mia looked at Zack's face. His blond hair was poking out from his helmet. He had crystal-blue eyes and must have been about thirty. She didn't think he was lying to her.

"What are you doing here?" Zack asked.

"I was coming to meet S," Mia said.

"S?"

"Someone I met online," Mia said. "I responded to an ad for The Guatemalan Way."

"A response that led the RAG agents to my house and got my dad killed," Carter said.

Mia looked over at him. He was leaning against a tree and the two other escorts lowered their weapons as well. The threat of danger was gone for now.

"Not possible," Zack said. "All our online correspondents are untraceable. We put a lot of work into that."

"So this is the right place?" Mia asked.

Her heart rose.

"Not yet," Zack said. "Why were you driving here? The instructions are to cross over the border and wait until we find you."

"I met someone in Mexico," Mia said. "She drew me a map to here."

Zack's eyes widened at this comment.

"She's a strategist for the Irish government," Mia said. "Her name is Riley."

"Great," Zack said. "Another confirmed country that knows of our location."

"You're hiding?" Mia asked.

"Not exactly," Zack said. "But we like to stay under the radar."

"Where's Andrew?" Mia asked.

"The doctor took him," Zack said. "I'd assume to the infirmary. If he's bad she'll transport him down the mountain to the hospital. Shouldn't you be more concerned about the man with the gunshot wound?"

The doctor was a female. Mia's eyes went wide for a moment, but before she could focus on that she needed to make sure Andrew was safe.

"Take me to him," Mia said. "I can't leave him."

"No," Zack said. "Sitting by his bedside isn't going to help him, and your story needs verification."

"You can't keep me from him," Mia said.

"Fine," Zack said. "Don't listen to me. Just stay here on this side of the road in a fancy dress with no shoes."

Zack started up the hill. His comrades followed him. They weren't so interested in guarding Mia and Carter anymore. She walked up to her friend.

"I am sorry for everything that happened to you," Mia said. "If I could change it I would."

"I want to hear his voice," Carter said. "I'd do anything to hear his voice."

Carter turned and wrapped his arms around Mia, burying his head in her shoulder. She ran her hand up and down his back, trying her best to comfort him. Mia moved her head to the side and saw that Zack and the other two guards hadn't stopped walking. Following them was the only way for Mia to get back to Andrew.

"I know this is hard," Mia said. "But your dad wouldn't want you to give up. He'd tell you to keep moving forward. We have to stick with these guys or we'll never get Andrew back."

"I have no one left," Carter said.

"You do," Mia said. "You have me and Andrew. We're your family now."

Carter lifted his head and let go of Mia. He didn't make eye contact with her but started nodding his head. The two walked fast to keep up with the guards.

Soon Zack turned off the dirt road and onto a path. Carter and Mia continued to follow Zack and his gang farther into the jungle. Mia heard strange noises coming from the trees and grabbed on to Carter's arm. He laughed a little; it was a pleasant sound to Mia's ears. Zack stopped walking. He was standing in front of a small cabin. It was surrounded by trees and Mia would have walked right past it. Zack pushed open the door and waved his arm for Mia and Carter to head inside.

There was nothing to the place. There was a desk with a couch in front of it. A few other chairs were against the walls and a small window was at the back. Mia noticed a closed door but thought it might lead to more impressive surroundings. Someone stood at the window. It was a woman. Her back was to them but Mia saw her brown hair was in a bun. She wore the same tan-colored clothing as the doctor who had assisted Andrew.

"Please," she said. "Have a seat."

Mia and Carter sat down on the couch. The woman spun around to face them and Mia let out a small gasp. She was older, the oldest woman Mia had ever seen in person. Her face had lines and her skin crinkled up at the corners of her brown eyes. Aging wasn't something Mia ever thought about, but seeing it face-to-face she felt overwhelmed by this woman's beauty. She looked determined and proud. More graceful than Mia could ever think of becoming.

"My name is Dina," she said. "Zack filled me in on your story. I'm waiting on confirmation from S right now."

"How?" Mia asked. Zack had been with her the whole time.

"We may live in the jungle, but that doesn't make us primitive," Dina said. "In other words, he sent the information over a radio. We're not used to recruits showing up on our doorstep."

"About my friend Andrew . . . ," Mia said.

"He is with the doctor now," Dina said. "I'll fill you in on any developments."

Dina paused and touched her ear.

"Yes," she said.

"Yes," she said again.

Mia looked at Carter, who shrugged. This woman was talking to herself.

"Perfect," she said. Then she directed her words to Mia. "S confirmed your conversations."

"When?" Mia asked.

"Just now," Dina said. She turned her head and Mia saw the clear earpiece. "So let's hear your story."

Mia remembered Riley's instructions.

"I didn't want to get married so I ran away. Andrew helped me, and Carter and his father took us in. My husband tracked down our location but the three of us were able to make it into Mexico. We were held up for about a month when Andrew and Carter were forced into a militia and I needed to pose as a woman willing to sell my body in order to rescue them. We drove here and had a car accident. Andrew injured himself in the process and our car ran out of gas."

"That is quite the story," Dina said. "And the man with the gunshot wound?"

"A friend," Carter said. "He helped us, got shot in the process."

Mia frowned and looked over at Carter; these people had a right to know how dangerous he was. Before Mia could correct Carter's story Dina moved her hand back to her ear.

"Yes," Dina said.

"Good," she said.

Her attention reverted to Mia and Carter.

"Andrew was severely dehydrated. He suffered a small concussion from the bump on his head and needed stitches. There was another injury that went unnoticed. He had a cut on the back of his knee where the blood didn't clot. It was the loss of blood that caused the blackouts."

Mia's mouth hung open. She shook her head, unable to believe she hadn't noticed the pain Andrew must have felt.

"He's resting now and expected to make a full recovery," Dina said. "You can visit him later."

Mia closed her eyes and felt the breath rush out of her body. She felt the tears well up.

"Thank you," she said.

Dina gave a pinched smile.

"Your other friend is being treated right now," Dina said. "He refused to have medical attention at first, even though his wound is much more severe. Why is that?"

"He's a selfless man," Carter said.

If Carter was looking for a surrogate father, Grant's bodyguard wasn't it. Mia didn't understand why Carter was covering for him. Still, Mia didn't want to volunteer the fact that she was the one who had shot him.

"We'll wait here for a moment," Dina said. "Then your orientation will begin."

"What orientation?" Mia asked.

"Into Affinity," Dina said. "That's why you're here. To join our revolution against America?"

"Revolution?" Carter asked.

"Our main priorities are to close the Registry and stop mandatory service," Dina said. "Take the government out of the picture and put the country back into the people's hands."

Riley had made some mention of these people being rebels. Mia hadn't realized they were this serious or well organized though.

"So you want us to join another army?" Carter asked.

"We are no army," Dina said. "You'll see once we start the tour."

There was something off about the way the woman discussed a revolt so casually.

"Everything here is voluntary," Dina said. "If you want to leave tomorrow, we'll let you."

"Why not now?" Mia asked.

"Do you? Want to leave now?"

Mia paused.

"No," she said.

Dina smiled again, never showing her teeth. Zack spoke up.

"Don't let her intimidate you," Zack said. "You're welcome to stay or leave, either way. That's my call to make these days."

"Are you in charge?" Mia asked.

"We have a system here," Zack said. "Nobody is in charge of everything. I run basic in-house decisions. Security, new members, anything that affects this spot right here."

"Yes, but this is a big area; you still have a lot to learn," Dina said.

Zack gave her the same pressed-lipped smile. He spoke to Mia and Carter without looking away from Dina.

"I was recently promoted," Zack said. "Dina here used to run things. She's sticking around to help with the transition."

"He'll escort you to the restrooms," Dina said. "I'm sure both of you would like a shower and a fresh change of clothes. Some shoes too."

Mia and Carter stood up and started toward the door. Whatever politics were going on here, Mia didn't want any part of them. She had enough of her own drama to deal with.

"I don't have a good feeling about this," Carter said.

"They helped Andrew," Mia said. "Right now what other choice do we have?"

Carter looked down at her. His eyes, one brown and one green, were vacant. He was floundering. Mia wished she could help but was at a loss.

Chapter **44**

Rumors continue to circulate about Grant Marsden's political prospects. Is he the new hope for the future?

—American Gazette

Grant walked Ian toward the door. His gaggle of females was already outside, standing by their car. Grant couldn't wait until he was alone; plastering a smile on his face was growing difficult. Ian stopped walking and started speaking again.

"I'd like to announce the engagement tomorrow," Ian said. "Which one do you prefer?"

"That soon?" Grant asked.

"Of course," Ian said. "Anyone who still remembers your old wife's name or face will have the memory replaced with the image of my daughter. It's important to wipe her away from the public's mind."

Saint Louis, Grant thought.

"What about her parents?" Grant asked. "What if they have any mementos or speak out?"

"Taken care of," Ian said. "A team was sent to their home and all evidence of their daughter destroyed. They will look crazy if they step forward with no proof. One of my daughters must be worthy enough for you. Please, name your choice."

Grant couldn't have cared less. All four were properly trained and looked alike. He just said the first name that came to his mind.

"Tamara."

"Splendid," Ian said. "The wedding will be next month. Here."

"I don't want my home invaded again," Grant said.

"Again?" Ian asked. His eyebrows rose.

"After the funeral," Grant said. "I'm a private person."

"Not if you want the title of grand commander," Ian said.

Grant's cheeks were starting to hurt from the fake smile. He did his best to keep it up and nodded his head.

"There will be television crews," Ian said. "A scene of you formally paying me and signing over the paperwork."

"The groom chooses his wedding," Grant said.

"Not when he's entering politics," Ian said. "I thought you would be pleased."

"I am," Grant said.

"I'll announce you as my successor," Ian said. "You won't officially take over for a few years, but the public will get used to your face. Do you need a coordinator?"

"No," Grant said. "Brandon can handle everything."

"Plan for two hundred guests," Ian said. "Then whoever else you want to invite, of course."

"How much is Tamara's fee?" Grant asked. It didn't matter; Grant could afford any woman, but he needed to ready the funds.

"It's all for show," Ian said. "She's yours gratis. But make the check out for one million. It will never be deposited, but the amount will earn you some esteem from your peers."

"Peers"—ha, Grant thought. There was no man or woman out there who was his equal. Grant had no peers. Ian smiled and shook

Grant's hand. Grant waved good-bye and closed the door. He let out a low growl. He couldn't wait until this showboating was over with.

He pulled his phone out of his pocket, surprised Rex hadn't called yet. Grant wasn't worried though; Rex never let anything lapse. Besides, Rex's call wasn't the one Grant was really waiting for.

Chapter 45

Constant communication between the Affinity camps is necessary to further our goals as a society.

—Internal memorandum from Affinity

Mia was alone in a communal bathroom. She saw cabinets built into the walls and wondered if they were going to assign her one. It was strange to have long hair again; not wanting to wait for it to dry, Mia made a thick braid down her back. She looked at herself in the mirror. She was wearing beige linen shorts and a white tank top. Her cut-up feet were secure in a pair of brown sandals.

When she exited the restroom Carter and Zack were waiting outside. They had both changed too. Carter wore a pair of brown shorts and a beige tank top, while Zack had on a similar outfit in shades of brown and beige. Standing next to Carter, Zack could have been his older brother, the two looked so similar.

"I left my clothes in there," Mia said.

"Someone will take them," Zack said. "I'm sure there's some use for the fabric."

"They're going to cut it up?" Mia asked.

"We don't have many formal events down here," Zack said. "Dina told you about the orientation? Well, I'm pushing that back."

Mia wasn't in a rush to have a formal introduction into Affinity.

"I'd rather wait until the four of you are together again," Zack said. "For now I'll start with a tour."

"Can I see Andrew?" Mia asked.

"Not until later," Zack said. "Doctor's orders. Here is a set of bathrooms," he continued. "There are three on the property. You'll get a locker assigned in one of them, but we share everything."

Mia noticed there was shampoo and soap, among other toiletries, sitting on the counter. They walked through the thick trees to the other side of the building. There was another steep hill and Zack led the way up the path. Mia was already sweating from the heat.

"You'll get used to things pretty fast," Zack said.

"How long did it take you?" Mia asked.

"I was born here," he said.

Mia had assumed everyone was a refugee. He read the shock on her face.

"My parents escaped America," Zack said. "They met down here."

"How many people live here?" Mia asked.

"Two hundred and forty-seven. Affinity has thousands of members across the world," Zack said. "This is just one of our camps, and not all the people who are active live here. My parents, they live about thirty minutes away on a beach. They're semiretired."

"Retired?" Mia asked.

"Means something different down here," Zack said. "They don't work full-time for the cause anymore."

Work for the cause. Mia didn't know what to take from that. They reached the top of the hill and the trees vanished. Mia stood next to Zack and Carter. They were on the head of a huge valley. Below were multiple cabins—Mia guessed about thirty. Zack pointed to his right. They were level with a giant lodge.

"That's the mess hall," Zack said. "You'll get breakfast, lunch, and dinner there. Also water or snacks. If we have an all-community meeting it'll be in there."

"Where is everybody?" Carter asked.

Mia hadn't noticed before, but the place was deserted.

"Work," Zack said. "Everyone has a job. We like to keep self-contained as much as possible."

"What are they doing?" Mia asked.

"All sorts of things," Zack said. "Some are training, others getting the meals ready—every person here is a part of the bigger picture. To take down the Registry."

"How do you get electricity up here?" Carter asked.

"Underground wiring," Zack said. "We're upgrading our systems, hoping to be fully wireless within the next few years. We may look simple, but all our resources go to more important things."

"To take down America," Mia said.

"The people who do the other work are no less important," Zack said. "Without them our world couldn't function."

He passed the mess hall. Another big building came. This was made of cement blocks.

"Bathroom number two," Zack said. "This is the busiest one since it's closest to the sleeping areas."

He continued his walk around the edge of the valley. There was a giant field. Mia thought it must have taken years to clear away the forest.

"This is a recreation area for the most part," Zack said.

In the distance Mia saw children playing.

"There are children here?" Mia asked.

"This is a full-fledged community," Zack said. "Our youngest member is six months old."

Mia thought she saw Carter's face lighten up. Families were together here. Soon his smile faded though. Mia's heart broke for him. She'd never had that type of bond with her parents. Mia had hurt terribly when she learned about her sister's death, but even Corinna and Mia weren't as close as Rod and Carter had been. She touched his arm, letting him know she was here for him. Zack turned away from the field and started down a path toward the cabins.

"That's it?" Mia asked.

"For now," Zack said. "The longer you're here the more you'll learn."

"Where's S?" Mia said. "I'd like to meet her."

"She's probably at work," Zack said. "Or sleeping if she has the night shift. We'd like you two to join us at dinner. People are waiting to meet you."

"Will she be there?" Mia asked.

"Almost everyone is there," Zack said. "We try to eat dinner as a group every night."

"Then we can see Andrew?"

"As far as I know," Zack said.

"Where's the farmery?" Mia asked.

"Infirmary," Zack corrected. "You'll see it later."

He stopped walking at a cabin. It was closest to the footpath that led up to the mess hall. Mia wiped the sweat away from her brow.

"Temporary quarters," Zack said.

He opened the door. It was cool inside. There was a small machine whining in the corner. One larger bed was on the floor, while one of the walls had three beds built into it. The opposite wall had one set of drawers, a desk, and two more bunks built on top of that.

"Big enough for six people?" Mia asked. "Are all the cabins the same?"

"No," Zack said. "This is the visitors' one. Some have families, others are groups of friends living together. Not a lot of privacy, but we make do."

"Doesn't seem like enough room to house two hundred fifty people," Carter said.

"There's another grouping on the other side of the field," Zack said. "At full capacity we could have five hundred people living on the premises."

Mia stopped at the desk. There was the plastic bag she had been carrying, and the queen. She wrapped her hands around the piece.

"We have to keep your gun for now," Zack said.

She opened the bag. All the documents were still there, including her letter from Riley. The phone was still in the bottom. Mia thought about calling her.

"There's a scrambler in the area," Zack said. "If you make a call they can't trace it."

"Aren't you scared we're going to tell people where we are?" Carter asked.

"No," Zack said. "You're not prisoners here. You can leave any-time. Plus we have two of your friends with our doctors. It's unlikely you're here to betray us."

"Thank you," Mia said.

"I'll let you two relax," Zack said. "Dinner is in a few hours."

Mia felt her stomach gurgle. She hadn't eaten all day. The door closed and she was left alone with Carter. He sat down on the lowest bunk and hung his head in his hands.

"What do you think, princess?" Carter asked.

Princess. That was Carter's nickname for her, one she hadn't heard in some time. She was grateful for whatever was making him comfortable enough to use the term.

"I don't think we can make any decisions until Andrew's with us," Mia said.

Carter didn't respond. Mia heard him let out a loud sigh.

"How are you doing?" Mia asked.

"I've had my brain messed with, I'm who knows where, and my dad is dead," Carter said. "I've been better."

Mia sat next to him and gave him a hug. She didn't know what to say.

"We have to look toward the future," Mia said. "Holding on to the past isn't going to help us. We still have each other."

"Do we?" Carter asked.

Mia wasn't sure what Carter was getting at. There were too many events happening for her to focus on the affection she'd once shared with Carter, or Andrew's reaction to it.

"I don't have any closure," Carter said. "Nothing. Whenever I try to picture the helicopter it hurts. I can't see anything, just a blank image, and that noise comes in."

Carter winced and his eyes shut in pain.

"Stop," Mia said. "There's a doctor here; maybe she can help you remember."

"Do I want to remember, though?" Carter asked. "My last memory is the truck flying off the road. Even that is hazy."

Carter leaned back onto the bed and turned to his side. Not able to offer any additional comfort, Mia leaned back against the bed, ready to listen if Carter wanted to talk.

Chapter 46

America is the only country in the world where all citizens have the right to arm themselves.

—American Gazette

Andrew's eyes blinked open from his dreamless sleep. He was lying in a bed. His intuition told him he was back in the militia headquarters and his body was filled with fury. He sat up and swung his legs to the side. He went to stand up and was met with a pull. He looked back; his wrist was handcuffed to the bed. He pulled harder, but the bed frame didn't budge. It was then he noticed it was made of wood, not metal like the militia's beds.

He took in his surroundings. This room was warm, a painting of a flower on the wall. There was a large window; he couldn't get close to it but it looked out over a jungle, not the desert scene from Mexico. The last thing he remembered was the men jumping out of the bush with guns. Was that a hallucination? Andrew started thrashing, trying hard to pull his wrist free or slide it out of the cuff. The door to his room opened.

"I see you're up," a woman said. "Here, let me get that for you."

She pulled out a key and went to Andrew's wrist. He pulled away.

"Well, if you want to stay chained to the bed you can," she said.

"What did you do to me? Where are my friends?" he yelled.

"They're eating dinner," she said. "I saved your life."

He heard the cuffs unlatch and grabbed his wrist away from her. There was a red mark going the whole way around it now, and it throbbed a little.

"We had to get stitches in your head," she said. "You're quite the fighter so we had to restrain you."

Andrew lifted his hand to his head and felt the stitches.

"Let me out of here," he said.

"You're not an inmate," she said. "But you were dehydrated and losing blood. I don't think you're all the way out of the woods yet."

Andrew stood up. The adrenaline was fading away and the wooziness was setting in. He leaned back against the bed again. He thought about Mia's last comments.

"Is this the American sanctuary?" Andrew asked.

"I suppose that's one thing to call it," she said. "I'm Dr. Drum."

A female doctor. Andrew looked her up and down. She wasn't dressed like a doctor. She was about ten to fifteen years older than him, with dark brown curly hair and a warm smile.

"Do you think you can keep food down?" she asked. "I'll bring you something."

"What happened to me?" he asked.

"I'm going to ask you something personal," she said. "Are you an addict?"

Addict? As in drugs? Andrew shook his head.

"I did a blood test on you," she said. "Not a full panel, but what I'm capable of looking at in my current facility. You've been dosed with several types of drugs."

During his time in the militia Andrew only remembered being given something to help him relax, to help with his recovery from his fever.

"I was sick," Andrew said. "They did give me some medicine."

"I wouldn't call it medicine . . ."

Andrew lifted his chin. He wasn't about to show weakness or let the doctor know how scared he was. Over his lifetime he'd met several people who were users. However good their drugs made them feel, Andrew didn't think it was worth the ailments they caused.

"There are four different detectable drugs in your system," Dr. Drum said. "I'm willing to bet if I took you to a hospital I'd find more."

"What are they?" Andrew asked.

"Methamphetamines, zomiotics—"

"In English," Andrew said. He turned his head toward the doctor slowly. He locked eyes with her and felt his gaze grow hard. It would be difficult for him to hide his rage soon.

"The side effects are memory loss, lowered inhibitions, heightened senses; some cause drowsiness, but one causes increased adrenaline," she said. "It looks like you were taking a variety."

"Do any of them make me more compliant?" Andrew asked, knowing the answer.

The doctor nodded.

"The mix of the drugs also made you less susceptible to pain," she said. "Your blood was having difficulty clotting too. You likely would have passed out, not woken up, and bled to death."

"I need to see my friends," Andrew said.

"Rex is nearby. He'll be fine. He was very lucky; the bullet only grazed him. It was a tender spot though. He needed some stitches and can't lift anything for a few weeks."

Rex must have been the big man's name. He was another threat to worry about.

"Where is he?" Andrew asked. Now that Andrew was thinking clearly it wasn't so funny that Mia had shot a man. They'd have been safer if he was left for dead.

"In the room next door," she said. "He's staying the night here too. For observation."

At least he had that. Rex could get nowhere near Mia.

"I don't think you should have any visitors yet."

"Take me to them," Andrew said.

"I can bring him in here," she said.

"Not him," Andrew said. "Mia and Carter."

He stood up again and walked a few steps before his legs gave out and he was on the ground. The doctor grabbed ahold of his arms to help steady him and guided him back to bed. She pulled out a penlight and examined his eyes.

"You pulled out your IV," she said.

Andrew looked down at his arms; there was a needle sticking out at the bend in one of his elbows. The needles. Images of a doctor stabbing him in the arm, the music, the bright lights—it came flooding back and Andrew sat up. He thought he might be screaming but couldn't hear his own voice.

Dr. Drum reached over him and reconnected a tube. He felt the cold liquid enter his bloodstream. He didn't like this and went to pull it out again. She put her hand on top of his arm. Everything vanished and the world was still again.

"Someone did this to you?"

"Not someone," Andrew said. "Something."

"Tell me," she said.

"I don't trust you," Andrew said.

"Why not?" she asked.

"Because you haven't given me a reason to."

"I took care of your injuries," she said. "And I took off your handcuff."

"You're the one who put it on," Andrew said.

He thought about how grateful he felt when the militia turned off the noise, not caring that they were the ones who turned it on. The brief thought was enough to make Andrew pull his head down to his knees and close his eyes in pain.

"Are you all right?" she asked. She bent down in front of him and tried to look at his face. "Where are you hurting?"

"My head," he said.

She ran out of the room. Mia. Andrew pictured Mia's face, back on her father's farm before all this started. The day he ran into her and his whole life changed. The noise faded away to a gentle hum and Andrew sat up again. Dr. Drum came rushing back into the room with some pills and water. Andrew ignored the medicine but grabbed the bottle and drank it down.

"What happened?" she asked. "Maybe your injuries are worse. We have to get you to a hospital if you have brain trauma."

"No," Andrew said. "It's not that."

"Well, what is it?"

"I'm fine now," Andrew said.

"You're my patient," she said. "We're going into town."

"No," Andrew said. He didn't want to head farther away from Mia or Carter.

"Unless you can give me a reason not to I'm taking you. Even if it means getting the guards in here and sedating you," she said.

"It's not the cut," Andrew said. "It's inside. It's something else."

"How do you know?"

"It was happening before the car accident," Andrew said. "There are guards here? I thought I was free to go."

"They're for my protection from you," she said. "Your friends filled us in on your journey, but you're still a stranger."

"Why would I hurt you?" Andrew asked.

He thought about all the people he had hurt over his life. He looked at this woman and realized she was right to fear him. His face went hard.

"Tell me about the mental pain," she said. "Maybe I can help you."

"No," Andrew said.

While the memory of the militia filling him with drugs and keeping him locked away in a room was painful, it was new. Andrew's memory was returning. He was pleased about that.

"Do you want food?"

Andrew couldn't stand being coddled this way. Having someone take care of him was unnerving. He wanted to get back with Mia.

"When can I pull this needle out?" Andrew asked.

"It's just fluids," she said. "I'm not sure how long you were on those drugs for; some might carry withdrawal symptoms. We'll know for sure by the morning."

"Withdrawal?" Andrew asked.

She let out a long breath.

"Anything addictive is painful to give up," she said. "Even if you didn't choose your addiction."

Andrew pressed his lips together. He wasn't an addict.

"Vomiting," she said. "Intense pain, fever, and a wide variety of other not-so-pleasant side effects."

"Carter," Andrew said. "They did this to him too."

"I already sent my technician to get blood samples from your friends," she said. "If he went through the same regimen as you, that's a good sign. He's showing no harsh side effects."

"They worked on him for three days, me for over two weeks," Andrew said.

The pain flashed in his mind again. He winced and closed his eyes. It passed and he blinked feverishly. Another new memory. Andrew was never sick; he was tortured.

"What are you feeling?"

He shook his head.

"I'm a doctor," she said. "I want to help, and I can."

"It's nothing," Andrew said.

"Well if they were only drugging you for two weeks, that's good," she said. "The shorter the addiction, the shorter the withdrawal period."

"The memories I lost, will they come back? All of them?"

"Not on their own," she said.

She was lying; he already remembered two new things. She saw his jaw clench and continued.

"Some may," she said. "When someone has been through a trauma, talking about it helps."

Andrew looked away. He was exhausted, and whatever adrenaline he had built up was working its way out of his system.

"Get some sleep," she said. "You may be in for a rough night."

"Mia—"

"Is safe," the doctor interrupted. "You can see her in the morning."

Andrew didn't have the strength to argue. Dr. Drum started walking toward the door and he lay back down in the bed. He couldn't believe anything was going to happen to him tonight. His body wasn't capable of anything but sleep.

Chapter 47

If a foreign national wishes to join Affinity they must partici-
pate in a thorough background check to ensure they're com-
mitted to the cause.

—Internal memorandum from Affinity

The dining room was filled with people. Everyone was chatting
among themselves, but as soon as Zack walked Mia and Carter in,
the sounds vanished. Everyone watched as Zack led them over to the
end of a long table. Mia and Carter took seats across from him. Soon
the interest faded and the noise of the conversations continued.

"Sorry about that," Zack said. "I brought you in after the an-
nouncements were made and assumed you'd draw less attention, but
I guess I was wrong."

Carter shrugged. Mia wanted him to perk up but didn't know how
to get through.

"Is S here?" Mia asked.

"She's working," Zack said. "It's important, or else she would be.
I think she's going to stop by your cabin later tonight. She wants to
meet you just as badly."

"But we're going to see Andrew later tonight," Mia said.

"Yeah," Zack said. "I'm sure you'll find the time to fit in both
visits."

A salad bowl was passed to Mia and she eagerly scooped the contents onto her plate. Next came some fish, and Mia took an equally large helping. She was hungry and took a big bite. It was fine, nothing special. She assumed it was hard to make enough to feed this many people, but knew she could do better than this. She spent the rest of the meal thinking about working in the kitchen. Mia had always loved to cook. Before, she had dreamed of making food for her husband and eventually daughters. Maybe in this place she could cook for all of the residents. Her eyes scanned the room. Preparing a meal for two hundred people would be a challenge, one Mia knew she would excel at.

Zack escorted Mia and Carter out of the mess hall. Some people waved and giggled as they walked by. Nobody said anything though.

"Are they not allowed to speak to us?" Mia asked.

"You guys broke protocol when you strolled up on us," Zack said. "Normally things are a bit more scheduled. We don't want a formal introduction until you're intact."

"Andrew," Mia said.

"And Rex," Zack said.

How could Mia forget the man she had shot? She cringed at his name, wishing she still didn't know it.

"He's okay?" Carter asked.

"He'll make a quick recovery," Zack said.

"There's something you should know," Mia said.

She felt a sharp pain in her leg. Someone had kicked her. She put her hand on her shin and Carter broke in.

"We don't know Rex all that well," Carter said. "He's another American who helped us and saved Andrew's life. He's a virtual stranger, but I think he's a good person."

"Well, everyone is a stranger when you first meet them. Talk to whomever you want and go wherever you want. Some people will get together in the field over the next hour and socialize. I'll be there," Zack said.

"When can we see Andrew?" Mia asked.

"In the morning," Zack said.

"No," Mia said. "You promised we could see him tonight."

"He's sleeping," Zack said. "The doc says if he gets enough rest she'll release him tomorrow."

"You're lying," Mia said. "You're doing something to him."

"Stop," Zack said. "You'll give yourself another panic attack. Keep breathing. We want to help him, and you too. It's one more night."

Mia tried to keep her breathing regular. She looked at Carter, who didn't seem concerned. Maybe she was overreacting. Andrew had been in bad shape earlier. These people hadn't done anything to earn her distrust—yet.

"First thing tomorrow," Mia said. "I get to see him."

"As long as the doctor's on board," Zack said. "I promise. Why don't you two relax a little and then go to the field. Say in one hour? I'll tell S you're going there. You must have a lot more questions for her."

With few other options, Mia nodded her head. Zack was right; she did have a lot of questions. He walked away, leaving Mia and Carter to head down to the cabin. Mia wanted to discuss his newfound admiration for Rex. She was about to give Carter the backstory, but when she looked up at him she couldn't do it. He looked so forlorn; he hadn't touched his food at dinner. Mia couldn't express her fears. That would make him worse.

"Socializing sounds fun," Mia said. "Maybe they'll play games or sing songs."

"Whatever," Carter said. "What does it matter anyway?"

"It will get your mind off of things," Mia said.

Carter pulled open the door to their cabin and stepped inside. Mia followed.

"Beating yourself up isn't going to help," Mia said.

"You don't have a clue how this feels," Carter said.

"When my sister died I—"

"Was living miles away from her and never expected to see her again," Carter said. "My dad was my life. I'm already forgetting him. His voice is slipping away."

Mia had lost other people too. Whitney, who was like family. Even parting ways with Riley was difficult, but of course Mia could always call her. Suddenly an idea hit her. Riley had shown Mia how to use the phone and programmed in her number. When Mia had called Riley's phone she didn't pick up. But it had clicked over to a message with her voice. She wasn't sure if it would help Carter cope or make things worse, but he needed something. She walked over to the desk and dumped out the plastic bag. The cell phone bounced across the table.

"Did your dad have a voice mail message?" Mia asked. "That he recorded himself?"

Carter nodded. Mia grabbed his hand and put the cell phone in it.

"Call it," Mia said. "At least that way you can hear his voice again."

"It's been inactive," Carter said. "I'm sure they canceled his number."

Mia didn't know about any of that, but if there was a chance to make Carter feel better he needed to try.

"You don't know that," Mia said. "It'll only take you a few seconds to find out."

He looked down at the smooth black phone in his hand. Mia saw his eyes well with tears.

"Tell him how you're feeling. It might make you feel better," Mia said.

Carter didn't look up.

"I'll leave you alone," Mia said. "Just for a few minutes though. Then I'll be right here for you."

"Thank you," Carter said.

Mia smiled at him and walked out of the cabin. She started up the hill toward the bathrooms, the whole time wondering what building Andrew was hiding in and hoping she was making the right decision by not demanding to see him tonight. Part of her wanted to sit by his bedside and wait until he awoke, but another part was too enthralled with her new situation. She sighed, deciding to focus on that evening, and smiled thinking of all the questions she had for S—questions she might finally get some answers to.

Chapter 48

Polls show Grant Marsden is truly America's new golden boy. He has the second-highest favorability rating of any American, after the grand commander.

—American Gazette

Finally Grant had some time to devote to his work. He was making progress on the knife and thought he was about ready to order some animals for testing. He feared the liquid would only inject the victim if the knife hit bone, though. The vibration of a cell phone sounded through the room. He dropped the blade. Grant was sure it was Rex checking in; hopefully it would be some good news. Still, he was annoyed with the distraction and walked over to the table.

His annoyance vanished when he saw his screen wasn't lit up, and instead the small black phone was vibrating. It was the first time it had rung since Grant had had it in his possession, and he had a feeling it was the call he was waiting for. He looked at the phone number and realized it wasn't an international line. His annoyance returned and he let the call hit voice mail.

Grant started to walk back to his work when the phone vibrated again. Someone had left a message. He decided it was best to get assurance. He flipped the phone back open and hit the "listen" button.

"Hi."

Grant was so giddy he almost dropped his favorite new toy.

"I know you won't get this, but I miss you so much. I'm safe, all three of us are. I keep thinking there is something I should have done, but I can't remember what happened. I know I let you down though. I promise—"

Disgusted, Grant cut off the message. He didn't need to hear any more. If the boy was calling from an American number in a foreign country that meant he was on a cell phone. Grant typed out a message to the phone number.

You didn't let me down.

He hit "send" and waited for the bait to get grabbed up. To his surprise the phone started ringing again. Grant declined the call and wrote another text message.

I can't speak right now. Don't tell Amelia or Andrew.

The message went through. A response came fast.

You're alive? I'm so sorry we left you. Can you come meet us?

Can't talk. Call me tomorrow. One p.m.

Okay. I love you, Dad.

Grant brimmed with repulsion over those three simple words. He felt dirty typing them but needed to send the message home.

I love you.

No response came. He put the black phone down and picked up his personal cell to make a quick phone call. The line rang three times.

"Dr. Schaffer," Grant said, "do you think it's time we woke up our patient?"

At last the wheels of Grant's plan were in motion. He could have everything again. The grand commander position, a doting wife, and the girl who had betrayed him.

Chapter **49**

Alcohol and recreational drugs are prohibited in all Affinity camps. They cloud the mind and interfere with our common goals.

—*Internal memorandum from Affinity*

"I have a feeling about this place," Carter said. "Everything's getting better since we arrived. Andrew's getting medical attention, nobody is forcing us into something. We have a roof over our heads, food."

The two were walking up toward the field. Mia was glad Carter was so happy, but she hadn't expected such a change in his attitude over a voice mail. Mia yawned and decided his emotions could be blamed on the lack of sleep. Any drowsiness she was feeling vanished when the field came into view. There was a group sitting around two men playing musical instruments, children kicking a ball back and forth, and a variety of other activities going on.

"Come join us," a woman said.

She was seated in the circle around the musician. Carter and Mia headed over and took a seat. The man was strumming and singing a song Mia had never heard before. She was a poor singer, so music had never been stressed for her. Mia wasn't sure what instrument he was playing; sometimes her mother listened to piano music, but most often the Morrisseys worked in silence. When her sisters were home from finishing school they would entertain the family with whatever music they'd learned. Corinna played the flute; Mia hated the way it sounded. So flighty and alone. The song finished and everyone clapped.

"Welcome to Affinity," the musician said.

"Thank you for your hospitality," Carter said. "You're very talented."

"Do either of you two play the guitar?" someone asked.

Mia shook her head.

"A little," Carter said.

The man handed over the guitar and Carter repositioned himself. He moved his hand quickly up and down the neck and played. Then he slowed down and started singing. His voice wasn't perfect, but Mia was impressed. He sang with a twang. Once Carter's song was finished everyone clapped, Mia especially hard.

"I didn't know you could do that," Mia said.

"I'm full of surprises."

He gave Mia a wink and went on to play another song at the behest of the crowd. Mia couldn't understand where he had even learned this type of music. She only knew the classic slow songs. Someone tapped on Mia's shoulder and she spun around. Standing behind her was a girl, slightly older than herself. The sun was behind her and Mia couldn't make out many of her features. She stood up and got a better look. The girl had shoulder-length brown hair and big green eyes. She was several inches taller than Mia. She smiled with perfect white teeth. Mia didn't say a word before the girl wrapped her arms around Mia in a hug.

"It's so nice to meet you," she said.

"S?" Mia asked.

The girl pulled away. "Yes," she said. "But you can call me Sarah."

Emotions overtook Mia. She couldn't pinpoint what she was feeling: relief, nerves, or a general breakdown. She let out a small sob and the tears started flowing. Sarah wrapped her arms around Mia's shoulders and led her away from the group who were still enjoying Carter's musical talents.

"Let's find a place to talk," Sarah said.

Mia nodded her head, unable to think of anything she wanted more in the world at this moment.

I'm not normally so emotional," Mia said.

"It's fine," Sarah said. "I'm so happy to meet you, and you've traveled such a long way."

"This place is . . . ," Mia said. "It wasn't what I expected."

"It takes some getting used to," Sarah said. "But it's home now."

"What's your job?"

"I'm in computers," Sarah said.

"That's a little vague," Mia said.

Sarah nodded. "I rotate between positions," she said. "I'm not one of the leaders, if that's what you're asking."

"Leaders?" Mia asked. This was the first she had heard of them.

"It's hard to explain," Sarah said. "There's no grand commander or anything like that. Everyone here has a say, or the option to have one, but there's a group of six with the highest positions."

"Like Dina?" Mia asked.

"No," Sarah said. "She's semiretired. Zack actually just replaced her."

Mia still cringed over the word "retired," even though Zack had informed her of the different meaning. Mia had picked up on some of the hostility between Dina and Zack, making her wonder if the other version of retired still had a more unpleasant meaning than Zack wanted to admit.

"What do you mean they have the option to have a say?" Mia asked.

"I'll just explain it all," Sarah said. "But act surprised when you hear it again."

Mia nodded.

"There is a board of six people," Sarah said. "They make all major decisions and report to each other. They each run a section of Affinity: Internal Controls, which is Zack; Internal Maintenance; Internal Software; External Planning; External Affairs; and External Tactics.

"It can get confusing and I have a tendency to babble, so stop me with any questions," Sarah said. "I'm stationed under Internal Software mainly; I do a little with External Planning sometimes. I'd like to move to that branch permanently."

"I don't know what any of this means," Mia said.

"IC handles our defenses here; IM covers the houses, meals, what we need to live; IS covers constant updates of our computer systems, technologies, makes sure we stay cutting-edge and integrates the new systems. I do a lot of converting things to wireless these days.

"EP works with bringing in the supplies we need, figuring out how to trade and raise money if we need more; they also handle all recruitment, which is how I met you," Sarah said. "EA deals with the other branches of Affinity, and ET are the ones you don't want to mess with. All they do is think about ways to take down the Registry."

"That's bad?" Mia asked.

"Well, all branches work toward that common goal," Sarah said. "But focusing on one idea all the time can make anyone a little . . . intense."

Mia thought everyone here fell into that category.

"So we have section meetings once a week, where the division heads report the goings-on and what we need to work toward," Sarah said. "Then once a month we have a mass group meeting. It's here that we're updated by the other sections. Mainly ET runs the meeting.

"Some people here want to take down the Registry," Sarah said. "But they're happy doing their part. They don't want to involve themselves further."

"Are you in one section forever?" Mia asked.

"Not at all," Sarah said. "With the exception of ET, you pick where you want to work, what you want to do—people switch all the time. We have a lot of interactions with each other too."

"Except for the people in ET?"

"It is considered a great honor to get asked to join ET," Sarah said. "They have so much information and technology at their disposal. But if I ever received an invitation to that branch, I don't know how I'd respond."

Mia didn't want to hear about any more tactical planning. She changed the subject.

"How long have you been here?"

"Three years," she said. "I was seventeen when I arrived."

"What made you come here?" Mia asked.

"My story isn't as exciting as yours," Sarah said. "Dina told me, but I want to hear details."

"I want to know yours," Mia said.

"I was in a car accident," Sarah said. "We were in the middle of nowhere. Someone pulled me from the wreck, and then it blew up. I remember seeing the flames with my parents and sister still inside the car. I fainted and my savior took me to his home. The nearest hospital was hours away.

"He didn't know what the procedure was, never having had any children of his own, so he let me stay for a few days while he figured it out. Then a few days turned into a few weeks. He lived in the Midwest Area, in the mountains. He worked with lambs and goats. My family was moving to the Southwest when the accident happened.

"One day he went into town and everyone was talking about the family that was killed in the car wreck. I was pronounced dead too. He found out I was supposed to go over to the government and they should raise me until I was ready for the Registry, but he liked having me around.

"He taught me so many things. I didn't even know how to read, and I was twelve. Nobody bothered us or knew I was there. I think he was lonely, and I didn't know what family was."

"What do you mean?" Mia asked.

"There's no real family in America," Sarah said. "Boys are kicked out so young they think it's right to throw their sons away. Daughters are seen as dollar signs and mothers are okay with that because they were treated the same way. When that car blew up, do you know why I fainted?"

Mia shook her head.

"It wasn't because my parents and sister were killed in front of me, it was because I was scared their deaths meant I couldn't enroll in the Registry."

Mia understood all too well. Throughout this whole journey she'd never given much thought to her mother or father. Mia's two living sisters weren't on her mind much either. Mia didn't wish them harm; she didn't care about them one way or the other. She looked over her shoulder at Carter. He and Andrew were her family now, and she loved them more than she thought imaginable.

"My time with Ernie changed me," Sarah said. "Soon I stopped caring about my appearance and started caring more about what he was teaching me. He wasn't my father; he was my dad."

Dad. That was the informal word Carter used to describe Rod. Mia knew it had a powerful connotation. One she'd never experienced.

"What happened to him?" Mia asked.

"He started getting sick," Sarah said. "We were both in denial over it, but he was older. He could have been my mother's father. I didn't want to leave him and he knew I never would. So he set this all up. There was a knock on our door and he told me to open it. On the rare occasion when someone came to our house, I hid in the basement. At first I suspected it was RAG agents and Ernie was turning me over to the government because he couldn't take care of me any-more. Instead it was Zack."

"I thought he was born here," Mia said.

"We used to sneak into America and bring people down," Sarah said. "The rules have changed though."

"So you just drove over the border with him?" Mia asked.

"Not exactly," Sarah said. "He had a huge cargo truck. I had to hide in the back. It was filled with American flags, ceramics, knick-knacks. Those things are very popular in most of Mexico. I was ter-rified when the border patrol opened the back of the truck. They just shined a flashlight and checked a few boxes. Our hearts were beating so fast."

"You weren't alone back there?"

"No," Sarah said. "There were seven of us."

"So you left Ernie?" Mia asked.

"He came too," Sarah said.

Her eyes started to water. Mia looked at the ground. She thought it might be a good idea to have Sarah talk with Carter. Maybe she could help him through his grief.

"Why does this place have to exist?" Mia asked.

"What do you mean?"

"The Registry," Mia said. "What caused it? Mandatory service too. Why does America operate the way it does?"

"After the conflict, or Great War, whatever you want to call it, an outbreak happened in America," Sarah said. "People were dying. It was bad, but the soldiers returning home weren't affected. Most of them were men, but not all. Either way the population was very low, between the war and the outbreak. Men outnumbered women at least five to one, maybe more.

"There was a concern that the population would go under. No country could give America any aid; people were scared. Those who'd just gotten back from war were too wounded, physically and mentally, and the ones left home were dying. Chaos broke out. The women who weren't infected were at risk of getting kidnapped and attacked. It wasn't pretty.

"There were military women too; they were strong and brave but so outnumbered. It turned out scientists were responsible for the outbreak. The man who was general of the army stepped up and took over the country. General Aaron Miller, or Grand Commander Aaron Miller. The government offered sanctuary. If you were a woman and made it to the capital they would protect you. Most went; their families back home were dead and they couldn't leave their homes without risk of getting gang-raped."

"Men aren't that brutal," Mia said.

"Not under normal circumstances," Sarah said. "But these men were scared. Their families were dead too. It wasn't about power or sex even; they wanted to keep the population going. It started to seem like a woman should be pregnant at all times.

"Once most of the women were in the capital it was decided that those who wanted children would be matched with a partner. It was seen as a duty back then, to carry on the lineage of America. Repopulate the country in a much more controlled manner. Those who didn't enter the program would never have children or families of their own.

"The logical way to determine which men got women was money. That meant the man could provide protection from those who weren't matched and the government could start collecting funds to rebuild the country. Women didn't see themselves as being sold yet."

"I'm sure some did," Mia said.

"Would you rather live your life alone and never have children when the population is dying out? Or go live with a man who could offer protection from the unruly mobs?"

"What about the women who had money of their own?" Mia asked. "Or were already married?"

"Most of the married ones fled the country," Sarah said. "As far as those with money, some ran and the ones who stayed went into protection. By the time they tried to access their money the government told them it was gone. There weren't a lot of wealthy soldiers anyway."

Mia thought about having children with Grant. A shudder made its way through her body.

"Keep in mind these people were living in a very different time and in a harsh environment. The capital could barely keep them fed, let alone clean," Sarah said. "It was a better choice than living out in the world alone, where you could get attacked at any moment.

"Slowly all the women were matched and the country started to pick up a little," Sarah said. "The government offered free housing and work to all single men who wanted to reenlist in the military, and most did.

"Then as the years passed the government asked that all daughters be turned over to the system," Sarah said. "It wasn't like these girls could go on dates. It still wasn't safe for them outside. Things were better but far from perfect. The population was still way overinflated with men. The government asked that daughters as young as twelve be turned over.

"Most parents objected, but the government gave the incentive of splitting the money the young women brought in," Sarah said. "Between that and the desire to keep rebuilding the population, it was seen as a duty almost. These girls were matched with the next round of rich men, but the military members grew angry because they weren't considered as potential husbands. So it became mandatory that a man had to serve in the armed forces to be eligible as a husband."

"So if a father wanted his son to land a wife, ever, the son needed to enlist," Mia said.

"That meant everyone made their sons join the service. But America was still vulnerable to attack. Over a decade had passed since the

Great War's end and other countries were starting to rebuild. By this point in time the population was still next to nothing. We had to keep up, to stay a global force. So the enlistment age was set at thirteen, and everyone had to sign up for a ten-year term."

"The youngest groom was twenty-three," Mia said.

"Once the men were released from service most didn't bother going home," Sarah said. "Their mothers and fathers were a distant memory. What they did remember was a loveless marriage where their father treated their mother like property. So they copied what they saw.

"By the time this generation had their sons some fathers started tossing them out like garbage."

"Why?" Mia asked.

"Well, just because you *could* get a wife at twenty-three didn't mean you were going to," Sarah said. "They needed to find jobs and make enough money to support their new purchases. The average groom was in his thirties. They saw a baby boy as another mouth to feed that wouldn't come home to them or bring anything to the family. The idea of family was destroyed, along with the notion of falling in love."

"When did appraisals come about?" Mia asked.

"So far this sounds like a happy coincidence, right? That the Registry was created by accident," Sarah said. "It wasn't. The first grand commander realized right away that men were paying more for the prettier girls. It was the girls who didn't understand this at first. They were kept in the dark. They didn't meet their husbands until a ceremony was performed at the capital. Some brides rejected their mates."

"What happened to them?"

"At first they were never matched again, but rumor is they were put to death," Sarah said. "It's not like any of this is written down anywhere. These are stories passed through generations."

"So marry this man or die?" Mia asked. "I'm guessing the twelve-year-olds were dragged away."

Sarah nodded and continued.

"Once it became obvious prettier daughters were bringing in more money, and those with appropriate qualities, as the grand commander saw it, parents started focusing on those characteristics."

"Like cooking and cleaning?" Mia asked.

"Yes," Sarah said. "There were a million things the grand commander could have done to rebuild the country. He could have screened these women and men and set up genetic compatibilities; he could have hosted controlled social functions for decent men to mingle with women their age. Instead he sold them right out.

"Once the population rose enough, the rules changed. The marriage and enlistment ages were raised to reflect the rest of the world's standards," Sarah said. "People became complacent with the way things were done. 'My parents did it to me so I'll do it to my children.' You teach your little girl to only love her husband and not love you and she will. You throw your little boy out and he'll throw his away."

"It doesn't make sense that people still go along with it," Mia said. "That nobody revolted."

"The military was huge," Sarah said. "They would crush any revolt and weren't about to turn on their superiors. There is always some discontent. Most of the people who make their way down to us are here because they found someone who loves them. Me and Ernie. You and your men."

"It was my sister," Mia said. "Not the guys."

"I just assumed," Sarah said. "I'm sorry."

"I do love them," Mia said. "More that I thought possible. It's different, too, than the way I thought I would love my husband."

"Because it's real," Sarah said.

She reached out and grabbed Mia's hand. She gave it a squeeze and Mia's body relaxed a bit. Mia thought about love. Corinna did love her, or else none of this would have been possible. Mia would have been someone else's property and happy about it.

Sarah's response was the first straight answer Mia had received. She needed time to process it all. Sarah recognized Mia's angst and leaned over, giving Mia's arm a squeeze.

"Now it's your turn," Sarah said. "Tell me about your journey here."

"After my sister left me an article about the way American women are treated, I recruited my best friend . . ."

Mia knew she should follow Riley's advice and stick to the main points, but her common responses overtook her training and she was happy to give Sarah every little detail.

Chapter 50

Rumor: Grant Marsden is wedding the daughter of the grand commander. It will certainly be the social event of the year.

—American Gazette

The cavernous east wing might have intimidated some, but not Grant. He walked through the giant warren of unused rooms. Sheets covered most of the furniture. He had planned to house his staff here, but so few lived on the premises. Once he was grand commander he would fill it with daughters and secret wives. Maybe even some female employees who could cook and clean for him. After all, he would be part of the government then.

He was getting closer to the occupied room and had to keep his pace normal, or else let Dr. Schaffer see how excited he was for this moment. He turned into the makeshift hospital room and saw the doctor standing over his unconscious patient. It wouldn't take long for Roderick Rowe to awaken, and find himself Grant's prisoner.

The pathetic man who had thrown himself from the helicopter had hit the ground with a thud. Grant was already down, having been kicked by the man's son. The helicopter took off and the sirens came closer.

Two ambulances arrived on the scene. As they loaded up Roderick into one, Grant insisted they ride together. Grant's ribs hurt from where he had been kicked, but Roderick was in far worse shape. He was unconscious and the paramedics were pumping air into his lungs. At first Grant wanted to offer them money to let Roderick die. This man who loved his son so much that he would sacrifice himself, he was responsible for Mia's escape. Then Grant remembered love wasn't a strength, it was a weakness. One he could exploit.

The hospital wasn't busy. Roderick was rushed away on a stretcher and Grant was treated for his bruises. He sat alone in the room until an administrator walked in.

"We received word not to discharge you," the doctor said. "Escorts are waiting outside your door."

"What about my friend?" Grant asked.

"He's in surgery," the man said. "It's looking fifty-fifty."

Grant reached into his pocket. He ignored the black phone he'd lifted off Rod in the ambulance and pulled out his own cell phone. The doctor looked impressed. Only Grant could have access to such fine equipment. A perk from the work he did.

"Have you seen one of these before?" Grant asked.

"No," the man said. "What is it?"

"Think of it as a tiny computer," Grant said. "It can do a lot of things. Take pictures and videos, access the Internet, make bank transactions. I think your hospital is doing a fine job. I'd like to make a donation, and a personal one to you as well."

"I'm sorry," the doctor said. "I have strict orders not to discharge you. This is coming from pretty high up."

Grant punched in a number and showed it to the doctor. His eyes went wide.

"Once that man is out of surgery you will send him and all his belongings to my home," Grant said. "A death certificate will be issued and no questions will be asked."

The man looked at the figure on Grant's phone. He smiled. "What's the address?"

A helicopter delivered Rod later that night. Grant already had his personal physician, Dr. Schaffer, at the house ready to greet his new patient. Under Grant's orders the man had been kept in a medical coma since then.

"How's our patient?" Grant asked.

"His brain is responding," said Dr. Schaffer. "Outside of the two broken legs and fractured ribs, he should be fine. I administered the medication to pull him out of the coma several hours ago."

"And he isn't awake yet," Grant said. He crossed his arms.

"Sometimes these things take time," the doctor said. "I wouldn't want to risk his health."

"You must be able to give him something," Grant said. "He's been asleep for over a month."

The doctor reached for a syringe and readied it to inject the liquid into Rod's IV. "A straight shot of adrenaline might do it," he said. "But it might also shock his system."

Grant rolled his eyes. He'd waited on the boy to call long enough. Grant waved his hand, signaling for the doctor to inject his patient.

"He'll be disoriented at first. Then I don't know what he'll remember," said Dr. Schaffer. "I would be better prepared at my lab."

"Well, this is all you have," Grant said. "He must stay here."

"As always, your requests will be honored," Dr. Schaffer said.

He pushed the plunger of the syringe down and the beeping of Rod's machines stayed constant. Then Rod's head rolled to the side. The beeping started increasing. Grant smiled as the man's eyes began to open. Dr. Schaffer pulled them open and shone a light.

"Where am I?"

He spat out the question with fury.

"You've been in an accident," the doctor said. "You're safe now."

"Where's my son?" Roderick said. He started to sit up in his bed. The doctor pushed him back and adjusted the bed frame so he was sitting up.

"He's fine," Grant said.

Roderick's eyes focused on Grant. He squinted. "Grant Marsden?"

This wasn't what Grant wanted. He had hoped for some memory loss. He was preparing to inform Rod of his hostage position when the man spoke again.

"You're a billionaire; what would you want with someone like me?"

Music to Grant's ears. It was only his notoriety Rod was aware of.

"So you follow the weapons business?" Grant asked.

"I like to stay informed," Rod said. "Where's my son?"

"Not here," Grant said. "He'll be in contact soon."

"What happened?"

"You were in a terrible car accident," Grant said. "I pulled you from the wreckage."

Grant felt his lips slide over his teeth as he tried his best to form a warm smile. Rod did not appear comforted. That was never a skill Grant had acquired.

A fishy smell had woken Grant up. He was seated at a long, fancy table, tied to a chair. He looked around and saw the other captive was already awake. Their host was seated at the head of the table, smiling as he ate his fish.

"It is so nice the two of you are joining me for dinner," the man said.

"Where am I?" the other man asked.

"You know the answer to that," the host said. "You broke into my house. Were you planning on stealing something or shooting me? Since you had the gun."

"Let me go, you sick piece of—"

"Now, now," the host said. "No foul language, please. That's no way to treat your host. How about you? Do you want to add to the conversation?"

He looked at Grant. Grant shook his head no.

"You're different," he said. "You don't look scared. Your coun-
terpart, on the other hand, is struggling against his ropes, trying to
break free. You are sitting calmly. Why is that?"

"I'm not scared," Grant said. "Of anything."

"How long have you been living here?"

"Two weeks," Grant said.

"You're good," the host said. "I didn't notice anything out of
place, not even food."

"I know," Grant said.

The other man continued to struggle. He started to yell again.

"Stop behaving like a boor," the host said. "Do you know what I
do for a living? How I have enough money to live in this lavish home
you were attempting to burglarize?"

The man continued to scream. The host stood up and yelled over
him. Grant saw a vein in his forehead bulge.

"I create things. I am an engineer. I work hard for my money
while you're content to cheat and steal for yours."

The other man did not stop yelling. The host grew more agitated.
He reached into his pocket and pulled out a small gun. He didn't
think twice before firing off two shots into the other man's chest and
head. The blast from the bullets rang in Grant's ears. The other cap-
tive slumped over dead.

"Now," the man said. "Where were we?"

I'd really like to speak with Carter," Rod said. "He wasn't in the accident, was he?"

"Safe and sound at home," Grant said. "At least a day's drive away
I might add."

"Where is this place?"

"An hour outside the capital," Grant said. "I assume you were
driving to bid on some sort of work—at least that's what your child
said."

Rod looked down at his nose, trying to process the events. Grant needed him alive and conscious, nothing else.

"Well," Grant said, "I'm sure you have a lot of questions. I'll leave the doctor to answer them for you."

"How long was I out for?" Rod asked.

"About eighteen hours," Dr. Schaffer said.

Grant nodded his head at the physician and left the room. His scheme was working and Grant was starting to feel like his old self again.

Chapter 51

The farmlands in America are better than anywhere in the world. We have the ability to grow such a wide variety of food that there is not a single dish anywhere else that cannot be prepared in America.

—American Gazette

"How did you become a doctor?" the man asked.

"You need to get over it," the doctor said.

"You're a female," he said. "It makes no sense."

"Oh, how you flatter me," she said. "Are you angry that a girl stitched you up?"

"Impressed," Rex said. "I thought all of you were mindless maids."

The doctor let out a loud laugh. Andrew sat up and leaned on his arms. Sun was pouring in from the slats in the blinds. His mouth tasted like death. Neither of the people seated in his room paid him any attention. They were both smiling at each other.

"Can I have some water?" Andrew asked.

He swung his feet over the edge of the bed and cradled his pulsating head in his hands.

"Look who's back to the land of the living," Dr. Drum said.

She walked over to him and bent down. She shone a small light in his eyes and he wanted to smack her away. He flinched and his foot hit a bucket. Rex walked over to him and picked it up.

"You shouldn't do any lifting," the doctor said.

"Katie, it's a puke bucket, it weighs a pound," Rex said. "I'm taking it to the bathroom."

"Katie?" Andrew asked.

"That's my first name," she said.

"What is going on?" Andrew asked.

The doctor continued her examination. "You don't remember?" she asked.

"I remember falling asleep after talking with you," Andrew said. "I felt better then."

She walked away toward a cabinet and came back with a syringe.

"I need to take some of your blood," she said. "Then I'll give you some water and medicine for the headache."

What Andrew really wanted was a toothbrush. He didn't even pay attention as she wrapped a tourniquet around his arm.

"Do you need me to hold you down again?" Rex asked.

He looked serious.

"Stay away from me, and you stay away from Mia," Andrew said.

"Whoa," Katie said.

"It's fine," Rex said. "I'll be in the next room."

"I thought you two were friends," Katie said.

"You thought wrong," Andrew said.

"I think you were a bit nicer going through the withdrawal than after," she said. "Rex helped you last night, against my orders. You ripped his stitches twice."

"What?" Andrew asked.

He squinted his eyes. He tried to focus on his last memory; it was of falling asleep. He wasn't met with a shooting pain attempting to think about anything else this time.

"We haven't been to sleep at all," she said. "You went through it pretty bad for about eight hours."

She finished collecting her vial and put a bandage on the interior of Andrew's elbow.

"Bend," she said.

He did as he was told.

"Keep that man away from me," Andrew said.

"I would have had my assistants help, but Rex insisted. I thought it would give you comfort knowing one of your friends was here."

"Stop using that word," Andrew said. "He's not my friend. He's dangerous."

Katie shook her head and came back with some pills and water. Andrew didn't want any more drugs.

"This is just headache relief," she said. "You can trust me. As soon as you feel better and I test your blood I'll clear you to get out of here."

Andrew reluctantly took the medication and drank the whole cup of water.

"Can you stand?" she asked.

"Yes," Andrew said with annoyance. Aside from the headache he felt fine.

"You kept trying to rip your IV out," she said. "We managed to keep it in most of the night. That should have helped with the dehydration. How is your appetite?"

As if on cue his stomach let out a rumble. It wasn't for food though; the idea of eating made Andrew queasy.

"It's fine," he said.

"It shouldn't be," she said. "The nausea will pass by dinnertime. Try to sit still for a while, force your body to keep the water down. I'm going to run a blood panel and check on your levels. Stay in bed until I get back."

Katie grabbed the vial and walked out of the room. Andrew wanted to get out of here, but puking on the floor wouldn't help him get released. He lay backward on the bed but kept his feet on the ground. A knock came outside his door and he propped himself up on his elbows. Rex didn't wait for an invitation as he walked in the room.

"You have every right to hate me," Rex said. "But we should talk."

"So you can convince me not to tell these people who you are? Who you work for? What you support?"

"Think past tense," Rex said.

"I should have left you to bleed to death in the jungle."

"I saved your life," Rex said. "Twice now if you count last night."

"After you took my friend's," Andrew said.

"That was an accident," Rex said. "I never wanted anyone to die."

"Why are you here?" Andrew asked. "What are you up to?"

"My former boss sent me down here to track and kill your girl-friend," he said.

"I should kill you right now," Andrew said.

"But," Rex said, "I didn't follow his order, did I? Instead I helped the three of you; doesn't that award me the benefit of the doubt?"

"You have it," Andrew said. "Why do you think I've kept my mouth shut this far? But your time is running out. Give me a reason to believe you."

"I've been a soldier my entire life," Rex said. "I'm good at it, fol-lowing orders, executing missions. After my time in service was done I reenlisted; once that was done I took a job in Grant Marsden's secu-rity. I never stopped being a soldier. I never will. I don't know how."

Andrew clenched his jaw. He knew not to trust Rex, but part of him knew how that felt. Andrew may have never made it to service, but even now he had a hard time turning off the man he was groomed to be. He nodded for Rex to continue.

"I don't care about owning a woman," Rex said. "I never have. I don't care about helping women either. A target is a target and a mission is a mission; Grant gave me that. Lately, I've started to think he isn't worth fighting for any longer."

"You're loyal to him," Andrew said. "As loyal as I was to America. It doesn't turn off that fast."

"It's been turning off for a while now," Rex said. "He lets emotions compromise his missions. I need a new general."

"And you think that could be me?" Andrew asked with a laugh.

"No," Rex said. "I researched your location. I traveled down here. The night of Mia's auction I was supposed to win it and kill her, but my plan was to win it and save the three of you."

"Mia's auction?" Andrew asked. He felt his stomach go queasy again. He didn't want to hear about that. "What did your boss think you were doing?" he asked. "If you did the research why did you tell him the truth about where we were?"

"It wasn't until after I told him that I changed my mind," Rex said. "He has some warped ideas about right and wrong that I no longer agree with. After spending one night here I realize that. This group is more deserving of my skills. I have Amelia to thank for leading me here. If she hadn't shot me I may have never discovered that fact."

"You just said a mission is a mission," Andrew said.

"Until it isn't anymore," Rex said. "Killing is not something I enjoy. Grant Marsden takes pleasure from the act, not me. He could not make up his mind as to whether I should kill you or follow you. Indecisiveness is not a quality of a leader."

Andrew felt the hairs on the back of his neck rise up and realized his knuckles were turning white from clenching his fists.

"This is a trap," Andrew said. "Why wouldn't he order us dead on sight?"

"I am not sure," Rex said. "A man cannot be loyal when respect is missing. Grant has shown his lack of respect for me, and mine for him has been vanishing."

"So what is your plan now?"

"I didn't think I would stay with you three," Rex said. "I assumed after I saved you we would part ways, but this place, these people, it's not something I expected."

"You don't know anything about this place," Andrew said.

"It's a tactical center," Rex said. "They're a well-trained and highly organized machine. I could help them."

"You know their goal is to take down the Registry? To stop your army?" Andrew asked.

Rex nodded.

"I am a soldier," Rex said. "My skills can be bought or my loyalty earned. I do not care who my opponent is, just that I have respect for my superior. I've been here for a short while and they have treated me quite well. I do not care one way or the other about the rationale for my fight. I only care that I have a fight and fellows who are worthy of my abilities."

Andrew locked eyes with Rex. He couldn't decide whether the man was telling the truth or not. He was like a well-trained soldier, impossible to read.

"I'm not asking for your trust," he said. "I'm asking for the chance to earn it."

Their conversation was finished when Katie came back in the room.

"Did you two make up?" she asked.

"No," Andrew said.

Even though his gut told him not to, part of Andrew understood what Rex was saying. Before Mia blackmailed him into helping her escape, Andrew hadn't really cared one way or the other about women either. He never saw their way of life as wrong or thought that anything was the matter with his. If Andrew had served his time there was a good chance he would have turned into someone like Rex.

"But he can stay here if he wants," Andrew said.

"Well, bad news for him then," Katie said. "Your blood work came back clean. No toxins in your system. As long as you feel up to it, you have my permission to rejoin the group."

Andrew stood up from the bed. The pills Katie had given him had made his headache go away.

"Take a shower," she said. "There are some clean clothes in there for you."

"Thanks," Andrew said.

He walked past Rex, who gave him a nod.

"I'm making you stay here for at least one more day," Katie said.

"I'm in better shape than he is," Rex said.

"You pulled your stitches twice," Katie said. "I know you're feeling fine, but if that happens again you could bleed out. You were shot; it was a through-and-through, but that doesn't mean you don't need further observation."

"Doctor's orders?" Rex asked.

"Besides," Katie said, "I think we both need some sleep."

Andrew walked into the bathroom and left the two of them in his room. He shut the door all the way and turned on the water. He had just started to take his shirt off when he thought he heard his name. He shut the shower curtain and held his ear to the door.

"Memory loss . . . long-term effects . . . permanent."

Andrew moved away and looked at the mirror. He had heard enough to get the gist of what they meant. He examined the gash in his head. His skin was stitched together. He lifted his head and stared at himself in the mirror. His brain was in trouble. He knew it, but Andrew couldn't focus on himself right now. He'd been to the brink of death and back over the past several weeks, but what mattered more than that was reuniting with Mia. Nothing was going to delay that event.

Chapter 52

While the community may assist in child rearing, it is important to foster the parent–child bond.

—Internal memorandum from Affinity

Fruit was set out in the mess hall. Mia didn't care about it though. Carter stopped to make a plate but Mia ran straight for Zack.

"Can I—"

Before Mia could finish Zack interrupted.

"You can't go see Andrew," he said. "Dr. Drum released him, so he's on his way to find you."

Mia felt like a fist holding her heart had released its grip. She let out a sigh of relief. Zack wore a goofy grin on his face.

"When?" Mia asked.

"After breakfast," Zack said.

"But he's okay?"

"He's fine," Zack said.

Carter came up behind Mia and took a seat at Zack's table. Mia followed his lead and started picking fruit off his plate. He didn't seem to mind. After hanging out with the group last night both of them had been exhausted and fallen right to sleep. Now they each had renewed energy.

"Rex has to stay in the infirmary," Zack said. "You're really not that concerned about him?"

"We just met him," Carter said. "We're glad he's fine."

"Well, we want to wait till he's out to introduce the four of you," Zack said. "So you three will have the next few days to yourselves."

"He's not staying here," Mia said.

Again Carter gave Mia's leg a kick.

"She means we're not sure of his plans," Carter said.

"Either way," Zack said. "Familiarize yourselves with this place, get to know some of the people, ask questions about their work, observe how we live. I'll escort you three this morning, then I have some work that needs my attention. Sarah had some of her duties reassigned, and starting this afternoon she'll be with you. I'll join whenever I can."

Mia couldn't think of a better guide. There was still a lot she wanted to learn about her new friend.

"Our blood tests," Carter said. "Did they come back . . . ?"

"You two are clean," Zack said.

Mia thought that was a formality. She was shocked to see the look of relief on Carter's face.

"About work," Zack said. "Do the two of you have any passions? Any skills you'd like to hone? I can tell you what to observe."

"I like music, art," Carter said. "I'm not a bad fighter."

"Well," Zack said, "everyone here knows how to defend themselves."

"Teaching," Carter said. He looked over at Mia and gave her a smile. "I'm a good teacher."

She nodded. Part of her was excited to demonstrate everything Riley had taught her.

"Mia is an amazing cook," Carter said.

"We can always use one of those," Zack said.

Suddenly cooking food didn't seem like such fun anymore.

"Driving," Mia said. "I like to drive."

"Hmm," Zack said. He gave her a head nod.

Carter looked over at Mia. She shrugged. If they were going to stay here she wanted a position with more action.

"Well," Zack said, "if you stick around the field you'll see the different groups working on their physical skills today. If you head down to the lake you can see the children and the teachers. We don't have any permanent driving positions at the moment, but that would be under my command so I'm sure I can set something up."

Before Mia could ask where the lake was, she heard the door to the mess hall open. She spun around and saw a figure standing with the sun pouring in behind him. Without waiting for confirmation she jumped up from her seat, knowing exactly who it was. She sprinted and as the doors shut the sun faded out and Andrew stood there. Mia almost knocked him over when she hurled herself into his arms.

She wrapped her arms around his waist and held him as tight as she could. His lean frame didn't seem real. She felt him return her grasp. His arms were around her shoulders. One of his hands went up the back of her head and into her hair. He held her close, her face pressed against his chest. Mia blinked away tears of happiness. They were together, and nothing would ever separate them again.

Chapter 53

Tonight on The Greg Finnegan Show, *an interview with Grant Marsden's superior during his tenure in service. Learn even more about the American Hero.*

—American Gazette

Frustration filled Grant. The boy was supposed to call an hour ago, and he hadn't heard from Rex in forty-eight hours. He didn't want to risk dialing out, in case the call was traceable. Too many people were watching him. Even though Grant had blocking technology, turning it on might signal something. He reminded himself Rex would have called if the situation had taken a turn for the worse, or maybe Rex was dead. Either way, the boy was more important.

On the plus side, if the boy met his demise at least Grant would have a new dummy to test his inventions out on. Human experimentation was something in which Grant hadn't taken part in some time.

*P*eace and quiet," the host said. "Still not scared?"

"No," Grant said. "I am hungry though; will you untie me?"

The host picked up his chair and set it next to Grant's. He cut up the fish and stabbed a piece with his fork, then fed it to Grant.

"Now everyone is happy," the host said. *"How many years until you report for duty?"*

"Six," Grant said.

"Don't talk with your mouth full," the host said. *"It's rude."*

Grant swallowed the fish.

"Do you know why you're still alive?" the host asked.

"Because you're having fun toying with me," Grant said.

"The young, so reckless," he said. *"I'm impressed with you."*

He held up another piece and Grant took a bite.

"Two weeks and I had no idea; you sized up that man right away for what he was, and you have no fear. What should I do with you?"

"If you aren't going to kill me, I guess let me go," Grant said.

"I never let anyone go. I don't like unserved men," the host said. *"I get one or two every year trying to break in or looking for work. They're dirty and lack potential, and are missing a certain amount of refinement. You don't show those qualities."*

Grant didn't know how to respond. Then the rapid-fire questions came.

"If I asked you to kill that man, would you have?"

"Gladly," Grant said.

"Why?"

"He was annoying."

"Have you killed anyone before?"

"Yes."

"How many?"

"One."

"Why?"

"I didn't like him."

The host smiled and leaned back in the chair.

"I can't kill you," he said. *"You remind me too much of myself."*

The host picked up a dinner knife and sliced through Grant's bindings. The ropes loosened and Grant lifted his arms. The host

still held the knife; he was ready to stab. Grant picked up his fork and
took another bite of salmon. The host laughed.

"I think we can have some fun together," the host said.

A vibration from Rod's cell phone brought Grant back to reality. He picked up the device and went into the room next door. Rod was awake, flipping through one of the old books Grant had found to keep him entertained.

"You're back," Rod said. "Any news on my son?"

"He's on the phone," Grant said. "I want you to tell him you're all right."

Rod nodded and Grant flipped open the phone, hitting the speaker button.

"Dad?" Carter said.

Rod was tearing up. "It's so good to hear your voice," he said.

"You're alive?" Carter said. "I knew you weren't dead."

"It was a bad accident," Rod said. "They're taking real good care of me."

"I'm so sorry I let you down," Carter said. "It should have been me who jumped out."

"What are you talking about?" Rod asked.

Grant pulled the phone away and switched off the speaker. He held the phone up to his ear and walked out of the room, ignoring Rod's calls.

"I can't have you upsetting my patient," Grant said.

"Who is this?" Carter asked.

"While we were never formally introduced, I think you enjoyed kicking me in the ribs several times," Grant said.

There was silence on the other end.

"Now that we're acquainted, let's get down to business," Grant said. "I have someone you want and you have something I want."

Still silence, but Grant could hear the boy's breathing.

"Bring me back my wife and you can have your father back. It's simple."

"She's not a thing," Carter said. "She's a person."

"She's a woman," Grant said. "But let's not get bogged down with specifics. She's mine and I want her back."

"Why?"

"I don't like these questions," Grant said. "I'd be more worried about my intentions toward your father. Do you know what I do for a living?"

Silence.

"I make weapons," Grant said. "I'm always on the lookout for someone I can test my models on. I have a knife that will shatter a bone as soon as it makes contact. I have a gun that will cause an infection to spread. A machete that is so sharp it can cut off an appendage with minimal effort."

"Enough," Carter said. "I can't bring her back. I wouldn't know how."

"You can and you will," Grant said.

"You'll kill us as soon as we get there."

"No, I am a man of my word. You and your father will go free. I'll fly you anywhere in the world you like; I'll even give you some seed money to start a new life."

"Never," Carter said.

"Okay." Grant let out a sigh.

"Wait, don't hurt him."

"I'm going to kill him in a very slow and painful manner."

"No," Carter said, his voice filled with urgency.

Grant rolled his eyes.

"I'm not unreasonable," Grant said. "You can call once a day and hear his voice, on speakerphone of course. The doctor expects his casts to come off in six weeks. You have one month until I start testing my weapons. Two months until he's dead."

"I can't bring her back," Carter said. "You'll do the same to her."

"No," Grant said. "While she deserves punishment, I gain nothing from it but personal satisfaction. Your father's torture, on the other hand, gives me something I want. His will be much, much worse than you can imagine."

"I need more time."

"This isn't a deal," Grant said. "It's a fact. Those are my terms and the clock starts today."

"Please let me speak to him again," Carter said.

"Once a day," Grant said. "Your father is quite happy here. He thinks he was in a car accident on his way to the capital to bid on a construction job and you're safe at home in the Southwest Area. If you say anything to make him think otherwise I'll make sure his stay here becomes less than pleasant. I know you are aware of the pain I am capable of inflicting."

"You're a monster," Carter said.

"Thank you," Grant said. "One piece of advice: I wouldn't let her know what you're up to. Talk to you tomorrow."

Grant hung up the phone. Now he had to fix the small problem with Rod. He pasted on a smile and went back into the man's room.

"Where's my son?" Rod asked. "Why'd you take away the phone?"

"He was upsetting you," Grant said. "Doctor's orders. He'll call tomorrow. Once a day until Dr. Schaffer says otherwise."

"Why was he talking about jumping?" Rod asked.

"He wasn't," Grant said. "You have a severe head injury. All he said was he was sorry you were hurting. It should be him hurting."

Rod's eyes were red. He looked shaken and leaned back in the bed.

"I can talk to him longer tomorrow?" Rod asked.

"Of course," Grant said. "As long as he doesn't upset you."

Grant's personal phone went off. He checked the screen; it was the grand commander calling. No doubt with another pointless lesson to teach Grant about politics. None of which mattered; once Grant was the grand commander he would run the country a different way. He left Rod's room and kept the plastic smile on his face as he answered his own call.

Chapter 54

Recruitment of new members must be handled with the utmost secrecy. Reaching out to people in the homeland puts their lives in great danger.

—Internal memorandum from Affinity

The morning went by quickly. Zack escorted Andrew on the same tour Mia and Carter had been given the day before. The three were so happy to see each other that they didn't pay much attention to the surrounding members of Affinity. After lunch Zack disappeared and Sarah joined them. Carter wandered off to use the restroom and everyone waited for him by the field. Mia was grateful Sarah was escorting them, but she was dying for alone time with Andrew. She had so much to ask him.

"I thought this afternoon we would go see the teachers," Sarah said. "Zack mentioned Carter expressed some interest in that position?"

"Position?" Andrew asked.

"Everyone has a basic job here," Sarah said. "If you decide to stay you'll have to learn a trade. More will be explained at orientation."

Mia wanted to interrupt and let Sarah know Mia planned on telling Andrew everything, but decided it was best to swear Andrew to secrecy.

"When will we have to make this decision?" Andrew asked.

Sarah shrugged. "We assume you're already on board," she said. "And you will be . . . soon."

Sarah flashed a smile and for a moment Mia felt the urge to grab Andrew's hand. She turned away. Mia didn't want to fall into that trap; she had nothing to worry about. Her days of competing with other women over men were long gone, and Sarah was no threat to what she and Andrew had.

Carter appeared in the distance. The three rose, but he didn't quicken his pace at all. When he neared them he held his chin high. Mia could tell something was wrong.

"Do you feel okay?" Andrew asked. Mia was surprised he felt concern for Carter; the two of them were normally at odds.

"I'm fine," Carter said. "Ate too much at breakfast."

"You guys want to head down to the school?" Sarah asked.

She didn't wait for a response and started walking across the field. Carter sped up to keep pace with her. In the distance Mia saw a group of people fighting.

"Should we break that up?" Mia asked.

"It's practice," Sarah said. "Every member of Affinity must know how to defend themselves."

"From what?" Mia asked.

"America knows we exist," Sarah said. "It's necessary we are prepared to take action."

"You think you could beat the American armed services?" Andrew asked.

"They'd never invade outright," Sarah said. "Fifty years ago they sent a convoy to attack us. It was the current grand commander's first act. We lost a lot of members, but the event was highly publicized. The world wanted to attack America over it."

"Did they?" Mia asked.

"No," Sarah said. "We were so close to having every country on the planet invade. The Registry would have been stopped then, but

America claimed it was rogue soldiers, on an unauthorized mission. Then the states of the United Kingdom declared war on each other and that took precedence. Ireland won."

Mia thought about Riley, how her country had grown in size since the Great War. Then she remembered what started this all: Corinna leading her toward a hidden magazine article. Mia had destroyed the pages, not wanting to get caught with them, but she'd memorized every word and remembered it was from the UK. She supposed if they were publishing articles like that, America would have reason for concern.

"A lot of people thought America instigated the UK war, but it could never be proved. Anyhow, we moved to this spot and have been left alone ever since, but all of us are skilled in defense tactics.

"It's not a stretch for the American men who defect to pick them up," Sarah said. "Carter and Andrew, I'm sure you two are capable fighters."

Andrew stopped walking and bent down. He held his hands over his ears. Mia saw him squish his face up. She put her hands over his.

"Come back," she said.

He opened his eyes and looked at her. The pain seemed to vanish.

"What's wrong?" Sarah asked.

"Nothing," Mia said.

Mia looked to Carter for verification. He kept a stone-cold face and his eyes diverted away from the incident.

"I'm fine," Andrew said.

Sarah raised the corner of her mouth and her forehead wrinkled, then she spun back around and continued walking. They cleared the field and started into the jungle on a path. Mia appreciated the shade. Soon the lake Zack mentioned came into view. Mia was sure he had meant to say "pond" though. She could see across to the other side. There was a clay building to their left.

"Once we get inside we'll stand in the back," Sarah said. "The kids might look at you, but try to keep your eyes on the teacher."

They approached the building and Sarah pushed the doors open. It was a giant room. The youngest child looked around five and the eldest was roughly ten. Slowly they turned their heads around and a hush fell over them.

"Ignore our guests," the man said. He was standing at the front of the room.

Mia locked eyes with him. There was an image projected on a giant white board. Mia didn't understand how it was there. She was more interested in the students than the technology. There were boys and girls mixed together.

"Who wants to name the eight old regions?" he asked.

A girl raised her hand.

"Ronnie," he said.

She rose from her seat.

"North America, South America, Antarctica, Europe, Asia, Australia, Latin America, and Africa."

"Very good," he said. "Now the current ones?"

A boy raised his hand. The teacher pointed and he stood up.

"Europe, Asia, Australia, and North America."

"And?" the teacher asked.

"Latin America?"

"Very good," he said. "Does someone want to explain what happened to the other three?"

The first girl raised her hand again; the teacher ignored her.

"Maura," he said. "Why don't you tell us."

Another girl stood up.

"After the Great War, Africa and South America became habitable. Parts of Asia too."

She took a seat.

"You're on track, but the word is 'inhabitable.' The opposite of 'habitable.' Benjamin, will you explain why?"

A small boy stood up from his seat.

"Because people can't live there," he said. "They don't have good water or food. They'd die."

He sat down again.

Mia felt her eyes go wide. These young people knew so much more about the world than she did. It wasn't fair. She felt a hand on her shoulder and looked up to see Andrew. He kept a blank face, but his eyes seemed warm. She turned and walked out the door; he followed her.

Once they were outside she felt like screaming; instead she paced back and forth. Carter and Sarah didn't join them. Andrew stood still with his arms crossed, watching her. Mia knew she'd have to speak first.

"It's not fair," Mia said. "A child knows more than I do."

"Don't you think they're too young to know that sort of information?" Andrew asked.

"Versus learning lies?" Mia asked. "I've never heard the words 'Africa' and 'Australia' before."

Andrew looked away.

"You knew," Mia said. "Nothing in there was new to you?"

"They were possible enemies. I didn't know about the old ones, or the inhabitable stuff, plus those were just regions, not countries."

"And it doesn't bother you?" Mia asked.

Andrew nodded his head. "Of course it does," he said. "But there are more important things to worry about than ancient history."

Then it dawned on Mia: Andrew was right, and they were alone. She felt the anger leave her body.

"Can you remember everything yet?" Mia asked.

Andrew shook his head.

"It's not pleasant to try," he said. "When I see you, part of me still thinks you're a ghost, or that I'm dead and living in some second world."

Mia walked toward him. She lifted her hand and brushed it against his cheek. His eyes locked with hers; they were sharp and his cheek-bones only added to his cold demeanor.

"I promise you," Mia said. "We are very much alive."

His facial expression didn't change, but his eyes broke from hers and he started looking at different parts of her face.

"Are we interrupting?" Sarah asked.

Mia broke eye contact with Andrew. Sarah had a playful smile, while Carter looked up at the sky. Mia didn't respond. She dropped her hand from Andrew's face.

"We're fine," he said.

"I thought we would check out some other areas of Affinity," Sarah said.

She started talking about checking on the older students. Mia tuned her out and kept her eyes on Andrew. He didn't seem interested in returning her gaze. There was so much she wanted to speak with him about—Rex, Affinity, the militia—but it seemed as soon as the chance presented itself, it vanished.

Chapter 55

POLLUTION PLAGUES MOST OF THE WORLD; AMERICA VOTED GREEN-EST COUNTRY ON THE PLANET

—American Gazette

Dinner made Andrew feel like an animal. All of the people of Affinity kept glancing over at their table. Neither Mia nor Carter seemed to mind. Zack and Sarah were nice enough, but Andrew wished he could be alone with Mia and Carter. They needed to discuss Rex and their future plans. Andrew wasn't sure joining another army was the right idea and Affinity seemed like a well-oiled machine.

"You seem nervous," Mia said.

"Stomach is upset," Andrew lied.

All day he'd been having flashbacks to his time in the militia. He kept reaching out to touch Mia, to make sure she wasn't a figment of his imagination. Then he thought about her auction and his anger would flare. It was turning into a cycle. He vowed that she would never come to any harm again.

"Excuse me," Zack said. He stood up from their table and went to the front of the mess hall.

"We are still missing a person," Zack said. "But let's take the time to welcome three people who traveled very far to join us this evening.

I'm sure you have seen them around, but please let me introduce Mia, Carter, and Andrew."

Zack held his hand out toward them. The whole room erupted in applause. Andrew felt a chill run up his spine. They were loud and their claps echoed off the ceiling. The lights started to get bright and Andrew had to close his eyes. The applause started to morph. It was the strange noise and it was deafening.

"Why won't you break?" the sergeant yelled.

Andrew didn't respond. He was having a hard time keeping his eyes open but wouldn't fall to the floor like his body was demanding of him. Not in front of this man.

"Do you want this to stop?" the sergeant yelled.

Andrew's knuckles were turning white. He raised his arm back and charged at the sergeant, but his fist never made contact. Two guards rushed over and held Andrew down to the ground. He struggled against them, but he was too weak. Then the doctor was leaning next to him.

"This will knock him out," he said. "Leave some bread in here, he'll eat it when he wakes up."

Andrew tried hard to kick and pull his arm away from the syringe. It did no good. As soon as the solution was inside his body he went limp on the floor. He felt his body shake before losing consciousness.

"Andrew," Mia said. Her hands were on his arm, shaking him.

He blinked several times, unsure of his surroundings. The applause was gone; nobody was paying any attention to them. People were filing out of the hall.

"You don't look well," Mia said.

"I'm fine," Andrew said.

"Tell me what's wrong," Mia said. "You had the same look earlier today."

Earlier he had flashed back to his training in the militia. Mia was talking to him then, and he'd seen her face vanish; she turned into the general, describing Andrew's new life. A feeling of dread came over him. If he didn't learn how to control his memories, he could hurt someone.

"I need some fresh air," Andrew said.

"I'll come with you," Mia said.

"Stay," Andrew said. "I'll be back soon. I need some alone time. I'm all right, I promise."

Mia looked hurt, but Andrew didn't want her to know how weak he was feeling. He thought about Dr. Drum's offer to help. It had seemed absurd earlier, but now all Andrew could think about was getting back to the infirmary.

Chapter 56

The most severe punishment Affinity will deliver is exile from the community. This may only be issued under extreme circumstances.

—Internal memorandum from Affinity

"Where's he going?" Zack asked.

"He's been through a lot," Mia said. "He needs some time to himself." She wasn't sure if she was trying to convince Zack or herself.

"I think I could use some of that too," Carter said.

He pushed himself up from the table and started for the door.

"Wait," Mia said.

She had let Andrew storm off because she didn't think she could help him, but maybe Carter could.

"Will you try talking with him?" Mia asked. "I mean, the two of you went through something together. Maybe he needs someone to talk with. I don't have a clue what you guys went through or how you're feeling."

"You're right," Carter said. "You don't."

He shook his head and turned around, leaving a stunned Mia standing alone.

"Men," Sarah said. "They think we're the fragile ones."

"Something is off about the two of them," Mia said.

"Well they were held hostage and tortured," Sarah said.

"It's something else," Mia said. "Like they're bothered by different things."

"Let them blow off some steam," Sarah said. "We have something fun planned for *you* now anyway."

Mia spun around to face Sarah. Zack stood up from the table and walked over to the girls.

"I thought you might want to take us for a drive," Zack said.

"Really?" Mia asked. "Isn't it getting late?"

"Not far," Zack said. "We have a couple hours of sunlight left. I want to see your accident site anyway. Rex said he left his truck there and maybe some supplies we can use."

Mia was worried about Carter and Andrew, but they were safe here and she didn't think either would try to leave. She did want to get behind the wheel again. The smile she was holding in came to her face and she nodded her head.

Zack had a vehicle ready down by the entrance to the camp. They stopped by the welcome building first and he went inside.

"Do you drive?" Mia asked.

"No," Sarah said. "Never felt the urge to learn. I'm sure I could figure it out though."

"It's not too hard," Mia said.

Zack came back from the building. He wore a holster over his arm with a handgun tucked inside. He tossed Sarah a matching belt.

"Sorry," Zack said. "You don't get one tonight."

"I don't want one," Mia said. Her experience with guns wasn't pleasant. "Why do we need those anyway?"

"Protocol," Zack said. "We always leave the camp armed."

"Do you think someone is going to attack you?" Mia asked.

"Guatemala is a pretty civilized country," Zack said. "But there aren't really laws or law enforcement here. We've run into trouble with people trying to rob us before. Think of it more as a formality."

"Just don't shoot me," Mia said.

"All members are trained in arms," Sarah said. "There's a shooting range on the other side of the camp. It can be pretty fun, letting off some steam."

"Have you ever shot anyone before?" Mia asked.

Sarah laughed and shook her head. Mia bet that if she had, her attitude about guns would be a bit different. Sarah went into the backseat and Zack jumped in the passenger side. Mia climbed in the driver's seat.

"Show us what you got," Zack said.

"It's not fingerprint coded?" Mia asked.

Zack shook his head.

"Too many people here," he said. "Any finger will start it. That's why someone always waits by the car when we take them out—no solo trips."

Mia pressed her finger down and the engine came to life. It was a quiet hum.

"Is there backup fuel in here?" Mia asked.

"Don't need it," Zack said. "This is the wave of the future. Totally electric cars. This guy can run for five hours before the battery dies out, and we have a battery pack in the back to give it a recharge."

Mia hit the buttons and they started down the drive.

"I'm surprised you know about that," Zack said. "In America the cars are strictly gas."

"Why is that?" Mia asked.

"America still has access to oil," Zack said. "They're the number one oil-producing country in the world. The electric vehicle is one of the few inventions that didn't come out of America. They have no need for them there."

"Before the Great War almost all cars were gas," Sarah said. "Most of the oil came from the Middle East."

Middle East. That rang a bell. Mia remembered seeing a headline on the Internet about America brokering peace there.

"Did the Middle East run out of oil?" Mia asked.

Zack and Sarah were quiet.

"I'm sure it's still there," Sarah said. "But not worth the risk of trying to recover it. Heavy radiation out there."

"What do you mean?" Mia asked.

"That's ground zero for the Great War," Sarah said. "It was actually over oil."

"But I read America brought peace there," Mia said.

"Don't believe anything you ever read in America," Zack said. "The Middle East is a barren wasteland. After the war the radiation went south, taking out Africa, which was pretty destroyed from the war too."

"Is that what happened to the rest of the regions?" Mia asked. "The ones the kids were talking about today?"

"With the exception of Antarctica," Sarah said.

"What started the war? Which countries? Over oil?" Mia asked.

"Let's focus on your driving," Zack said. "You have the rest of your life to learn world history."

Mia realized she was driving slowly. Being behind the wheel did bring a level of comfort. She pressed her foot down on the accelerator and felt her ponytail fly behind her in the wind. The simple act gave her some peace of mind as she drove them back down the mountain.

Chapter 57

We should never be afraid of foreigners; they should be afraid of us.

—American Gazette

It took longer for Andrew to walk back to the infirmary than he thought it would. He spent the time rehearsing what he was going to say to Dr. Drum. Now that he had made it here, he forgot everything he'd planned. Andrew swung the front door open and was surprised to see Dr. Drum sitting on a couch in the front room and Rex sitting next to her. Both of them stood up.

"Andrew," she said. "You're back. Do you feel all right?"

"Are you two alone here?" Andrew asked.

"I sent the technicians back to the group," Katie said. "I thought I would keep Rex company."

Andrew didn't like that. He was giving Rex some freedom, but leaving him alone with the doctor wasn't on his list.

"You shouldn't be alone with her," Andrew said.

"It's better that I let her stay by herself in an empty building away from everyone else?" Rex asked.

"Wow," Katie said. "You two have some strange ideas. I might be female, but remember, we're not in America. I'm capable of anything either of you are. I don't need someone to tell me what I can and cannot do."

Rex's face did not relax. Andrew kept his eyes glued to the large man.

"Is that what you came all the way out here for?" Katie asked. "To check on me?"

"No," Andrew said. "Can we talk in private?"

"I was going up to my room anyway," Rex said. "I never went to sleep today and I could really use some. Good night, Katie."

Andrew cringed at the way he said her name. He couldn't lose focus though. He did have a reason for coming here tonight.

"Please," Katie said. "Sit down."

Andrew walked over to the couch and had a seat.

"I want you to give me something," Andrew said. "I was thinking . . . if drugs did this to me, maybe there's something that can fix me. Reverse everything that happened."

"Back up," Katie said. "What makes you think you need fixing?"

"I've been having flashbacks," Andrew said. "To my time with the militia."

"What are you remembering?"

"They played noise, loud," Andrew said. "Then they would check on me and inject me with medications, leave me a small piece of food for when I woke up, but I was always hungry. It felt like I never slept."

"Sleep and food deprivation, manipulation of your senses," Katie said. "I have to say it's a good sign this is coming back to you."

"No," Andrew said. "It's not. I feel like I'm slipping into another reality when it happens."

"I was concerned you weren't going to be able to form new long-term memories," Katie said. "This is positive. If your old ones are coming back, that means your new ones aren't in jeopardy."

"Can't you give me something to speed this up?" Andrew said.

"It's a natural process," Katie said.

"I don't want to hurt anyone," Andrew said.

"What makes you think you will?"

"Just a feeling," Andrew said. "I go back to that spot. I react like I wanted to then. If I'm alone with the wrong person I might attack . . ."

"The odds of that happening are slim to none."

"But they still exist," Andrew said. "Please, you must be able to give me something."

"I want to tell you a story first," she said.

Andrew was willing to listen to anything if she made the flashbacks stop.

"During the Great War, a lot of people lost their lives. North America was the only continent that didn't see battles," Katie said. "A lot of Americans died fighting, but the ones who made it home returned to a horrible surprise."

"What?" Andrew asked.

"The same thing they saw overseas," Katie said. "Death and destruction. The world was in ruins, so nobody paid much attention. They had their own countries to fix. Rumors fly around about what happened."

"So nobody knows?" Andrew asked.

"I didn't say that," she said. "America was on the forefront of modern technology. They always have been; the refrigerator was an American invention, along with countless others. The brilliant minds left at home during the war were trying to create a superweapon. Do you know what biological warfare is?"

Andrew shook his head.

"Countries used to think about releasing a disease on their enemies, one that had no cure and would take out the whole population."

"So America released one at home by accident?" Andrew asked.

"Even way back then the world knew this was too dangerous," she said. "What if it spread and took out the whole planet? But all is fair in war, so America was trying to prepare for an attack like that. You know how people receive vaccines? Shots you probably got when you were young and some boosters along the way?"

Andrew nodded.

"It was that," she said. "A single dose of medicine that wards off fevers, infections, viruses, and bacteria. You can still get sick, but nothing like people in the past were scared of. Back then the flu could kill you."

The flu. Andrew was familiar with that term. The government had found a cure. Now most diseases were hereditary and didn't strike until old age. If someone got an infection, all it took was some medicine to clear it up. Katie continued with the story.

"America developed a cure. One shot and biological warfare wouldn't be a threat. It passed with flying colors. They sent it out to everyone who was at home first, in case America was attacked. People were lining up at clinics everywhere. But the scientists were under such pressure to do this quickly that the drug wasn't well tested.

"Your leg got a scratch and the blood wouldn't clot because of a drug in your system," Katie said. "Now it's a minor side effect, but before this medicine actually made blot clotting impossible. Anyone who had received a shot was in grave danger of bleeding to death even from minor injuries. There was no cure."

"So what happened?" Andrew asked.

"People died," Katie said. "Others went crazy with fear and locked themselves inside. Nobody wanted to have children because it meant a sure death for the mother. There was a fear the population would disappear. America would be no more."

"How did they stop it?" Andrew asked.

"They didn't," Katie said. "All those affected were gone and it wasn't communicable.

"The reason I wanted to tell you this story is because sometimes a quick fix isn't the best answer," Katie said. "If you want help getting through this, drugs aren't a solution."

"What is?" Andrew asked.

"Talking," Katie said. "You can come see me and we can work through your memories together."

"Why isn't this happening to Carter?" Andrew asked.

"Maybe it is," she said. "Did you try asking him?"

Andrew shook his head.

"People react to trauma in different ways," Katie said. "But talking it through always helps. We can start tonight if you want."

It was hard for Andrew to admit he wanted the doctor's help, but that concern wasn't as large as his fear that he risked hurting Mia. He nodded his head.

"Tell me everything that you can remember," she said. "Once you get to a point where your head starts to ache and the noise comes back, we will stop. I promise, nothing bad will happen to you here."

Andrew took a deep breath before starting in on his story.

Chapter 58

Mia slowed the vehicle down. She didn't stop completely but was sure they were coming up on the break in the trees. She tried to look at the ground ahead for the broken auto-drive.

"Affinity doesn't use the auto-drive feature?" Mia asked.

"That uses satellites," Zack said. "A lot of these roads are unmarked; it wouldn't do much good up here."

Mia had no clue what a satellite was but felt like she had learned enough new information for today. Then she spotted the broken piece of equipment in the road. She looked to her left and saw the break in the jungle.

"It's up there," Mia said.

She pulled the car over to the side and killed the engine.

"Sarah, you guard the car," Zack said.

All three stepped out. Sarah stayed by the vehicle and Mia walked Zack toward the trees. The sun was starting to set, lighting the greens with an iridescent glow. Mia walked down the path and it wasn't long before Rex's truck came into view, or at least what was left of it.

The windows were smashed in, pieces of paneling were missing, the hood was popped open, and the insides were gone. It was destroyed.

"Someone beat us here," Zack said.

Mia ignored him. She walked over toward the cliff; the tire tracks were still visible. She closed her eyes and saw Rex crouched down and the militiaman reaching for his gun. Mia heard a weapon cock. Her eyes flew open. That was a real sound. She turned to see Zack holding his hands in the air, backing away from the truck. Three men came out from the trees; they were wearing a familiar uniform.

"Where is our vehicle?" the man asked.

Zack stood next to Mia now.

"Wherever you left it," Zack said.

The three men were far more interested in Zack; no eyes were on her. The men kept moving closer and Mia stopped backing up. One was right next to her now. She knew this was her chance. She took a moment and worked out a strategy, like Riley had trained her to do.

Mia leaned forward and stomped on the back of the man's heel. He let out a wail and Mia jumped behind him. Some gunshots went off and she felt his body move, like he was a human shield. Zack got his chance and Mia saw him bring out his gun and fire two quick shots.

"Run!" Zack said.

Mia let the man's body drop to the ground and didn't look back to see whether the other two were dead. Zack moved fast and Mia struggled to keep up. Sarah was standing in the back of her car with her gun drawn. Zack ran to the passenger side.

"You want me to drive?" Mia yelled.

"You're unarmed," he said. "There might be more of them."

Mia turned the car on and started back toward Affinity. She didn't waste any time driving slow. They sped up the hills, but one glance in the rearview mirror showed a car coming up to the spot they had just left.

"Sarah, stay down," Zack said.

He stood up and aimed his gun behind them. More death was coming. Mia felt her fingers going numb. These people chasing her had gone through the same training as Carter and Andrew; she didn't think they deserved to die.

"Are you going to kill them?" Mia yelled.

"Not unless I have to," Zack said.

Mia tried to look in her mirror, but the car wasn't behind them yet. She pushed the accelerator down and they started going faster.

"Don't let us fall off the road," Sarah said.

"I know what I'm doing," Mia said.

She hoped she could outrun whoever was trying to tail them. It didn't take long until they were on the main road back toward Affinity. She couldn't hear anything over the wind. Zack turned around and sat back down. He didn't put his gun away.

"Did we lose them?" Mia asked.

"I'm not sure they were ever after us," Zack said. "That was a poor job of keeping up."

"Did you kill those men?" Mia asked.

Zack didn't respond. Mia took that as a yes.

"Slow down," Zack said. "Pull over."

Mia slammed on the brakes and they all went forward. Then the car was still. Her fingernails were digging into the bottom of her palm from gripping the wheel too hard.

"Friends of yours?" Zack asked. "They had matching uniforms."

"The militia," Mia said. "What were they doing there?"

"It looked like a trap to me," he said. "Waiting for someone to come back for Rex's belongings."

"Are you two all right?" Sarah asked.

Mia nodded.

"That was an impressive move," Zack said. "Where did you learn how to do that? And how did you know I'd fire?"

"You're a trained gunman," Mia said. "I knew you needed a window."

Zack's breathing slowed down and he closed his mouth.

"Keep this between us," Zack said. "I need to bring it up to ET before we alert everyone."

Sarah nodded.

"Try to look calm," Zack said.

Mia took a few breaths before starting the car again. She didn't know what would be worse, keeping the militia's presence hidden from Andrew and Carter or what would happen once the two of them found out about it. Mia had a feeling this wasn't the last time she'd have a run-in with this group.

Chapter 59

The American government wants its people free and happy. That is why there is as little involvement as possible in a citizen's everyday life.

—American Gazette

The sun shone down on Andrew. Even in the morning its rays were powerful in the tropical heat. He was glad they were starting orientation today. He'd had enough of wandering aimlessly around Affinity, following Sarah or Zack to the next work spot, none of which offered much of interest to Andrew. He glanced over at Mia. She wore the same worried expression he had seen on her face over the past twenty-four hours. Carter was walking several feet in front of them, his head held high. The three of them hadn't been talking much at all. When they were alone it was like everyone just wanted to sleep. Andrew didn't want any questions about the state of his emotions, but he wondered what Carter and Mia were hiding.

"What's wrong?" Andrew asked.

Mia turned her head toward him and put a smile on her face.

"Nothing," Mia said.

Andrew frowned.

"I'm a little nervous about orientation," Mia said. "Choosing a division."

It seemed decided that they were staying here, though none of them had discussed the topic. Andrew wasn't sure where else they would go anyway. He still believed Mia was hiding something, but she wasn't questioning his disappearances to speak with Katie and he didn't want her to ask, so he dropped the subject.

He hated to admit it, but after two nights of speaking with the doctor he was already feeling a little better. The headaches still came when he thought back to his time in the militia, but he was getting better at controlling his memories.

They walked down the hill and made it to the entrance of Affinity. Rex was standing outside waiting for them. He didn't smile. Instead he wore the same blank face as Carter.

"Don't let him get to you," Andrew said.

"I think Affinity has the right to know what type of person he really is," Mia said.

Andrew and Carter had convinced her he deserved a second chance, but she wasn't on board yet. Andrew didn't think Mia would ever understand Rex the same way he and Carter did. Andrew saw the man as a possible future version of himself and part of him needed to believe Rex was capable of redemption.

Mia took the lead and pushed past Rex, opening the door to the room. Carter paused to talk with the man; Andrew decided it was best to follow Mia.

"Give him a chance," Andrew said.

She frowned, but before they could continue the conversation Zack popped his head into the room.

"Right on time," he said. "Have a seat."

There was a large table. Andrew and Mia both pulled out chairs and sat down. Rex and Carter were in the room now and they did the same.

"Welcome to Affinity," Zack said. "Today we're going to fill you in on some details of our society, our goals, and what will be required of you if you choose to stay."

Zack was energetic. Andrew could tell he enjoyed his occupation.

"We are a free society," he said. "Everyone here is your equal. There are no divisions on the basis of gender. You must treat everyone accordingly."

Andrew wondered how hard that was for Rex. Zack opened his mouth to continue, but before he could speak the door swung open and Zack stopped. Andrew turned around to see a woman at the back of the room. She was older, her hair pulled up in a tight bun.

"Good morning, Zack," she said.

"Eleanor," he said.

"It's come to my attention that two of our newest recruits require a private orientation," she said. "I'd like to take them to my office, if that's all right with you."

"Why . . . er . . . of course," Zack said.

The woman moved to the front with Zack. He bowed his head. The speech Zack had just delivered didn't apply to this woman; she was obviously Zack's superior.

"Amelia," she said. "And Millard. Please follow me."

Rex and Mia started to stand up.

"No," Andrew said.

Mia looked down at him. Her eyes told Andrew she didn't mind leaving. She wore a small smile of reassurance.

"I'm not leaving you," Andrew said. His voice was firm.

She bent down and whispered in his ear, "We're always together."

Andrew didn't respond. He looked at her; she wore a soft expression. Her lack of argument told him she wanted to follow this woman, even if it meant being alone with Rex.

"I promise you she will return to the group by the end of the day's activities," Eleanor said. "Zack, please continue."

She walked toward the door and didn't turn around to make sure Rex and Mia were following. Andrew felt like she had brought iciness to the room. The doors closed and they were gone.

"Can you believe Rex's real name is Millard?" Zack asked.

Carter let out a little laugh. Andrew turned his attention toward Zack. He wanted some answers.

"Who was that?"

"Let's get back to orientation," Zack said. "By the end of the session all your questions should be answered, including her role in Affinity."

With few other options, Andrew gave Zack his full attention. Whoever that woman was, Mia didn't mind following her; Andrew needed to focus on that. Mia was turning into a capable person, and she deserved some deference.

Chapter 60

The world is excited for the imminent announcement about Grant Marsden's future. Will he be our next grand commander?
—American Gazette

The boy was still in denial. Grant could tell after yesterday's phone call. He didn't want to discuss the terms of his surrender yet. Grant had anticipated that, but Roderick's clock was already ticking. He had a few hours to kill until the boy's next phone call, but Grant wasn't in the mood to work. It was the lack of a phone call from Rex that was bothering him.

Rex was as loyal as they come, and it was unlike him to wait this long to check in. Grant would miss him if he were dead—at least Grant thought he would. It would be an annoyance replacing him, one Grant didn't want to deal with at the moment. He didn't want to call Rex. Even though he had technology masking the source of his calls, if there were any way to trace a phone call to Mexico from Grant he would have to face some questions. But not knowing was getting to Grant. He decided if there was a safe place to make the phone call it was from his systems. He picked up the phone, took a breath, and dialed out. The phone rang.

"Hello," a voice said.

Grant didn't recognize whoever was on the other end.

"Hello," Grant said.

The two were silent. They were at a standoff; Grant didn't want to show weakness.

"Your friend has caused me a lot of trouble," the person said.

Grant didn't respond.

"I know he's your friend since this is the only phone number stored in his phone," the voice said. "Do you care about him?"

"He's a good employee," Grant said.

"So you sent him down here?"

"To track something," Grant said. "That was stolen from me."

"Well, now he has stolen from me," the voice said. "Who am I speaking with?"

"That's not a concern of yours," Grant said. "Is my employee dead?"

"Not yet," he said. "Soon. We know where he is."

"How do you have his phone?" Grant asked.

"He and those three clever imbeciles think they're safe," he said. "But I am coming for them. Unless you are willing to pay for your employee's transgressions?"

"Tell me something," Grant said. "How is someone a clever imbecile? It's a contradiction."

"They're clever because the four of them managed to screw me over, but imbeciles because they think they can get away with it."

"What makes you think the four of them are a team?"

"He saved the life of one of the men," the man said. "Andrew Simpson may think he has cheated death, but it is still coming his way if I do not receive my goods."

This was news to Grant. Rex was working with Amelia and the boys. Grant felt a bit of rage bubble but swallowed it back down. He did instruct Rex to keep their unit intact. The man on the phone was of no concern to Grant, and Rex was more than capable of taking care of himself.

"Consider him fired," Grant said. "Feel free to kill him."

The man on the other end started to talk, but Grant had had enough. He had heard all the information this man had. Grant hung up and dropped his phone on the table.

I hope you slept well?" the host asked.

Grant nodded. The food on the enormous dining room table smelled wonderful. The table looked different in the light of day, especially without the dead body slumped over.

"I have a team of groomers coming over this morning," he said. "If you're going to work for me you have to present yourself better."

Grant took a seat. He started to reach for some food.

"Uh-uh," the host said. "Learn some manners. Sit straight up, put the napkin in your lap, keep your elbows down. Don't they teach you any of this in those schools?"

Grant looked at the man with confusion.

"It is polite to answer all questions asked of you," he said.

"No," Grant said.

"Maybe this was a mistake and I should just kill you," he said.

Grant didn't respond to the man's threat. He wasn't about to live his life in constant fear that it could be ended in a moment. The host smiled at Grant's lack of reaction.

"You have something that none of the others had," he said. "I like to have an apprentice. Normally I choose someone right out of service; my last young man didn't fare too well and I am looking for a replacement. It's you."

Grant stayed silent.

"Aren't you going to accept?"

"You didn't make an offer," Grant said. "You gave an order."

The host smiled.

"My name is Victor Marsden," he said. "I've decided you can call me Victor."

Grant nodded. The door to the dining room opened up and a young woman came in. She was in her twenties, with beautiful long blond hair and bright blue eyes. Grant felt his back straighten as soon as she walked in. Her eyes were glued to the floor. She pulled out the chair next to Victor and took a seat.

"Grant, please let me introduce you to my wife," Victor said. "She was good last night, so I'm allowing her to eat at the table with us this morning. Her name is Daphne."

She still didn't look up from the table. Grant watched her cast-down eyes; they were filled with fear. Grant tried to cock his head to get a better look.

"Pay her no attention," he said. "Please, Daphne, serve us now."

She rose from her seat and picked up one of the dishes from the table. Then she started spooning out three portions.

"You seem fascinated with Daphne," he said.

"I'm not used to being in the presence of women," Grant said.

"It's easy to adjust to them," Victor said. "Just forget they exist."

He smiled at his wife. She nodded her head, but Grant could see she was holding in her emotions. Daphne's face was still, but her eyes gave her away. She looked like a bomb, ready to explode. Grant thought Victor should keep her away from knives.

"Let's discuss your new position," Victor said. "For the first few weeks you will tail me. Everything I do, you do. Everywhere I go, you will accompany me. Then I can see your weaknesses and strengths."

Grant nodded his head. He wasn't certain what Victor's occupation was or what Grant was about to learn. At the moment he didn't care. Daphne held much more fascination for him.

Chapter 61

In order to stop the Registry, Affinity must be stronger than the enemy. If that includes sacrificing our own, so be it.

—Internal memorandum from Affinity

The walk was quiet. Mia didn't want to strike up a conversation with Rex, and Eleanor seemed unapproachable. They were going up a path, higher into the mountains. Every time a building came into view Mia hoped they would stop, but instead Eleanor kept on walking. The air felt thinner up here; Mia couldn't tell if they had been walking for thirty minutes or an hour, but either way it would be difficult to make her way back to Andrew. Finally Eleanor took a turn. They were off the main path and into the jungle. Mia was happy to have the shade. A fence came into view; there was a keypad and Eleanor pushed her palm against it. Mia heard a buzz fade away and the fence open. Eleanor walked through and Rex and Mia followed. When the gate shut the buzz returned. While Affinity felt like an open community, this place was more like a prison.

There was a larger building in the center of a clearing and several smaller ones surrounding it. The trees weren't completely cleared away. Eleanor made her way to the larger building; another palm scan and a door opened up. They walked inside and Mia was happy to feel the blast of air-conditioning on her face.

They entered a large room that must have taken up the entire first floor. There was a giant conference table in the center and screens on all the walls. They walked toward the table, passing a door leading to a flight of stairs.

"Please have a seat," Eleanor said.

Mia pulled out a chair and Rex sat opposite her. The table was elegant. Mia thought it belonged in a fancy office more than a room in the middle of the jungle. The chairs had wheels and were large and comfortable. None of this fit in with the rest of Affinity.

"You are in the External Tactics division of Affinity," Eleanor said. "Do both of you know what we are?"

"Yes," Rex said.

"I assume Dr. Drum filled you in?" she said to Rex.

"Yes," Rex said.

"And you learned of us from young Sarah?" Eleanor asked Mia.

"Yes," Mia said.

Sarah had told her to act surprised, but Mia didn't think it was worth trying to lie to Eleanor. The woman carried a level of intensity Mia had never seen before; she would likely be able to read any lies. She walked over to the table with a tray of water glasses. She handed them out before having a seat.

"Let's start with Millard," she said.

Mia didn't notice a remote, but one of the screens came on. There was a picture of Rex.

"How do you know my real name?" Rex asked.

Eleanor smiled and ignored Rex's question. Sarah had mentioned ET had access to impressive technology.

"You served multiple terms in the American military," she said. "Then you were head of security for Grant Marsden."

The screen switched. There was a box with a giant question mark.

"Mia," she said. "You have been much more difficult to find information on. Your companion Andrew CMW1408 is impossible to track, since his release from the orphanage, because America doesn't keep records on their young men. Carter Rowe, on the other hand, was raised by his father, who recently passed away in a car accident. Miles away from the spot where Mr. Marsden's wife lost her life."

The screen switched again. There was a picture of Grant on the screen.

"There is much to be said about this man," she said. "His recent tragedy is big news to the American people. However, it is impossible to find a picture of his wife or confirmation of her name. At first we thought it might be a publicity stunt to gain public appeal, and there was no wife."

The screen changed. This time it was Mia's Registry photo.

"One of our members uploaded this to us," she said. "It was circulated around the city of Saint Louis, along with a hotline to call regarding your disappearance. As far as I can tell it is the only photo of you in existence."

Mia hated that photo.

"The American government is going to great lengths to make sure you don't exist," Eleanor said. "If you came forward as Mia Morrissey there would be no photo or person to back up your claim. Why is that?"

Mia was uncomfortable. Eleanor waited for a response.

"Because I made it out of the country," Mia said. "My story might inspire other girls to run."

"We know you are Grant Marsden's wife," Eleanor said. "And I think Millard was sent down here to execute you; why he hasn't remains a mystery."

Grant did say he had friends in the government, but Mia thought he was a private citizen. She didn't know why her identity required erasing.

"I am no longer in Grant Marsden's employ," Rex said. "I am looking for a new life to lead."

"And you care about stopping the atrocities happening in America?" Eleanor asked.

"No," Rex said. "I am a soldier looking for a new general. Affinity has shown me respect and I would like to serve them in return."

"Why should we trust you?" Eleanor asked. "I believe Mia does not."

"Because being in Grant's employment for so long has taught me many personal things about him. I know his habits, his weaknesses. I can be a great asset."

"How do I know you're not still working for him?"

"If I was, I would have killed her," Rex said.

The room went quiet.

"Grant Marsden is cruel," Rex said. "He is on his way to political power. I have been growing uncomfortable living under his leadership. My plan was to make it out of the country, to help Mia, and to make a new life for myself. Somewhere else."

"Why help Mia?"

"I felt I owed her that," Rex said. "I don't enjoy death. It is part of the job, but I take no pleasure from it. My actions resulted in the death of one of her companions. If I was going to live a new life I had to make amends."

Mia was shocked. Her heart was breaking again, thinking about Whitney's death. Rex had a heart? He felt guilty for Saint Louis. Mia didn't know how to feel about his admission. While he was trying to make it right, Whitney was still gone.

"So you're not passionate about stopping America," she said. "How do you feel about stopping Grant Marsden?"

"The man deserves no respect," Rex said. "He shows none to any other people, regardless of their status in the world. His actions involving Mia's disappearance were poorly planned and executed. Above that he fails to admit fault and learn from his mistakes. He is indecisive. If Grant Marsden rises to power America will burn to the ground and destroy the rest of the world in the process. I do have a problem with that."

The screen changed again to show Grant's face.

"We are anticipating an announcement," Eleanor said. "That Grant Marsden will be declared the next grand commander of America."

"No," Mia said.

Rex was right about one thing: if Grant led the country, that would mean a darker, harsher reality for America. Mia didn't want to imagine the possibility that her home country could become an even more horrible place to live.

"We need to stop him," Mia said.

"How?" Eleanor asked.

"I can come forward," Mia said. "If I'm still alive it will destroy his credibility."

"But how do we prove you are who you say you are?"

"He has a file on her in his house. Complete with pictures, fingerprints, her blood analysis," Rex said.

"Wouldn't he destroy it?" Eleanor asked.

"Not a chance," Rex said. "He won't stop trying to destroy her. If that file disappeared he would be throwing away any leads and any way of gathering information on her whereabouts."

"Interesting development," Eleanor said.

"You two are discussing me like I'm not in the room," Mia said.

"The two of you are a great asset," Eleanor said. "During your tenure at Affinity I would like to invite you to join the External Tactics division."

Mia's heart jumped into her throat. This was the branch Sarah had warned her about. Rex agreed quickly, but Mia wasn't sure this was the life she was after. She thought about learning computers with Sarah or driving for Zack. Those options still left Mia with a somewhat normal life.

"I need to think about it," Mia said.

The corner of Eleanor's lips curled upward.

"Take all the time you need. The offer does not expire," she said. "I think that is all for today."

Eleanor rose from the table. Rex and Mia stood as well. They walked back outside in silence. Once they reached the fence Eleanor placed her palm on the keypad and the fence opened again.

"Mia, can you make it down the mountain by yourself?" she asked.

"You're not coming with me?" Mia asked.

"Rex made his decision, and I'd like to spend some time picking his brain," she said. "We need to move forward with our plans. Once you have made your choice, please let Zack know."

Mia felt out of sorts. She nodded and headed through the gates and back to the main path. Part of her was angry she wasn't asked to stay with Rex and strategize on how to stop Grant. But then she remembered she had been asked; it was she who had turned down the opportunity. Mia had an important question to ask herself, one whose answer she was unsure of. What would be better: living a life aiding a noble cause or living a life fighting for the noble cause?

Chapter 62

*As soon as a member is no longer capable of completing all the
physical requirements of Affinity, he or she will transfer into
inactive status, unable to hold positions of authority.*

                              —*Internal memorandum from Affinity*

"I don't want to take orders," Andrew said.

Mia walked back into the meeting room, a little shocked Carter
and Andrew were still seated.

"It's not like that," Zack said. "We have to defend the camp. That
means learning combat skills. There are no sergeants or generals.
Everyone must go to training though."

"It sounds like an army to me," Carter said.

"We'll check it out this afternoon," Zack said. "And you'll see
then."

None of them noticed Mia walk in. Then Zack looked up and saw
her.

"Mia," he said.

Andrew and Carter turned around to see her. She saw some relief
on Andrew's face, but Carter seemed indifferent.

"Where's Rex?" Zack asked.

"He stayed with Eleanor," she said.

"We were about to break for lunch," Zack said. "Meet me in the fields in two hours. We'll catch a training session and you two will understand."

Carter and Andrew stood up. Zack went to the back of the room with a stack of papers.

"How was your morning?" Mia asked. She tried her best to smile.

Before either of the men could respond, Zack spoke. "Mia, could I speak with you in private?"

"Wait for me outside?" Mia asked.

Carter didn't respond, he just walked toward the door.

"What is with all the secrecy?" Andrew asked.

"It's not secret," Mia said. "Just a job offer."

Andrew raised an eyebrow.

"I'll tell you everything after dinner," Mia said. "When we have some free time."

"I'm not free then," Andrew said.

Mia knew he had disappeared last night after dinner too.

"I can come with you," Mia said.

"No," Andrew said. His voice was sharp. "I mean, after everything I need some space. We'll talk about it later tonight?"

Mia nodded. Andrew had been known to want alone time, but Mia didn't know why he would have it prescheduled. He raised his hand and gave her arm a quick squeeze for reassurance before walking out. Once his hand was gone Mia looked down at where he had touched her. It was tingling. Even with everything that was happening he could still ignite something in her. She didn't want the feelings to fade.

"Mia?" Zack asked, breaking her out of her trance.

She walked up toward him.

"Did Eleanor ask about the militia?"

"No," Mia said. After this morning Joseph's militia didn't seem as big a priority as yesterday.

"Good," Zack said. "ET was informed, but they haven't commented."

"Why is that good?"

"They're leaving it to Internal to handle," Zack said.

"Is there any news?" Mia asked.

"There is a convoy," Zack said. "Stationed right outside our borders. They won't step foot onto the land though. They must have some type of electronic sensors. They're staying just beyond the view of the cameras."

"How did they find us?"

"I think we were followed," Zack said. "Remember how we heard the car, but then it never attacked? Stayed out of sight?"

Mia nodded.

"Did you give any more thought as to what they want?" Zack asked.

"I still think it's me, Carter, and Andrew," Mia said. "We escaped."

"No," Zack said. "That doesn't make sense. You're just three people and they are a business almost. It would be a waste of their resources to track you. Did Carter or Andrew take something from them?"

"The clothes and the car," Mia said.

"We searched the vehicle," Zack said. "Nothing important in there."

"They asked about it though," Mia said.

"If we give it back my guess is they'd leave us alone," Zack said. "I still have the ban in place on anyone leaving camp, but soon the people will have to know what's happening."

"Do you think the militia will attack Affinity?" Mia asked.

"I don't know," Zack said. "They'd regret it if they did, but I'd like to avoid that at all costs."

"Why would they regret it?" Mia asked. "Aren't you scared? What if they win?"

"Let me show you something," Zack said.

He pushed open a side door and walked into a computer room. There were screens all over the wall.

"The whole jungle is wired," Zack said. "Everyone here is a trained fighter. If they step foot on our land in a hostile manner we can detonate bombs. We know our jungle. The rest will infiltrate from the trees. Even if they sent all their forces here we could still take them out."

"But your land would be destroyed," Mia said. "And they're trained too. What if someone from Affinity is hurt in the process?"

"That's why I want to figure out how to make them go away," Zack said.

"Did you try talking to them?" Mia asked. "Point-blank ask these men what they want?"

"Too risky," Zack said. "Our security system can halt all electronic devices that cross the threshold, but they can't stop bullets. I'm not sending anyone down there; it's too big of a risk. I was hoping they would send one man in here, but so far nothing. I'm going to drive down there soon, so I can get a better look and make sure their numbers aren't growing."

"What happens if they are?" Mia asked.

"Then we will prepare for battle," Zack said.

"Maybe I shouldn't have been so aggressive," Mia said. "When they had their guns on you. If we'd only talked to them then instead of attacking . . ."

"You did the right thing," Zack said. "When someone has a weapon pointed at you it's the only way to react."

"I'm having a hard time keeping this from Andrew," Mia said.

"Don't tell him," Zack said. "He's still recovering. Finding out the men who tortured him are so close might make him snap."

"Snap?" Mia asked.

"If I were him I would want some revenge," Zack said. "Wouldn't you?"

Grant. He had tortured Mia in a way. Chased her across the country, taken her friends' lives and almost her own. Mia had the chance to get some revenge; by joining ET she could accomplish that goal. Revenge wasn't what she was after though. Mia wanted a stable, normal life, away from him and the horrors of her past.

"They're waiting for me outside," Mia said.

"I'll see you at the fields this afternoon," Zack said. "Keep thinking about the militia. What could they want?"

Mia nodded. She went back into the main room and out the front doors.

"You're popular today," Carter said.

He was leaning up against the building. Andrew was standing next to him.

"Zack wanted to know about Eleanor," Mia said.

"What about Eleanor?" Andrew asked.

"I'm really hungry," Mia said. "Can we go eat?"

Andrew nodded and Carter kicked off against the building. Mia knew Andrew wanted to protect her. He'd always made that clear. Now Mia had the opportunity to protect Andrew, but keeping this information from him still felt a lot like lying.

Chapter 63

All American refugees must be given asylum in Affinity camps. They may not be permitted to join our ranks, but we will give them the chance to prove themselves regardless of any previous affiliations.

—*Internal memorandum from Affinity*

Lunch was awkward. Carter, who normally provided the conversation topics, was staying very quiet. Mia didn't want to accidentally tell Andrew about the militia or go into her meeting this morning, leaving little to discuss. Once they were done eating the group left the mess hall.

"We still have an hour," Carter said. "I'm going to take a walk around."

"Do you want some company?" Mia asked.

"No," Carter said. "I'll see you two at the fields."

He ran off, leaving Andrew and Mia alone.

"Just the two of us," Mia said. "It's been a while."

Andrew's eyes shifted back and forth.

"Are your memories coming back?" Mia asked.

Andrew nodded. "Not all of them," he said. "I still don't remember you on the beach, or my arrival at the militia camp. It's like they're coming in backward too."

"And the headaches?" Mia asked.

"Better," he said.

"Good," Mia said.

She knew his memory of kissing her was gone. She wondered if Andrew remembered walking in on Mia and Carter. That was the night Mia's world collapsed for the second time.

"What are your thoughts on Affinity?" Mia asked.

"Where else would we go?" Andrew asked.

Mia shrugged.

"Travel the world," Mia said. "Just the two of us. Start a life together."

Andrew's eyes widened. Mia wondered if his feelings for her were lost as well.

"Could you do that?" Andrew asked. "Knowing what you know now, could you walk away from the fight?"

"Do you think Affinity will win?" Mia asked. "Stop the Registry and mandatory service?"

"I'm not sure," Andrew said. "And I'm not talking about me. I'm talking about you."

"What do you mean?"

"Mia, you care about people," he said. "Would you be happy knowing there was suffering going on in the world? When you had a chance to help stop it, even if you were doing something small like cooking food for a group of rebels, could you walk away?"

Mia didn't have a response. Cooking food didn't seem like a good way to help when she had the option of contributing so much more.

"What I'm trying to say," Andrew said, "is that I know you. If we left this place you would be miserable."

"I'd be miserable without you," Mia said.

Andrew smiled and kicked the ground a little. He put his hands in his pockets and looked at the sky.

"I'm not good at this," he said.

"At what?"

"That night in Saint Louis," he said. "When you tried to kiss me I should have let you."

"You did," Mia said.

Andrew's eyebrows scrunched up. His lips pressed together in a quizzical look.

"You kissed me once," Mia said. "It was right before Grant attacked."

Mia hoped this would bring some comfort to Andrew.

"So you don't need to worry about being bad at this," Mia said. "You showed me how you feel already."

Andrew's lips flattened out and his eyebrows relaxed. Instead of seeming calmer though it was like a new anger ignited inside of him. Mia could tell he was clenching his jaw.

"What's wrong?" Mia asked.

She lifted her hand to touch his cheek. He stepped back.

"They took that from me," Andrew said.

His eyes went vacant. He was somewhere else.

"I'm still here," Mia said.

"They ripped everything from me," Andrew said.

"It's over," Mia said. "Look to the future."

Mia saw Andrew's fists were clenched into tight balls. He lifted his arm and Mia took a step back. He turned around at the last second and slammed his fist into the wooden building. Mia heard the sick crack of his knuckles making contact with the wall.

She rushed toward him and grabbed his arm, pulling his hand into hers. All four of his knuckles were sliced open. The skin around them was growing red. Mia expected to see a dent in the wall after how hard he had hit the building. Mia looked at Andrew. He didn't appear to be in any pain.

"Why did you do that?" Mia asked.

He kept his head straight. Mia pried his fist open. His fingers were shaking and some blood was starting to roll down. His hand was starting to swell up.

"You need a doctor," Mia said.

"What?" Andrew asked.

He shook his head and pulled his hand away. She saw his face fill with pain and shock.

"Andrew, what's going on?" Mia asked.

"Tell Zack I'll be late," he said. "I need to see Dr. Drum."

Andrew started walking away, cradling his hand.

"Wait," Mia said. "I'll go with you."

Andrew didn't stop or turn around; instead he picked up his pace. Mia was too stunned to chase after him. She had just witnessed the effects the militia had had on Andrew. Zack was right; if he discovered their existence right outside the gate, Andrew would be likely to burn the whole jungle down to get back at them. Now the militia rose as a priority on Mia's list. She needed to find out what they wanted.

Chapter 64

It is crucial we do not worry ourselves with the problems of the world. Affinity's only concern is for our brethren back home.
—Internal memorandum from Affinity

It didn't take long for Mia to find Sarah. She was stationed at the same computer tower she'd shown Mia yesterday. Mia arrived at the building and walked inside the circular section. There was Sarah, seated in front of a screen, typing away. Mia's presence startled her.

"Mia," she said. "How is orientation going? Are you on your lunch break?"

"Is anyone else here?" Mia asked.

"No," Sarah said. "What's wrong?"

"I need to figure out what the militia wants," Mia said. "I need them to leave us alone."

"Zack thinks they'll give up and leave soon," Sarah said.

"Or they'll get reinforcements and attack," Mia said.

"I'm more of an optimist," Sarah said. "Affinity has never had a full-scale attack. Not in our lifetime at least."

"Is there any way to talk to them remotely?" Mia asked.

Sarah shook her head.

"Not unless we threw them a radio," Sarah said. "But Zack would never let you get that close. It's too dangerous."

"What about their car?" Mia asked.

Sarah turned around to the computer and the screens changed. The image of a parking lot showed up.

"We searched it," Sarah said. "There was nothing in there."

"I want to get a better look," Mia said. "Can you take me there?"

"It's a far walk from here," Sarah said. "It's near the infirmary."

"Please," Mia said.

"You'll miss your afternoon orientation," Sarah said.

"I don't care," Mia said. "This is important."

Sarah glanced around.

"I'm not supposed to leave this place unmanned," she said.

Mia didn't stop pleading.

"Fine," Sarah said. "But we need to move fast."

Sarah jumped up from her chair and Mia followed her back outside. Sarah started through the jungle and Mia was close behind.

"I don't know what you think you'll find," Sarah said.

Mia didn't know either, but it was worth a shot.

They arrived in the carport and Mia saw her getaway vehicle. She jogged over.

"Nobody's guarding the cars?" Mia asked.

"No," Sarah said.

She pointed to a house next to the lot.

"That's the infirmary," she said. "If anyone needs anything they can radio from there."

Mia climbed in the jeep. She opened the interior compartments and lifted up the floor mats. There really wasn't anything in here.

"Was this cleaned?" Mia asked.

"No," Sarah said. "Once we have some time someone will reprogram the fingerprint sensor. It's not a priority."

Mia was frustrated. She jumped out of the car and started walking around. It was just like the one she learned to drive on. When Riley had first shown her the vehicle Mia thought it was a shell of a car. Someone had ripped off all the exterior panels even. That was a bit odd actually; what use would those have? Mia ran her hand along the paneling. Her hand went over a division.

"Do you have a tool?" Mia asked. "Something I could use to wedge this open?"

Sarah walked over to another car. She came back with a thin bar. Mia stuck the tool inside the division and wedged the paneling off. It didn't take much effort. Two large cellophane bricks fell out.

"What is that?" Sarah asked.

Mia bent down and picked one up. She turned it over and over, examining the contents.

"I think it's whatever the militia is after," Mia said.

She felt some relief. There would be no attack. Andrew was safe from having any more harm done to him and Mia could focus on her other looming decision. Sarah started jogging toward the infirmary.

"Where are you going?" Mia asked.

"To call Zack," she said.

"Tell him to hurry," Mia said.

Sarah waved and disappeared into the trees. Mia started to crack open the rest of the panels. She needed to move the bricks into an operational car. This would end today.

Chapter 65

When will multiple wives be permitted? The question every male wants an answer to.

—American Gazette

After an hour of examining his hand, Dr. Drum was starting to bandage it up.

"It's good you came straight to me," Katie said.

"When Mia told me," Andrew said, "I lost it. I saw red."

"Your hand will be fine," Katie said. "You didn't break anything. I'm more concerned about how you're channeling your rage."

"I felt like I had no control," Andrew said.

"Think about how much progress we've made in a few days," Katie said. "These things take time. There is a chance all your memories will return."

"When I came out of it, I was scared it was Mia I had punched, not the wall."

"But you didn't," Katie said. "Focus on that."

"Hello?" someone called from downstairs.

"I'll be right back," Katie said. "Stay here and we'll finish our conversation."

Andrew sat in the chair. He heard Katie walk down the stairs. She left his door open a crack and he recognized Sarah's voice. He wondered what she was doing here. He walked over to the door frame.

"I need your radio," Sarah said.

"There's a receiver on my desk," Katie said.

"You don't have the portable one?" Sarah asked.

"The whole infirmary is wired; I need to hear it everywhere in case there is an emergency," Katie said. "My portable is upstairs. I can get it."

"No, this is fine," Sarah said.

Andrew heard footsteps. Then a box in his room let out Sarah's voice. He turned his head and walked over toward it.

"Zack?" Sarah asked.

"I'm here," he said. "Are you with Mia, Andrew, or Carter? They've missed their afternoon session."

"I'm with Mia," Sarah said. "She found it, what the militia wants."

Andrew felt like the air in the room was standing still. The militia wanted something? Were they here?

"We're down at the carport," she said. "We need to transport it to the entrance."

"It's too dangerous," Zack said. "Wait for me. I'll be right there."

The source of Andrew's problems was right here. He hadn't even realized it. They needed to pay, deserved to feel the same suffering he did. Andrew turned and ran down the stairs and out the front door. He went over toward the carport and spotted Mia. He ran over toward her.

"You knew?" Andrew asked.

Mia stopped what she was doing.

"You knew that the people who did this to me were here and kept it from me?" Andrew asked.

"I wanted to protect you," Mia said.

"By lying to me?" Andrew asked.

"I didn't lie," Mia said.

Andrew walked over to the car she was loading up and sat in the driver's seat. He looked around for keys.

"What are you doing?" Mia asked.

"I'm going to see them," Andrew said.

"You can't drive," Mia said. "Not this car."

He ignored her and continued looking for a way to bring the machine to life.

"We have to wait for Zack," Mia said.

Think, he told himself. He'd been in these things several times now. How were they started? Then he noticed the center panel. He started to push the buttons.

"Andrew," she said, "this is all ending today. You won't have to worry about the militia anymore. We can go back to the way we were."

None of the buttons had worked thus far. Then he tried pressing his hand against the small screen. He heard the car come to life.

Mia opened the passenger door and climbed inside.

"Stop," she said.

She grabbed his good hand and pulled it up to herself. He turned his head and looked at her.

"I know you're angry," Mia said. "But you're not thinking clearly either. What will you do if you see them? You're unarmed. If we give them this stuff they will leave us alone. For good. We can move forward."

Mia glanced away. Andrew turned to see Zack, Sarah, and Katie standing watch. Andrew stood up and moved into the backseat, next to the cellophane bricks. He didn't make eye contact with Mia. Zack approached the car.

"I'm coming with," Andrew said.

"No," Zack said. "I'm going alone. It's too dangerous."

Andrew turned and looked at Zack. The man examined Andrew's face. Andrew didn't waver. He stared at Zack with intensity. The man would have to kill Andrew to get him out of the car.

"Fine," he said. "Sarah, I need you to cover me."

Zack climbed in the front seat.

"I don't think that's a good idea," Katie said.

"I don't have time for this," Zack said. "This morning there were four of them, now there are fifteen. We need this to end now."

Sarah walked over to their car and climbed in next to Andrew. He was smashed between her and whatever Mia had loaded into the car. He watched as Zack pushed a button and the car started backing up.

"All three of you stay in the car," Zack said.

He drove down the road. Andrew was filled with rage. He wanted nothing more than to kill these men. He'd take out the entire army if he had his way. Because Mia had kept this information from him, Andrew had missed an opportunity to get some relief. To have a sense of justice for the atrocities done to him. He didn't understand why she would deny him that satisfaction. The car started to slow down. Andrew saw figures come out of the jungle and stand in a line blocking the road. They had their weapons drawn.

Zack stopped the car about twenty-five feet away.

"Stay in the car," Zack said. "Mia, if anything happens to me drive them out of here."

Zack opened the door and stepped out. He raised his hands in the air. Mia slid over to the driver's seat and Zack walked around toward the back. He stopped to pick up one of the packages in the backseat.

"I have what you want," Zack said.

He kept his arms up and started walking toward them.

"Who is in charge?" Zack asked.

Then the unforgettable face walked out from the side of the road. It was the sergeant. Memories of the noise came flooding back. His evil laugh at Andrew's initial discomfort.

"I am sure you're a reasonable man," Zack said. "Let me give these back to you and leave us in peace."

"Or I could kill the four of you and take back what is mine."

"Look at the trees," Zack said. "They are filled with my best men. You're smart enough not to cross onto our land. Why is that?"

The sergeant laughed. He signaled for his men to lower their weapons.

"Are there really people in the trees?" Mia asked.

"Yes," Sarah said. "Zack wouldn't have moved so fast without adequate protection."

Andrew didn't care about Affinity's defenses. He couldn't keep his eyes off the sergeant. The rest of the world seemed to fade away. Andrew kept having flashes go off in his head. Bouts of intense pain that vanished as soon as they started. He needed to get closer and he needed a weapon.

Andrew opened the side door and started to gather the packages from the car. He didn't listen to Mia or Sarah's protests. Once his arms were filled he walked over behind Zack, never taking his eyes off the sergeant.

"Take these and leave," Zack said.

Andrew walked closer, until he was right next to Zack. The sergeant finally looked at him and broke into a smile.

"Private Simpson," he said. "You really were quite remarkable. It's a shame we lost you."

"Andrew, put the man's packages down and let's get out of here," Zack said.

"They are so informal here," the sergeant said. "We would have turned you into a man. They'll keep you a little boy."

Andrew walked forward and threw the packages down. The sergeant kept his smile and signaled for his men to gather up the bricks. Andrew was still seeing red, but then he felt a hand on his shoulder. He turned around to see Mia. She looked up at him with open eyes and a soft smile. Andrew realized he had won already. He wasn't stuck with the militia and Mia was alive. The work they had done on him was already fading away. His anger started to subside. Her hand slid down his arm and stopped when it met his. She started to walk back and Andrew followed her.

"I guess you were a weak one after all," the sergeant said.

The rage bubbled back up. Andrew dropped Mia's hand and spun back around. He saw Zack's gun hanging from his holster, and in a fluid motion Andrew reached out and grabbed it up. He cocked the weapon and pointed it at the sergeant. The man was laughing. Andrew didn't care who else was there. In his mind all he saw was one of the men responsible for his current state.

"Pull the trigger," the sergeant said. "Then you and all your friends will die."

"You're wrong," Andrew said. "You are the weak one. You have no principles or purpose to your life. There is nobody who cares about you. You live your life for yourself. You're everything that is wrong with this world."

The sergeant didn't stop smiling, but reality was coming back into view. Andrew thought about Mia, Katie, and Affinity. They wanted to help him. They wanted to help the world. He lowered his weapon.

"I feel sorry for you," Andrew said.

"We'll meet again someday, Private Simpson," the sergeant said. "You can count on that."

"As far as I'm concerned you're not worth my time," Andrew said.

He handed the weapon over to Zack and turned around. He grabbed Mia's hand again and walked back toward the car. Sarah moved into the passenger seat and Mia and Andrew slid into the back.

Zack waited till the men backed away from their standoff before coming back to the car. He got behind the wheel and watched as the militia disappeared.

"Is it over?" Mia asked.

"It's over," Andrew answered.

Andrew had faced the manifestation of all the hatred he held inside of himself and beat it down with the realization that he had people who cared about him. He closed his eyes and felt the wind blow over him. Everything he had been through had taught him one valuable lesson: he was loved, and that was something he'd never thought possible.

Chapter 66

IT'S OFFICIAL: GRANT MARSDEN TO WED; YOUNG LADIES ALL OVER AMERICA IN MOURNING

—American Gazette

"Really, sir, this isn't necessary," Grant said.

"I insist," Ian said. "It was no trouble at all."

No trouble for Ian, but Grant didn't want to drive into the capital in the first place. Once he arrived and discovered the purpose of his visit was to have dinner with his bride Grant had almost reached out and strangled Ian. The man Grant once saw as a respected authority figure was becoming nothing more than a nuisance.

"Two weeks until the wedding," Ian said. "I want you in the public eye nonstop until then. Tomorrow you'll tape another interview with Greg Finnegan. The two of you have a great rapport."

Another person Grant detested. How was he supposed to get any work done? Still, he gritted his teeth and smiled. Ian opened the door to a small room with a table. There was a candle lit and two place settings. Grant wasn't hungry.

"I hope I'm not interrupting," a female said.

Grant turned around to see his future wife. She was dressed in an orange ball gown that didn't do much for her figure or complexion. He almost had to lift his hand to block the glow of her dress. Grant looked down at his red polo and plaid shorts. He wasn't even dressed for the occasion.

"You look lovely, Tamara," Ian said.

He went and gave his daughter a kiss on the cheek. Grant wasn't sure which one he had picked. Part of him was hoping for a twin, but Tamara was stunning. Her dark hair was pulled up, showing off her thin shoulders. She smiled and Grant pulled out her chair.

"I'll let you two get to know each other," Ian said. "There's wine in the bottle and someone will be by with your food in a few minutes."

After Tamara sat down Grant took his seat. He didn't like his lack of control over the situation. This was pointless; he had already picked her, so he sat wasting time.

"Wine?" she asked.

Grant nodded and she poured him a glass first, then herself. He'd had wine at his first meeting with Mia. She'd been so outspoken and rude. That was one of the reasons he had picked her. She would be fun to break. Tamara, on the other hand, was more than ready for the role of subservient wife. She didn't even make eye contact with Grant.

"So, Tamara," Grant said, "why don't you tell me about yourself."

"I'm a very skilled singer," she said. "And I am more than prepared for any duties you request of me."

"Anything?" Grant asked.

"Of course," she said. "Once you're my husband."

He felt a vibration go off in his pocket. He pulled out his cell phone and saw a blocked number. He watched his high-tech phone scramble the digits until the actual number showed up. An international line. His curiosity was piqued. Grant stood up from the table and walked to the corner of the room.

"Hello," Grant said.

"Hi, boss," Rex said.

Grant turned around and saw Tamara sitting still, staring down at her plate. She would be nothing but a dutiful wife who would offer little entertainment for Grant. He walked farther out of earshot.

"And to what do I owe the pleasure of this call?" Grant asked.

"I needed to get some alone time," Rex said. "I lost my phone and had to acquire another."

"What are the newest developments?" Grant asked.

He didn't want Rex aware of his knowledge.

"I was attacked by the same group who held your wife," Rex said. "I've taken refuge in the same sanctuary as her."

"And she's aware of your presence?"

"She is under the impression I've sworn off my allegiance to you," Rex said. "What better way to watch her?"

"How ingenious of you," Grant said.

"What's the next step?" Rex asked.

"Monitor her closely," Grant said. "My strategy is already in play."

"What is your strategy?" Rex asked.

"Something you're not privy to," Grant said. "Tell me, what is the nature of your sanctuary?"

Grant knew exactly where Rex was. He was with a rebel group; it was obvious.

"A village in the mountains," Rex said. "A harmless group of ex-patriates."

"How does that make you feel?" Grant asked.

"Disgusted," Rex said.

Something rang false with Grant. The man on the phone did not make this group sound harmless. Grant didn't know what his former employee was up to but decided it was best he keep up appearances until his questions were answered.

"Tell me," Grant said, "did the opportunity present itself to terminate any of the travelers?"

"Negative," Rex said.

He was lying.

"So none of the men were at risk of being injured either?"

"We all made it out unscathed," Rex said.

"And this group, who was holding the young men hostage, are they a threat? Something worth worrying about?"

"Amateurs," Rex said.

Grant was quiet for a moment. Rex hadn't admitted his betrayal yet, but the shortness of his answers and lack of suggestions told Grant something was wrong.

"Keep doing the same," Grant said. "Monitor the situation, stay close. Check in as the situation develops."

Grant hung up the phone and walked back to his table. He needed to put the phone away before this girl reported back to her father that Grant had spent the whole meal ignoring her. He still wanted the grand commander position and had to keep playing along until the announcement was made.

If Rex betrayed him it would change nothing. Before he became irate, Grant took a breath and reminded himself of his current situation. Grant would become grand commander and get to kill Mia, making sure she never reappeared. Roderick Rowe would ensure that outcome.

"Do you not like salmon?" Tamara asked, pulling Grant out of his mind.

"Not particularly," he said.

"I can get you something else," she said. "I'd like to hear about the food you like."

How boring, Grant thought to himself.

"You have a lifetime to learn everything I like," Grant said.

"Did the phone call upset you?" Tamara asked.

"A friend may have moved on," Grant said.

"How terrible," Tamara said.

She assumed Rex was dead, and he might as well have been.

"Please," Grant said. "Tell me about yourself."

Tamara started to babble on about her singing skills. Grant couldn't have cared less.

*W*hy are we learning about weapons?" Grant asked.

"We aren't," Victor said. "I know about them already. You only have two years until you report for service. The more prepared you are, the better the placement, and the better the placement, the better your quality of postservice life."

Over the past four years Grant had already learned a great deal. He enjoyed his work. He spent most of his time studying chemical reactions and how to improve roadways. His favorite assignments were those involving technological advances, but those were few and far between.

The two were at one of Victor's retreats. This one was in the hills, half a day's drive away from Victor's home. They were lying on the ground, guns in hand waiting for their prey.

"Release the next one," Victor yelled.

A door lifted and a boy ran out. He was about Grant's age and dirty. He had a black eye and was filled with confusion, just like the rest of them. He stopped and stood still in the open grass.

"This one isn't even trying," Victor said. "Release a dog."

Grant heard the barking coming and the boy started to run.

"See if you can get him with one shot this time," Victor said.

Grant looked through the scope of his gun. He watched as the boy tried to run in a zigzag pattern across the grounds.

"Are you sure this isn't illegal?" Grant asked.

"Of course it's illegal," Victor said. "But not for a person like me. One day it won't be for you either. Remember that. You are better than everyone else."

Grant continued to follow the boy through his scope. He saw his shot and took it, this time hitting the boy in the head. He fell to the ground.

"See?" Victor said. "Each time you take a life it gets a little easier."

"It doesn't seem like a fair fight," Grant said.

"That's because it isn't," Victor said. "I think that's enough for today."

Everything Victor taught him over the years came with a harsh sense of cruelty. Grant didn't mind, though. He looked forward to getting home. All the horrors Victor had exposed him to were worth it. Not because Victor was teaching Grant a skill or preparing him for a successful tour in service, but because at the end of each day Grant came home to Daphne.

Grant had had enough of this dinner. He stood up from the table. Tamara kept her head bowed and rose as well.

"I had a lovely time tonight," Grant said. "Business calls me away."

Tamara curtsied and Grant walked out of the room. He started down the hall toward his car. He didn't care if Ian got upset. Tamara might have been his daughter, but she was still a woman and not a priority on Grant's list.

Grant needed to get home. He wanted to start making preparations for Amelia's return. Grant wanted everything perfect for her, including the decision on which weapons he would use with her.

Chapter 67

All members must complete core education requirements. For new members these may be completed concurrently with their work assignments.

—Internal memorandum from Affinity

The doctor was waiting outside the infirmary for the car to return. Mia saw her rise as they pulled into the lot.

"I think we all deserve a break after that," Zack said. "We'll finish orientation tomorrow."

"Andrew," the doctor said, "what happened? Are you all right?"

"I'll tell you all about it tonight," he said.

He looked down at Mia and watched her reaction. She was proud that he was seeking help in others. She gave him a smile. There was new warmth in his eyes. Almost like a spark had been reignited. He looked away to step out of the car; Mia did the same.

"Someone should tell Carter," Mia said.

"You don't know where he is?" Zack asked.

Mia shook her head.

"Probably looking for us," Mia said. "We were supposed to meet him at the field."

"I think we could use some time to ourselves," Andrew said.

He was looking at Mia. She felt he was ready to continue with their conversation from earlier.

"I'll find him," Sarah said. "See you guys at dinner?"

Mia nodded. Zack, Sarah, and Dr. Drum walked off.

"Come on," Andrew said.

He walked away from the carport. Once they reached the road he walked in the opposite direction from the camp.

"Where are we going?" Mia asked.

"Just walking," Andrew said. "Not far."

Mia kept pace with him.

"I've been speaking with Katie," he said.

"Katie?"

"Dr. Drum," Andrew said. "I call her Katie."

"Oh," Mia said.

"She's helping me deal with my time in the militia," Andrew said. "That's what I've been keeping from you."

"Oh," Mia said. "How is she helping you?"

"We're talking mainly," Andrew said. "When the memories come back, they aren't as painful."

"That's good," Mia said.

"That response is the exact reason I didn't want to tell you," Andrew said. He had a pressed smile on his lips and shook his head.

Mia stopped walking. She placed her hand on his face and turned it toward her.

"There's nothing wrong with talking to someone," Mia said.

"I know," Andrew said.

"I'm surprised it's not me," Mia said.

He grabbed her hand with his own and gave it a quick kiss before dropping it. Mia felt like her skin was on fire. All of her concerns over Andrew speaking to the doctor instead of her vanished. If that was what he needed, she would support him. They continued walking.

"I've been asked to join the External Tactics division," Mia said.

"The most prestigious branch," Andrew said.

"And the most intense," Mia said. "Sarah says you never see those people. They follow a different schedule. I wouldn't be with you as often."

Andrew frowned.

"I told Eleanor I'd think about it," Mia said.

"Is that where Rex is?"

"He joined," Mia said. "He said he saved your life to try to redeem himself for Whitney."

"Do you believe him?"

"I think so," Mia said.

"Yeah," Andrew said. "Me too."

They walked in silence for a few more minutes. On the side of the road were two large rocks, sitting just outside the jungle. Andrew led Mia over and took a seat. She sat across from him. Mia looked into his eyes; he was staring at her. His jaw was relaxed and there wasn't a crease on his face.

"I don't know what you're thinking," Mia said.

"I'm thinking that I missed you," Andrew said.

Mia thought he was moving closer, but at such a slow rate she couldn't be sure if she was imagining it. She started to lean in a little.

"I missed you too," she said.

Suddenly it wasn't in Mia's imagination. Andrew leaned closer and brought his hand behind her head, pulling her toward him. Mia let her eyes shut and when their lips met she felt like her whole body was exploding. He rested his other hand on her leg and she returned his kiss, parting her lips just a bit. He did the same and Mia felt a shiver run through her body. Then he gave her a quick kiss and pulled away. Mia knew her lips were in a pout. Andrew smiled and laughed a little.

"Now that we're alone," Andrew said, "with no dread looming

over us, I want you to tell me in great detail what you've been doing for the last month. Including how you got this back."

Mia looked down and saw Andrew holding up a piece of her hair. Mia blushed and grabbed his other hand. She would tell him everything. Riley, Joseph, Dalmy, and why she was valuable to External Tactics. She didn't want any secrets between them.

Chapter 68

The names of our members stationed in America must be kept hidden. They should exist on no piece of paper or electronic document.

—Internal memorandum from Affinity

"I know that most of you have had the pleasure of meeting our newest recruits, but tonight please allow me to formally introduce Mia, Andrew, Carter, and Rex," Zack said.

The four of them rose from their table. The whole room was clapping. Andrew didn't seem upset this time, more embarrassed by the attention. Carter cracked a small smile, the first Mia had seen in days. Rex's smile was almost too large. His toothy grin made him look like an eager child.

"As is our way," Zack said, "tonight there will be a celebration in the field in their honor."

Now everyone really clapped. This was news to Mia. All of her colleagues seemed surprised too. Mia saw Carter's smile fade though. He was always so social. It didn't make any sense.

"We hope to see everyone there," Zack said.

The applause died down and people started leaving. A small girl came running up to them. She had a piece of folded purple paper in her hand. She handed it to Andrew and then ran off right away.

"What was that?" Mia asked playfully.

Andrew opened the paper up. Mia leaned over his shoulder to read. In childlike handwriting it said:

Welcome to Affinity Andrew. We are happy you are here. Love your friend Stella

"I think someone has an admirer," Mia said.

"She must be seven," Andrew said. He looked concerned.

"When I was her age I had crushes on all the older farmhands," Mia said. "I guess that's just human nature."

"What?" Andrew asked. "Liking older men?"

"Liking attractive men," Mia said.

Andrew shook his head, but Mia watched as he folded the note back up and slid it into his pocket.

"Can we talk?" Carter asked. "Just the three of us."

Rex had already walked away. He was speaking with Katie. Andrew looked concerned.

"I'll be right back," he said.

He walked away from the table and over toward Katie and Rex.

"It's important," Carter said.

Andrew didn't seem hostile. In fact the opposite; he seemed almost happy.

"Mia," Carter said.

"What?"

She turned her head back to look at Carter. His forehead was crinkled up and his arms were crossed.

"Do you ever pay attention to anything I say? Or are you too obsessed with Andrew to spare me any thoughts at all?"

"I care about you," Mia said. "That's not fair."

"I want to talk to both of you," Carter said. "Before the party."

Andrew came back over. Carter pushed away from the table and walked toward the door.

"What's his problem?" Andrew asked.

One detail Mia had left out when she was describing the past month to Andrew: her fling with Carter.

"He's feeling a little left out," Mia said.

She started after him and Andrew followed. Carter went straight to their bunk. Mia pushed the door open; Carter was pacing back and forth.

"We're here," Mia said. "Our attention is all yours."

"They introduced us as recruits," Carter said. "When did we agree to stay here?"

"Where else would we go?" Mia asked.

"I don't know," Carter said. "Anywhere. We could go back to Mexico. We could stow away on a boat. Anywhere."

"That's crazy," Mia said.

"I'm not crazy," Carter said.

"I didn't say you were," Mia said. "Sit down."

Carter stopped pacing and took a seat on the lowest bunk. He hung his head between his legs, then brought his hands up through his hair and down his face.

"I don't want to stay here," he said.

"Why not?" Mia asked.

She glanced toward Andrew. He was silent, leaning against the door.

"I feel trapped here," Carter said.

Mia didn't understand. They had a lot of freedom here. Carter seemed very frustrated.

"Are you two together now?" he asked.

Mia's eyes widened. She was going to have to find time to tell Andrew everything, before Carter did and Andrew hated her for it. She remembered the look of betrayal on his face when he'd walked in and Mia was on top of Carter.

"Yes," Andrew said.

"Perfect," Carter said.

"It doesn't mean we care about you any less," Mia said.

"Get over yourself," Carter said. "Everyone thinks your life is so precious. That you are worth more than anyone else. I don't see what the big deal is."

"Hey," Andrew said.

He started to walk over from the door. Mia felt guilty. She hadn't realized Carter's feelings for her were that serious, but she wanted to avoid having this conversation right now.

"Carter," Mia said, "you're frustrated. I understand."

"You don't have to stay," Andrew said.

"Andrew," Mia said. She shot him an angry look. "If one of us leaves, we all leave," Mia said.

Carter seemed to relax a little at that comment. His face loosened up and he sat up tall.

"I want to leave," Carter said. "Tonight."

"Give it a week," Mia said. "Let's spend one week here and then have this conversation again. Can we all agree on that?"

Carter glanced around the room and nodded his head. Andrew was indifferent.

"But you have to give it your all," Mia said. "Is there any position you're interested in?"

Carter shrugged.

"Teaching," he said. "I like the kids."

"Tell Zack that," Mia said. "Then spend the week at the school."

Carter nodded his head.

"We should get to the party," Andrew said. "It is in our honor."

Carter stood up from the bed and walked toward the door. He brushed past Andrew on his way out. Whatever camaraderie the two had built over the last few weeks was dwindling down.

"Why did you say that?" Mia asked Andrew.

"What?"

"That he could go off on his own?"

"I don't want him to," Andrew said. "But I also don't want him to feel like a prisoner. If he's not happy here or happy about us he needs to know he has options."

"Well, there are better ways to say that," Mia said.

"Why are you so upset?" Andrew said. "He just insulted you."

Mia took a breath. Now was her moment to come clean.

"Andrew, I didn't tell you everything earlier," Mia said. "Before we left America . . . Carter and I were . . . together."

Andrew looked like he'd been punched in the gut.

"Did I know?" Andrew asked.

"You found out," Mia said.

In true Andrew fashion he sucked up whatever he was feeling and his face went blank.

"We should get to the party," he said.

"Does this change anything?" Mia asked.

"No," Andrew said.

Mia knew he was lying. He wouldn't look at her as he turned and left the cabin. Mia stood alone in the empty cabin, regretting her time with Carter and her decision not to tell Andrew about it this afternoon.

The party was in full swing. There was a campfire set up with people sitting around it. A band was playing music on the field and people were dancing. Children were running all over the place. Mia watched as Andrew chatted with Rex and Katie, while Carter played games with some kids. Mia sighed and decided it was best to give Andrew some time to digest the news. She spotted Sarah sitting by the campfire and went to join her friend.

"Congratulations," Sarah said.

"For?"

"Joining Affinity," Sarah said.

"We haven't yet," Mia said. "Well, not officially."

"Oh," Sarah said. She crinkled her nose, then let out a small laugh. "Did you give any thought to your job?" she asked.

Apparently formal acceptance was a minor detail.

"I was hoping to talk to you about that," Mia said. "I received an offer, from ET."

Sarah's eyes bugged out of her head. "Are you going to take it?"

"I said I needed some time," Mia said.

"You're crazy not to," Sarah said.

"You said you would be unsure."

"I said that because I'll probably never get asked," Sarah said.

"I thought you said they were so intense."

"Well, it depends on your goals," Sarah said. "You'll be separated from the group some of the time, but you'll be in on everything. You'll have a say in the master plan."

Mia looked over at Andrew. He smiled and laughed.

"Part of me wants a somewhat regular life," Mia said. "I wouldn't get that if I was focused on America all the time."

Sarah shrugged. "I think you're worried you won't get enough time with Andrew," she said.

"No," Mia said. "He knows and said he'll support whatever I choose."

"See that man dancing?" Sarah asked. She pointed her finger at someone who was waving his arms in the air, carefree. Mia nodded.

"He's a member of ET," she said. "And that woman over there? She is too."

"How many members are there?"

"Eleven," Sarah said.

"Eleanor said my invitation was open-ended," Mia said.

Sarah's eyes popped back out again.

"That's unheard of," she said. "You must be pretty special. Did someone else join too?"

"Rex," Mia said.

"Well, if you don't accept by next week someone else will get an invite," she said. "They always have an odd number."

"What if I change my mind?" Mia asked.

"I don't know," Sarah said. "Eleanor doesn't lie, but she doesn't mess around either. Maybe they'd kick someone out?"

Mia glanced at the two ET members. They seemed fairly happy. Maybe it would be possible to have both. A normal life and one devoted completely to the cause. She stopped glancing around the crowd when Andrew came into view again.

"I'll be back," Mia said. "Thanks."

She stood up and made her way toward Andrew. He saw her coming and broke away from Rex and Katie.

"Can we talk?" Mia asked. "Somewhere private?"

He nodded his head and walked along the jungle, away from the party.

"I'm really sorry," Mia said. "I should have told you right away. I was nervous about how you would respond and—"

Before she could finish Andrew wrapped his arms around her waist. He pulled her forward and up on her tiptoes. She met his mouth with hers and wrapped her arms around his neck. She felt like she was flying as his energy made its way through her body. After a few moments he pulled back, giving her a tiny kiss to end their embrace.

"You should have told me," Andrew said. "But it was in the past. You're my future."

Mia felt like her body was melting. She went back up on her toes and he met her kiss. They moved their heads in a rhythm and Mia felt like it was only the two of them left on the planet. She pulled away this time.

"I'm not going to join External Tactics," Mia said.

"Why not?" Andrew asked.

"Because I want to stop the Registry, but I want this too," Mia said.

"You'll have me either way," Andrew said.

"Not just you," Mia said. "I want as quiet a life as possible. At least for a little bit."

"Nothing about you is quiet," Andrew said.

A ball came sailing across the grass, stopping right beside them. Andrew broke away and picked up the toy, tossing it back. He came over and grabbed Mia's hand.

"Come on," he said. "It's our party."

Mia was happy to follow him. This was what she had been waiting for. She felt like she belonged here. She had the best of both worlds. She was able to continue fighting injustice while starting something more with Andrew. She couldn't imagine anything more perfect.

Chapter 69

GREG FINNEGAN PREVIEW: GRANT MARSDEN HOPES TO HAVE SONS,
SO HE CAN TURN THEM OVER TO THE GOVERNMENT AND ENSURE OUR
GREAT NATION CONTINUES ON WITH A STRONG ARMED SERVICE
— American Gazette

The drive home from the studio cleared Grant's mind. It was his
third interview with Greg Finnegan in four days. He was looking
forward to his wedding night. That meant no more forced public appearances and no more *Greg Finnegan Show.* He would be named
the next grand commander and this tasteless display could stop.

At least the public was informed about his dress choices; he didn't
need to wear a suit tonight. No doubt after the show aired tomorrow
night Grant's look would be the newest trend among young men.
A tan cardigan was tied around his shoulders, blowing back in the
breeze from his convertible sports car. The sky was covered with
stars but Grant never took his eyes off the road.

He wondered what Rex was doing. The man hadn't made contact
since his initial phone call. Grant wouldn't let Rex bring him down.
He was on the cusp of getting everything he wanted. Carter's phone
calls were regular and he promised Amelia's return. Roderick was
becoming a bit of a pain. He was starting to question his confinement
and lack of access to the outside world.

Talking about his past wasn't something Grant enjoyed. Whenever Greg got a little too personal Grant got more and more vague. Tonight Greg had asked about Grant's premilitary life; of course Grant had lied, but the memories kept coming back.

Daphne was beautiful. The longer Grant stayed with Victor the more that became the ultimate truth. Grant wanted her. He wanted everything she represented. He looked forward to meals; they were the only times he was able to see her. He waited patiently at the breakfast table. Victor came in and took a seat.

"How are you feeling?" Victor asked. "One week until you report for service."

"Confident," Grant said.

Victor picked up a dish of eggs and put some on his plate before handing them to Grant.

"No Daphne to serve us this morning?" Grant asked.

She was there most of the time, but at least once a month she was absent. The next day her arms would be covered in bruises. Victor liked her to show them off; it let the world know what a poor wife she had been. Grant always hated those mornings.

"Daphne is no longer my wife," Victor said.

"What?" Grant asked.

Marriage was only severable by death.

"In five years she's produced three sons," Victor said. "And she's started to get a little old. I think I deserve an upgrade."

"What happened to her?"

"I told the authorities she slipped and fell down the stairs," Victor said.

He gave Grant a mysterious grin.

"But I have a surprise for you," Victor said. "Finish your eggs and come with me."

Grant ate with speed. He thought about Daphne. Over the last sev-

eral years he'd never spoken to her directly. But he liked looking at her. She was a flower in Victor's palace of rage and cruelty. Grant knew he didn't have much of a heart, since he had little problem inflicting pain on innocent people, but Daphne was different. He felt they had some unspoken bond. Like they were both prisoners here. Both of them were kept with golden handcuffs. If Grant left he would have returned uneducated and poor, while Daphne didn't even have that option.

Breakfast was done and Victor led Grant out of the kitchen. They walked down the long hall and toward the basement. Victor always kept that room locked. He punched in a code and the door opened up. Grant had never been down here before. He had always wondered what was beyond that wall.

When they reached the bottom of the steps he saw a big empty room with cement walls. It was the opposite of Victor's home. There was a tool bench and a drain in the middle of the room. Outside of that Grant didn't see much. His eyes stopped wandering when he saw her. Daphne was strapped to a pole in the middle of the basement, clad only in her undergarments. Makeup was running down her face from her tears; a piece of tape covered her mouth.

"I thought you could have her as a going-away present," Victor said.

Grant looked up at him, confused.

"Of course you'll have to kill her at the end of the week," he said. "But maybe release some desires. I know you harbor them. It's only natural. My gift to you."

Grant was mortified. The woman he fantasized about was helplessly tied to a pole. He couldn't let Victor know his pain.

"Thank you," he said.

"I'll leave you two alone for a few hours," Victor said.

He patted Grant on the back before walking up the steps. Grant waited until the door was closed, then he ran over toward her. He ripped the tape off her mouth.

"Are you okay?" he asked.

She was shaking. Grant ran over to the tool bench. There were pliers, saws, and a variety of knives set out. Grant picked up a large knife and ran back toward her. She let out a scream.

"No," Grant said. "I'm not going to hurt you."

He started sawing at her bindings.

"We have to get out of here," Grant said. "Both of us."

He cut through the last strap and she fell forward.

"I'm going to check upstairs," Grant said. "Make sure we have a way out. Then we'll run."

"Where will we go?" Daphne asked.

"Steal a boat," Grant said. "Make our way across the ocean."

Grant picked up her hand and led her toward the stairs. He signaled for her to wait at the bottom and checked the door. It was unlocked. He peeked his head out, then waved for her to come up.

They moved quietly down the hall; Grant still had the knife in his hand. The silence shattered when Daphne started screaming.

"Victor," she yelled, "he's trying to run!"

Grant turned around and grabbed her, covering her mouth with his hand. She looked at him with intense hatred and pushed him away.

"Victor!" she screamed again. He got his hand over her mouth again.

"I'm trying to help you," Grant said; she shoved him again.

"You're a traitor," she said. "I don't want your help. I want to serve my husband."

She took off running through the halls. Grant chased her, hoping to stop her. She turned into the main room and Grant followed. There was Victor, seated in his favorite chair with his legs crossed, a cruel smile on his face. Daphne ran over to him and kneeled down.

"I did just like you said, and he wants to escape. He talked about running away from service."

"Is this true?" Victor asked.

Grant looked back and forth from Victor to Daphne. Victor looked smug and Daphne pleased with herself.

"No," Grant said.

"Then prove it," Victor said.

Grant looked down at Daphne. The woman he had been willing to sacrifice his life to help was nothing but a lapdog. He had wanted to give her everything, and she didn't care about him at all. He gripped the knife in his hand and ran at her. She let out a scream as he brought the weapon down into her back, stabbing over and over again. Her blood sprayed back in his face. Her screams stopped soon and she lay in a pool of blood, gurgling away. Grant was breathing heavily. He moved back and stood up.

Victor came up behind him and placed his hand on Grant's shoulder.

"This is the most important and hardest lesson to learn," Victor said. "Love is unnecessary, and it will make you weak."

Grant looked over at Victor. This man who had given him every-thing, who taught him how to live. He was the closest thing Grant would ever have to a father. But Grant wasn't him. Victor had noth-ing but true hatred in his heart. Grant still had some semblance of a soul left. If he ever wanted to become Victor he needed to destroy it all. He turned toward the man and brought the knife up with speed. He drove it straight through Victor's chest with a single motion. The look on Victor's face was a mix of confusion and anger.

"On some level I loved you too," Grant said.

He pulled the knife out and Victor started backing away. Grant dropped the blade and sat next to the man while he died. It was over. Grant spent the rest of that day hiding the bodies and the evidence of the murders. That night he went to the recruitment station early. He never once looked at the news to see what was reported about Victor's death.

At that point Grant hadn't known what was in front of him. Looking back, he should have been afraid. Armed with the knowledge of the future, Grant realized that night had changed everything for him. It had made him the man he was today.

He parked the car in front of his house and turned off the engine. The newspapers were calling Grant a hero, but that wasn't a title he was after. Grant was much more interested in being a winner. That crown was headed his way.

Chapter 70

Affinity is made up of individuals, not governments. If another country offers aid we will accept and become allies, but we will not directly affiliate ourselves with our host countries.

—Internal memorandum from Affinity

The days were flying by so fast Mia was having a hard time telling them apart. Carter didn't mention the ticking clock on his ultimatum, and Mia took that as a good sign. He was at the school today, where he spent most of his time. Andrew was starting to fit in as well. Mia stood on the field watching him train with his group. They were practicing defensive moves and even from a distance Mia could see the joy on his face. After training he would speak to Katie for a while, then join Mia at dinner. It was a simple, easy routine.

"You ready?" Sarah asked.

Mia had forgotten that her purpose in the field was waiting for her friend. Without a permanent workstation chosen, or even one in mind, Mia spent most of her time shadowing Sarah.

"You don't have to come with me today," Sarah said. "I see you eyeing Andrew; you can spend the whole day with him if you want."

Mia shook her head. She enjoyed practicing her defensive and fighting skills, but not enough for full-time work. Mia turned and started walking toward Sarah's workspace.

"Did you stay up too late last night?" Sarah asked. "You seem really out of it today."

"I stay up too late every night," Mia said.

Sarah let out a laugh. It was true. Mia's favorite part of Affinity was the nights. Whoever was free gathered in the field and socialized. Mia was always one of the last to head to bed. She loved hearing about everyone's days and the general experience of getting to know people, which she'd never had before.

Last night she'd spoken with two sisters; they were young and both were born here. They teased each other and each took turns trying to surprise the other by pulling on her hair. Mia laughed as she watched them, but part of her core stung at the sight. She had been robbed of those types of interactions with her own sisters, and the young women in America would never know that type of bond existed.

"Zack thinks you should sample some of the other areas," Sarah said. "It's obvious you lack a passion for computers, and driving can't be a full-time occupation. Carter mentioned you liked to cook before. Do you want to spend a day in the kitchen?"

Mia almost spat. The kitchen had always been an escape for her, where she could focus on one task and excel. Now that she had escaped the Registry she didn't need to clear her mind. Armed with the knowledge she now had, any time her mind was clear, thoughts of America filled the space.

"You don't want me following you?" Mia asked.

"Maybe you should think about Eleanor's offer," Sarah said.

"I want a quieter life," Mia said.

"Do you?" Sarah asked. "I mean, you have everything you were after—you're in a safe place, the people who love you are protected, you're forming new friendships—but you're not letting yourself go. I can see it, the way you carry yourself. What could be eating away at you?"

"Nothing," Mia said. "It's just an adjustment, that's all."

Sarah shook her head. "You're not adjusting well," she said. "At least not when it comes to picking a path."

"I'm learning something about what you do," Mia said.

"Like what?" Sarah asked. "Give me an example."

The two entered the jungle and started up the hill to Sarah's tower.

"I can type better," Mia said.

"Do you have any interest at all in learning how computers work or staying at the forefront of technology? I showed you a lot of new things, inventions I couldn't wait to get my hands on when I was as new as you, but you look unimpressed when I show you."

"If I'm bothering you, let me know," Mia said. "I can shadow Zack, or someone from his team."

"I think it will be the same," Sarah said.

Mia wasn't sure if Sarah was right. When she saw the advances all Mia could think about was the poor people in America who would never know this type of technology existed. Sarah stopped walking and Mia looked up. They were in front of the electric gates of ET. Mia whipped her head toward Sarah and gave her a suspicious look.

"I did this for your own good," Sarah said. "Ask Eleanor if you can spend the afternoon here. I'm sure she'll agree. Then maybe you will have your answer regarding your place in Affinity."

Before Mia could respond the gate started to open. Sarah waved and turned, walking down the hill. Mia redirected her gaze toward ET. The gate was open now. Without thinking Mia's feet dragged her across the threshold, her body knowing what she wanted more than her mind.

This is against protocol," Eleanor said. "And unfortunately since you are not a member of External Tactics yet, you are not privy to certain parts of the facility."

"I don't want to see everything," Mia said. "Just an idea of what my life would be like if I joined ET."

They were in the same room Eleanor had escorted Mia and Rex to earlier in the week. Mia was seated at the table and Eleanor walked over to the control panel for the screen. She started typing.

"There is no typical day here," Eleanor said. "At one point you may be brainstorming, looking for weakness in American defenses; at another you may speak with one of our contacts. It varies depending on where we need help."

"If I were a member of ET," Mia said, "what would I be doing right now?"

Eleanor spun around and showed her pressed lips. She looked like she wanted to scream at Mia but instead broke into a smile. She hit a button on the remote in her hand and the screen changed, displaying hundreds of small pictures. Mia couldn't focus on a single one; they kept shifting.

"These are the images we receive from America," Eleanor said. "Some are feeds hidden by members of our organization who reside inside the country, others are satellite images where we found weakness in America's defenses, and others are from television programs and private security devices we have been able to hack."

"How many people does Affinity have?" Mia asked. "On the inside at least? Why don't you evacuate them?"

"Those are the types of questions that only get answers if you're a member of External Tactics." Eleanor pushed another button and the screen went dark.

"We are not pioneers, living in the wild trying to think up schemes," she continued. "We are an advanced society, more so than most others in the world. If you join us this will all be at your disposal."

"Why me?" Mia asked. "I'm not good with electronics; I'm uneducated."

"Outside of your connection to Grant Marsden?" Eleanor asked.

Mia nodded; that couldn't be the only reason they saw her as worthy.

"You managed to escape from confinement twice; you rescued two men from a dangerous situation and since then have stopped an attack on Affinity," Eleanor said. "There is a difference between intellect and education. You are a great asset, for many reasons."

There was warmth growing inside Mia over Eleanor's compliments. Something she felt selfish for embracing.

"That being said, coddling is not in my job description," Eleanor said. "You already know more than the average Affinity member. I'm afraid I cannot give you further details without hearing your decision."

Eleanor stared at Mia, her arms crossed over her chest. This was the moment Mia needed to pledge her allegiance to ET, but before she could speak Andrew's face came to her mind. She thought about the time they'd spent together this past week. How nice it was to have him by her side, without any doom looming over them. If Mia knew everything ET and the Registry were up to that blissful ignorance would vanish forever.

"I need more time," Mia said.

"Then you can spend it elsewhere," Eleanor said.

Mia stood up from the table and Eleanor walked toward the door, holding it open for Mia as she left. No more words were exchanged. Mia regretted coming to the ET compound. She walked to the fence and waited for it to open. Even though the information she had gained today was minute, Mia knew that instead of satisfying her craving to know the Registry would be destroyed, it had only intensified it.

Chapter 71

Each Affinity camp can set up their village how they see fit, as long as the shared priority remains working toward the downfall of America.

—Internal memorandum from Affinity

Tonight was her first meeting. The entire organization was invited and External Tactics would run the event. Two days had passed since Mia's time with Eleanor and still she couldn't make up her mind. Mia thought about Rex saying Grant was indecisive and not worthy of loyalty; she wondered what the big man thought of her now.

"What is this about?" Mia asked Sarah.

"It's a special meeting," Sarah said. "I'm not sure what for. It must be big news though."

Mia looked around the room. There were about one hundred people in attendance. She was surprised more didn't attend, but Sarah did tell her some of the people wanted to stay in the dark on some of the larger issues. Before Mia could make it to her seat Eleanor intercepted her.

"Mia," Eleanor said, "have you given any more thought to my offer?"

"I'm still deciding," Mia said.

"I hope you don't wait too long," Eleanor said.

She continued walking up to the front of the mess hall. There was a large table set up and the other eleven members sat down. Eleanor's seat was in the middle.

"She's never spoken a word to me before," Sarah said. "I doubt she knows my name."

"Maybe you should rethink joining ET," Andrew said. "You'd fit in nicely at the head table."

"I think I like it better down here with the minions," Mia said.

Sarah and Andrew laughed at her joke. Carter walked in and sat by them.

"I thought you weren't coming," Mia said.

"It beats sitting alone in the cabin," Carter said.

"I'm glad you're here," Mia said.

Carter looked away. She wanted him to feel like he belonged.

"Can I have your attention?" Eleanor said.

The whole room stopped talking in an instant. Mia had never seen anyone control a room with such power.

"It has come to our attention that the rise of a new grand commander is imminent. This individual is more ruthless than is imaginable."

Grant. Mia knew Eleanor was right. She glanced over at Andrew, who gave his full attention to the ET panel.

"We have some inside access to him," Eleanor said. "We are looking for volunteers for a mission. We need to send a group across the border, into America, to retrieve some files."

The files on her. Mia looked around the room. Nobody had raised their hand yet. This was crazy. People could lose their lives, and there was no way everyone would survive the return trip. Mia wouldn't have that blood on her conscience. Eleanor couldn't think simple files were worth the loss of innocent people.

Carter stood up. "I volunteer," he said.

Mia reached over and tugged his clothing. He brushed her off. Eleanor nodded at him. Someone else stood up. These people were going to risk their lives. Mia didn't think they understood what they were giving up. She stood up.

"Stop," Mia said.

Everyone turned and looked at her.

"Excuse me?" Eleanor asked.

"Nobody is going back," Mia said.

"That is not your call to make," Eleanor said.

"Then I would like to accept your offer to join External Tactics," Mia said.

"Consider yourself a member," Eleanor said. "But this has been decided."

"Then I'm going back too," Mia said.

"No," Andrew said.

"Unfortunately your presence will do more harm than good on this mission," Eleanor said. "We need you for something else."

"You want me to present myself as the grand commander's deceased wife," Mia said. "And I need to go back there to do it."

There was an audible gasp from the room.

"Mia, what are you doing?" Andrew asked.

Eleanor glanced at the panel members.

"We're listening," she said.

"No," Andrew said. He stood up. "If any of you go back they'll kill you. He'll kill you."

"I'm not letting anyone else sacrifice themselves," Mia said.

"I'm not letting you sacrifice yourself," Andrew said.

"As moving as this display of affection is," Eleanor said, "it doesn't concern us. Everyone, thank you for your time tonight. Volunteers, please meet at ET tomorrow morning. This meeting is adjourned."

The people took Eleanor at her word and started standing up, talking among themselves.

"I won't allow this," Andrew said.

"It's not your call to make," Mia said.

"Mia, you said you wanted a quiet life," Andrew said. "What would you call sending yourself to certain death?"

"I can't let another person die because of the Registry," Mia said. "I do want a quiet life, but this week has shown me I can never find true peace until the Registry is done."

"So you think exposing Grant's lies will put a stop to it?" Andrew asked.

"No," Mia said. "But I think if we're going to stop the Registry it has to happen from inside. We need to strike soon. Once he takes over, those people back home, they're in grave danger. The whole country."

Andrew didn't argue with Mia. He looked away. Eleanor approached them.

"That was brave," she said.

"Some files on me aren't worth people's lives," Mia said.

"What about the women trapped in America? Is risking a few lives worth their freedom?"

"I'm going back," Mia said. "I'll expose Grant from the inside, but I'm going alone."

"Rex is a crucial part of this mission," Eleanor said.

"Just the two of us then," Mia said.

"I won't leave you," Andrew said. "I'm going too."

"Me too," Carter said.

Eleanor glanced around. She let a smile curl up on her lips.

"You underestimate the capabilities of Affinity," Eleanor said. "Four members will not take down a massive government. We have much at our disposal."

Mia thought about the video feeds. That was impressive, and it was only a fraction of their capabilities. Still, Mia didn't feel more confident.

"If you three are volunteering you will be informed of our proposal," she said. "However, input from members outside of ET is not welcomed."

"So you want us to risk our lives without a say?" Andrew asked.

"This is voluntary," Eleanor said. "I hope to see you three in the morning. Mia, welcome to External Tactics."

Eleanor turned and left. The rest of the room emptied out. Sarah stayed with the group until Zack walked over. He put a hand on her shoulder and she left the room. Her eyes stared into Mia and they were filled with concern and worry.

"We can't do this," Andrew said.

"We already have," Mia said. "There's no other option."

Andrew's face was hard. He wouldn't make eye contact. Mia knew he wanted to scream at her. Carter, on the other hand, could barely contain his grin. It was like he felt relief at returning home.

"It's up to us," Mia said. "We have to go back. We have to stop this. All of it. The Registry, mandatory service, the way America works."

"You heard Eleanor," Andrew said. "We're only three people, four if you count Rex."

"Affinity is behind us," Mia said. "I wouldn't underestimate their methods."

"And what are those?" Andrew asked.

"I don't know yet," Mia said.

She knew sitting idle wasn't an option. Mia did her best to hide her fears and show Andrew and Carter her determination.

"But no matter what, we are going to do this . . . together."

None of them spoke a word. Mia knew Andrew didn't agree with their plan. When Mia had landed in Mexico she was a terrified, help-less girl paralyzed with fear. Now she was about to mount a rebellion against the most powerful country in the world. She knew she should be terrified, but instead she felt a strange sense of calm. The quiet life Mia dreamed of would never be possible until the Registry ceased to exist. This time Mia wasn't alone. She was part of something larger; she was part of Affinity. Mia could do this—she could go back. The Registry would be stopped.

Don't miss the explosive final installment in

THE REGISTRY TRILOGY

Coming Fall 2014

When she escaped to Mexico for a new life, Mia Morrissey wanted one thing: freedom. But now she must risk her hard-won liberty for the freedom of others . . . and the end of the Registry.

Undercover as part of a diplomatic mission, Mia returns to America, where the walls have grown ever taller, and the forgotten country faces its most ruthless leader yet. With Andrew, Carter, and the members of Affinity by her side, she embarks on a dangerous journey to defeat Grant, bring down the government, and destroy the Registry once and for all. But when a terrible betrayal blows the operation wide open, Mia discovers she's been used by friends and foes alike. As unsure of her allies as her enemies, Mia doesn't know who to trust, where to turn, or whether the mission she's risking everything for is even worth the sacrifice.

The fate of her friends, her country, and her own humanity hangs in the balance—and Mia is the one who will seal that fate, for better or for worse.

From William Morrow

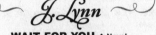

Sophie Jordan

FOREPLAY A Novel
Available in Paperback and eBook Fall 2013

J. Lynn

WAIT FOR YOU A Novel
Available in eBook
Available in Paperback Fall 2013

BE WITH ME A Novel
Available in Paperback Winter 2014

TRUST IN ME A Novella
Available in eBook Fall 2013

Molly McAdams

FROM ASHES A Novel
Available in Paperback and eBook

TAKING CHANCES A Novel
Available in Paperback and eBook

STEALING HARPER An Original eNovella
Available in eBook

FORGIVING LIES A Novel
Available in Paperback and eBook Fall 2013

DECEIVING LIES A Novel
Available in Paperback and eBook Winter 2014

Shannon Stoker

THE REGISTRY A Novel
Available in Paperback and eBook

THE COLLECTION A Novel
Available in Paperback and eBook Winter 2014